# AN AMISH CHRISTMAS TABLE

MINDY STEELE    RACHEL J. GOOD    JENNIFER BECKSTRAND
TRACY FREDRYCHOWSKI

Cover design by Tracy Lynn Virtual, LLC

ISBN: 979–8-9906105–4-5 (paperback),

979–8-9906105-3-8 (ebook)

# AN IDEAL CHRISTMAS

## MINDY STEELE

# CHAPTER 1

*H*azel Fisher stood at the large window of Miller's Bakery, admiring the calm December day. Now that the morning rush was over, she took in the changing scenery of the Christmas season and trimmings along the street. When she spotted the open buggy parked a few doors down, her heart tugged at seeing her new stepson on the sidewalk just outside.

"Hank, fetch a half dozen cinnamon rolls. Abner's outside. Surely, he could use something sweet today," she called out to her husband. It had been two whole weeks since either of them had laid eyes on Abner, and since the community had split, placing him in the Locust Creek community where few families remained. She hated to see him further isolated than he had already made himself.

Hazel watched Abner hand over the keys of Fisher Furniture to the new owners. Another act of self-seclusion, she concluded. "I can't believe he sold it." Hazel clicked her tongue. "We don't need an auto parts store next door."

"Pleasants County doesn't have one, dear, and it's a long drive for my *sohn* every day." Hank settled to her right, a cup of *kaffi* in one hand and a small box of cinnamon rolls in the other. "Abner

3

would rather work from his shop at home. He makes a good living selling at the market too."

"He worries my heart," Hazel admitted, though she had never been a worrier.

"Don't fret. He always took his time at things. It's what makes him a better furniture maker than me."

Hazel straightened. "That's not true. You taught him well and good, but I do worry he's keeping to himself too much. Lloyd's *fraa*, Jeralyn, said he never attended any of the fall weddings and seldom leaves his farm."

"He lost his *fraa*," Hank reminded her. "And it doesn't help that you keep trying to match him up." Hank sipped his *kaffi*. He never lifted his tone, even when he was trying to make a point.

Hazel loved how easy their love was. "Only because I love him. I have three *dochters* and no *sohns*, until now. I missed years of mothering him. I want him to know he has a mother who cares for him." Hazel knew Abner had struggled with the loss of his wife, Cilla, years ago, yet *Gott* insisted we not linger in the past, but live in the present. After seven long years, it was clear that Abner was stuck and not moving forward.

"He knows," Hank assured her. "He just needs time."

"*Jah*, grief has no clock for sure. We know that for sure and certain, but our *sohn* needs love in his life, Hank."

Hank took another slow sip of his *kaffi*. Evidence speckled his beard that he had already scarfed down a sweet roll this morning. Hazel reached out to brush away the crumbs.

They watched Abner climb into his buggy and aim for the first of three traffic lights. Here he was, right next door, and hadn't even stopped by for his favorite cinnamon rolls. *Jah*, Hazel had reason for her concerns.

"At least he took the sign with him," Hank mumbled, noting the long wooden Fisher Furniture sign pointed upward in the buggy.

"He didn't even pay us a visit, and here our buggy is right outside. Is he trying to worry us?"

4

"Why should I get an ulcer when you worry plenty for the two of us?" The glint in his eyes was playful. It was one reason Hazel agreed to remarry after turning sixty. Who didn't want to be smiled at like that for the rest of her days?

"If you get an ulcer, it's because you don't eat right. Do you want him alone"—she motioned out the window—"forever?"

Hank scratched his beard again. More crumbs cascaded down, latching onto his shirt. "There isn't much we can do about that. You saw how he reacted when Grace invited him over for supper to meet Susan Keim. We'll pray and trust *Gott* to help heal his heart."

"*Ach*, Grace thinks herself a matchmaker, but *mei dochter* forgets that only *Gott* makes matches. Susan Keim is too quiet. They'd have nothing to talk about." Hazel turned.

"*Fraa*, I love you, and I see you're thinking of match meddling here, but we shouldn't meddle in *mei sohn*'s life. You *were* terribly wrong about Nelly and Levi."

"Nelly snuck up on me. That one was never easy to predict." She did get it wrong, but sometimes the Lord didn't explain His plans to her understanding. Hazel was determined to be a better listener this time.

"I plan to see him happy with a family," she informed her husband with a lifted chin. There was no ignoring the Lord when He asked for help. "You can help or not, but *Gott* says we must have love."

"Do I have a choice?" Hank laughed. "If you're... If *we're* going to do this, let me pay a visit to the market tomorrow and invite him for supper."

"That's a good idea, and you can see if he's caught anyone's eye." Hazel was blessed to be married to a husband who understood matters of the heart and was equally inclined to help her spread love amongst their community.

# CHAPTER 2

"*I* can get a dozen donuts for eighty cents less at Miller's bakery," Eliza Lapp quipped. If she hoped to earn Ina Graber's sympathies, she'd just as well head into town, a whole seven miles from Troyer's Marketplace.

It might only be Ina's third day working at her sister's donut shop, but Ina wasn't in the business of bargaining. Not when every dollar earned prevented Lavina and her three *kinner* from leaning on the community. Lavina wasn't proud, but since her husband vanished in the night over four years ago, she'd been forced to accept help from the benevolence funds more than she wanted.

"*Jah*, but they'll not taste as good," Ina replied. "And your driver will charge you at least ninety cents a mile to get there. It's a deal, considering you are already here." Ina shrugged.

"Yer a *schmaert* one." Eliza was prone to stating the obvious.

Ina liked to think she was smart. When you were the fifteenth of twenty-one *kinner*, it was easy to be overlooked. That's why Ina had to rely on smarts to find her place amongst her lot. Unfortunately, her ideas also earned her plenty of Mamm's worrisome looks.

When she quit working at Miller's Bakery to help *Aenti* Elvesta

6

sell fresh-cut flowers, Mamm insisted it was because Ina feared the local matchmaker would turn her attention on her. She had only been eighteen then, and Hazel had been set on matching her with Sam Lewis. No *maedel* wanted to hitch a buggy to a Lewis, and Ina already knew where her heart aimed. Unfortunately, it was in the direction of the only man who didn't even know she existed. In fact, it was the very week she graduated from eighth grade that he married another. Her heart broke that day and broke further just a year later, when his *fraa* died unexpectedly.

So, Ina focused on work, learning new things, and forgetting about the young widower with soft brown eyes and a broken heart. Selling flowers was a dream job, but soon after the sneezes started, it became necessary to find a new job. Ina didn't want to spend another year at home learning to be a proper *fraa* when her future clearly wasn't aiming that way. That's how she found herself painting houses with her *bruder* Henry's work crew. *Mamm* fretted terribly over that rash decision and Ina's future. Ina's future was fine, and *Mamm* needed to focus more on Della and Esther getting married before her. Those two were terrible at knowing their hearts.

Ina could paint and forget all about the young boy who carried her home after she'd broken her ankle. But painting was harder than she had predicted, and after one little spill, Ina was mucking stalls for Cecil Delegrange. It was honest work, and Cecil never minded that she was a girl, even if her siblings thought she was soft in the head.

Ina liked fresh starts. Clean beginnings. Mucking stalls wasn't clean. Which was why Ina was thankful Lavina mentioned she was struggling with work and tending to her *kinner*. Ina happily agreed to help in Lavina's donut shop at the local market. It was clean work and a job that put her in the shadows of seeing Abner Fisher two days a week. Since the community split, she'd not seen him at all.

Masking her elation at making another sale, Ina boxed up

one dozen sugary glazed donuts, fried perfectly this morning. Lavina insisted December was her slowest month, and Ina was determined to prove differently.

"*Danke*, Eliza." Lavina offered Eliza her change. The sisters retained pleasant smiles as Eliza disappeared around the corner to the Bee and Honey shop.

"Perhaps you're better suited for selling donuts than painting houses." Lavina giggled. Her darker hair matched that of the Graber lot, whereas Ina and sister Esther had lighter hair.

"It was one mess," Ina reminded her and turned her focus to mixing up more glaze. At this rate, they might sell out before noon. "Henry never fired Matthew for that time he painted all the doors on that house or Enoch for leaving the drywall mud lid off, costing him plenty." It wasn't Ina's fault the ceilings were so high and the ladder too short. "I could have broken an arm." She tilted her head to her sister.

"You should focus on a husband, not jobs not fitting for you." Lavina sounded much like *Mamm* when she offered gentle reminders, but she wasn't *Mamm*. Having older siblings was a thorn. Fourteen to be exact, and none missing a chance to remind Ina she had too many big thoughts.

"Why should I worry about marriage when Esther and Della are older yet? It's good to know how to do things. I fixed your supper table. It no longer wobbles," Ina said convincingly.

"It doesn't wobble, sure enough, but we need more than a few pieces of cardboard to make it worthy before Christmas supper."

Each year, Christmas supper was held at a different house. Ina thought it wrong that anyone expected Lavina to host the meal, considering her unusual circumstances. Yet Lavina happily accepted that it was her turn and seemed eager to have Christmas in her home.

"You could use a new one," Ina suggested. Surely glasses would spill and gravy land in laps if they dared let any of their *bruder*s sit there.

"I can't afford a new one," Lavina said flatly. Lavina's

concerns over her recent finances were valid. With all three *kinner* now in school, there was the monthly school donation and driver's fee. Seth, only being nine, couldn't handle the congested road to school each morning, so having a school driver was also a cost for the added safety.

"You can if we sell more donuts," Ina smiled encouragingly and pointed at the new sign she was sure would encourage more customers. Then she noted a long, tall silhouette step into the market and pause in the doorway before turning down the first aisle to her left. Her heart kicked up a few beats.

Abner had been known to hide away for days since Cilla's death. The lonely widower tugged at her heartstrings as he marched, head down, to his booth. If only she could help him. If only he'd turn around and see that someone was there willing to.

"How good that would be," Lavina said dreamingly, pulling Ina back to the present.

Abner Fisher was not a good idea. Ina wanted a family of her own and had already wasted too many nights dreaming of a different future than the one handed to her. *Mamm* said she needed to put away her childish thoughts, if she wanted any future at all. The trouble was, Ina had no idea how not to love the man who'd stolen her heart as a girl.

A strong stench of vinegar filled the market, and Lavina's face pinched. "Ach, smells like little Sara Beth was trying to help Kara again." Lavina's smile was motherly. "I best go see if they need help cleaning up." Kara was the eldest sister among them and ran The Pickle Jar just two booths down.

"I can handle the stand alone." Ina wasn't a fan of vinegar or pickles.

"It's your third day. I sure hope so." Lavina hesitated before leaving. Her lack of faith in Ina was apparent.

Three women and a young girl walked up to the counter, and Ina put on her best smile. The more donuts they sold, the more Lavina could rest easy.

"Made fresh this morning," Ina began her well-rehearsed

jingle. She had thought it up the night before her very first day, and it had proved reliable. Now if only she could think of an idea to help her sister this Christmas. It was only three weeks away. Surely, God would reveal it to her.

# CHAPTER 3

*A*bner Fisher stepped into Troyer's Marketplace and let his eyes adjust to the dim, wide metal building sectioned off into various booths. A strong stench of vinegar filled the air, making his stomach turn. He'd looked forward to a warm cup of coffee and a donut, but now, not so much. Perhaps he should have stopped at the bakery yesterday. Hazel always saw fit that he had plenty, but another conversation with his stepmother about his future was harder on his digestion than eating cold pizza.

Since selling the shop in town, which was too far to travel by buggy each day, Fisher Furniture still had to make a profit. That required showing up here two days a week. There were a gazillion things he'd rather be doing, like catching up on furniture orders.

"Abner." Surprisingly, his father welcomed him when he reached his booth.

"Hi, Daed." Abner shuffled his feet in the doorway. Surely, Daed was here to address his absence lately.

"Morning, Abner," Lewis Milford also greeted, walking their way. The young minister rented a booth close to Abner's, a toy shop sitting between them. Lewis sold homemade bookshelves,

11

clocks, and small wooden items when he wasn't working at the Shed Shop in town.

"You had a couple in here about an hour ago eyeing that bedroom set," Lewis said as he turned to the barn wood set—a bed, dresser, and nightstand made out of refurbished barn rafters. "They didn't flinch at the price, so I gave them your card. Hi, Hank. What are you doing with yourself since it's too cold to fish?"

"Fishing is easy work." Hank grinned. "Helping out my *fraa*. Now that takes a little more." The men laughed, but Abner hoped part of Daed helping his *fraa* didn't include him.

"I imagine so," Lewis added.

"Watch it, mister!"

A young girl, no more than seven or eight years old, pushed between the men. Abner collected his balance as a pair of red sneakers rushed toward the exit. The donut in her hand sparked a laugh out of him.

"Those must be tasty donuts," his father commented.

"Tastier when paid for," Lewis said with a scowl. "She was here on Tuesday, and I'm pretty sure she swiped one then, too. Lavina should have never left her stand unattended. I should go see if she's missing a donut." Lewis turned and aimed for the other end of the marketplace.

"I hope he remarries someday. He'd make a fine *daed* the way he worries over *kinner*," Hank commented as he watched Lewis aim down the long aisle.

"Not everyone remarries," Abner remarked. "Are you missing the work?" Abner turned, motioning to the display of furniture. Without his work, Abner wouldn't know what to do with himself.

"Nee, just my *sohn*," Hank replied. "I like married life too much to miss working all day. I no longer have to fret over cooking, and my socks never get holes in them." Hank chuckled.

"I don't recall ever going hungry," Abner assured him. It was hard growing up without a *Mamm*, but as far as Abner was concerned, *Daed* had filled in those empty spaces well.

"I came to ask you to supper. Hazel insists. She would have asked you herself when you were in town yesterday, but you must have been in a hurry."

Abner didn't bother mentioning how uncomfortable he was around his stepmother. Hazel tried terribly hard to make Abner feel included, and it often felt like a blanket was being pulled tightly around his head. "I've much yet to see over in the shop."

"Which will be there when you get back. I miss seeing you, so you best come by at seven. She's planning on a nice meal since it's her day off." Hank placed a hand on Abner's shoulders, which clearly meant he'd hear no excuses this time.

"Now, I best be going. Hazel sent me with a list for shopping, and I've been hoping to try out one of those donuts." Hank pointed a thumb toward Lavina's Donut Shop.

"You didn't have a sweet roll already?" Abner grinned, knowing his father's fondness for sweet breads.

"I did, but what Hazel doesn't know won't hurt." Hank winked and made his way down the aisle.

Abner chuckled. How his father stayed in such fine health, eating like he did was a wonder. Perhaps marriage was good for some. Just not all.

Before slipping into his shop, Abner watched his father step in front of a small Amish woman. Whatever he said had her laughing. It had been years since Abner made anyone laugh.

Slipping inside his 20 x10-foot booth, Abner scanned his stock. The furniture practically sold itself. Already, a set of end tables were missing. He'd need to stop by the house before leaving today and collect his check from Leon and Hannah, owners of Troyer's Market and Orchards.

Collecting a rag hidden in a dresser drawer, Abner began dusting off the pieces as he contemplated what he needed to fill the empty space next. He had little time to build extras, not with so many orders awaiting him.

At the oak table with rounded corners, his eyes immediately landed on an ashen ring at one end. Burning irritation engulfed his usual subdued demeanor. It was obvious someone had sat at the table and had a snack.

Setting down the rag, he went to a dresser in the far corner where he stashed supplies for just-in-case. He ripped out a sheet of paper from the notebook and grabbed a permanent marker. NO EATING OR DRINKING OR SITTING ON FURNITURE. It was sad that common sense and basic morals had to be penned and hung up.

"The little thief!" a voice called out from somewhere toward the basket shop.

"She went that way!" another voice called out.

Stepping out of his booth, Abner witnessed a small crowd forming. It was none of his concern, though he did suspect a pair of red sneakers might be involved. He taped the paper sign on the wooden post entering his booth.

"She took a whole jar of *Mamm*'s jam too," Addie Troyer, owner of the Honey Shop, announced.

"Perhaps to put on the donut she took from Lavina's," someone said.

*Jah*, they were all speaking of the young girl with unruly blonde hair and high-water britches. Abner scanned the crowd. He didn't like a thief any more than he did someone who disrespected his furniture, but it was hard to feel anger towards children. Children made mistakes, especially when not raised to know right and wrong. He'd sure made a few, and he was thankful *Daed* had a patient hand and a big heart during those running-around years. Now, Abner's heart was soft as a mushroom for children.

"She ran past our table and knocked jars everywhere. I've not got a jar of pickled corn left to sell!" Kara Smoker crossed her arms over her chest.

*Did folks really eat that stuff?*

"Let's not let our tempers best us," Lewis spoke up, reminding everyone that customers still needed to be tended to. Abner admired Lewis's abilities. Little ruffled his feathers. Perhaps

Abner should take the sign down. After all, he had written it with anger in his heart.

"I think we should call the sheriff. She can't be stealing without facing the consequences, or she'll keep doing it."

*Actions did have consequences. It was better for the child to learn now than later.*

"I think she needed those things more than we did." A small voice spoke up above the rest. She barely reached Lewis's shoulders, and beside her stood his father. Her identity hid behind a rich blue dress and matching apron and his father's frame, who seemed to be there for moral support.

"I need things too, but I have to pay for them," Addie spat out.

"*Jah*, but you have a job," the woman quickly replied. "Did you see her shoes? Her hair? Did any of you see a *mamm* or *daed* or anyone with her?"

The crowd grew quiet as such details hadn't been noticed by anyone, including Abner. After further convincing by the minister, everyone returned to their booths, but not before the woman turned, and their gazes collided. She looked to be one of Freeman Graber's *schwestern*. The young one, he recalled, who'd slipped on a patch of ice and broken her ankle years ago. Abner had to carry her all the way home from the school that day, seeing as none of her siblings had stuck around to let her catch up to them. He'd seen her in passing over the years. He remembered her as one of the many who prepared food the day Cilla was put in the earth, but his last seven years had been no more than a blur.

She had a sweet look to her, fine features, and a gentleness in her gaze that warmed him. Abner broke the contact, ripped down the sign, and strolled back into his quiet booth.

At three, Abner pulled his watch from his pocket. It was finally time to close up and get back to his shop. Work was waiting on him. He was also…starving. Since the uncomfortable incident with the young *maedel* earlier, Abner hadn't dared venture out of his booth. Thankfully, supper awaited him, even if eating with his new family might cause indigestion. They were simply too happy all the time, but he'd endure it for sustenance.

Stepping out to exit the booth, someone smacked into him. What was it with everyone running into him today? Abner reached out to hold on to the person when a pair of the brightest blue eyes he'd ever seen stared up at him widely.

"Hiya. Guess in my hurry to catch you before you left, I caught you," she greeted.

Abner dropped his hold on her immediately and took a step back.

"I've only been working here for a few days, but you didn't wander out, even though I didn't see you had any customers, and I was too busy to wander your way with the donut shop having so many. So. it's a good thing I caught you. Hank said you'd leave right at three and not one minute later. So, I hurried." Her smile blossomed over her unblemished cheeks.

"Did you need something?" He sounded like he had a cold, and he cleared his throat.

Without an invitation, she stepped inside. "I've spent most of my day thinking and sorting through ideas, and I've decided on the best one."

She was chatty and spoke in endless circles, and her fingers went straight to the water ring stain on his table.

"Shame folks don't have a care for beautiful things." She collected herself and turned to him. "Of course, with all the commotion earlier, it's a wonder I could think at all. Lavina said much goes on here at the market, but I had no clue how exciting it could be. It's like I never left home, but you get to see fresh faces instead of the same old ones."

Abner tried not to grin at her chattiness. He also suspected that if one forced her hands to still, she'd have fewer words to say. "*Jah*, I heard some of it. It was kind of you to come to the child's defense even though she'd done wrong."

16

"We all fail. How could I not?" She shrugged innocently, as if her thoughts knew no other way. "*Kinner* make mistakes."

"Especially when not taught properly."

"Exactly!" Blue eyes landed on him again, and he wanted nothing more than to distance himself a little further. The last thing Abner needed was to think she was pretty or want to keep looking at her.

"What is it that you need?" At least he sounded more like himself now.

"Nothing at all," she replied with another signature smile, and his heart kicked up.

"But I could use a table." They both looked at the one currently there. "*Nee*, not that one," she scoffed, then quickly gathered herself. "*Ach*, it's a fine table. Don't get me wrong. You do wonderful work. That's why the idea finally came to me when I saw you looking at me."

"I was looking at everyone," he quickly put in.

"But you stared long enough that the idea came," she said, lifting her chin slightly.

*A bold one for sure*, he thought, and stiffened. "What size table are you looking for?" He didn't have time to build any more tables right now, even if she did study him as if trying to memorize all his expressions and movements. Abner was accustomed to a few *maedels* giving him a second look, but she was studying him like all her next words were written between his brows.

"About a hundred feet." She chuckled. "I'm Ina Graber."

*Ina.* He now recalled the name of the little girl. Then again, the Pencil Grabers, a nickname given to the widespread lot, were too many to recall so readily, and Abner wasn't in the market for making new friends. Peace. Quiet. That's what he would rather have. "Pencil Grabers?"

"Yes, those Grabers." She hid another laugh behind her hand. "I'm number fifteen," she replied, as if the question had been asked. Abner had no business noticing the little dimple on her right cheek. He might be a widower now, but he still felt like a married man.

"I can see you are uncomfortable. I was just foolin'. Just a regular table will do fine. You see, my sister deserves better than she's got."

"I'm not…uncomfortable," Abner told her, though he was feeling a little exposed. Glancing over Ina's *kapp*, he noticed Lavina gathering up her son and daughter. He remembered Ruben Miller and the day folks awoke to find he had left Miller's Creek. Abner ignored all the rumors, doing his part and helping where he could as far as Lavina and her *kinner* were concerned.

"She doesn't have a table?" Abner asked. How had he missed that detail the last time he and a few of the *menner* put up winter wood for her?

"*Jah*, she does, but it's barely enough for them, and it wobbles."

Abner had a tight deadline to finish orders already in the works. If Lavina had a table, she could manage until he could get to it. "That's an easy fix."

"*Jah*, and I fixed it," Ina said proudly. "But that's temporary. I want to have one built for her as a Christmas present. She's hosting Christmas this year and is a great bit excited about it." Her nose crinkled. "I don't know why. It will be crowded, and *Mamm* will insist on doing most of the cooking. Lavina needs this, and I want to do this for her. It's the best idea I've had yet!"

It was sweet that she wanted to help her sister, but Abner had no spare time for such a project. "I'm sorry, but I have orders backed up. I can build it, but not by Christmas." A ridiculous deadline, considering Christmas was just three weeks away.

All the joyful light drained out of her.

"But it's a Christmas present. I can't give it to her after we've already eaten."

"But I don't have the time to build it right now."

"Your *daed* thought you'd say that," she quirked a brow. "That's why I'm offering to let you take my time too," she said, as if time was something to barter and trade and share. "It really has to be ready for the meal."

"You're asking for me to do the impossible." He reminded her.

"Of course I'm not. You're not God. I'm only asking for help, and I am paying for it. Nothing is impossible. You just have to consider new possibilities."

Abner blinked in confusion.

"Hear me out." She held up a hand. "You can have my time, literally. If you had help, you could do it."

"Did that idea just come to you too?"

"I have lots more if you need one," she returned with equal pluck. "Lavina needs that table. I have my whole savings put up for it. I know the costs, and I'm willing to help do the work."

"I work alone." He rubbed the back of his neck, the tension there only strangling him tighter. "I can try and squeeze it in, but no promises."

"I work for free." She was desperate and beautiful. Beautiful in the way of Plain women, without makeup or fancy jewelry adorning them. Why couldn't Lavina have asked for the table herself? Abner had at least known Lavina, Beth, and Martha Kate over the years. Long enough to know none of them caused his throat to catch.

"Have you ever built a table before?" Surely, *Daed* didn't plant this whole idea in her head.

"*Nee*," she replied. "Have you ever made donuts? I could teach you, if you're willing to learn."

What a proposition. "I'm not interested in making donuts."

"Good, because we have no time for me to teach you. I'm off Monday, Wednesday, and Thursday. See ya then," she said and quickly scampered off before he could stop her.

Abner was certain that he'd just gotten pulled into a problem, and he was certain his new step-mother had a hand in it.

# CHAPTER 4

*I*na took up two bowls of fried corn and carried them to the tables. What a change of events her life had taken on. Just when she'd decided to move on with her life, Hank Fisher bought a glazed donut. How did he know she was searching for a good idea for Lavina? When he suggested Abner, Ina thought she might swallow her tongue. She appreciated his advice on how to convince Abner to help. Maybe she'd set aside her childhood crush too quickly. Why had she doubted God's timing?

Trying to suppress her giddiness, she placed one bowl of corn on the family table and the other on the fold-out table that held the spillage of her family on a regular Saturday evening. She'd not dwell on the way Abner's gaze looked through her as if trying to be politely present and fifty miles away at the same time. She'd certainly not dwell on how funny he'd looked when she'd mentioned she'd caught him staring at her. Abner hadn't a clue how often she'd gazed at him over the years or how God blessed her with the gift of patience, and Hank Fisher with a sweet tooth.

"Ina," *Mamm* called out, despite Rachel and Kaynoshia standing about doing nothing. "Can you grab more butter for the second table?"

"*Jah*." Ina swiveled around, careful not to run over little Lisa,

Andrew's youngest, and went to fetch more butter. Fifteen-year-old Enoch could eat a whole block alone when sister Esther made her heavenly biscuits, but Enoch was on another of *Mamm's* strict diets to curb any chance he'd gain over the winter months when selling birdhouses kept him indoors more than out.

Supper for thirteen adults was a chore, and tonight Andrew and Beth paid an unexpected visit with their four *kinner*. Ina didn't mind the size of their family, but it did leave little elbow room at the table.

Rachel was already seated next to her twin, Stephen. Even at home, she was terribly shy and always trying to hide in his shadow. Paul was going on about some gypsy colt that he was eager to start working soon, and Kaynoshia was filling glasses with water, all the while rambling on about tonight's sleepover with friends. Ina never had time for such things. Not with so many siblings to help look after. She seldom went to ball games or singings because when she did, she'd rather play and sing than deal with young boys flirting and winking at her. Most had no more sense than a head of cabbage.

Ina took a seat. Since Henry married Kate and started his own drywall and painting business, she earned a new seat closer up the table. Andrew and Beth would just have to be happy with the folding chairs between them all.

A full minute of silence started the meal, just as another minute would end it. The in-between was nothing short of normal chaos. The joys of a large family sometimes weren't joyful at all. Not when you were born toward the end, and sort of in the middle. Talk of roofing jobs, favorite cookies, and ducks filled the air. Della had a thing for ducks, but Ina doubted her newest scheme to finally turn Val Beechy's head would even work.

"I heard there was quite the commotion at the market today," *Mamm* said as plates began being filled. If a Graber name was mentioned outside these walls, *Mamm* knew.

"Ivy Troyer heard a group of *youngies* ran in and broke up a bunch of Kara's goods," Esther added.

"I heard they stole a bunch of stuff, and the minister was there and did nothing about it." Freeman woke ready for each day, but by supper he was often cranky. Ina reckoned it had to do with putting in such long working hours or the mention of the newest minister. Freeman tended to draw more eyes on him than any Graber before him.

"It was just one girl," Ina answered, spooning corn on her plate. "She swiped a donut from Lavina's shop while I wasn't looking, but Kara said the jars were an accident."

"*Ach*, the poor child." *Mamm* clicked her tongue.

"You mean poor thief," Stephen corrected.

"*Nee, Mamm*'s right. She was alone and looked to be in more need of a donut than anybody I ever saw. I reckon most thieves are poor." Ina never understood why folks always assumed the worst.

Andrew, as the eldest, did that a lot. Ina still remembered when she caught him reading her journal. It was private, and yet he read all her heartfelt thoughts. Then he proceeded to tell her that Abner was not worth her time. It was embarrassing and not very nice, but soon after, Abner started courting, and Ina was sure all her hopes for a future were gone.

"You have big thoughts, but you also have a good heart, Ina," Beth offered up in a left-handed compliment kind of way. Her knack for sharing kindness and truths never went unnoticed.

"How's the store?" Ina shifted the conversation to The Bent and Dent, Andrew and Beth's favorite subject, considering the small store was prospering well. Talk further shifted to how Enoch wished folks bought birdhouses in winter and how cold his little workshop was now that winter was on their doorstep. There were two spills, no leftover potatoes, and forks clattering on empty plates before Ina wished to escape to her shared room for a moment to gather her thoughts. She'd have to inform her family of her newest intentions and hope for the best.

"If you don't mind," Paul said, clearing his throat. "I promised Sam I'd give him a lift to the ballgame tonight."

"Me too," Michael put in as he started scooting his chair away from the table.

"Don't you think to leave without me, *Bruder*."

Michael rolled his eyes at Kaynoshia's reminder.

"Supper's not over, *kinner*," *Mamm* said softly, and all movement ceased. "We prepared a fine meal, and we are all together at the most important time of our day." The supper table was *Mamm*'s favorite piece of furniture in the whole house. Having her *kinner* around her was her biggest joy. Ina knew this because *Mamm* said it so often.

Eating dessert quieted her family more than not. Ina decided now was a good time to tell her parents about her newest idea. "I offered to help Abner Fisher in his woodshop." Usually, little of what she said was truly heard and seldom addressed. This evening was the exception.

"Abner Fisher?" Andrew spoke up. As if being the eldest gave him a right to say anything at all.

Ina tossed him a glare.

"And why did you offer to do that?" *Daed* leaned back in his chair and gave her a look that required a long-winded answer.

"Because I need him to build something, and he's too far behind if he doesn't get help." Short and to the point always worked best.

"Abner builds nice things," Enoch spoke up. Though Enoch was born with Down Syndrome, he was a wonder with wood and knew every bird and their migratory pattern.

"Abner is a widower. Folks would talk," *Mamm* said, then set down a large sheet cake that looked to be apple. Ina knew that, but how else would she get Lavina's table done before Christmas and find out if God was pointing her in Abner's direction?

"I wonder if Sam Lewis might like hearing that you plan on helping Abner in his shop," Andrew put in.

"I'm not courting Sam, and that's none of your business," Ina said bluntly.

"Maybe so, but yer *Mamm* is right, Ina. I do trust Abner and think he could use more friends, keeping to himself as he does, but I cannot allow this." *Daed* accepted his slice of cake.

"But it's a table for Lavina." The secret was out. "Please don't let her know." She glanced around to all her siblings. "I've saved up, and she really needs one." She returned her pleading blue eyes on her *daed*, the final answer would be his after all. "*Mamm* says the table is the center of the home, and well... Lavina needs centering. Don't you think? Ruben sure didn't see she had one worthy of eating on."

The table grew solemnly quiet in the truth of her statement.

"We *are* having Christmas there this year," Della put in. "Wouldn't it be nice to see the look on her face?" More supporting comments followed, surprising Ina with what a great idea she had come up with. No one supported her when she wanted to start a worm farm, and yet she had made good money setting up at Twin Fork Lake every Saturday morning to sell worms for two whole summers.

"I can see you want to do more for her. We all do. It's a terrible thing she must face, but Lavina knows our love for her, and she's never been one for fanciful things," *Daed* said.

"*Nee*, she hasn't. That's why she deserves it. I agree with Ina. I had to put three new screws in her table leg a month ago. I know *Mamm* meant well gifting it to her, but you cannot even add the leaves in it without worrying they'll fall to the floor," Michael said.

"I can help Abner Fisher. I can make tables," Enoch interjected. He pushed his glasses higher on his face, a few crumbs of spiced apple cake at the corners of his mouth. Ina reached over and swiped them away. She adored her younger brother. More than Andrew, who was still eyeing her with fatherly contempt.

"*Daed*, you can't think it's okay. She's barely twenty. He's..." Andrew stopped when *Daed*'s hand went up.

"You married at her age," *Daed* reminded him before looking over all his *kinner* present. As a minister, he knew the importance of helping others, but Ina wasn't sure why his face looked so sad. "Lavina is a good example to each of you of how we should reach out to the Lord in times of hardship. Young Abner could benefit from such a project. This may be Ina's idea, but I do feel *Gott* presented it to her."

"Not like you think," Andrew muttered under his breath.

Ina ignored further mumblings from Andrew and held her breath. Andrew's problems with Abner were beyond her, and Ina refused to dig into the past that broke their friendship.

"I will allow you to help, if Abner agrees for Enoch to help too," *Daed* said.

Andrew stood from the table and, without a word, marched from the room.

"Really?" Ina got up and kissed *Daed*'s cheek.

"So, you wanna help too?" Ina looked to Enoch, who was clearly more intent on a second slice of apple cake than noticing all the mixed expressions at the tables right now.

"Sure. He might teach me something I don't know." Always-positive Enoch.

"I'm sure Abner will welcome the help," *Mamm* said with a hint of uncertainty.

Ina hoped so too. Once she convinced him what a great idea it was.

ABNER FINISHED the baked chicken and rice on his plate, thankful Hazel's *dochter*, Grace, hadn't insisted on him trying her broccoli casserole again. Growing up an only child, he'd always wanted siblings, but not three grown sisters who spent far too much time focusing on a grown *bruder*.

Lydia, just a year younger, was of the mind that any leftovers had to be carefully wrapped for him to take home. She fretted too much over Abner's appetite. Grace was always talking up her single friends in hopes to match him up. That

one was much like her mother. Then there was Martha, who
exuded melancholy. She and Cilla had been close since
childhood and just seeing her reminded Abner of his and Cilla's
first visits.

"If everyone is finished, I'll just see to wrapping up the rest of
the casserole." Lydia stood, shooting him a smile.

"I bought some of those plastic containers, so he can freeze
them if he wants," Hazel told her.

Abner failed to mention he hadn't even cared to fill up the
icehouse this year. A waste of time for only one person. Hazel
embraced finally having a *sohn* entirely too much. There was no
sense in refusing, he knew. Refusing their kindness only
encouraged them to try harder.

If only he could find a good excuse to leave before dessert
and avoid hearing Hazel talk up another single *maedel*. She was
relentless in seeing that every Kentucky heart found love. Abner
was fairly certain she had suffered a terrible head injury in the
past. Hazel was of the mind that God spoke to her personally,
and that everyone had a love match.

His was gone.

The only reason Abner even crossed over to this side of the
community since it split into two church districts was to make
*Daed* happy. Who, if he was being honest, looked happier than
Abner had seen him in years.

"I'm sure Abner appreciates all your concerns," *Daed* winked
at his *fraa*.

Abner lowered his gaze. At sixty-five, his father was in love
and had a house full of children and grandchildren. Something
Abner had never managed to give him.

Abner was twenty-nine, had an empty house, never-ending
work, and barely remembered what marriage was like. The
memory wasn't everlasting. Visions faded, and moments became
a blur. Yet Abner remembered well how it felt to have someone to
talk to and share his days with. He hadn't forgotten that.

"Have you hired help yet?" Hazel asked from across the table as she tried spooning broccoli casserole in little Emily Grace's mouth. She clearly wasn't a fan of her mother's casserole either.

"I know you have orders to fill. Hank thinks he should come to help you."

Abner glanced at his father.

"You know how his hands give him fits," Hazel quickly added. "We had hoped you would've hired help by now."

"I'll get around to it." Abner didn't want help, listening to folks talk about family, *kinner*, and all the things he had been cut short of having. Work was constant and dependable, and grief was better nursed in private. Life was easier if he focused on creating something of use. Something that lasted when nothing truly did.

"If you had help, you'd have more time to focus on other things," Grace put in. "I heard Miriam Strolfus has returned from visiting her *aenti* in Ohio," Grace continued.

Abner's face pinched at the name.

"*Nee*," Hazel quickly interjected. "She's too flighty. Our dear Abner needs..." She pointed her eerie gray eyes into him. "Someone who likes what he does. Someone who knows the value of family. I can find someone who'd be best to work with you."

Abner often liked to think before he spoke. Ponder before he decided. But he knew his stepmother, and the last thing he wanted was her deciding on his first employee.

"I had someone offer to help out for a spell," he quickly put in and shot his *daed* an *it's-your-doing* look.

"Who?" Martha inquired.

Now he'd done it. "Ina Graber needs a table built in a hurry and offered to help in the shop long enough to see it finished." In four years of sitting at this table, Abner had never known his family capable of complete silence.

"*Gott* has a match for that one. Sam Lewis is perfect. Ina is the only one out there who can convince him to follow his heart and not the path his *bruders* keep pulling him down," Hazel said.

"Sam and she would make a fine match," he agreed with a nod, but inside he couldn't see pretty little Ina Graber and any Lewis matching. "I just said she offered to help."

"But then your match will still be waiting. Abner, dear, I just want you to be happy." There it was. Hazel's ultimate concern. Abner's heart.

"*Danke*, but I'm not unhappy. I'll be going." Abner fetched his hat. If he hurried, he could finish the railing on a bed a local Englischer ordered two months ago.

"Before you leave, help me hitch up Martha's and Grace's horses," *Daed* said. It was code for let's talk, and even their husbands knew not to follow and do it themselves. Abner thanked the women for supper, slipped on his boots since Hazel frowned on shoes on her freshly cleaned floors, and followed his father to the barn. He enjoyed any alone time they could squeeze in. After all, it had only been the two of them since *Mamm* died when he was only seven. Well, until Cilla, that was.

"You were more quiet than usual tonight. Is something wrong?"

"*Nee*. It's just been a long week, is all, but you should tell Hazel to stop worrying about my love life. Meals go down better when everyone isn't focused on me," Abner told his father.

"Hazel will never stop being the face of love in these parts. It's why I love her so much. She knows what you have endured, and yet she opened her heart to an old coot like me."

"Not so old," Abner replied, though he couldn't ignore his father's stiffer fingers and his more uneven gait. They made quick work hitching both buggies. Cool night air reminded him he should see to a winter coat soon.

"It is good to have a family who loves you. You and I have spent many years without it."

"We did all right." Abner tethered Martha's horse to a round ring hanging on the side of the barn.

"You do need help, but if Amos Graber's *dochter* won't work, I can speak with Silas. His *buwe* are of age. Gideon seems to have taken a liking to building things."

Abner turned down his father's offer. He'd rather work with Ina and her infectious eyes than have his nephew, Gideon, anywhere near his things. If ever a boy was bent on calamity, it was Gideon.

"You are like a wheelbarrow, *Sohn*. You don't go anywhere unless pushed."

"I don't need to go anywhere," Abner replied. "Nor do I need you sending pretty *maed*'s my way."

"*Schee*, huh?" His father smiled. Abner should have left that thought to himself. "I only suggested you'd be good to build the table. I call that promoting you." He winked. "I've always been fond of her. She's a hard worker and spent all last year mucking stalls at the horse farm."

"Hazel's rubbing off on you." Abner wasn't blind or deaf. He knew his *daed* was up to something.

"*Nee*, I just see what is plain to see. You need help. She needs a table. I reckon she can sand and varnish and help you catch up."

It made sense, though Abner was a bit skeptical of his father's reasoning behind steering Ina his way. "Good, because I'm not interested in Ina Graber. I'm fine with how things are."

"I miss her too, *sohn*." Hank placed a hand on Abner's shoulders. "But Cilla would never want to see you alone. You make yourself scarce even now that you have a big family." That was an understatement. "You find no joy in it. Stop hiding, accept help, and God will take it from there."

"I will," Abner assured him, though more to ease his father's worries than anything else. Abner didn't mind being alone.

"Well, that's good to hear. I will see you Tuesday for supper. Their cousins will be here."

Abner nodded, though he didn't want to meet any more extended family. "I'll try. See ya soon."

"Abner," his father said, stopping Abner just shy of the door. "If you keep doing what you're doing, nothing will ever change."

Abner considered his father's words as he drove home. Blue danced across a light bed of snow, but warmer temperatures were expected for the next week that would melt it all away. He liked the snow. The way it muffled out noise and held a calm that was impossible to put into words. The sun forced a man to see more clearly. He didn't want to open his eyes any wider than they already were.

# CHAPTER 5

*A*bner studied the door all morning, waiting for Ina Graber to come barging through it at any time. She didn't strike him as someone who knocked first. By nine, he let out a breath and focused more intently on his work. He didn't need help building furniture, and he certainly would not be rushed.

Outside, rain continued to pounce on the metal building while thunder rumbled overhead. The rising temperature had turned winter into a fall thunderstorm. He turned on the generator located under the short eave connected to his shop and flipped on the wood planer that had been converted to work off an air compressor. That's why Abner had a subscription to The Busy Beaver buy-and-sell magazine. Unlike his father, Abner embraced a few new ways to be more productive, all the while keeping within the necessary confines of the *Ordnung*.

Shoving aside any concerns, since Ina hadn't made good on her threat to help him, he pushed the first board through the planer. He was well into work when movement caught his attention. The man was bent over a stack of pre-cut boards for a set of end tables at the far end of the shop. Customers usually didn't walk into his shop freely. There were dangers. In fact,

Abner had hung up a sign especially to prevent sudden barge-ins. They had to wait in the small office like every other customer.

He finished taking another eighth of an inch off his current board, turned off the planer, and removed his safety glasses. "Can I help you?" When the man turned, Abner recognized him immediately. Enoch Graber never missed hitting home runs, built birdhouses for a living, and was born with Down Syndrome.

"That'll make a lot of birdhouses," Enoch pointed. In his coat, he looked much larger than Abner remembered.

"*Jah*, but it's for a set of end tables," Abner replied. Enoch pointed at another stack. "That's for two bench seats." Abner was about to inquire about the purpose of Enoch's visit when his sister stepped into the room. She was here, and she was late.

"I reckon I should have tried in here first." Ina appeared from the side door that led to his humble office. Her cape was soaked, her shoes were sopping wet, and her dark blue dress clung to her small frame. But her laugh brought a smile to his face.

"I went to the house first." She removed her black bonnet and began shaking rain from it. She looked as if she had just swum Twin Fork Lake. Disturbingly, it didn't take away the look of her.

"I found him first," Enoch insisted. "He uses maple, hickory, and cedar. I don't like cedar. I like maple, but I make my birdhouses out of oak. Robert gives me all his leftovers when he does big jobs. So, I have to use oak or pine. I like maple."

Abner blinked at the mouthful. "I like maple too, but folks want the cedar for certain pieces," Abner replied, ignoring how Ina's eyes brightened as she looked at her *bruder*.

"'Cause it keeps bugs away, but maple is better." Enoch continued to explore the shop's inventory.

"I see you brought reinforcements for your cause," Abner muttered to the woman at his right, her gaze solely on her brother.

"Not my idea, but he is in his element." She sighed affectionately. "I reckon that's why *Daed* insisted he come along, on account folks might think we are sweet on each other," she said, grinning as she looked up at him.

"We're not," Abner said bluntly. The last thing he needed was for anyone to get the wrong idea.

"Exactly! Where do we start?" She rocked on tiptoe, eager, or perhaps she had a dangerous *kaffi* habit.

"I told you I can't build a table in three weeks. I have other orders." He waved a hand over the crowded, vast room, dozens of projects in various stages of completion. To his right, Enoch was on his knees, studying all the details of a bandsaw.

"But now you can. We're here to help you, Abner. Hank said you like working alone, but that helping one another is important and you might need the reminder."

"I don't want help." He was certainly not missing the next family supper. *Daed* had some explaining to do.

"But you need it and how will Lavina get her Christmas present if you don't? I'm paying you."

"It's not about money," he told her. Her confusion showed in the way her brows gathered.

"I spent all night thinking of ideas to help you accept our help, but none of them will work if you don't try to look at it from my point of view." Her nose wrinkled disapprovingly.

"Your view isn't the only one there is. Leave me your order, and come back after Christmas." Abner turned to walk away. Hopefully Enoch wasn't readjusting touching anything too sharp.

"It's because I'm a woman, isn't it?" Her hands exclaimed her words. "Andrew and Henry always say I can't do things, yet I do. Are you of the same thinking? I know Hank doesn't think so. He said I'd be a great help to you. I worked for Henry's painting crew, and when my family came down with the flu, it was me and Robert who had to finish that addition to our house. When Michael and Timothy are out doing no telling what"—she rolled her eyes adorably—"I see to chopping the firewood for *Mamm*, and Esther seldom helps out."

"It's not because you are a woman." A fact that was more

apparent the longer she stood there. And with so many *bruders*, why was she chopping firewood? "Your *bruders* should be seeing to the chores and not telling you such things."

"*Nee*, they shouldn't, but *bruders* can be a thorn." Her hands finally rested.

"So can *schwestern*." Abner had a sudden vision of Grace and Lydia smiling, but quickly shook it off.

"*Ach*, you're worried about your shop. You have many fancy things here." She took in the room. "Is that it? You don't trust others in your shop? Is that why you're always alone?" She eyed him curiously.

Being alone wasn't his choice. Not really. "I'm not worried about my shop." They both glanced at Enoch again. He clearly was in awe of the machinery.

"Enoch will be of help too. No one taught him to build birdhouses. Refusing help is...prideful." She squinted judgingly. "I can paint, varnish, sand, and follow orders. I can even tackle that desk of yours. You know, you wouldn't be so behind if you organized better."

"When do you breathe?" Abner said in complete astonishment. How did she expel so many words without air?

"After I'm finished." Offense showed in the tightening of her lips. "When you're number fifteen, it's best you get it all out before someone else starts up. If my talking is a deal breaker, then you'll not hear another word out of me."

He doubted that, but was surprised she was so willing to please him. "I like being alone." Could he be any more clear?

"No one likes that," she said as she waved a hand towards him and laughed.

"I do. This" —he motioned between them—"will not work," he told her as he tried not to decide if her eyes were blue green or just an unnamed shade of blue.

"Why?" Her head tilted curiously.

Abner wasn't about to tell her that he didn't like change, and she clearly would bring a lot of that to his routine. "Because."

"It will work how *Gott* sees fit," she said with an unusual sadness he hadn't expected. "Please help me, for Lavina's sake, of course." She pointed to her *bruder*. "Enoch knows his way around, and I'll stay out of your way, if that's what you want. This is important to me."

The begging in her tone tugged his softer side. It wasn't Enoch that concerned him. This wasn't an apprenticeship. Abner started to reroute her thoughts once more when she turned and walked away. That's what he got for hesitating, but those eyes were definitely blue green. She whispered something in Enoch's ear, and they both turned to him and smiled. Hers with an extra dose of sweetness.

*Now why did she have to go and do that?*

"You know your *Englisch*?" Enoch marched towards him, his shoes smacking hard on the concrete floor. "I do because I read a lot, but Ina says you're smart too," Enoch quirked a grin.

Abner lifted a brow. Enoch was clearly part of her plan to distract him. "I know enough," Abner replied, curious where the odd question was going.

"Which is proper? Is the egg yolks white, or, are the egg yolks white?"

Abner gave it some thought and replied, "Are."

Enoch's laugh erupted. "Told you he wouldn't get it. Can we build tables now?" Enoch asked his sister. His mind already focused on the next task.

"How about you show us what we can easily help with? You have us all day," she said seeing that he was growing more frustrated the longer they kept him from his work.

"And tomorrow. You promised I can be in a real shop tomorrow too," Enoch reminded her. "*Daed* said you have to let me help, and Andrew says I have to watch you."

"Andrew isn't your boss," Ina said sharply, a hint of red warming her cheeks.

"You tell me what to do all the time. *Mamm* says to listen to my siblings."

Now it was Abner's turn to laugh. "Fine. You can sand," he told Ina. Sanding would tire her out real quick, and she'd likely not return. He turned to Enoch. "And you can varnish." Abner had seen the man's birdhouses enough to know he had some talent with a brush, and Abner was behind on the chore.

"Will I get to work on the bandsaw?" Enoch asked eagerly.

"I'm sure Abner will get around to showing you later," Ina told him. "Remember, we are here to help Lavina, not to enjoy ourselves."

"That's a secret. Lavina's table is a secret. Andrew said we can't share our secrets with Abner."

Why Enoch's comments about Andrew troubled him, Abner wasn't sure. He and Andrew had been boyhood friends, but after Cilla, Abner let that friendship fall away. No matter. That was long ago, and Abner couldn't hash out burned-out friendships.

By the end of the day, Abner had to admit the two had made a difference. Ina hand sanded every board for a bookshelf without complaint. Once varnished, set to dry, and revarnished, he could assemble everything and call up Mr. James, who thought himself a bibliophile, *whatever that was*, and let him know he would finally have somewhere to place his beloved treasure trove of books.

Enoch too had made a lot of headway. The bed ordered by the young couple would be ready to assemble tomorrow. All the posts, railings, headboard, and footboard glistened sharply under the gas lighting. Enoch had even finished the matching men's dresser, with all its drawers and corners. That's why Abner said nothing when Enoch waved goodbye and said, "See ya in the morning."

# CHAPTER 6

*B*y Friday, Abner was beginning to admire the siblings' dedication and how quickly two more tables had been assembled. He was further surprised when Ina brought lunch for them. It had been some time since he'd eaten roast beef sandwiches and raspberry bars. She must have gotten up real early to prepare everything.

"I reckon you should decide what sort of table you want me to make," Abner told her.

"That would make building it a bit easier, don't ya think?" She grinned, wiping her mouth. Her sarcasm was deserved, considering both siblings had been here all week, and Abner had yet to start on Lavina's Christmas table.

In his office, Abner fetched two magazines he often let customers sift through, and for reasons he didn't understand, he collected the yellow binder filled with his own personal sketches. Some pieces he'd built already. Some, he hoped to one day.

Setting her lunch aside, Ina sifted through the magazines while he and Enoch returned to work. The more Abner got to know the two, the more he discovered Enoch Graber was wasting his days on birdhouses. He never had to be told twice what to do, and his eye for detail was impressive.

MINDY STEELE

"You drew these?" Ina strolled up behind him, his design folder in her hand.

Abner set down the large clamp in his hand that he used to join glued boards into one large piece and he turned to her. "I used to have time for sketching out a few ideas."

"Each one is amazing, Abner!" Her gaze held the pages, and his heart surprisingly accelerated.

"I love them all, but this one," she pointed, "is practical. I like how the legs allow for extra sturdiness. Can two leaves fit on this one without falling to the floor?" She presented him with a Dutton design, one of his most treasured table designs with carved edges and square legs. He'd hoped to build it one day in rough, sawn lumber, varnished in rich mahogany or walnut. The way she tilted her head struck a chord in his chest.

"Four," he said as he cleared his throat and focused on the sketch. "It can take up to four leaves, but I'd have to attach drop-down legs for extra support. I know you have a big family, but the extra leaves will take longer. We can build it at seven feet. Not too big. Not too small, and add two leaves. Should seat around... sixteen or so."

"Can we do *that* in two weeks? I know you have others who've been waiting." She ducked her head and tucked a corner of her mouth between her teeth, hopeful he'd say yes.

He liked the sound of "we" and how she smelled of sawdust and jasmine. "We did finish the bookshelf and two more pieces today, and if Enoch doesn't mind helping me with that new bedroom set and table tops, it's possible."

"He would. He talked all night about that bedroom set."

"He's been a help," Abner admitted. "*Daed*'s been hounding me to hire help, and I am considering offering Enoch part-time work. I should really put him on the payroll for all he's done." It was true. The young man could stick to a task and see it finished in a timely manner. Abner also enjoyed Enoch's company. It had been years since he let a silly joke spark a laugh out of him, and Enoch had a pocketful of reasons to laugh.

38

"And what of your sander?" She lifted two fine brows playfully.

Abner's palms began to sweat as she awaited his answer. Not very safe for working with saws and sharp objects. He was in danger of letting all those adorable quirks make him keep smiling. He admired her zeal for trying new things and her deep love of family. He didn't even mind the way her hands flowered her words. Her attentive nature, seeing that he and Enoch had warm *kaffi* and a full lunch, despite her working too, spoke volumes to the woman she was. She had a way about her that made each room brighter.

"You could probably sand faster if I showed ya how to use the battery sander." *Had he said that out loud?*

"What a trick, Abner Fisher." She narrowed him a look. "I reckon I can be pushy when my mind is set on something."

That was putting it mildly. A laugh barreled out of him like steam from a hot kettle. He liked the banter between them, and as she continued to study the design her heart was set on, he tried not to study the way her finger traced down the page.

"I want to help with the process."

*Of course she did.*

"It's not like building a pole barn or putting on an extra room."

"*Nee*, it's not," Abner replied.

"Robert and his crew are always trying to hurry and put those up. He'd get angry at me for pointing out missing screws or uneven cuts."

"They are contracted to finish in a timely manner."

"But one should always do their best," she added, giving him another intense stare. "Furniture…isn't hurried."

"*Nee*, it takes time and patience." Two things Abner had plenty of. He walked her through the process, picked out his best boards, stacked them by the planer, and let her decide on what varnish they would apply.

"I think the darker one would look better, don't you?"

His opinion mattered. It had been years since his thoughts carried any weight. "I do."

"Danke for letting me help. It makes it all the more special by being a part of Lavina's ideal Christmas. Helping others is such a blessing."

"I'm learning it can be." Abner now understood her willingness to be here. Ina liked to see a thing from start to finish, to learn the steps that shaped something useful.

"You're the best furniture maker I know. You know your purpose."

"You don't have to keep sweetening me up, Ina. Besides, we're all good at something." Like making his thoughts wander as to whether or not she would accept a ride from him one late evening.

"I've tried everything, but once I learn it, I'm ready for something else."

"Perhaps you're meant for coming up with good ideas," he suggested and watched her appreciation brighten her eyes.

"I'm not sure that's really a trade that will support me one day, but I do have lots of ideas." Her face bloomed.

"You'll marry," he said abruptly. It was a wonder she hadn't already. "And you'll need all your ideas to run a household and a family."

"*Mamm* says the same, but I don't know. I can't see getting married without a perfect partner."

"You cannot tell me no one has asked you on a date before," Abner said aloud. He seldom let his thoughts escape so forwardly, but he found her comment hard to believe.

"They ask, but..." She lowered her gaze. "But I've yet to say yes."

"Afraid they won't like a pushy girlfriend? Could be a deal breaker for some men."

"Not funny. I'm waiting." She turned her eyes from him, a hint of longing behind long lashes.

"For what?" He truly wanted to know.

"I'm waiting for... well, for Della to marry first." She didn't sound so sure. "I mean, she's twenty-five, and if her baby ducks don't land her a husband soon, I may never marry at all."

"Baby ducks?" Abner had heard plenty of excuses why one waited to start a family, but Ina's excuse made no sense at all.

"It wasn't my idea," she made sure to point out, "but Della thinks her Muscovy ducklings will work. She dropped three of them off at Val Beechy's Harness Shop for him to watch over them while she was shopping. She wants to know if he has a gentle spirit, she says, because he always looks so temperamental."

Abner knew of Val and his sour looks, but now he had more questions. "Did he tend to them?"

"*Jah*, but that was three months ago. She's waiting to see how long it takes him to come calling," she said as she cocked her head towards him with a playful flicker of amusement in her eyes, "or return them."

"Well," Abner said in surprise. "Never heard of such a nudge for courting." Abner chuckled.

"I'd never do something so foolish, but Della has been sweet on Val for a while, and I pray it works out for her."

"Me too," he said, shooting her a smile. "I'll pray that baby ducks bring on a spring wedding, but I'm glad to hear you'd never try something so foolish." Silence lingered between them for a few seconds before she spoke again.

"Will you be at the recital next Friday?"

"I don't have *kinner*."

"Neither do I, but we never miss it. If you come, you can try my brown sugar cookies," she said with a hint of hope. "The *kinner* do a wonderful job. I'd hate to see you miss it."

Abner remembered when she worked for his stepmother at the bakery. If lunch today was any indication of her cooking abilities, he imagined her *kichlin* were just as tasty. "I live in this church district now. My step-sisters," he shook his head. "They

41

tend to try pushing me towards their single friends. I'd rather not give them any false hopes by showing up."

"Oh," she replied. Her downcast expression quickly perked up. "I have an idea."

"I reckon you do."

"If I invite you, then maybe they won't try that."

It would surely convince Grace and Lydia to not push Miriam Strolfus his way, but… "Are you asking me on a date, Ina Graber?" *Was she?* Part of him hoped not, but the other part, the part who found her forwardness refreshing and those adorable grins enchanting, was itching for a different response.

"*Nee*, I just wanted you to try my brown sugar cookies. Women don't ask men on dates," she said as she rolled her eyes.

"*Nee*, they don't, and if I were interested, I'd rather do the asking." But that he couldn't do. What was wrong with him? Abner had no business standing here flirting with Ina, talking about marriage, dates, and ducks. He had no business daydreaming about spending more time with her. Cilla was who mattered. His heart belonged to another.

Stepping away, he collected himself. How could he have let this slip of a woman make him forget? "We'd best be getting back to work."

# CHAPTER 7

*S*hame heated Ina's cheeks as she worked a fresh battery onto the sander. She truly wanted to see Abner be a part of something with others, even if it didn't include her. Her invitation came out wrong. Didn't it? She had tried so hard not to show her true feelings, but that one long look had her forgetting. What was she thinking of asking Abner Fisher on a date? What happened to being patient and letting God direct their paths? *Mamm* said her forwardness fenced on the edge of invasiveness. She was…incorrigible.

She flipped on the switch, gently maneuvered the rotating sander over the edges of a desktop, and considered the man. She'd give him credit. Abner was wiser than Sam Lewis and less noisy than her *bruder*s. His shop was a declaration that the man liked exploring new things. She remembered him as one of the men who helped build a new room at the school, and he was there when the Lambright's horse barn had to be rebuilt after a storm.

Ina bounced between jobs in hopes of finding her place. Abner knew his place. He looked at a piece of wood, put it in his hands, and with tender steps, nurtured and transformed it. She could probably learn a thing or two from that.

43

The sound of something smacking concrete drew Ina's attention. She flipped off the sander, removed the oversized safety goggles Abner insisted she wear, and went to investigate. Oh, she hoped Abner wasn't so upset at her boldness that he'd slipped and cut off a finger. What if he bled to death? What if she killed the only man she truly loved?

Behind a moving wall that prevented dust from settling on furniture during the varnishing process, Ina noted the dark maple syrup seepage from under the wall. Just then, Enoch stepped around the corner, and it was much worse than a missing finger.

"It's broken. Help me, Ina." His front was covered in varnish, and his arms and hands were dripping onto the floor. "Abner's gonna be angry."

Ina hurried to her younger sibling.

"What happened?" Abner appeared, a worried look on his face.

Ina hoped her *bruder* wouldn't get too upset. Accidents happened. Unfortunately, she could already see Enoch's bottom lip push out and his head droop. He was prone to sudden outbursts of tears when frustrated or overwhelmed, though it had been some time since he had done so. By the look of him, Ina knew a flood was coming.

"I got it all over *mei* shirt. *Mamm* will be mad too. Ina, I'm sorry. I tried to refill the can like Abner showed me, but my fingers got slippery, and I dropped it." The tears finally came, but Ina was proud to see Enoch try to remain calm. As a child, it had been much harder for him to do so.

"Slippery hands would make it difficult." Abner stepped forward and helped him out of the puddle. "Let's get these shoes off." He turned to Ina. "We can't let this soak through, or I'll have to scrub him down with gasoline."

Fear struck Enoch in the mention of gasoline instead of soap. "But that will hurt! Will it hurt?"

"Don't fret. I've spilled my share of paint and varnish. Have you seen these floors?" Abner turned to her. "Run into the house and fetch my extra boots by the door. Perhaps a change of clothes, rags, and soap, too. You can find everything in the washroom at the back of the house."

Ina hesitated only briefly before she darted out into the cold and into the two-story house next door. She hated to leave her *bruder* alone with Abner. Having never grown up with siblings of his own, she didn't know if he would show the patience required when dealing with Enoch, but she reminded herself that Abner was the epitome of calm as she rushed across the yard. Cold wind snapped at her kerchief. *Daed* always insisted that being too kind to Enoch would only make him think he wasn't normal. No one wanted Enoch to feel that.

The two-story house was long and narrow. A saltbox design like her grandparents' home had been. She pushed through the back door and immediately spotted two piles of laundry. After a few minutes, Ina determined which was clean and which wasn't and selected a pair of trousers, socks, and a shirt. It had been years since she'd been inside the home. With that, the memory of Cilla's death swarmed over her. *If Abner wanted to court you, he would have asked.* What a dumb idea, hoping this time together would show Abner she was no longer a small girl clumsy on ice.

Aside from the piles of laundry, the rest of the room was tidy. Floors were swept, and everything was in its place. Turning, she found the pull-on boots and collected those as well.

It was curiosity that forced her to take two steps into the kitchen. Empty counters and sparse furnishings spoke of the widower. She noted two aprons hanging from a wooden hook on the pantry door. She started to giggle, imagining him cooking in them, but once more, reality gutted her heart. Those could be Cilla's.

Death was forever. She'd been taught that from the cradle. Sucking in a sorrowful breath, Ina knew that Abner was clinging onto the memory of what he lost, and she feared he'd never embrace a new future. They'd finish the table, and he'd return to being but a blur in her life.

"*Gott*, help my heart to be thankful for what time we have together. Help me accept Your will in this."

~

"She likes you," Enoch said as Abner pulled off his socks. The varnish had found its way in, leaving his socks dripping, and his feet black. As much as Abner didn't like having the sticky substance on him, he was sure Enoch didn't either.

"Who?" Abner replied despite knowing who Enoch was referring to.

"My *schwester*, Ina. Andrew says you can't like her back. Are you going to fire me? Henry fired me." Enoch's shoulders curled, and his head hunkered between them.

"I'm not firing you. I've made bigger messes than this. You're gonna have to take off that shirt and your trousers." Without hesitating, the grown man stripped awkwardly. Abner was thankful he was behind the wall in case Ina returned.

Abner tried not to let Andrew's disapproval trouble him, but he was but flesh and had never recalled doing anything to warrant Andrew's disapproval. "Why does Andrew say I can't like her back?"

"He says yer old, but I don't think yer old. You don't even have white hair."

Abner's brows gathered. He was two years younger than Andrew, which made him fairly young.

"I have the clothes," Ina called out, shutting down any further talk.

Abner stepped out from behind the wall to collect the extra set of clothes. "I'll take those."

Bits of snow sprinkled her shoulders and kerchief, and he thought about the little girl who bravely held back tears of pain as he carried her home. At seventeen, Abner hadn't been eager to start courting, but Andrew encouraged him to court Cilla so he could court Beth. Cilla was pretty, sweet, and shy. Abner had been taken with her immediately. Ina was nothing like that, yet he couldn't deny the attraction between them.

"Wait here," Abner told her, taking her armload from her. When his fingers raked over hers, his face warmed. "Did you get the soap?"

"It's in one of the boots. I'll go fetch some water." She hurried off again.

The shop wasn't as cold as the outside. Not with the potbelly stove burning nearby, but Enoch shivered, his teeth chattering uncontrollably. Abner helped him remove most of the stain from his arms. His belly and legs would take more than soap, but Abner knew it was best to let the young man see to that himself. After all, Enoch might be one of God's special children, but he was a man now.

"I want to go home now," Enoch said as he put on a fresh shirt. He was wider in the shoulders, and the tight fit was apparent.

"We finished a lot today. We can start back Monday."

"Will I get to use the planer?" Enoch asked.

"Depends on what jobs I get lined up by then, but I'd be happy to teach you." This earned Abner a wide, toothy smile.

"I'll fetch the buggy." Enoch put on his coat and left Abner to see to the rest of the spilled mess. Abner chuckled. Enoch wanted to get home before folks saw him in clothes that were not his.

Abner collected the soiled garments and stepped out from behind the wall. Bent at the knees, Ina was working a stack of shop rags over the spilled varnish. Like a bee on a flower patch, she fought to clean up as much as possible. Maybe Andrew had a reason to worry.

"I say we call it a day. He could use better fitting clothes and went to hitch up the buggy."

Ina jumped to her feet. "Enoch always gets upset, but working will help him move on and forget it. That's why he started building birdhouses."

"Kind of a therapy?" *Was that why she was always trying new things?*

"*Jah*, exactly. So, if you make us leave, he'll only worry more." She gave him her most pleading look. "Enoch loves working with you. Please don't make him leave. It's my fault anyhow."

"How so?" As far as Abner knew, she was at the other end of the shop when the sprayer broke.

"Well, if I didn't have the idea to build Lavina a table and to have you build it, then *Daed* wouldn't have made him come. So, in a way, this whole mess"—she motioned about her—"is my fault."

"I think…" *That Enoch is blessed to have her as a sister.*

"I'll pay for the varnish plus what I already owe you, and we can stay later and try to get this up before…" She looked at the mess at her feet. It was hopeless, but the color did give the concrete an oddly nice appeal.

"Just let us finish the table at least. I'll keep quiet and watch over Enoch better. Don't make me… I mean, us leave."

Abner couldn't help but smile. He doubted she knew the definition of quiet, but he admired her dedication to her family.

"I'm apologizing, Abner Fisher. It's not funny. It wasn't my idea to let him use a sprayer."

"Because your ideas are all failproof," he replied playfully, noting the way her scrunched-up expression was cute.

"I have many great ideas. Once I made plastic boot covers for Henry's work crew so they didn't get paint on their shoes."

That would have come in handy currently, Abner mused. "Did they work?"

"*Jah*, of course," she shot back quickly. "Well, until Timothy and Michael slipped and fell and…"

"And…" He leaned in closer. So close, he caught another scent of jasmine.

"And they fell in the paint." She let out an exasperated huff. "Do you like making me doubt my own ideas?"

"*Nee*." In fact, Abner wanted to nurture them, but telling her so felt like a betrayal to Cilla. She'd often begged for his opinion on her sewing. Abner didn't know one stitch from another, but he always encouraged her interests.

"I'm not making either of you leave, but Enoch's eager to get home, wash up, and put on clothes that fit him. Your help has made a difference." Abner didn't think she could get any prettier, but when her shock replied with a silent *O* shape on her lips, he laughed again. "In fact, I like having you around. It gives me a reason to laugh," he said, feeling his own face heat.

"I like being here too," she said with a wide smile.

How did she so easily help him forget his promise?

"Ina, I have to take you home. Abner said so." Enoch yelled from the office door, but her eyes held his for a moment longer.

49

# CHAPTER 8

*I*na hated missing going to the woodshop today, but in the last week, she had come to know the widower better than the boy of her schoolgirl crush. She cherished their time together. She'd learned how to build a table from start to finish and even discovered Abner's love for cocoa and frosted brownies. She organized his books as well as all the hardware he used on dressers, doors, and handles. Abner was currently stumped on Enoch's newest riddle. "*When is a door, not a door?*" Ina hated to admit it, but she too was stumped by that one. Perhaps her head was in the clouds, her love for Abner growing deeper. He didn't have to stop at the donut shop two mornings in a row or compliment the sign she painted for Lavina. Was it possible that Abner was ready to open his heart to love again?

"You've been spending a lot of time at the furniture shop lately," Della said, pulling Ina back to the present and the fact that her last batch of cookies were burning. The school recital wasn't until noon, but making three dozen brown sugar cookies and two pans of cookie bars took some time.

"Perhaps her thoughts are more on a handsome widower and not on baking," Twelve-year-old Kaynoshia further remarked.

"It takes a lot to build a table, and Enoch really enjoys being there." Ina tried sounding convincing, but her *schwestern* weren't convinced her recent joy had anything to do with Enoch's enthusiasm over working at a furniture shop.

"Abner isn't interested in anyone," her *schwester* Joan remarked.

"He has been visiting my donut shop more too," Lavina revealed. "What are you helping him with?" she asked while feeding soupy oatmeal to three-year-old Naomi.

"It's a little Christmas project. Nothing important." Ina shrugged, hoping Lavina didn't ask more.

"If you are thinking to catch his eye, you'd best pay better attention to your baking," Esther pointed at the overly brown cookies.

"Now, Esther. I remember when you burned cookies because you were more concerned with your sewing than your baking." *Mamm* smiled tenderly before turning to Ina again. "I think Enoch is learning much under Abner's teachings, but there is talk that Abner is slipping from his faith. He has many fanciful things in his shop, and he's asked his *Englisch* neighbor to create a website for his furniture."

"What a great idea," Ina blurted out. "He could double his orders." *Mamm*'s frown had Ina wishing she kept the thought to herself. "I mean, it isn't against the rules, as long as he doesn't *use* a computer and all of his tools and machines run off air or batteries. It's no different than what Robert or Henry do for their work."

"You're defending him." Della slipped cooled *kichlin* onto a tray and covered them before shooting Ina a sneaky smile. "None think he'll ever remarry. You'd be wasting your time."

"You're wasting your time waiting on Van to bring your ducks home," Esther shot back.

"Many remarry after a loss. It is our way," *Mamm* informed her daughters.

"But some focus on the blessings around them instead of what is gone," Lavina muttered as she brushed a finger over

Naomi's chubby cheeks. Such talk clearly made her think of Ruben.

"*Jah*. It can be hard to accept *Gott's* plan." *Mamm* patted Lavina's hand. "You have been a great example to others of how our faith can carry us through hard times."

"How can some remarry and some *naet*?" Kaynoshia snapped a lid on the half sheet of cookie bars to keep them fresh. She was already dressed in her favorite blue dress, and Ina had heard her practicing each of her lines for the recital up into the night.

"I think sometimes love can be so beautiful that once a partner is gone from us, we struggle to recognize love again." *Mamm* turned to Ina. "Are you concerned that Abner may never find love again?" *Mamm* lifted a brow. "I have always known you've had eyes for him."

"You did?" Ina shouldn't have been surprised.

"Whatever!" Della laughed. "We all know."

"Well, he may never feel the same, but I think everyone deserves to be loved. Even Della and her ducks." Ina giggled, earning her a narrow look from Della.

No longer wanting the attention on her, Ina quickly changed the subject to who was riding to the youth recital with whom. The men would be there just before it started, seeing as they had drivers hauling them from a job site, but the women had to be early to make sure all was ready for the break after the recital.

Ina held the reins firmly in her hand as she followed *Mamm's* buggy toward the school. The wind was terrible today—a coldness that could move quickly into your bones if you let it. Beside her, Lavina sat, staring out at the landscape, a knitted scarf wrapped snuggly around her neck.

"Winter is here, I'm afraid."

"Winter can be as beautiful as summer if you look at it right," Ina replied. She never understood why folks complained about the seasons. Sure, some were better than others, but all were beautiful and necessary for life to thrive and survive.

"You're not the one who has to depend on others to chop

your wood." Lavina straightened. "Sorry. I'm just not myself today."

Just as Ina suspected, all the earlier morning talk had soured her sister's mood. "Is it because talking earlier made you think of Ruben?"

"*Jah*, but he is seldom far from my thoughts." Her cape hid strong shoulders that had borne much weight the last few years. Ina prayed God would help her sister. A sister who understood matters of the heart more than anyone she knew.

"Can I ask you a question without you getting upset?" Ina gave her a sidelong look.

"Of course. I can't imagine you purposely upsetting anyone."

"Did you truly love Ruben—I mean, with all your heart?"

"Of course I did, and in my heart, I still love him."

"But he left you and the *kinner*." Ina didn't understand. If love wasn't returned, how could one keep on loving the person?

"Love stands even in the darkness, Sister. We cannot make our hearts stop, even if it is one-sided."

"Even when they don't love you back?" Ina wasn't sure letting Abner consume her heart all this time was best. What if he never came to care for her? Could she risk having a family of her own if he didn't?

"Even then. My friends tell me they don't understand either after everything Ruben has done—is probably still doing." Lavina stared forward and shook her head. "Yet, I stood before our community and *Gott* and promised to love him all my days."

"He made that same promise," Ina remarked.

Lavina turned to her swiftly. "*Jah*, but I don't have to answer for Ruben's choices."

That was true. *Gott* didn't hold you accountable for the mistakes of others. "Will you keep loving him?" Did that mean Abner would always be in her heart? That, if she continued her girlhood fantasy, her future would be as lonely as Lavina's?

"Until death." The finality of it was a hard fact. Her sister would be forever yoked with a ghost. Ina wondered if Abner felt the same and would forever live a life without love in it.

"If *Gott* ever gave you the choice to have love a second time and to be happy again, would you accept it?"

"That's a strange question. Are you asking me if I'd accept love again and go against our faith, or...?" Lavina narrowed her gaze as one side of her lips hiked slightly. "Are you asking if Abner Fisher could love again?"

"The second one," Ina shamefully admitted.

"I thought so. We could have gotten to this sooner if you didn't dally so long," Lavina scoffed. "*Gott* gives us what we need and no more than we can handle. If our heart has been taken, we can't very well deny it. Do you love him, Ina?"

"I do. I have for some time."

"Since that day you fell running after us to get home, and he carried you all the way home," Lavina said as if suddenly recalling the day. "I'm sorry we left you. I should have paid closer attention."

"Since then." Ina blew out a breath. "I never blamed any of you for leaving me. I was too young to keep up, and I let Enoch get lost twice. Remember when I lost Kaynoshia, and *Mamm* found her sleeping in the laundry basket? It's *narrish*, loving someone at six."

"It's sweet, not crazy at all."

"I want a family, but I want love in return too. Abner may never be able to do that. Right now, I am nothing more than a sander to him."

"I see. We all have our idea of what our life should be." Lavina shifted in the seat to face her. "Ruben's *Mamm* asked me a question back then, and I didn't want to hear it, but for you, I think it's a good question. Are you willing to be Abner's friend, even if he can never give you more than his friendship, even if he never loves you the way you love him?"

It was hard to fathom a life without loving Abner Fisher in it. Ina had done so for as long as she could remember. When he married, it nearly broke her, but when he lost Cilla, it tore open her young knowledge of life, love, and the unpredictable tomorrow. She had witnessed siblings marry and grow families. Her heart ached for that, but she also knew love wasn't always romantic.

Ina loved Enoch, Joshua, Stephen, Paul, Michael, Timothy, Henry, Freeman, Robert, Allen, and even Andrew, despite him being so bossy. She loved her *daed*. Lavina's question sat between her ears the rest of the way to the school. Though her heart had always been set on the romantic, Ina knew she'd rather love Abner as a friend than to never love him at all.

"I am willing."

"Oh, Ina." Lavina leaned over and draped an arm around her. "I love you, *Schwester*, and I pray all will *kumm* right for both of you. I truly feel you are the healing Abner needs."

Ina wanted to be more than his need. She wanted to be his choice, but just as she accepted her faith, she had to accept God's answers.

# CHAPTER 9

*A*bner hated to admit it, but the shop was quieter without Enoch and Ina about. For a man who craved quiet, it was suddenly too quiet, and he missed them. But letting Ina take up any room in his heart meant he had to let go of the parts Cilla consumed.

"Lord, I'm torn between holding on and letting go. Give me peace and understanding."

"It's a fine thing to hear you're talking to the Lord, *Sohn.*"

Abner startled as his stepmother stepped into the shop. In her hands was a tray of something covered with a pink lid. The woman did like the color pink and tried incorporating it where she could. Abner glanced behind her and let out a breath. None of his stepsisters accompanied her. Neither did any unwanted *maedel.*

"He and I have our talks. I know you didn't stop by on your way home, since the bakery is the other way," Abner grinned. "Is everything alright?"

"*Jah.* The Lord tends to see all things come out right, eventually. I brought you these." Hazel lifted the lid to reveal a few dozen frosted brownies. She had discovered them as a favorite of his and often saw to it that he had plenty on hand. "I should have *kumm* sooner," she glanced at his work clothes. "You best hurry, or you'll be late."

"Late for what?"

"The school recital. You can take these for the snack afterwards. The *kinner* love them." She shoved the pan into his hands. Abner had to accept it lest it fall to the floor, and he wasn't one for wasting frosted brownies.

"I have a lot of work to do and…"

"And work will wait. God gives us enough time to do all the things He needs us to do. He doesn't need you hiding away in here and avoiding all the things He has planned, either." Her smile was a tad cocky, as if she did speak directly with God for all her wisdom.

"I know I haven't been the best stepmother."

Abner started to explain that it was him who hadn't been the best stepson when she held up a hand to keep him quiet. "But you do give me a few challenges. I shouldn't have invited Miranda for supper a few weeks ago. I sometimes forget to listen to God more than my own thoughts. Pride is such a sinful thing, but I've learned my lesson."

"Have you?" Abner wasn't sure. Give Hazel an inch, and she took a whole foot.

"I have. I will not meddle in your love life any longer, even though I know what a terrible mistake you're making."

"Is that so?"

"*Jah.* You're hiding, and you're missing everything. I tried that already, and it doesn't work. I loved Joseph with all my heart. We had so many good years together. Many memories, and when he died, I was lost. I had no one to tell about my day and no one to listen to my thoughts or encourage me to keep baking. I had *kinner* missing their *daed* to see over."

Shame washed over Abner at her heartfelt words. Hazel always appeared confident and the center of everything around her. Hazel had built a whole life with her late husband, only to have it cut short.

"That was a lonely season in my life, but I prayed for guidance and for God to help me find my purpose as a widow."

Abner traced his foot over a pile of wood shavings. "Did He answer?" Abner had yet to hear God's instructions after a prayer.

"He always answers. We just don't always like to listen. We have many roles in our lives, but none of them are to be alone."

"I reckon I've been guilty of that," he admitted. "How did you...?" He wanted to say get over it, but no one truly got over losing someone they loved.

"Heal?

"*Jah.*" *That was a better word.*

"I sold everything we had and moved into a small cottage with barely enough room to bake a cake. I traded my view of the world with a new one." Her laugh was one of Abner's favorite things about her. In fact, Hazel had many great qualities. He had just been too reluctant to accept them.

"Then I put my focus on helping others. Lydia first, of course, because she blamed herself for Joseph's death, though she had no part in it. I wanted everyone to know the love Joseph and I had, so I started matchmaking, or match meddling, as some seem to think of it." She straightened, knowing Abner was part of those someones. "Love is stronger than death." She placed a hand on Abner's forearm. "I know what it's like to feel lost without your spouse. I know how it feels to fear loving another, but love cannot be wasted, or bottled up and put on a shelf."

"I've done that, haven't I?"

"I did for a time too, but you're young yet. There is still time for you and your match."

So that's why Abner stood outside the school with the pink brownie tray in his hand and wearing his Sunday clothes. He waited until the last family walked in before he gathered up the courage to go inside. Hopefully, the recital had already started, drawing fewer eyes on him. Unfortunately, that wasn't the case, since one of the scholars had eaten something blue, and much of the focus was getting her cleaned up. He slipped by a group of elders and made his way toward the line of windows aligning the back wall.

"You're here!"

Abner looked across a sea of *kapp*s to see Ina pushing her way over to him. His heart kicked up its pace seeing her. A laugh filled his heart as she hurried to his side.

"Hazel wanted me to deliver these," Abner said just as the *kinner* lined up along the front of the room. For the next thirty minutes, they stood together, laughing at funny jokes and feeling the warmth of Christmas surround them as young voices sang praises to a birth that changed the world.

When Kaynoshia sang next, Ina whispered in his ear. "She's been practicing for two weeks." Her love for family told Abner all he needed to know. Ina loved. She knew no other way. But could she love him, a man struggling with his own heart?

At the end of the recital, Teacher Lydia instructed everyone to go downstairs for snacks, but a familiar voice had Abner and Ina pausing where they stood.

"Abner. What are you doing here?" Andrew questioned, without the welcoming tone Abner would have expected from an old friend.

"I invited him," Ina said, lifting her chin.

Abner could speak for himself, but he liked that Ina stepped in for him.

"I see," Andrew glared at Abner as folks hurried downstairs. "Ina, you best take those on down before folks start eating."

With that order, Ina took the brownies and scurried off down the stairs, but not before glancing over her shoulder and smiling. Abner liked that she was happy to see him.

"I've noticed it's taking you longer than usual to finish that table."

"Actually, I've never finished projects so fast with Enoch there. Your *bruder* has a mind for the work."

"My *bruder* has plenty of work of his own. He's only there because you agreed to Ina's stupid idea."

"She's full of ideas for sure and certain, but I've not seen a stupid one yet. She's trying to do something kind for Lavina. Why don't you want me helping her?"

"Just because she still has stars in her eyes for ya doesn't mean you're right for her."

"What are you talking about?" *Ina cared for him...still?* "She's old enough to decide, and I haven't said I was interested." No, but he had done everything to show her his feelings for her had been growing.

"Which is why she won't stop." Andrew sighed heavily. He looked around the room, noting they were now alone and missing the snacks below. "If you're no longer grieving Cilla, then I'm glad to hear it, but Ina isn't for you."

"I'll never stop missing Cilla," Abner admitted.

"Exactly!" Andrew leaned closer, his white-hot temper showing. "Ina deserves *that* kind of love."

So that's why Andrew was opposed to Abner caring for his *schwester*, and Abner couldn't argue with that. Ina did deserve more. More than Abner might ever be able to give her. "I had no idea she had feelings for me."

"You really are blind then. She's been sweet on you since you saved her." Andrew rolled his eyes. "She used to write your name all over her little idea book she kept as a young *maed*." Andrew wagged a finger towards Abner. "Best you keep to your end of the shop and finish that table soon."

Andrew stomped off down the stairs, leaving Abner to sift through knowing Ina had cared for him for years. Siblings were a thorn, he was learning. Protective brothers stepping on toes, but Andrew was right about one thing. Abner was struggling with letting Cilla go, when she wasn't ready to leave. Ina deserved someone who'd love her without restraint or confusion in his heart.

～

INA POURED soda pop into paper cups that were lining the table, her smile too big to contain. Abner had accepted her invitation. Hope winked her way. As folks collected their snacks in line, Ina noted Andrew stepping into the room. "Can you finish this? I have to speak with our *bruder*." Ina didn't give Kaynoshia a chance to complain or refuse as she walked Andrew's way.

"Where's Abner?"

"How should I know? Where's Beth? I should probably help her with Lisa. She's teething."

"Andrew David! What did you do?" Ina planted her fist on her hips. She didn't care how many heads had turned. "Why is Abner not here? You were just talking to him. Do you know what a step it was for him to come? Do you know how long we have all been waiting to have him join us?"

"We? Don't you mean *you… schwester*?"

"That is none of your concern."

"I see that Sam Lewis is here today," he tried shifting her focus.

"I don't like others thinking they know what and who is best for me."

"Sam is a nice fella. Only a year older."

"*Jah*, but Sam has eyes for another. This is you stealing my idea book all over." She watched Andrew's grin fade regrettably.

"Now, Ina, I told you I didn't take it. Freeman and Henry did. I returned it to you."

"After reading it. Since I was knee high, you've tried watching over all of us."

"There were a lot of you to watch over," he said unflinchingly. He didn't even see the wrong in his older brother ways—that privacy was private and making choices that were not his to make.

"*Jah*, but now you have the Bent and Dent, Beth, and four *kinner* to worry over."

"You forget I grew up with Abner. I know him well. Ina, he won't love you enough."

Ina had her own reservations about that, but Lavina's words had helped her next response come easily. Andrew thought he knew best for her still, just like when she was young and he thought she was too young to ride a horse or too small to lift bales of hay onto a wagon.

"You think you know how much love I need? *Ach, Bruder. Gott* loves me more than enough. Worry over your friend. It's Abner who needs all the love we can give him." Ina pivoted and ran up the stairs and out the school door. Hopefully, Abner hadn't left yet.

"Wait!" Ina ran into the snow without caring if she had her coat, but he was gone. He'd slipped through her fingers... again.

# CHAPTER 10

*H*ank Fisher didn't like when his *fraa* was quiet, a sign they weren't in agreement. He also didn't like eating whatever Grace planned on cooking for supper tonight. Grace wasn't the most graceful in the kitchen and tended to spill too many strange flavors into her dishes.

Hazel insisted that Abner join them. Hank knew his son. Abner liked to focus on his work, but Hank agreed his son deserved the same second chance he had been given. Ina was a fine *maed*, and it hadn't escaped Hank how often he caught the young *maedel* asking over Abner.

WHEN THE OFFICE DOOR OPENED, revealing his father, Abner turned off the bandsaw, removed his glasses, and went to click off the gas generator that kept it all in motion. He'd been so busy working, he'd forgotten to feed the potbelly stove. A chill rolled over him.

"I was here just a few days ago, and you had orders stacked against the corners." Hank looked over a dresser set, bookshelves waiting to be delivered, and two tables waiting for a final finish, before shooting Abner a worried scowl. "You clearly haven't left this shop in days."

"I live fifty feet away. I'm not far from the bed," Abner said. "And thanks to you, I've had help," he added with a knowing brow.

"We all need help from time to time, and it's good you are getting to know each other." Hank studied the carved scrolls along one table's edges. Abner had finished those last night. When he couldn't sleep, work always soothed him.

"You should leave the matchmaking to Hazel," Abner remarked, brushing sawdust from his trouser legs.

"I'm retired. I don't know what to do without keeping busy." Hank chuckled.

"You now have ten grandchildren and three *dochter*s. I'd say you're plenty busy."

"*Jah*," his father smiled tenderly. "I have been blessed for sure and certain, and one day I hope you will give me a few more gross*kinner* to love. I do enjoy having such a big family."

"I'm sorry to disappoint ya, but we both know I won't be having *kinner*."

"I know nothing of the sort. You've plenty of time for that, and folks seem happy that you and Ina Graber are spending time together. She's a fine woman."

Abner shook his head. It had been four days since seeing Ina and Enoch. "We're building a table, and..." Abner pointed to the table top before them. "We're almost done. She'll be gone, and things will get back to normal."

"She doesn't have to be. Do you have feelings for her?"

"I can't," Abner replied honestly.

"You won't. That's what you are saying. There's no wrong in love, Abner."

"Yet, Cilla can never do that. She can never feel anything at all!" The admission took weight from him. Andrew was right. Ina deserved true, endless love. Abner didn't believe it existed.

"*Ach*, Abner. Cilla is not the one without love. You are."

"How can you say that? She's gone."

"She knew love just as your *Mamm* did. They had family and friends to love them, as well as us. Now they are with *Gott*. How much more love can we ever dare to be given?"

Abner hadn't thought about it like that. He only saw all the things Cilla had missed and would never know.

"You can't have that perfect love until *Gott* calls you home, but you can try to find room in your heart for loving others. How could you even think it's wrong to love others? Our faith demands it of us. Ina comes from a good family and can bring much to your life," *Daed* continued.

Being born an only child, Abner always wondered how big families did it. From his view, the family unit worked like sandpaper over wood. A few rough pieces always smoothed out the grain.

*What of your sander?* Ina's words barreled into him now.

"If you care for her, then don't waste any time. You and I know, we cannot know how much time we are given."

Abner lowered his head and shoved both hands in his pockets. His father was the wisest man he knew. Abner wanted love in his life once more. It wasn't betraying Cilla; it was loving Ina.

# CHAPTER 11

Thirty minutes and the market would open, and nothing was going as it ought. Ina had never overslept in all her life, but since the school recital, sleep had been much sought after. She was still torn between missing Abner and never speaking to her *bruder* again. Andrew had crossed a line, and taking Enoch to learn how to stock shelves at the Bent and Dent recently only meant she couldn't help Abner finish Lavina's gift. Andrew was meddling with Enoch's work, ruining Lavina's perfect Christmas gift, and making a muck of Ina's ideal Christmas.

On a tempered breath, Ina watched six rings of dough sink to the bottom of the fryer. "Oh no!"

"*Ach*, please tell me you remembered to bring a new tank of gas with you," Lavina said as she paused from cutting out the next run of donuts.

Ina closed her eyes and cringed. Lavina had only asked one thing of her, and she'd forgotten. "I'm sorry. I'll run back home and fetch it." Ina tossed aside her full apron. It would take a good half hour if she hurried her horse, but the roads this morning were already slick with recent rain and snow and dropping temperatures.

She looked past the counter. A line was already forming.

66

Marketers eager for a fresh donut before eight o'clock when the booths officially opened. They'd sell out quickly and have to close until Ina returned and more donuts were made. She glanced at the dough currently rising to her left. Not only would Lavina lose money closing temporarily, but much of the work she had done this morning would be wasted.

"Problems?"

Ina turned. Her breath catching. "Abner." Oh, how she'd missed him.

"Ina forgot the extra tank, and we just ran out of gas." Lavina waved a frustrated hand in the air.

"I've got an idea." Abner smiled. He really did look more handsome when he smiled.

"I'm sure Leon and Hannah have gas up at the house or maybe in the canning shed." The Troyers canned applesauce and sold fresh cider from their vast orchard. "I'll run up there and see."

"*Danke*, Abner," Lavina quickly offered. "That's *verra* kind of you."

Abner nodded and shot Ina a half-hearted smile before turning toward the door. Now why hadn't that idea come to her? *Because you're not yourself.*

While Lavina assured everyone they'd soon open, Ina focused on fetching half-fried dough from the bottom of the fryer. She wasn't accustomed to anyone helping her out of a fix no matter how many times she found herself in one.

"Looks like your boyfriend might save our morning," Lavina teased.

"Friend," Ina responded, but hope lifted in her heart that Abner felt more than friendship for her.

Twenty minutes later, Abner had a fresh tank installed, and the grease heating. "May I speak to you for a minute?" he asked.

"Go on," Lavina urged her. "I still have to get everything ready… again." Lavina smiled, but it didn't take away how her morning had already been ruined by Ina's lack of responsibility.

"Let's talk over here." Ina led him to a corner that allowed a little privacy. "*Danke* again, Abner. If you hadn't come along…"

"You would have come up with one of your ideas and figured it out." He smirked, twisting his straw hat in his hands. "I missed having you and Enoch this week," Abner said. "I have the tabletop joined and glued. It looks good."

"I missed being there. I know we have so little time, and I'm sorry, but Enoch had to go to the Bent and Dent and help Andrew, and *Mamm* wouldn't allow me to come without him."

Abner's lips pinched firmly. Folks busied about as the smell of hot grease and strong scents carried from the candle shop next door filled the area.

"Abner, I'm sorry if Andrew said anything that…"

"Andrew cares for you," he said flatly. "He thinks he's doing the right thing."

"He's not. He should focus on Della and Freeman. Those two could use his brotherly attention." Ina rolled her eyes.

"I'm learning a little about siblings and how they tend to meddle. I had supper at Grace and Michael's last night, and she invited Miriam Strolfus."

Ina tried not to look surprised, but how did one hide worry and fear?

"Don't fret." He leaned in closer. "I don't like Mariam Strolfus." His eyes traveled to her lips, and Ina knees weakened.

"Siblings can make a problem where there isn't any." Ina held his gaze, the sounds of a busy marketplace disappearing in the way he looked down at her.

"Andrew is dealing with his own guilt. He was the one who told me Cilla liked me. She and Beth were close. He wanted to date Beth, and I think he matched me up with Cilla so we both could court. Women tend to like doing things in pairs."

"Not all women," she said matter-of-factly. "But I'm glad you had Cilla in your life then." Ina meant it too. Despite her young heart aching each time she saw them together, she thanked God. Abner gave Cilla love and was loved in return before her life was cut short. *Gott*'s plan wasn't always easy, but it was always necessary.

"Cilla and I loved each other. I was blessed to have her."

"I don't know what to say." Ina wasn't accustomed to not finding the words she needed.

"Say you will be at the shop tomorrow."

Her head shot up. Did he want to see her or ensure he had plenty of help finishing Lavina's gift? "I will do my best, but if Andrew keeps needing Enoch, well..."

"You're one of those Pencil Grabers, are you not? I imagine you have more than one *bruder* who'd be willing to chaperone." Abner grinned. He reached out, touched the tip of her *kapp* string, and rolled it around his finger before dropping his arm back to his side.

"Not if Andrew finds work for all of them. He can be *verra* stubborn." She was being honest, despite the shivers running over her.

"He thinks I'm too old for you."

"Our parents have nearly as many years between them. It only matters if you think that."

"I don't think that at all," he smiled before strolling off toward his own booth and leaving her breathless. Was it possible Abner was growing a new heart?

# CHAPTER 12

On Christmas Eve, while most families focused on baking and readying for the morrow, Ina Graber entered his furniture shop at seven-thirty with Enoch and Andrew. When Ina set her heart to something, she was certainly committed to it. Abner found he could learn something from her determination.

While Enoch spread glue over the top of a butcher block cart, he and Andrew worked to install all the hardware on the lower section. The owners had gone to visit family for the holidays and wouldn't return for a full week. In the far corner, Ina put on the last coat of polyurethane. She had insisted she'd see to the final steps of the Christmas table herself, and Abner had to agree. This was her ideal Christmas gift for Lavina. Suddenly, Abner wondered what gift was perfect for a woman like Ina Graber. It had been years since he even considered such a thought, and now it was all-consuming.

"I reckon I have an apology to give you," Andrew said on a bent knee as he tapped another wooden plug into a hole. Once two pieces were screwed together for a tight hold, glue would be put in the hole, and a wooden peg would fill in the area to give each piece a more polished, homemade look.

"*Nee*, you don't," Abner replied. He understood Andrew's

love for Ina now that his heart had opened to what a gift she was to him as well.

"I do. It wasn't even about you, but my own guilt for setting you and Cilla up. Beth thought she was too shy and knew she had eyes for you."

"I'm glad Beth did. I loved her. We may have only had a few years together, but I've cherished them."

"And…" Andrew rubbed the back of his neck and the tension burrowing there. "I didn't like how sweet Ina was on you either. Since that day she broke her ankle, she's stared after you like a puppy waiting for snacks. Ina is…different."

Abner knew that, but she was the right kind of different that he loved. Abner glanced in Ina's direction. "That's what I like about her."

"Even when she was young, she'd get a thought and cling to it until it worked out."

"She still does. You should have heard her convince me we could finish this by Christmas." Abner smiled recalling her fast talking ways.

"She's had stars for you for a long time." Andrew looked away, intent on his work.

"She was just a girl grateful I carried her home when you all left her."

"She was in first grade, but by the fifth grade, Freeman snuck into her room to hide a roach in Esther's bed." Andrew chuckled, his eyes crinkling in the corners of his smile. "Esther hates roaches. He found Ina's idea book and took it. I thumped his head for it."

"But not the roaches?" Abner lifted a brow. The world of siblings still eluded him.

"*Nee*. Esther was quick to tattle on us. I'm certain I even helped him catch those bugs." Andrew stood and stretched out his back. "I read her idea book and knew then that she thought of you as more than a boy who helped her. Little hearts and the like. The older we got, the more I caught her staring at you. It was embarrassing."

"I never knew." Abner looked toward the corner. He had always thought those were looks of appreciation for helping her, but now Abner knew better.

"I shouldn't have meddled, it's just..." Andrew searched for the words.

"I forgive you, if..."

"If?" Andrew asked.

"If you let me and her deliver the table to Lavina's this evening." Abner watched Andrew's stern frown curve slightly.

"It's heavy."

"I'm strong," Abner countered.

"You want my blessing or something?" Andrew waved the small hammer Abner's way, "She's my *schwester*."

"How could I forget?" Abner chuckled and went to call his driver.

Ina stood back and admired the glossy sheen of maple. She wanted the hickory top, but Enoch was set on maple. Abner assured her it would be sturdy and long-lasting, and she trusted him. Lavina was going to be surprised for sure and certain. Just as surprised as she was when Andrew arrived at the house this morning with a heartfelt apology for meddling into her life and a willingness to help her and Enoch today.

Running her fingertips along the carved line along the edges, she heard Abner's approach. "It's not sticky, so I reckon" —she turned to him—"it's finished." That reality made her heart sink.

"It went faster than I thought," Abner admitted. He stood at her side, admiring what they had accomplished together.

"*Jah*, it did." If only he knew how much more they could accomplish together. She tried to hold back her swirling emotions and remember Lavina's wise words. His friendship was all that mattered.

Suddenly, Ina noted how quiet the shop was. No motors running, no laughter from just on the other side of the movable wall. "Where are *mei bruders*?"

"They left. Andrew wanted to drop Enoch off before going to the school board meeting."

"They forgot me!" *Of all the stuff.* For a *bruder* who tended to include himself too much into her life, Andrew showed just how easy she was to forget!

"*Nee*," Abner reached out to take her hand. "I asked if you and I could deliver the table together. After all, it is your gift to Lavina."

The warmth of his fingers, combined with the love in his eyes, made Ina light-headed.

"Scotty will be here in a few minutes with a trailer."

"Should I sweep up before he comes?"

"I'd rather talk." His hand still held hers firmly as he led her toward a bench nearby. She liked the dark walnut color. Perhaps he'd build her one for *Mamm* and *Daed* one day.

"Oh, I reckon it's time to discuss what I owe you." She owed him more than any number he might give her.

"I think we should discuss… this." Abner gave her hand a gentle squeeze as he studied how easily their fingers fit together. "I spoke to Andrew." His tone was even, unsurprised.

"Andrew?" Ina gulped a bit of air.

"He's of the mind you have feelings for me."

Ina's heart fluttered, and her stomach twisted. She wasn't raised to speak untruths no matter the cost. "I do, but I know you're not interested in me…like that. I just hope we can be friends."

"I don't want to be just your friend, Ina. I do cherish our friendship, but I hope you would consider courting me."

Ina hesitated. She wasn't sure she'd heard Abner correctly. She had so much love in her heart for his woundedness, but it was the man staring at her intently right now that had her toes tingling.

"You really want a pushy girlfriend?" She smiled over at him. "You should know I have ideas."

Abner reached out, pushing a loose thread back under the cotton knitting of her drab blue kerchief. "Do you have any that include me?"

"I may have a few." Ina's eyes blurred with tears. "You should build a showroom here for folks to come buy your furniture. I know you don't like going to the market each week."

"That was before I had a reason to go," he confessed. "I'm becoming rather fond of donuts." He grinned playfully.

"You can hire help," she added.

"Perhaps someone who has a way with talking folks into things they don't know they need."

"*Jah*, someone like that." Ina refused to let a single tear fall. She'd not cry on the happiest day of her life. "Consider opening… consider opening up your heart again."

"I have my own ideas about that. I know this woman," he began, his gaze turning solemn. "She's pushy and full of big ideas, but she's wiggled her way into my heart. I want nothing more than to earn her love."

Flabbergasted at his confession, words she dreamed to hear, Ina melted. "Look at me!" She swiped her wet cheeks with her sleeves. "Who cries at a time like this?"

"Someone who's waited a long time for me to come to my senses." A fraction closer, and they would kiss. "I do love you, Ina."

A hundred times she had imagined her first kiss, and each one belonged to him. He loved her despite her flaws. That's why Ina leaned closer and met him the rest of the way. His lips were warm, like a heavy blanket on a cold morning. Ina wanted to linger in that kiss longer, but found his slow, tender approach something she'd savor for a lifetime.

"I hear the driver," Abner said in a low, deep tone. "We should get this loaded before someone sees us."

Ina giggled, noting his own cheeks blushing. "That's a good idea. I do have something to ask you first."

"I'm not surprised." he laughed.

"Would you join us for Christmas? I'll warn you, though, that eating with us Grabers can get noisy and hot, and there will be barely any room to move."

"I wouldn't mind a chance to sit close to you again."

# CHAPTER 13

$S$now fell softly outside of the small two-story home. Vast aromas of sugared ham, spiced apple dumplings, and warm cider wafted through the air as Ina glanced out Lavina's kitchen window with a thankful heart. This would be her first Christmas with Abner, and if that second kiss this morning as they drove here was any indication of his feelings for her, she anticipated many more Christmases together.

"I still can't believe you did this without me knowing," Lavina repeated.

"Our *schwester* is one for secrets," Andrew teased, giving Ina a playful pat on her *kapp*. "I'd best go round up all the little ones." Andrew aimed for the sitting room, where cousins shared new toys and the joy of the season sparked in laughter.

Kaynoshia sang as she readied tables set up along the far kitchen wall. Della had added cranberries and sprigs of holly down the table center. Candles flickered as doors opened and closed when the older *kinner* came in from playing outside. Oh, how Ina loved the chaos of a large family.

"Henry, will you see to taking the ham to the table?" *Mamm* asked. A few hairs of brown and gray flitted about as she mashed the last bowl of potatoes.

"I'll go check on Lilly before we start eating," Ina told her sister, Joan, before slipping into the small bedroom nearby, where Lilly napped. The one-year-old looked so much like Joan, though she did have Jason's round cheeks. An ache stirred in Ina's belly as she looked down upon the child.

"She is beautiful," Abner whispered as he entered the room.

"*Jah*, and sleeps like her *Mamm*. I don't know how anyone could sleep with such noise going on."

"She's at peace, perfectly content in knowing she is loved. I happen to know how well sleep comes when one's heart's content."

Ina's cheeks warmed at his affectionate words.

"I have something for you." Abner pulled a gift from his coat, wrapped in perfectly pink paper.

"You didn't have to give me anything. Knowing how you feel makes my heart happy."

"My heart is happy too. Go on and open it," he encouraged.

Ina tenderly pulled the ends loose and slowly revealed the leather-bound notebook with an engraved butterfly on the front. "Oh, Abner, it's beautiful."

"I thought you could use a new idea book, and this one has two keys, so no one can read your thoughts ever again." He offered her two tiny keys. What a thoughtful gift. A place to store all her new ideas. All of which included him and their future together.

"Well, I don't mind if you read my thoughts." Ina returned one key into his hand. Her heart was his. There would never be secrets between them.

"*Danke*, Ina. That means more than you know." He leaned toward her. It wasn't terribly private, but Ina felt as if they were suddenly the only two people in the world. Abner placed a soft kiss on her cheek before they joined the rest of her family at the table.

When heads lowered for the silent prayer, Abner squeezed her hand. His love for her no longer a dream.

As plates were being filled, a knock at the door quieted everyone. "I'll see who it is." Andrew stood and went to the door. A few seconds later, Val Beechy walked inside. He was on the short side of tall, with unruly black hair. Removing his black hat, his gaze sought out Della.

"I didn't mean to interrupt," Val said. "Hazel asked that I deliver this," he offered up a box that Ina suspected was filled with red velvet cupcakes. Hazel had a thing for red velvet cake and love matches, claiming the two went hand in hand.

"You aren't interrupting; there is always room at the table for one more," Lavina welcomed with a bright smile. Ina wasn't sure if she imagined it or not, but Della looked shorter in her seat when Timothy fetched a fold-out chair and pushed it closest to her.

"*Danke*, but I didn't come to eat, but to return something. Or a few somethings," he shot Della a crooked grin.

"It's about time," Esther spoke out, causing the room to erupt in laughter.

"We can discuss that after supper," *Daed* said to quiet the room. "Have a seat young man. Supper's getting cold." Even *Daed* felt sorry for how red Val's face had become.

"The ducks worked," Abner whispered in Ina's ear as he passed her a plate of warm sliced bread. Indeed, the ducks had worked, to Ina's utter shock. Perhaps Della wasn't so bad at finding love after all.

"This table is beautiful, Lavina," Henry's *fraa* commented, noting the fine groove along the edging. "I've never gone so far as to gift something this nice to one of my *schwestern*."

"Ina knows what is needed at the right time," *Daed* replied, casting her a pleased look.

"She does," Abner spoke, not concealing his feelings. Ina's heart swelled knowing how love had sparked more than her heart this Christmas.

"This table will serve us for years to come and keep my *kinner* close to my heart," Lavina added. "Ina knows the importance of what that means to me."

"How can a table do that?" twelve-year-old Christina asked curiously.

All eyes found the matriarch of the Graber lot, Ada Graber. *Mamm* was far from dainty with her lofty height and strong shoulders, but her voice always carried a soft lullaby that soothed even the most stubborn of her *kinner*. She was especially fond of laughing, and now that she had stepped over fifty, fine lines marked the number of laughs she had been blessed with.

"The supper table is the most important piece of any home. It's where problems are solved and friends are made," she shot Ina and Abner a tender look. "Life gets busy. Some days stretch out longer than others, but at the table, we all *kumm* together. We talk about our day, celebrate new *bopplin*, and pass potatoes. We hear silly jokes," *Mamm* looked to Enoch, her motherly heart exploding with how much she loved each of them in their unique way. "That keeps us young. We clean up messes, thank *Gott* for our blessings, and always love each other. Like the nails that hold together each board, the table holds us together, when the outside world tries to separate us."

"It's all of yesterday's love and tomorrow's hope in one place," Ina concluded.

\*\*\*

I hope you enjoyed your visit in two wonderful Kentucky, Amish communities. Want to read more about the Amish of Kentucky, follow my author page at MindySteele.com, or dive into the first books of the Miller's Creek Amish.

# HAZEL'S FROSTED BROWNIES

**Ingredients:**
  1 ¼ c. sugar
  1 c. all-purpose flour
  ¼ c. cocoa powder
  ¼ tsp. baking soda
  ½ tsp. salt
  ⅓ c. vegetable oil
  ¼ c. milk
  2 tsps. vanilla
  1 egg
  ¾ c. chocolate chips

Preheat oven to 350°. Mix dry ingredients, then add oil, milk, vanilla, and egg. Beat well before folding in chocolate chips. Cook until done. Let cool before adding frosting.

### Hazel's Chocolate Frosting

¾. c. sugar
3 T. milk
3 T. butter
½ c. chocolate chips
½ tsp. vanilla

Stir together milk, sugar, and butter in a pan over medium heat. Bring to a boil. Cook at a rolling boil for one minute, then remove from heat. Add chocolate chips and vanilla. Stir until chips are melted. Pour over cooled brownies.

# INA'S BROWN SUGAR COOKIES

3 cups brown sugar
1 cup lard or butter, softened
2 eggs
2 teaspoons baking soda
2 cups sour milk
2 teaspoons baking powder
5 cups flour, sifted
pinch of salt

Cream together brown sugar, lard or butter, and eggs. Stir baking soda into sour milk. Sift baking powder, salt, and flour together. Add milk and dry ingredients alternately to the creamed mixture. Drop by teaspoonful onto a greased cookie sheet. Bake at 350° for 7–8 minutes.

# ABOUT THE AUTHOR

Best selling and award-wining author, Mindy Steele is a welcomed addition to the Amish genre. Not only are her novels uplifting and her characters relatable, but she touches all the senses to make you laugh, cry, hold your breath, and root for a happy-ever-after. Her storyteller heart shines within her pages. Research for her is just a fence jump away. Her relationships with the Amish contributes to her understanding of boundaries and traditions, giving readers a Plain life view of the world.

Her series include the Millers Creek series, The Heart of the Amish collection, and the Mountain Protector series. Her standalone novels are *An Amish Flower Farm, His Amish Wife's Hidden Past*, and *Christmas Grace*. She also has stories in several anthologies, "A Brookhaven Christmas" in *Christmas Cookies and Mysteries*,"The Cookie Thief" in *Amish Christmas Cookie Tour*, and "Leaving Lancaster" in *A Lancaster Amish Christmas*.

# GATHERED AROUND LOVE'S TABLE

RACHEL J. GOOD

# CHAPTER 1

*B*risk December winds swirled a few dried autumn leaves past the window, and Miriam Lapp shivered as she packed snacks for their long trip. Temperatures had dropped last night and iced the windows with lacy designs. Sautéing onions, bacon, and hash browns for the breakfast casserole had steamed the inside panes, so small drips ran down the glass.

*Inner and outer.* Like my life. Icy, but appearing lovely on the outside, hiding the steaming and melting on the inside, while drips slide down like tears.

If Miriam repeated those thoughts to her family, they'd stare at her as if she made no sense. She didn't fit with her practical family and had no way to express her passion for beauty and poetry, a longing she kept hidden, though it blazed and bubbled within.

Miriam pinched her lips together to prevent the inner raindrops from slipping down her face. Her fiancé had broken up with her several weeks before their wedding, so she welcomed this chance to get away. It had been painful seeing him and her best friend together.

*Mamm* entered the kitchen, balancing two-year-old Lizzie on her hip and carrying two suitcases. "Is everything ready?"

Glad her back faced *Mamm*, Miriam blinked hard. Then she nodded and bent to remove the casserole.

While her mother set the suitcases by the door, Miriam hustled past and called up to the second floor. "Breakfast."

A thundering herd pounded down the stairs. Four of her five younger brothers rushed to their places at the table. Softer footsteps followed. Two of her sisters entered the kitchen, one holding the hand of five-year-old Beth. Both carried overstuffed duffel bags they set by the back door.

After *Daed* dropped several suitcases onto the pile of luggage and sat at the table, only one place remained empty. Abraham's. *Daed* raised his voice. "Abraham, get down here now. We're all at the table."

No answering sound came from upstairs.

Miriam's stomach clenched. Since her brother had turned sixteen last year, he'd used *Rumspringa* as an excuse to break all the rules. Several times she'd seen him sneaking out after their parents went to bed.

Last weekend, he'd stumbled in drunk. Miriam had helped him to bed, and he'd begged her not to tell their parents. She agreed if he'd promise never to do it again. As far as she knew, he'd kept his word, but what if he hadn't?

*Daed* pointed at Luke. "Go upstairs and wake your brother."

Luke bounded up the stairs two at a time and banged the door open. "He's not here, but he left a note." Luke raced down and handed *Daed* a paper.

As *Daed* read, his face turned ashen. "I don't believe this."

"What is it?" *Mamm* leaned over to see. She sucked in a breath. "What are we going to do?"

A chorus of questions spilled across the table. "What's wrong?" "Where's Abraham?" "Is he sick?"

His eyes wide, Luke announced, "Abraham says he doesn't want to go to Pinecraft with us. He's staying with an *Englisch* friend's family at a Ski Roundtop vacation rental for a week."

"What?" Cries and squeals erupted around the table. "Ski

Roundtop? He doesn't know how to ski." "Will we have to stay home?" "We don't know most of his *Englisch* friends, so how will we find him?" "We don't have time to get him, or we'll miss the bus."

"That's enough," *Daed* boomed. "Everyone quiet down. I need time to think. We'll pray and eat our breakfast."

An uneasy quiet fell as everyone bowed for prayer. After they lifted their heads, they cast anxious glances at each other.

Miriam's stomach clenched. She never should have kept Abraham's drinking from her parents. If she'd told, they'd have grounded him, so he'd be here now with the family. And he'd be heading far away from the troublemakers he'd befriended.

*Mamm* took a few bites and set down her fork. "I'd hoped we could all spend Christmas with your grandparents." Her voice shook.

*Dawdi* and *Mammi* were both ill, and *Mamm* worried about them.

With a sympathetic glance at *Mamm*, *Daed* said, "We can't disappoint your parents, not when they need us. Besides, we paid a lot for this trip, and it's not refundable, so we're still going."

"But we can't leave Abraham alone all that time. We won't be back until after Christmas." *Mamm*'s eyes filled with tears. "All of you go. I'll stay home."

"Absolutely not." *Daed*'s words rang with finality. "They're your parents, and this might be the last—" He broke off as moisture glistened in *Mamm*'s eyes.

He didn't need to finish. Everyone understood what he'd been about to say. This might be the last time *Mamm* got to see her parents.

His face grim, *Daed* said, "I'll stay home. You go and take the children."

"But our anniversary."

Miriam's guilt had built to an unbearable level. She was to blame. "*Daed*, this trip is special to you and *Mamm*. I can stay here."

"But you're not old enough," *Mamm* protested.

"I'd have been married in November with a house of my own if. . ." Miriam didn't want to bring up being jilted, but she had to convince her parents to go.

*Daed* looked thoughtful. "That's true." He turned to Mamm. "Miriam's responsible. And Abraham listens to her better than he does to us."

"But you'll miss Christmas with us." Tears trickled down her mother's cheeks.

"I'll have Christmas with Abraham." Miriam tried to sound cheerful about the idea, although she dreaded it.

They'd been so busy talking, they hadn't finished breakfast when the van crunched up the driveway. *Daed* had hired a fifteen-person van, expecting it to hold him, *Mamm*, and all ten of his children, along with extra room for their luggage.

"Hurry," *Daed* ordered.

Everyone shoveled down the last bites of breakfast and jumped up from the table. Miriam pulled her duffel bag from the pile at the door and set it aside. While *Daed* and the boys donned their coats and loaded the van, Miriam and her sisters whisked the dishes into the sink, dried them, and put them away. Meanwhile, *Mamm* bundled up the two youngest and strapped them into car seats.

Miriam longed to spend a little more time with her family. "May I go along to see you off?"

*Mamm* hesitated, but *Daed*, who was returning from a quick trip upstairs, overheard. "Of course. Elmer doesn't live too far from here. I'll pay him to drop you off afterwards."

*Daed* handed Miriam a small metal box. "There's money in here for groceries for the next few weeks. Keep it in a safe place, and whatever you do, don't let Abraham know you have it."

*What?* Miriam tried not to let her shock show. Perhaps *Daed* knew more about Abraham's worrisome behavior than she'd realized.

"Hurry and get your coat on, *Dochder*. We need to leave."

Miriam sprinted upstairs, hid the box in the drawer where she kept recent sketches and poems, and then rushed back down to pull on her bonnet, coat, and scarf. She stepped into her barn boots near the back door.

Before she went outside, she paused to run a finger over the scarred oak table they used for every meal. Her heart ached. All the chairs around it would be empty this Christmas. All except hers. And Abraham's. . . if he showed up.

A hollowness in her chest, she headed out the back door and climbed into the van. The windshield wipers ticked back and forth, wiping wet flakes into splotchy puddles. Snow flurries dusted the corn stubble and fallow fields they passed.

Elmer cleared his throat. "It's already laying. You're getting out of here before the worst of it. Bet you'll be glad for Florida sunshine."

*Daed* nodded, though his brow remained knotted. Was he fretting about Abraham? His *sohn*'s rebellion and today's defiance? Or did *Daed* have other concerns, the way Miriam did? Suppose Abraham got hurt at Ski Roundtop? How would they find out? Would he decide to stay with his *Englisch* friend for the rest of December? Or even worse, what if Abraham came to love *Englisch* ways and chose to leave the Amish?

With each mile that passed on the way to New Holland, Miriam's spirits sank lower. She'd miss her family. And the Florida trip. Not only had she lost her fiancé, but she'd probably spend Christmas alone. She tried to shake off her gloom and count her blessings, but by the time Elmer dropped them off beside the Elite bus in the Yoder's Market parking lot, she was fighting back tears.

Keeping herself busy would stem their flow, so she rushed to help everyone unload their bags and stow them in the bus's cargo hold. Then while *Daed* went to explain they'd have two less passengers, Elmer left to find a parking place in the busy lot.

"Take as long as you need," he'd told Miriam. "I'll keep the van warm."

Grateful for his kindness, she huddled deeper into her heavy wool coat as icy winds whipped her scarf in her face. Her mood drooped even lower when the winding line boarded the bus, and one by one, her sisters and brothers climbed the steps. After some rearranging by *Mamm* and *Daed*, everyone settled into their seats.

Her siblings pressed excited faces against the window. Their first bus trip. Their first visit to Pinecraft. Miriam longed to be riding with them. She'd never been out of state, never seen a beach. She'd been looking forward to this adventure and to visiting *Mammi* and *Dawdi*. Most of all, she'd wanted to get away from Lancaster and her heartache.

Her eyes swam with unshed tears. This was so unfair. Abraham's selfishness had deprived her of this vacation. And now she'd be stuck in an empty house over the holidays taking care of an unruly brother—if he even bothered to return. Why had she volunteered to stay?

Miriam's toes and nose stung from the cold. A few tear droplets trickled down and froze on her cheeks.

The bus driver shut the door, and a few moments later, gears ground. The idling bus lurched forward. Fumes belched from the tailpipe, clouding Miriam's view of her family waving frantically as they pulled away. Shivering, she waved back until the bus pulled onto the main road and disappeared.

By tomorrow, they'd be a thousand miles away, and she'd be alone in the house for the first time in her life.

# CHAPTER 2

*I*nstead of going straight to the van, Miriam dashed into the market to warm herself. Elmer said he'd wait, and she needed groceries. They'd emptied the refrigerator last night except for this morning's breakfast ingredients. Other than the home-canned goods on the pantry shelves, she had no food.

She'd only buy a few staples now because the snow had already started coming down harder. The rest of her shopping could wait until she knew Abraham's plans. What if he stayed with his *Englisch* friend the whole time her family was gone? She'd have no guests for Christmas Day or Second Christmas. Their relatives expected her family to be away, so they'd all made plans to travel elsewhere this year.

Praying that shopping might distract her from the loneliness chilling her heart, Miriam moved around the market briskly. Rather than lessening the iciness, though, each time she pulled an item off the shelves, it increased her aloneness. Rather than buying the large family sizes, she selected small portions for one person. Abraham wouldn't be here this week, and she didn't know how much he'd be around after that.

By the time she reached the check out, her eyes were so blurry she had trouble counting out the money. Her whole body dragging under the weight of her gloom, she stumbled out of the store, clutching her change and her purchases.

In the covered brick archway, guitar music floated through the air. *Christmas carols.* She winced, but not because the music sounded bad. Actually, it sounded *wunderbar.* But it only scraped her heart raw. She battled the waterworks threatening to fall.

~

JERRY GINGERICH STAMPED his feet to bring feeling back into them as frigid gusts blew snow into the brick archway of Yoder's Market. At least this spot provided some shelter from the impending storm. While Jerry hung their sign, his friend Logan Sheaff, hunched in a wheelchair beside him, huddled deeper into his blankets, but he kept his pinned-up pant leg visible.

Shivering, Jerry slung his guitar strap over his shoulder and blew on his stinging fingertips, poking from his fingerless gloves. When he'd thawed his hands a bit, he limbered up by strumming a few chords. Meanwhile, Logan reached down and set the glass tip jar between them.

"Ready?" Logan asked.

Jerry nodded and launched into a medley of Christmas carols. That should please the usual crowd passing through here. He preferred stores like this that drew customers from the Amish and rural Christian communities. With all the generous givers, he and Logan did well in these places. On good days, nobody complained, and management didn't discover they were there. Jerry hoped today would be one of those days.

Through the glass doors of the store, he spotted an Amish girl wearing a red wool scarf leaving the checkout. He wished he had his glasses on to see her more clearly, but his lenses fogged up in this weather.

When she emerged from the exit, head down and shoulders sagging, he had an urge to brighten her day, though his own life was far from cheerful. Maybe "Joy to the World" would do the trick.

He strummed faster, picking up the lively tempo with his voice. He might not have the golden voice of the Amish Rebels' lead singer, but Jerry had served as drummer and sometimes backup vocalist in that rock group before it disbanded. Since getting dumped—and duped—by their manager two years ago, Jerry had been working on his vocals and guitar skills. The guys who listened to him regularly claimed he'd improved and said his rough, but mellow, voice had a hypnotic quality.

Evidently, it didn't appeal to the girl. She winced and scurried through the glass exit doors as if eager to get out of the brick archway to the outside. He lowered his volume, but her squinched face revealed it hadn't helped. She did look up, though, and her gaze flitted from him to the sign he'd hung overhead, "Help Feed a Homeless Vet," then landed on Logan, sitting in the wheelchair beside him. After she noticed his missing leg, her face softened in sympathy.

She hurried toward them with a handful of bills. A store employee had salted that morning, but the wind had been blowing a steady coating of snow across the floor for the past two hours. Jerry had slipped there earlier.

He broke off the song to shout, "Careful!"

Her eyes flicked up to him instead of down to the slick entryway floor. Next thing he knew, she was skidding toward him, arms pinwheeling, money and groceries flying. Potatoes and apples flew out of her bags. Coins and dollar bills rained down around them.

In one swift movement, he flipped his guitar to one side to prevent damage and extended his arms to stop her slide, but one of her bags whopped him in the stomach. He doubled over. She slammed into his lowered head.

The impact knocked him staggering back. *Crash!* He banged into the metal carts behind him and whispered a muttered *Ach!*

She crouched over, clutching her stomach. One plastic bag

had split. Tuna cans clattered to the floor and rolled. Other items scattered around them. A small jar of honey crashed beside her, oozing out stickiness.

A woman wheeling out a grocery cart got a wheel stuck in the golden goo. "Help!" she yelled, as her cart slipped sideways, blocking the exit doors.

"Are you all right?" Jerry asked the girl. "I didn't mean to hurt you."

Her eyes showed she understood, but she appeared too winded to speak. He must have hit her hard in the stomach. Not that he'd tried to. Actually, she'd banged into him, but it didn't matter. All that mattered was that she was all right.

She lifted her head, and when she did, a shock jolted through him. Miriam Lapp. They'd played volleyball against each other as *youngie*. And he'd had a major crush on her. He hoped she didn't recognize him. His scruffy beard, mustache, and shoulder-length hair threw most people off.

Small frown lines appeared between her brows as she looked him over. *Please, please don't figure out who I am.* Most of the time, he disguised the shame of who he'd become with his changed appearance. Being homeless also helped him stay anonymous. Few people looked closely at him. They ducked their heads and dropped money in the jar or scurried by, pretending not to see him or Logan.

She was still hunched over, and her eyes glimmered with moisture.

Was that wetness from running into him? "I'm so sorry." He wished he could take away her pain. "I hope I didn't hurt you too badly."

Miriam waved away his concern and stared at her groceries littering the floor, his identity forgotten.

"Manager!" the woman stuck behind them shrieked. "Someone get the manager. Look what she's done." She wagged a finger at Miriam.

Jerry frowned at the lady. It wasn't like Miriam had gotten in this customer's way on purpose. He swooped down and scooped up rolling potatoes and tuna cans. The ripped bag still dangled from her arm.

He had some bags he'd brought to protect his shoes from the snow later. He dumped the handful of goods into the bag behind Logan's chair, then reached for the two nearest apples.

A manager slithered through the crowd of shoppers waiting to exit and reached the screaming woman. "What can I do for you, Ma'am?"

"Call the police and arrest that man." She pointed straight at Jerry. "He headbutted that girl to get her money. You can see she's still holding her stomach. And now he's trying to steal her groceries."

"*Neh.*" Miriam's breathy protest was barely audible.

"I stopped a robbery and assault. In broad daylight." The woman crowed to the cart pushers behind her, drowning out Miriam's protests. "Do you believe the nerve of these homeless people?" the woman asked.

Jerry's face burned. He always tried to keep a low profile, so he didn't get kicked off sidewalks outside of businesses. But now they'd drawn too much attention. If it hadn't been snowing, Jerry would have picked up and moved to a new location, but finding another sheltered place like this would be difficult. He spread out his hands to beg for understanding. "I didn't headbutt her. At least, not on purpose. It was an accident."

The manager, his name tag too hard to read after the blow to Jerry's head, inspected him with narrowed eyes. "An accident? That's hard to believe. Bumping into someone maybe, but knocking into her with your head. Were you standing up?"

"*Jah, vell, neh.*" He stopped himself. Under stress, he often thought and spoke in his more familiar childhood language. He had to speak in *Englisch* to explain. "I bent over because I'd been hit in the stomach, so when she slid, my head hit her."

The skeptical look the manager shot him worried Jerry. If this guy believed Jerry had deliberately hurt a customer, he might call the police.

Miriam's eyes widened when Jerry lapsed into *Deutsch*. She studied him even more closely than before, seeming most interested in the legs of his broadfall pants. He'd worn this same sturdy pair for years. With no money for replacements, he made do. Jerry relaxed a little. His oversized thrift-shop parka covered most of his clothes.

She opened her mouth to say something, but the woman yelled over her. "That man pretending to be a veteran is pocketing all the money, while the guitar player's been stealing her groceries."

Jerry turned, his blood boiling. Logan wasn't a fake. His friend had only been collecting the scattered bills and coins to return them to their owner. So far, Logan had been setting all the money in his lap rather than in their jar.

"He's only trying to help," Jerry protested. "So was I."

"Of course he is," the woman said sarcastically. "If I hadn't called you out, this poor girl would be hobbling home minus her cash and groceries."

Miriam, who was still struggling to suck in air, shook her head. She jabbed a finger toward the money Logan had gathered and the coins that remained. Then she waved toward their donation jar. She meant to give all the cash she'd dropped.

Jerry's eyebrows rose.

"It's for you." Her grimace of pain lifted into a small smile.

"Are you all right?" he asked again, concerned. How hard had he hit her? Hard enough that he'd knocked into a line of carts and crashed them into the wall. His back still ached. He might even have bruises tomorrow. Not that he had any way to check. Which meant she'd taken quite a blow.

"Look behind the wheelchair," the woman called. "That grifter hid the groceries back there."

"Can I see?" the manager asked.

Jerry bent to scoop up two more apples rolling toward him

and dropped them into the bag behind the wheelchair. Then he lifted the plastic bag and handed it to Miriam with a flourish.

He motioned to her broken bag. "She couldn't put her groceries into that one," he explained.

The manager's side eye signaled he didn't believe Jerry originally intended to give Miriam the food. But with the groceries restored to their owner, the manager could do nothing about that. Instead, he called for maintenance to clean up the honey. Then, he shifted the accuser's cart out of the way, so other people could get past, releasing the bottleneck. After the waiting customers exited, the manager shuffled through the accumulating snow to carry the grouch's bags to her car.

As he picked up the last load, the woman made one final complaint. "I can't believe you let these filthy, shabby pickpockets stand in the doorway blocking traffic. I was stuck here for more than twenty minutes because of them." She shivered with disgust. "They're probably infested with lice, diseases, and cockroaches. If I get anything from them, I'll sue your store."

"I'm sorry your visit has been so unpleasant, Ma'am." The manager handed her a store gift card. "Here's a little something for your trouble." Then, he escorted her to her car and set the final two bags in her trunk.

As he crossed the parking lot, he waved at her departing car. "Have a good rest of the day."

Meanwhile, Miriam stooped to retrieve a carton of oatmeal that had rolled under a row of carts and winced.

Jerry beat her to the spot and fished it out for her. "Is that everything?" he asked, handing it to her just as the manager returned.

The manager stopped to check if Miriam had been accosted. After she assured him she was fine and had appreciated the help the guitar player had given her by gathering her items, the manager turned to address Jerry and Logan.

"Look, guys, I hate to turn you out on a day like this, but

we're very busy with holiday shoppers, so I'm going to have to ask you to leave."

Deep down, Jerry had been expecting this ever since that grouchy woman started squawking, but he and Logan would be hard pressed to find a warmer spot.

Usually, when they got shooed off, they moved to a new location down the block, but today they'd trekked all the way out here because the store would be busy. Jerry had hoped to make enough to pay for a room for Logan tonight.

While Jerry stowed his guitar in its battered case and pulled down the sign, Logan picked up the jar and deposited Miriam's money in it. He tucked it under the blanket. Then Jerry trudged out into the frosty air, one hand assisting Logan in propelling the wheelchair through the rapidly falling snow.

Jerry heaved a sigh. Parking lot traffic had already thinned out. Most people had rushed out this morning to do their emergency shopping. Few would venture out this afternoon, now that the storm had worsened. He and Logan would have to give up busking for today. They had a bitter-cold walk back to their camping spot, followed by a snowy, twenty-degree night.

# CHAPTER 3

*M*iriam checked under the carts and in the entryway corners for possible missed groceries before heading out and slogging through the drifting snow to the van. An inch or two had fallen already, but wind whipped across the parking lot, piling flakes into small mounds. She ducked her head so the brim of her black bonnet shielded her face from tiny stinging ice pellets.

Ahead of her, the guitar player pushed his friend across the parking lot. She'd been so busy feeling sorry for herself this morning. Shame filled her. The plight of those men made her realize she should be counting her blessings. Many people in this world had worse problems than she did, so she had no business wallowing in self-pity.

She hurried after the two of them. Earlier, she'd been so flustered by dropping her groceries and holding up traffic, plus fending off that *Englischer*'s accusations, she hadn't thanked the two men properly for their help. She should do that now before she lost sight of them.

"Wait," she called after them.

The guitar player partially turned, and she squinted at him, her gaze running the length of his profile from forehead to nose, skimming the mustache, his lips, and beard. Next, she mentally sketched the line of his neck and curve of his hunched shoulders. A distant image tugged at her memory. Miriam had a vague notion she'd seen or met him before.

Her bags bouncing against her sides, she caught up with them. "Thank you again for helping me. I'm so sorry I got you kicked out of here."

"Not your fault," the vet mumbled.

"Don't worry about it." The guitar player burrowed deeper into his parka and pulled the hood strings to cover most of his face.

"Do I know you?" she blurted out.

His hollow laugh sounded mocking. "Not unless you hang around with homeless people."

"Are you really homeless?"

Now it was the vet's turn for a sarcastic laugh. "You think we'd hang around outside stores in a snowstorm if we didn't have to?"

Miriam's cheeks, already burning from the cold, flushed with heat, making them sting. She couldn't believe she'd asked that question, but it didn't stop more from crowding out of her lips. "Where do you sleep?"

"Here and there." The vet waved a vague hand. "Why do you care?"

She did, though. "Outside in weather like this?"

"The plan was to get enough money so Logan could sleep indoors tonight." Bitterness tinged his words. "That didn't work out so well."

All they'd gotten this morning had been her change. Miriam wasn't sure how much had scattered, but it certainly wouldn't be enough to pay for a place to stay.

"Look, we gotta go. It's too cold to stand out here and talk." The guitar player waved his hand. "Glad we could help with the groceries. Thanks for the donation." He turned his back and started pushing the wheelchair.

"Just a minute," she said, pattering after them. She reached deep into her coat pocket for the twenty she hadn't used for groceries.

They looked eager to get away, but when the guitar player saw the money, he stopped. "You already gave us some."

"It wasn't enough." She wished she had more.

He reached out and took it with bare, red fingers.

"Your gloves don't cover your fingers." Miriam couldn't keep the shock from her words.

The vet laughed. "That's so he can play the guitar."

She tugged off her stretchy black gloves. "Here. Take these. I have another pair at home. You can pull them over those gloves."

The guitar player pulled his hands back as if reluctant to take them.

"Come on, man," the vet said. "Just take 'em, and let's go. The snow's sliding down my neck." He wriggled in the chair, trying to tug his collar higher.

Miriam plopped the gloves into the guitar player's hands, then reached out to help Logan. Wasn't that what the guitar player had called him? After a few yanks, he'd gotten his collar a little higher around his neck. Quickly, she undid her scarf and wrapped it over the collar to keep it in place.

Logan blinked at her. "But it's yours."

"Not anymore."

With gruff *thank-you*s, the two men hurried away.

She headed for the van. If only she could do more.

Climbing inside the warm vehicle was heavenly. Although her fingers and toes stung, Miriam thanked God for the heat. Something those two men wouldn't have. But why couldn't they?

"Elmer," she said after she'd stowed her bags behind her and dropped into the passenger seat. "Could you do me a favor? You see those two men over there? Would you be able to drive them to where they're going? I'll pay you extra when I get home."

"Sure. Looks like they're struggling to get through the snow

103

with that wheelchair. That's got to be a freezing ride. No need to pay me. God would want me to help."

He eased the van into gear and drove slowly. The wheels slipped a little as he drove up the slight incline toward the main street. "It's getting bad."

Miriam bowed her head and prayed for their safety as well as for the homeless men. *Lord, please help them find a safe shelter from the storm.*

When she lifted her head, God seemed to be whispering in her ear. She knew the perfect place for them.

Elmer eased the van next to them just before they reached the parking lot exit. He rolled down the window and called, "Want a ride? I'm happy to take you wherever you want to go. No charge."

Logan looked up. "Man, that'd be awesome."

Miriam hopped out to open the back door, and Logan gave her a grateful smile.

The guitar player's back went rigid. "No, thanks. We can walk."

"Jerry, for God's sake, don't be so stubborn." Logan dropped his voice low, probably to prevent Miriam from hearing, but his words carried. "I know you don't want to associate with the Amish, but I'm freezing."

"You take the ride then. I'll help you in, but I still intend to walk."

*Jerry?* The wave and earlier flourish came back to her. She'd sketched those gestures, that profile, minus the beard and mustache. Even the broadfall pants should have given her a clue. All the hair had thrown her off. Amish men never had mustaches. She'd definitely seen him before. He'd been in another *g'may*, but they'd played against each other in baseball and volleyball.

Miriam leaned out. "Jerry? Jerry Gingerich? Is that you?"

Jerry scrunched his hands into fists in his coat pocket. Hands covered in the black gloves she'd given him. So much for keeping his secret.

Logan stared from one to the other. "You know each other?"

"Could we talk about this in the van?" Elmer asked. "We're losing all the heat out the door. Need help with the wheelchair?"

No point in denying the ride now. "*Neh*, I can get it." Jerry helped Logan up and onto the van seat, then he collapsed the chair, and lifted it in.

While Logan guided it behind their row of seats, Jerry hopped in and closed the door.

"Where to, gentlemen?" Elmer asked.

Logan and Jerry stared at each other. A message passed between them. Logan nodded to show he understood. Jerry didn't want anyone to know about his living conditions, especially Miriam. "Maybe you could drop us at the corner of—"

"I have a better idea," Miriam chirped like a happy bird. "Elmer, can you take me home?"

"*Neh!*" The word exploded from Jerry's mouth. He'd never go into an Amish home. He hadn't been baptized, so he wouldn't be shunned. But he wanted nothing to do with the Amish. Never again.

Elmer's eyebrows shot up almost to his hairline. "Miriam, your parents would not approve."

That was for sure. If Jerry remembered right, Miriam had a lot of younger brothers and sisters. And her parents had always been strict. They wouldn't want him setting a bad example for their children. He no longer went to church, and the life he'd been living would be unacceptable. Besides, he couldn't walk into her house with scruffy clothes, a mustache, and shoulder-length hair. And he had a beard when he was unmarried. They'd all be shocked.

"They aren't here to ask."

Jerry hadn't kept up with anything in the Amish community. Had something happened to her parents? If they weren't home, he couldn't possibly go into their house. He couldn't believe she'd even considered it.

She turned around in her seat, and Jerry wanted to duck and hide. He felt exposed, unworthy of even being inside this van. Despite the air being too warm for his hood, he kept it closed so she couldn't see what he looked like.

"Listen, you need a roof over your head. We have plenty of room."

Elmer tutted. "Miriam, it wouldn't be proper. Not with your whole family gone and you alone in that house. I know the Amish church and your parents would never approve.

Jerry wasn't sure what to think. Surely, this driver hadn't meant they'd all died. But he couldn't picture an Amish family going off and leaving her alone. "Your whole family's gone?"

A shadow flitted across her face. "They went to Pinecraft to take care of *Dawdi* and *Mammi*."

"And they left you here by yourself?" None of this made sense.

"Someone needed to stay her for my brother Abraham." She waved an impatient hand, but her eyes shone with tears. "Now's not the time to talk about all this. The snow is getting worse."

"Absolutely not. We can't sleep at your house." Jerry issued the flat denial. As wonderful as it would be to spend the night in warmth and comfort, he wouldn't let her break *Ordnung* rules.

"You wouldn't be staying in the house. You and Logan could sleep in the *dawdi haus* out back."

Elmer hesitated. "I guess that would be all right." He didn't sound too certain.

"It's either there, or they sleep on the street," Miriam pointed out.

"I'd offer to have them at my house," Elmer said, "but my daughters and all the grandkids are visiting. We don't have enough beds, so the kids are using sleeping bags. They've pretty much taken up every spare inch of floor space."

Jerry broke into the conversation. "We're used to sleeping

outside." He wouldn't let other people make his life decisions. From a young age, he'd always been set on doing everything his way. That's why, during *Rumspringa*, he'd broken with his parents. He'd been bound and determined to join a rock band, and no amount of his parents' begging, pleading, or punishing persuaded him otherwise. Jerry had pursued his dream for two glorious years.

Miriam shook her head. "You may be used to it, but I can't let you do that during a snowstorm when I can give you a roof over your heads." She sounded as determined as he was.

"Don't be ridiculous, Jerry," Logan said. "She has a place to keep us out of this storm. Just say thank you, and be grateful for a roof over our heads for a night or two."

Jerry grumbled to himself, but Elmer had already turned the van in the opposite direction of their small encampment. It looked like Jerry had lost the argument, and they were heading for an Amish house. He had a very bad feeling about all of this.

# CHAPTER 4

*D*espite its snow tires, the van fishtailed as it rounded the final curves in the country road. While Elmer turned the wheel to straighten the car, Miriam tensed and gripped the door armrest, grateful no vehicles occupied the other lane.

"It's getting slippery out here." Elmer's usual cheery voice held a note of strain. "Glad I don't have far to get home."

"You can let us out here." She pointed in front of the house. "I don't want you to get stuck in the driveway." She'd have to clear it once the snow stopped. *Daed* had set the shovel on the back porch before he left, but Miriam missed her brothers, who usually did that job.

When she reached for her grocery bags, Jerry waved her away. "We can get those. I'll just hang them on the wheelchair."

"You don't have to—"

"Least we can do." Jerry's gruff response and fidgeting revealed his nervousness.

Was he anxious about being around her or being away from his usual surroundings? Or maybe heading into an Amish home brought up old memories along with guilt about leaving the community?

Jerry struggled to push the wheelchair through ankle-deep

drifts to the back door. He insisted on depositing the grocery bags inside her back door before she showed them to the *dawdi haus*.

"Make yourselves at home, and feel free to use anything in the house," she told them. "I'll stop over with some food once I put away the groceries."

While Miriam unbagged items, she regretted not purchasing more at the market. but she set aside most of it to take to them. Loud scraping on the back porch startled her.

Outside the window, Jerry was shoveling snow from the porch and clearing a path to the *dawdi haus*. The falling snow would soon coat it again, but it would make her task easier once the snow stopped.

She tucked several jars of homemade canned soup, fruit, and vegetables into a basket with the groceries. When she opened the back door, the wind smacked her in the face and nearly ripped the screen door from her hand.

"It's too cold out here," she called. "Shoveling can wait until the storm ends." She held up the basket. "This is for you."

"*Danke.*" Jerry kept his head down as he came over and took the basket. "I'll do more later," he said. He hung the basket over his arm and pushed the shovel ahead of him all the way to the *dawdi haus*, swiping it sideways to remove a wide swath of snow on either side.

Throughout the chilly afternoon, Miriam kneaded large batches of dough for bread and sticky buns. While the dough rose, she made two chicken-and-rice casseroles, but the whole time, memories niggled at the back of her mind.

After she shaped the dough, she went upstairs and dug through old boxes on her closet shelf. She'd labeled each container with the year, so she tried to guess which one held what she wanted to find.

In the second box she selected, she sifted through piles of poetry and sketches. Her parents had been against her drawing people, so most were landscapes, animals, and objects around the house. But this box contained many, many forbidden pictures.

Most showed the same young man—playing volleyball and baseball, eating an ice cream cone, climbing into a buggy, laughing at a joke. . .

She unearthed the one she'd been searching for. That day, Jerry had made a home run in baseball. She'd captured his powerful swing, the lines of his motion, the perfection of his profile. A profile she'd never forget.

Because she couldn't draw people in public, she'd mentally traced every detail of his form and movement, storing them all in her memory. That night she'd tiptoed downstairs, taken the DeWalt into the pantry, shut the door so the light wouldn't escape, and sketched him again and again. She'd crumpled up many of the sketches and buried them under potato peelings and other scraps from their dinner. One sketch, though, stood out from the rest.

Miriam caught her breath. She'd found it. Even now, years later, it still moved her.

Although it had been the best portrait she'd ever done, embarrassment flooded through her at the tiny hearts on each corner of the paper. She'd been sixteen and sure she was in love.

She'd learned the hard way that her choices couldn't be trusted. Shortly after she fell for Jerry, he left the community to play in some rock band, and look where he'd ended up. Far from the faith.

In her next attempt at a relationship, she hadn't fared much better. He'd jilted her for her best friend. Miriam might be better off avoiding love.

Yet, when she'd looked across the Yoder's Market parking lot, Jerry had turned his head turned at the exact angle in this picture. Her heart had fluttered the way it had when she'd drawn his portrait.

Her fingers itched to record Jerry's profile from today and compare the two. She took out a pencil and paper, and let muscle memory take over. The lines flowed from her mind to her hand. An image took shape. When she finished, she compared the two.

Jerry's beard and mustache covered his lower face, but the way he carried himself matched. So did his features, but they had a sharper edge.

The major difference between sixteen-year-old and present-day Jerry, which Miriam's side views didn't show, lay in his eyes. The mischievous twinkle had changed to a wary, haunted expression.

That saddened her. The only way to bring back the old joy to his face would be if he surrendered to the Lord, but Jerry had made it clear years ago he'd broken with the Amish for good. Today, he'd preferred to stay outside in a snowstorm rather than in an Amish home.

*Lord, please soften Jerry's heart and bring him back to You.*

A noise outside startled her. She dropped her pencil and hurried to the window. Jerry was shoveling the driveway. A knit cap covered his hair. Her red scarf wrapped around his lower face hid the beard and mustache. In his parka and broadfall pants, he appeared to be an Amishman doing chores.

Eager to get this transformation down on paper, Miriam grabbed her art supplies and returned to the window. She'd never had a chance to draw from life, so she reveled in the opportunity. After a few scribbled sketches of Jerry in motion, she worked on a more precise drawing, comparing the man in the snow to the one taking shape on the paper, painstakingly recording every detail.

If only this image of Jerry could be real. . .

Miriam jerked her mind away from that thought and stopped to massage a crick in her neck. *Ach! The time.* She'd gotten so engrossed she'd forgotten about the rising dough. Dropping her pencil, she berated herself for focusing on a frivolous activity instead of working and raced down to the kitchen.

Several hours later, the aroma of yeast and cinnamon filled the air from rows of loaves and pans of sticky buns cooling on the counter. Miriam set most of the baked goods in a basket.

A plow rumbled down the street with a loud rasp as it shoved walls of snow to each side of the road. Miriam thanked the Lord for clear roads. She could get to the store for additional groceries to feed her guests.

Her head snapped up at a rap on the back door. *Jerry.* Her pulse sped faster, but she shook off her childhood attraction. Her heightened feelings had been fueled by her drawings and his appearance as a typical Amish man. Unwrap that scarf and take off the hat, he'd reappear as an ex-Amish homeless man. Despite picturing him that way, her heart longed for the *youngie* he'd been before he'd gone wild during *Rumspringa.*

When she opened the door, he inhaled deeply and closed his eyes. "Smells delicious in here."

His snow-crusted eyelashes fanned across his ruddy cheeks, and Miriam longed to paint them and write a poem about the emotions they stirred within her.

"*Danke* for clearing the driveway." Her words came out breathless, and she hoped he wouldn't guess why.

MIRIAM's lilting voice strummed chords in Jerry's soul he thought he'd never hear again. It started an unbearable longing for home and family. After so many road trips with the band and the hardships of the two years since, he'd missed a warm kitchen and a kind heart. Miriam would never know what the roof over his head meant to him. And not just to him, but to Logan. For that, he'd do whatever he could to help.

He opened his eyes. "*Gern geschehen.*" The *Deutsch* "you're welcome" had just popped out. He reverted to *Englisch.* "It's not much, but I wanted to repay your hospitality."

"I didn't expect anything in return."

Jerry had been cheated by so many people in the past few years, he'd almost forgotten the honesty and charity he'd grown up with in the Amish community. He swallowed hard. "We appreciate it." That barely expressed a tiny portion of his gratitude. His heart overflowed at her generosity, but he had no way to put it into words.

"I just finished baking."

"Mmm, I can tell." He smiled, attempting to hide his longing for even one bite of those tantalizing baked goods. Despite Miriam's warming and filling spaghetti soup he'd heated for Logan and gobbled down himself a few hours ago, his stomach grumbled.

"I packed a basket for you to take back to the *dawdi haus*."

"You didn't have to—"

Before he could finish, she bustled over to the counter, returned with a full basket, and handed it to him.

Once again, she'd overwhelmed him. "*Danke.* You don't know what this means to us."

Her eyes brimmed with sympathy. "If you need anything at all, don't hesitate to ask."

He shuffled both feet on the snow-dusted porch, reluctant to ask for another favor. "I, um, wondered. . . if you'd mind if I invited several other people to join us. Just until this storm is over. I'm especially worried about an older couple and a young girl. They could take my place here."

His plea touched Miriam. He'd be willing to sleep in the snow to help someone else. That reminded her of the Jerry she knew as a *youngie.*

Still, she hesitated. Should she put her own safety over the life-threatening cold homeless people endured during a snowstorm?

Other people might warn her against having a crowd of street people living here while her parents were gone. What would *Mamm* and *Daed* say if they knew? More importantly, what would God say?

The words of Proverbs 19:17 echoed in her mind. *He that hath pity upon the poor lendeth unto the Lord.*

Miriam tamped down her fears. She would do God's will.

"*Jah*, you may invite all of them who need shelter, but you stay too. Do you want to take the family buggy to bring them here?"

Jerry stared at her in astonishment. "You'd trust me with it?"

"Of course." If they had more guests, she'd need additional food. "Would you be able to stop at the store for milk and other supplies if I give you a list and some money?"

He frowned. "How do you know I won't take your money and flee?"

His question puzzled her. Was he warning her not to rely him? Or was he testing her confidence in him? That had an easy answer. "I trust you, Jerry Gingerich."

Pressing his lips together, he lowered his head. "Not everyone does."

At the sorrow in those words, Miriam's heart ached for him. What had he been through the past few years?

# CHAPTER 5

*A*lthough Jerry appreciated Miriam's offer of the buggy, it had been years since he'd been in one, let alone driven one. Instead, he offered Elmer the tip-jar money to drive to town. But once Elmer found out why they were going, he refused payment and insisted the Lord expected him to help.

Jerry tried to convince people to come with him, but many refused. Some didn't want to leave their familiar surroundings. Others were too suspicious. He didn't ask any troublemakers because he didn't want any problems for Miriam. In the end, he rounded up six people—an older couple, another vet, a runaway teen, and a couple with a young daughter who'd recently joined their circle. On the way back to Miriam's, they stopped for her groceries.

After they returned, Jerry showed everyone into the *dawdi haus*, then asked Inez, the older woman, to accompany him to take the groceries to Miriam. When Miriam called for them to come in, she was pulling several casseroles from the oven.

"*Gut.* You can take these back with you." She motioned to the pans, then she removed a few items from the grocery bags. "The rest is for all of you."

RACHEL J. GOOD

"Are you sure?" Jerry didn't want to leave her hungry. He'd experienced that enough times to know what it felt like.

"I have more than enough."

Her sunshiny smile flipped Jerry's stomach. He'd always loved that smile. He forced himself to focus on the potholders she was holding out to him. As he reached for them, his hand brushed hers.

Sparks zinged up his arm. He steeled himself not to react, not to jump back. But it took all his willpower. He hadn't expected her to still have the power to attract him. If anything, her pull had only grown stronger. Or maybe in his loneliness, he missed experiencing a gentle touch.

To get his reaction under control, Jerry passed the potholders to Inez. "Could you carry the casseroles? I'll get as many grocery bags as I can. We can come back for the rest."

Inez tipped her head in Miriam's direction. "Thanks for the food and place to stay."

"You're welcome. I'm glad you're here. I'm Miriam."

Jerry's cheeks stung with heat. "I'm sorry, I forgot to introduce you. This is Inez."

"Glad to meet you." Miriam's greeting sounded genuine, not like so many of the patronizing people who asked prying questions of the homeless.

As he and Inez picked up the last of the groceries and casseroles, Jerry asked, "Do you have enough for yourself?"

She nodded and pointed to two loaves of bread and a pan of sticky buns. "And I have the cans and food that rolled away at Yoder's." She giggled.

The sound bubbled through him like joyful music. "If you need anything, let me know," he teased. For the first time in years, his spirit lightened. He hadn't joked around like this since the Amish Rebels disbanded.

116

MIRIAM LAUGHED as Jerry walked out the door. He still had some of his old lighthearted ways. His joking and teasing often got him trouble as a *youngie*, but she'd seen the loneliness and insecurity underneath. She understood his need to be the center of attention to make up for his judgmental family and overbearing father. Being in a band that toured the country must have validated Jerry after all the criticism at home. Too bad he hadn't looked to God for his self-worth instead of the world.

After Miriam cared for the horses, she fixed herself a plate and sat alone at the huge, empty table. Looking at all those seats with nobody in them made her eyes sting. How would all the people in the *dawdi haus* fit around the small table in her grandparents' kitchen? They only had chairs for four.

Miriam had counted six people streaming from the van. And where would they all sleep? They were probably used to sleeping on the ground, but it didn't seem right. She'd seen a couple with a child, and Inez had been walking beside a man. Her husband perhaps? This house had plenty of beds.

After Miriam finished her lonely meal and washed the dishes, she made up her mind to issue an invitation. Darkness had fallen, so she carried a flashlight to illuminate the snow-drifted path to the *dawdi haus*. She knocked, introduced herself, and suggested some of them could sleep in the house.

Jerry's eyes widened. "I'm not sure——"

"I am." She remained firm.

"All right. But the young men will all stay here." He pointed to the teen and the other vet. "They can take the two beds, and I'll get Logan set up on the couch here. We'll be fine."

"What about you?"

"Don't worry about me. I picked up my sleeping bag." He tipped his head to the rolled-up bag in the corner.

Miriam opened her mouth to protest, but he shook his head. "I'm sure your parents wouldn't approve of me sleeping in the house."

She frowned. "I don't like thinking about you on the floor."

117

Jerry laughed. "If you saw where I've been living for the past two years, you'd understand sleeping on the floor here is a blessing. A roof over my head that doesn't drip or rumble. Warm, dry ground under me. A rug to cushion the floor. No freezing drafts or drifting snow. No exhaust fumes choking me."

Though he kept his tone bright and cheerful, Jerry's descriptions horrified Miriam. "But why did you stay there?" It made no sense to her.

With a quick glance toward his friend in the wheelchair, Jerry lowered his voice. "I need to keep an eye on Logan at night. Sometimes he needs help. Most nights, he won't agree to sleep indoors. Today's snowstorm changed his mind."

So, Jerry stayed outside in all kinds of weather to care for a friend? He had a good heart and many fascinating sides to his character. Miriam longed to get reacquainted with him. Not as a crush anymore. That was impossible. But she did want to be friends.

Jerry picked up several black plastic trash bags from the floor. "Why don't I help people carry their things?"

When they reached the house, Miriam led them into the dark kitchen.

"Where's your light switch?" the little girl asked.

Her mother hushed her, but Miriam explained that Amish didn't use electricity.

"We didn't have 'lectricity either," the girl confided in a low voice, "'cause we didn't have money to pay the bill."

A short while later, everyone had been settled in their rooms. The mother with the young daughter cried when Miriam led them into her parents' bedroom and suggested their daughter could sleep in the bedroom next door.

"We've hardly ever slept in beds after we got evicted six months ago. We lived in our car until that got repo'd. Grayson and I have been looking for jobs ever since the restaurant closed, but most places aren't hiring."

Her husband put his arm around her. "We'll get something

soon." He turned to Miriam. "It's hard to find family shelters with openings. And Janece didn't want to go to a woman's shelter and be apart from me."

Janece nodded. "Come on, Willow, let's get you washed up before bed." Janece shot Miriam an apologetic smile. "It's hard to get clean in public bathrooms. And washing clothes is a trial. Tried to save money for the laundromat, but every penny went for food."

Miriam had never considered the problems homeless people faced. "We can do laundry tomorrow." Others probably needed clean clothes too.

"It's warm in laundry-mats," Willow said. "And in libraries. And the train station."

It broke Miriam's heart to think of this family searching for warmth in winter. Where would they have slept tonight?

Once she had everyone settled, she headed for her room. Grateful nobody had come in there, she gathered the drawings she'd left scattered around, intending to stash them away. Instead, she directed the flashlight beam over her drawings of Jerry. Her heart pitter-pattered at each one, but the final one, where he looked like an Amishman shoveling snow brought tears to her eyes. What had driven him from the Amish faith?

SNUG IN HIS SLEEPING BAG, Jerry relaxed for the first time in years. Tonight, he didn't have to be on alert for thieves or drunks. Or drug users on a bad trip. Or cops who'd arrest them for vagrancy. All he had to worry about were Logan's PTSD nightmares. Maybe sleeping on a comfortable couch out of the weather and city noise—no backfiring cars, drag-racing teens, loud music blasting from cars, or angry arguments—might give him a peaceful night. Thankful for the warmth and safety, Jerry drifted off.

A car pulling partway into the driveway startled him awake.

Always a light sleeper, he woke on high alert, ready to jump into action. His watch glowed 1:18. What would someone want at an Amish house this late at night?

To his relief, the car backed out and drove away. Must have been someone turning around. Although he tried to slow his racing heart, the adrenaline rushing through him kept him tense and awake. He took several deep breaths to calm his pulse.

Were those shuffling sounds on the driveway? In one fluid motion, he jumped to his feet. Tiptoeing so he didn't wake Logan, Jerry inched his way to the door. He pulled on his boots and coat, then felt for the flashlight he always kept in his pocket. He fumbled through tissue packs, a lighter, folded trash bags, a rain poncho pouch, a whistle, a handful of bandages, and the gum they chewed to lessen hunger pangs when they had no food. Finally, his hand closed around the miniature flashlight.

By this time, the footsteps had reached Miriam's back porch. *Thud.* Something heavy smashed to the ground. Jerry eased open the door. In the moonless night, a shadowy figure struggled to stand, but kept slipping on the ice.

Instead of turning on the light, Jerry crept closer. An *Englisch* teen dressed in jeans, boots, and a hooded parka hauled himself to his feet, his steps unsteady. Drunk, for sure. Jerry reached the teen just as he rattled the doorknob, trying to get in.

Jerry grabbed the boy around the waist. "What are you doing?"

# CHAPTER 6

$\mathcal{H}$eadlights shining into her window woke Miriam. A car backed up and drove away. Just a driver lost on country roads. She lay back down, but sleep eluded her. She'd been dreaming of Jerry, and she longed to drift back into his arms, where she'd been before she'd jolted awake. As tempting as it was, Miriam shouldn't let herself return to that fantasy.

Soft shush-shushing sounds in the driveway made her tense. Someone seemed to be slipping and sliding toward the house. The intruder reached the back porch. Had Jerry invited another friend to spend the night? Maybe the person needed a bed.

Miriam slipped her dress over her nightgown, tucked the braid she wore to bed under a kerchief, and headed downstairs.

*Thud.* Something hit the back porch.

What was that?

She stopped. The doorknob rattled. Someone was trying to get in.

Low, growling voices came through the door, along with more thumps.

Miriam stood motionless, unsure whether to enter the kitchen.

Suddenly, something bumped against the back door.

∾

THE KID JERRY had nabbed twisted away.

"Who are you? And what are you doing here?" The boy's words came out slurred. Definitely drunk.

Jerry had been attacked in street fights before. He didn't like this boy's attitude or the way he crouched as if readying to land a blow. Raised a pacifist, Jerry took a step back, hoping to cool down the teen's temper. But backing off didn't mean he'd let anyone bother or hurt Miriam. Or go into her house without permission, especially not a tipsy *Englischer*.

Maybe the kid was so out of it, he'd mistaken this for his house. "Are you sure you're at the right place?" Jerry made his question friendly and nonthreatening.

The boy looked around with a bleary expression. "Yep. But you sure aren't." He narrowed his eyes. "Who are you?" he demanded again. "And what are you doing here?"

"I'm Jerry, and I've been invited to stay—"

"Liar." The kid wobbled as he tried to pull himself erect to appear more imposing. "This is my house, so get out of here." He staggered back to the door.

"I'm not letting you disturb the people inside." Jerry slid in front of the teen and blocked access to the door with his body.

"People inside?" The boy laughed. "Nobody's here. Now get out of the way. It's my house."

"This is an Amish house, and you're not Amish."

"I am too. Now go away before I—I. . .

Suddenly, the door opened, and a flashlight flicked on. "What's going on?"

The kid paled. "Miriam?"

The light wavered. "Abraham?"

Jerry stepped away from the door. "You know him?"

"He's my brother."

Feeling like a fool, Jerry mumbled a quick apology and rushed toward the *dawdi haus*. He couldn't even imagine what

Miriam must think of him, stopping her brother from entering the house.

~

"Jerry," Miriam called after him, "*danke*." She appreciated his desire to take care of her. He knew her family was gone, so he must have assumed Abraham was a burglar. She opened the door wider to let her brother in.

"Who is that guy? And what's he doing here?" Abraham stumbled into the kitchen and nearly fell.

Miriam's stomach curdled at her brother's slurred words. He'd promised not to drink again. "Jerry's a guest." She slammed the door against the freezing gusts of air carrying snowflakes into the kitchen, then regretted it. She hoped she hadn't woken anyone.

"How come you're here?" Abraham whined. "I thought you'd all be gone."

"Why? So you could have parties?"

From the guilt in his eyes, she'd guessed right. "You really think *Mamm* and *Daed* would leave you here alone?"

Abraham's face fell. "Everyone's here?" He looked like he did whenever *Daed* grounded him. "You're not gonna tell them about this, are you?"

"I told you I would." It irritated Miriam that he expected her to cover for his wrongdoing. "What happened with Ski Roundtop?"

He flapped his hand. "I said that so *Daed* wouldn't try to find me. I can't believe you all stayed home." Bitterness edged his words. "How angry are they?"

"They're very upset. *Mamm* cried about not getting to see her parents. You messed up the Pinecraft trip." Miriam wanted him to be aware of how his behavior affected the family, but her conscience nagged her about letting him believe a partial truth.

Abraham swallowed hard. "They're going to be furious."

"Do you blame them? You should be grounded for months. I'm sorry I didn't tell them you came home drunk. If I had, we might all be in Pinecraft, but I'll tell them the minute they get back."

"From where?"

"Pinecraft."

"But you said—" His brow furrowed. "They went? Then why are you here?"

"I volunteered to stay so *Mamm* could go. I didn't want them to miss their anniversary together."

His eyes gleamed. "Then I have three weeks."

"*Neh*, you don't. You'll behave yourself the whole time they're gone or else. . ."

Abraham swayed when he stood. "Or else what? You can't stop me."

"They left me in charge, and they expect you to listen."

As her brother lurched toward the stairs, Miriam lowered her head into her hands.

*Lord, I don't know what to do. Please help me handle Abraham and keep him from getting into trouble.*

After she left her worries in God's hands, she rose and caught up with Abraham. "Be quiet when you go upstairs so you don't wake anyone." If they hadn't already been awakened by the scuffling outside, the slamming door, and the argument just now.

"You said they all went to Pinecraft."

"They did. We have guests."

"What? Who?"

"You'll find out tomorrow."

Abraham stared at her in disbelief, but to her surprise, he tottered quietly to his room.

*Thank you, Lord.*

She'd might have more problems with him tomorrow, but at least she'd sleep peacefully tonight.

~

Outside, the wind howled. Inside, windowpanes rattled. Jerry struggled to fall back to sleep. Despite the comfort of having a warm, dry place to sleep, he tossed and turned.

Each time he closed his eyes, images of Miriam came to mind. The smiles she'd given him today. Her generous offer to stay here. She'd always been caring and kind. If he'd been different as a *youngie*, maybe he'd have joined the church and dated her. That opportunity had passed him by. He had no chance with her now.

The memories saddened him. Since the band folded, he'd been living one day at a time, only concentrating on surviving for the next few hours. For the first time, he pictured his future. He'd grow old on the streets. Is that what he wanted? What choice did he have?

He could get a job, even an entry position. If he did, who'd take care of Logan? Maybe they could find a way to make a better life for themselves, but how?

A thunderous crack ripped through the night. Jerry stared through the frost-fogged window in horror as an uprooted tree crashed onto the barn roof.

At the bang, Logan bolted upright on the couch.

Jerry knew from experience to stay back. Getting close agitated Logan. "You're okay, Logan. You're safe. It's only a noise outside," Jerry said in a calm voice over and over.

Logan's restlessness might lead to a fall. Usually, he slept on the ground, but tonight he was on a couch. Jerry sat beside Logan to prevent an accident. At first, Logan fought, hitting and shoving Jerry. As the blows rained down, Jerry repeated soothing phrases and endured the pain.

All at once, Logan collapsed back, covered his head, and whimpered—a signal he'd soon stare blankly into the distance.

Herb, also a veteran, opened the bedroom door. "Can I help?"

"Can you keep him from falling? And ground him when he's ready? I'll go check out the damage."

"Sure. I've done this with some of my buddies." Herb sat facing Logan and murmured to him.

Jerry bundled up and raced out the door, almost running headlong into Miriam.

"The horses," she gasped as she ran toward the barn. She slipped on the slick driveway.

Jerry took her hand to keep her upright. "Careful. Watch for black ice."

Miriam clung to his fingers, and they entered the barn. A large branch had punched a hole through the rafters, and all the snow from the roof had showered down on the farm equipment in the back of the barn.

"It missed the stalls." Jerry exhaled a pent-up breath, but with Miriam's soft hand in his, adrenaline still sent fire through his veins.

Nostrils flared, the three horses snorted, stomped, and pawed.

"They're scared." Miriam broke free from him to pet and settle the horses.

Her gentle words touched a hardened, locked-up place deep within Jerry. If he stayed around her, sooner or later, she'd turn that key, and all his bottled-up pain would spill out. He backed away. He wasn't ready for that and never would be.

Keeping his voice brisk, he assessed the damage. "We'd better move the tree before it crushes that whole side of the barn. Can you get your brother and Grayson? Also, I'll need rope, a ladder, and a tarp.

She waved a hand toward the corner under the fallen tree. "They'd all be back there." As she spoke, the barn wall creaked and groaned, and the tree shifted. More snow plopped through the hole. "But you can't go back there, it's not safe."

"We have to hurry. Can you call everyone? We'll need lots of help."

While Miriam hurried off, Jerry whispered a prayer. He might not have joined the church, but he still believed in God. If the tree smashed down, the barn wall would crush him and the horses. He had to move the horses outside first.

By the time, he'd tied the first horse to a hitching post by the house, Grayson joined him, staying way clear of the horse.

"You know anything about horses?" Jerry asked.

Grayson took a step back and held up his hands. "Never been around one in my life."

Jerry couldn't send a family man into the barn under that tree for the supplies. "Gather everyone near the root end of the tree."

Abraham and Miriam emerged from the house. Jerry called to them, "Get the horses outside."

A sulky look crossed Abraham's face. He also looked nauseous. Miriam's brother must have a nasty hangover. Doing this job would be hard for him.

"Come on, Abraham." Miriam rushed toward the barn. "The horses'll die if the roof caves in."

That spurred him into action, but he took slow steps and winced. Jerry dashed past him and into the barn for supplies, casting a wary eye at the tree as it shook under the weight of snow cascading from the roof.

Although he had no right to ask the Lord for favors after the way he'd turned his back on God and his faith, Jerry murmured a prayer.

*Lord, I deserve nothing from you, but Miriam does. She needs the supplies back there. Please keep the tree from smashing down.*

Heart pounding, he ducked underneath. When he picked up the coil of rope, a load of snow slid off the roof and onto Jerry's head. He brushed it off, but icy trickles slid down the back of his neck, and he shivered.

He grabbed a tarp and lifted an extension ladder from its wall hooks. Grunting, he swung the heavy ladder down. This should be a two-person job, but he couldn't ask anyone else to endanger their lives.

Another load of snow landed on an outstretched branch with

a plop. The branch snapped, sending shudders through the trunk. If the tremors brought it down. . .

*Please, God. . .*

Throat dry, Jerry moved as fast as he could to exit the barn. Outside, he exhaled a long, relieved breath. He'd made it. His life had flashed before his eyes, and his heart still banged against his chest. His eyes stung. So many things rose from his past that he wished he could undo. How different his life might be now if he hadn't been blinded by bitterness and a rebellious spirit.

Jerry shook off the cloud of depression. They had to move the tree before it destroyed the barn.

# CHAPTER 7

*J*erry stretched his aching muscles. They'd roped the tree, and with everyone pulling, even Logan, they'd managed to raise the tree, shift it, and lower it to the ground near the barn. They'd all been sweaty and sore, with rope burns on their hands, but they'd cheered as they lowered the tree the last few feet. Sawing that massive trunk into firewood would be a major job, but they'd saved the barn. Except for the hole in the roof, it was still intact.

As the sun rose above the horizon, shedding a golden glow on the snow, everyone traipsed inside Miriam's house and gathered around the old oak table to warm their hands on mugs of coffee or hot chocolate. Jerry had never seen such a large table, but if he remembered right, they had ten children. This table was the perfect size for all his friends.

Grayson, a short-order cook, insisted on making pancakes, while Miriam set the table. Jerry went to the *dawdi haus* to shower while they fixed breakfast. Gratitude filled him for the spray of hot water. Most public restrooms had only lukewarm water at best, and he struggled to get clean with paper towels. After having a roof over his head and running water, he'd have trouble going back to the streets.

He'd also miss these delicious meals. A heavenly aroma filled the air as Jerry, his damp hair tucked under a knit cap, entered the kitchen. Grayson piled everyone's plates with pancakes and slathered on butter and syrup. Only one awkward moment occurred. Miriam and Abraham bowed their heads. Jerry nodded to encourage everyone else to close their eyes and bow their heads.

Once they all lifted their heads, Willow's forehead wrinkled. "Ain't you going to pray?"

Miriam smiled at her. "We pray silently."

Willow thrust out her lower lip. "But I like to pray out loud."

Jerry sat uneasily while everyone closed their eyes their eyes again and Willow said grace. Once, he would have smiled at the small girl's earnest thanks for the pancakes and a warm bed. Instead, he *rutsched* guiltily. How far he'd come from his childhood beliefs.

He pushed aside those niggling thoughts and concentrated on savoring his breakfast. As soon as everyone finished and ended with another prayer, Jerry rose, grateful for a full stomach. "Come on, Abraham, let's get a tarp on the roof."

Abraham scowled and looked ready to protest.

Jerry cut off the boy's defiance. "With your parents gone, you're the man of the family now."

Miriam's brother blinked. Then, to Jerry's relief, Abraham pushed back his chair and headed for the door.

In companionable silence, they climbed to the roof and tacked down the tarp.

"That'll hold for now," Jerry said as they returned the ladder to the barn, "but we should repair it as soon as possible."

"We won't have any money until my parents get back in three weeks." Abraham's jaw hardened. "*Daed* puts all the money we earn in the bank and only gives us a little pocket money every week. I already spent mine."

Jerry could guess where that money went. "I'd offer to pay,

but all I have is a small amount from the tip jar." He didn't add it had come from Miriam.

"Tip jar?"

Shame washed over Jerry, and he hung his head. "I play the guitar on the street for money.

Abraham's eyes widened. "You're like a beggar?"

Viewing his life as an outsider, Jerry had to admit he basically had been. He'd always seen it as payment for entertaining people, like when he'd toured the country to play music. "I used to be in a band."

"That's why you look familiar. You were in the Amish Rebels, weren't you?"

Jerry nodded. "How did you know that?" Miriam's brother would have been a young teen when the band was together.

This time, Abraham was the one to look ashamed. "I sneaked out with my *Englisch* friends to hear you play a few times."

So, Abraham had been rebellious long before *Rumspringa*. "How old were you?" Jerry asked.

Abraham mumbled, "Fourteen."

"Pretty young to be sneaking out."

"You must have done it too," Abraham shot back.

"We were sixteen." Jerry wished he'd had a different past so he could be a better example to Miriam's brother.

Abraham's eyes narrowed, "But you must of made a lot of money with the Amish Rebels."

Jerry's mouth twisted. "We did, but our manager took off with all of it."

"Can't you get it back?"

"*Neh*, we didn't sign a contract, so we couldn't sue. Besides, Mark Troyer'd never agree to that."

"So how come you didn't get a job?" Abraham's eyes bored into Jerry.

Jerry looked away. "I got a job at a nightclub, but they mostly paid me in alcohol. I ended up too drunk to hold a job. I played guitar for drink money. I couldn't get through a day without it."

Abraham avoided Jerry's eyes.

Jerry didn't want to talk about those dark days. "Logan and I went to AA together. He got kicked out of his apartment after a bad PTSD episode, and we ended up on the streets."

The pity on Abraham's face mortified Jerry, but maybe he could give this boy a life lesson. "I rebelled against my family's rules and turned my back on the church. My poor choices cost me the woman I loved, my home, my family. My father will never speak to me again, and he won't let anyone else in the family contact me."

He had the teen's full attention, so Jerry pinned Abraham with a serious look. "Keep heading the way you are, and you could end up like me—sleeping under a smelly underpass in freezing weather, shivering in a sleeping bag, terrified of getting robbed or thrown in jail."

From the shocked look in Abraham's eyes, Jerry's story had made an impression.

As INEZ, Jenece, and Willow washed dishes with Miriam after breakfast, a deep contentment settled over Miriam. Yesterday, she'd been expecting a lonely Christmas at the big table, but this morning, almost every seat had been filled. Since her family left, she'd been feeling sorry for herself. Now, she had a purpose. Helping these people who were now becoming friends filled her with joy.

When they finished, they did laundry for everyone who wanted it. Then Miriam needed to buy meats and more vegetables to feed her guests. "Would anyone like to ride along to the farmer's market?"

The two women and Willow agreed, and they all headed to the barn, where Jerry and Abraham seemed to be having a serious discussion. Miriam prayed her brother wasn't admiring Jerry's choice to leave the faith.

Willow jumped up and down when Miriam pulled out the buggy. "We're going in that?"

Jenece looked nervous. "I'm not sure that's a good idea." She backed up further when Miriam brought out her horse.

"A horsey," Willow squealed and charged over.

Miriam let Willow help hitch up the horse, but it took a while to coax the two women to climb into the buggy. They both sat rigid and fearful for the first several miles, while Willow bounced on the back seat. As they neared the Green Valley Farmer's Market, the women relaxed a little, although they tensed or sucked in breaths whenever cars zipped past.

Once they entered the market, everyone stayed close to Miriam as she headed to the stands. While she waited in line at Lapp's Pastured Pork, Miriam got lost in thought. She could house Jerry's friends until her family came home in a few weeks, but what then? No way could she throw them out into the cold.

*Lord, please show me what to do.*

She was so engrossed in prayer, she almost knocked over an elderly lady with a cane. Miriam reached out to support the teetering woman, who beamed at her.

"Ah, just the person I wanted to see."

Miriam craned her neck behind her to see the person the woman had addressed.

The gray-haired lady patted Miriam's arm. "I meant you, dear. I'm Mrs. Vandenberg."

Maybe this lady didn't see well at her age. "Perhaps you've mistaken me for someone else."

"My eyes are fine. I'd like to get in touch with Jerry."

"Jerry Gingerich?"

"Of course. I have some questions for both of you. Will you be at home this afternoon?"

"Um, yes, but—"

Mrs. Vandenberg's face settled into a contented smile. "I'll stop by around two."

Miriam stared after her as she hobbled off. The poor woman hadn't even asked for an address.

The girl at the meat stand studied Miriam. "Mrs. Vandenberg's interested in you and this Jerry, huh?"

"I think she's mistaken. I don't even know her."

"You will," the girl said. "Mrs. Vandenberg's never mistaken. She must have had a nudge from God. She's not only the owner of this market, she's the richest woman in the area and known for her charity projects."

Still befuddled about why a rich woman had approached her, Miriam placed her order.

When the girl handed Miriam her bag, she waggled her eyebrows. "Mrs. Vandenberg's also famous as a matchmaker. You and this Jerry better watch out."

*Me and Jerry?* Miriam hid a smile. That might have been a possibility at age sixteen, but now? Too many obstacles stood between them.

She turned to find Inez and Jenece giggling together. "That old lady's gonna match you and Jerry?"

Jenece sobered. "Actually, it would be nice if you can convince Jerry to get off the streets."

"He'd never do that," Inez said. "He's too committed to caring for Logan."

Miriam had to stop their joking before they got home. "I can't marry Jerry. He's not with the church."

"But he used to be Amish," Inez pointed out.

"He's not Amish anymore, so it's impossible." Though Miriam said it with finality, she drifted off into daydreams of Jerry, clean-shaven and faithful to the church, all the while she finished her shopping.

SEVERAL NEIGHBORS JOINED Abraham and Jerry, bringing axes and battery-powered chainsaws. All the homeless men, including

Logan, came out to help cut and stack wood. They'd finished half the tree when Miriam's buggy pulled in the driveway.

Twenty minutes later, she called everyone in for a hearty meal of soup and sandwiches. After the silent prayer followed by Willow's audible prayer, they passed around the food, ate, and joked.

The Amishman sitting next to Jerry studied him closely. "You one of the Gingerich boys from Ronks?"

Jerry cringed and wished he could hide. While they'd been working, nobody had asked any questions. He'd hope to pass for *Englisch* with his beard and mustache.

When he nodded, the man continued, "You used to work with the Yoder boys and their dad in construction?"

"*Jah.*" The word came out choked. Jerry had apprenticed there after he'd finished school at fourteen. Even back then, he'd been as rebellious as Abraham, but he'd worked hard for the Yoders.

The man nodded. "Thought so. You all helped me build the addition on my house." He peered closer. "You must be the one who run off."

Jerry wished he could deny it. "I am."

"Heard that band broke up, and most of them went back home. Sorry to see you never came back. What are you doing now?"

How did he answer that? "Still playing guitar," Jerry mumbled.

The man's brow crinkled in disapproval, but before he could answer, someone knocked.

"Mrs. Vandenberg," Miriam faltered when she opened the door. "Come in. Would you like something to eat?"

"No, no, I had plenty earlier. I'll just sit here until you're done." She shuffled toward one of the empty chairs directly across from Jerry.

He gulped. Years ago, he'd heard of her reputation as a

matchmaker. But she couldn't possibly be here for him. Maybe for Miriam? That sent a pang straight through his heart.

# CHAPTER 8

*M*rs. Vandenberg's presence made Miriam so nervous, she almost dropped the dishes as she cleared the table. The men headed out the door to work on the tree, but Mrs. Vandenberg stopped Jerry.

"Perhaps we could talk in the living room?" She pushed herself to her feet.

Jerry froze like a raccoon caught in a flashlight beam. Wary, but curious.

"I'd like you to come with us, Miriam."

Miriam gestured toward the sink. "But I have to—"

Inez shooed Miriam toward the living room. "We can handle this. Spend time with your company."

Reluctantly, Miriam headed to the living room.

Mrs. Vandenberg sat in an armchair. "It was lovely to see a full table, Miriam. I'm so glad you're open to the Lord's leading. Otherwise, you might have had a lonely holiday. This year, you'll make many people happy."

Miriam froze in the doorway. Had this woman been spying on her?

"Sit down, dear." She gestured toward a chair as if this were her house instead of Miriam's. "Jerry, I want to start with you."

He squirmed and appeared ready to flee.

Miriam didn't blame him. She'd also be happy to escape.

"Relax." Mrs. Vandenberg laughed. "You both look like you're facing a serial killer."

Jerry's uncomfortable laugh echoed Miriam's nervousness. She twisted her hands in her lap and worried about inviting this woman into the house. Miriam's trust in the Lord had overcome her fears about asking the homeless people to stay. If she relied on God for that, she should trust Him for courage now.

"First of all, Jerry, I think you did a good job of selecting the people you brought into Miriam's home. All of them trustworthy, and most haven't been on the street long."

"How do you know that?" Miriam burst out.

"I trust God to guide me." Mrs. Vandenberg's calm answer made Miriam feel guilty for asking.

"Now, I know you're both worried about what will happen when Miriam's parents return. None of us want to see these friends of yours back out on the streets, so I have a proposal."

Miriam had been concerned about that all morning. She tried to push aside her wariness to listen.

JERRY LEANED FORWARD in his chair. If Mrs. Vandenberg had ideas for helping, he couldn't wait to hear them. She'd done so many good things for the community.

"I've opened the STAR center downtown to keep youngsters out of gangs. And the training center for gang members has been placing their graduates in jobs. You were there, Jerry, right?"

Miriam sucked in a breath.

Did she think he'd been in a gang?

"I spent one night there after our manager took off with our money, and we had no place to stay." He checked to see if his explanation had calmed Miriam's alarm.

Her furrowed brow worried him. He wanted her to have a

good opinion of him. Not that it mattered, because he'd never see her again after his stay here ended. That thought filled him with despair. More than anything, he longed to be around her for the rest of his life.

Mrs. Vandenberg cleared her throat. "All in good time. Right now, I'm ready for a new project I'd like your help on, Jerry."

He tensed. What help could he be?

"I want to open shelters for the homeless. I've researched available programs, and many offer only temporary assistance. Some allow a few days before people must leave. That isn't usually sufficient. And there are more people on the streets than the shelters have room for."

Jerry nodded. He knew that firsthand. "But what do you want me to do?"

"I'd like your recommendations as to what programs are most needed." Mrs. Vandenberg pulled a pen and tablet from her purse.

He didn't hesitate. "Somewhere vets can get help for PTSD." He'd often wished he could find a place for Logan.

"The government has assistance for vets."

"But some vets like Logan don't trust it, and others don't know where to go."

"Hmm, good point. We should assist people in applying for benefits and government programs. Not just vets, but everyone." She jotted notes. "We can help those who don't read well enough to fill out the forms or don't have access to a computer."

Over the next half hour, Mrs. Vandenberg took Jerry's ideas and expanded them until she had three pages of notes. And not just on transition housing and shelter needs, but many of the other things that could help: food, toiletries, mailboxes, employment and resume services, warm daytime shelters, bathrooms with showers, private lockers for possessions, drug and alcohol rehab, education opportunities, mental health counseling. The list went on and on.

Jerry couldn't believe she was willing to provide all these

things free. He brought up problems with violence, thievery, and predators. They discussed people who preferred to live on the streets and those who preyed on street people. He'd expected her to be unaware of safety concerns, but she brought up some he'd missed, and she already had plans to address many of them.

He admired her stamina, her generosity, and her genuine caring. "This all sounds wonderful, but won't it take a long time?"

"Let's start tomorrow. Would you be willing to supervise?"

"I've never been in charge of anything."

Miriam broke in. "You did a great job getting everyone to work together to move the tree."

"See," Mrs. Vandenberg said, "you have the skills. And it's never too late to learn more." She rose. "I'll send a van tomorrow at nine for anyone who wants to work. We can use help cleaning, painting, organizing paperwork, planning meals, making phone calls, buying bedding and furniture. . ."

His mind spinning, Jerry walked Mrs. Vandenberg out to her car, elated by all the possibilities, but for years, he hadn't interacted much with people, other than the friends he'd made among street people. He wasn't sure he was ready for a project this ambitious. What if he failed again?

MIRIAM COULD BARELY BELIEVE what had happened. Mrs. Vandenberg had swept into their lives like a whirlwind. In a short time, she'd arranged and paid for the barn roof repairs, which *Daed* could repay when the family returned, and she convinced everyone in both houses to help with her homeless project.

Because Miriam and Abraham had taken three weeks off work for the Pinecraft trip, they were free to join the crew. She'd expected her brother to protest, but he shocked her by getting up early and caring for the horses before breakfast, then joining everyone as they boarded the van the next morning.

Miriam tamped down her jealousy when Abraham sat next to

Jerry on the bus, and the two of them chatted the whole trip. She had no idea what they even had in common. She wished she could hear what they were saying, but even more, she longed to be talking to Jerry herself.

When they arrived at the building, she was astonished to see a gigantic rundown hotel with several wings.

"Separate women's and men's sections," Mrs. Vandenberg explained. "And we'll turn suites into family quarters. I have contractors working on that."

After a brief conference with Mrs. Vandenberg, Jerry assigned people to different jobs, depending on their skills. Miriam couldn't help but admire the way he took charge, but not in a bossy way. He genuinely cared about everyone and made sure they were happy in the jobs they were doing.

"He's a natural at that, isn't he?" Mrs. Vandenberg asked.

Miriam jumped. She hadn't heard the elderly woman come up behind her. "Um, *jah*, he is."

"I'm hoping he'll agree to work here permanently, so he'll no longer have to live on the street."

"It'd be a great job for him."

"I think so too. He'll also make a fine husband, don't you think?"

He definitely would. Since Mrs. Vandenberg was a matchmaker, did she have someone in mind for him? The thought choked Miriam up. She swallowed hard. "He would."

Mrs. Vandenberg beamed. "I'm glad you think so."

She moved to the front of the room, leaving Miriam downcast, picturing the sweet *Englisch* girl Jerry might marry.

After Jerry finished assigning jobs, Mrs. Vandenberg held up her hand. "I believe in paying people fairly, so all work will paid at five times the minimum wage."

Everyone, including Jerry, stared at her, stunned. They'd all assumed this volunteer work might help them as well as others in the future. A smattering of applause broke out. The clapping grew to a wave of cheers, stomping, whistling, and loud *thank yous*.

Jerry couldn't believe it. All of them could use the money, and many had been struggling to find jobs. They'd all earn more here than at most jobs.

"Thank you," he told her.

Mrs. Vandenberg smiled. "No, thank *you*. You're a good judge of character. Feel free to invite more people to join us. They can stay here in the building while they work."

"That would be great." He had a long list of people he'd trust in here, but what about the others?

"Something's bothering you."

"I'm worried about the ones who aren't stable. And a few will never come inside. None of them should be out in this cold."

Her brow wrinkled in concern. "Do you have any suggestions?"

"What about putting a roof over the courtyard out back and making it like a park? Maybe add benches and heating grates or a fireplace."

"That's doable. It'll keep everyone out of the rain and snow. We could get several enclosed outdoor heaters. We also need to work out something to help those with mental health problems or drug and alcohol addictions."

"Not everyone wants help." He should know.

"True. But we'll do what we can. My goal is to give this to the community as a Christmas gift. Think that's possible?"

Was she serious? That sounded impossible, but Jerry broke into a grin. "I'll do my best."

"I know you will." Mrs. Vandenberg's gaze drifted across the room. "Aww."

He turned. Miriam knelt beside Willow, helping her label cubbies behind the reception desk. When Willow succeeded, Miriam glowed and hugged her. Willow threw her arms around Miriam's neck and hugged back.

"She'll make a good mother, won't she?"

"The best." The words brought a stab of pain. Miriam deserved to have a lot of children. But it meant seeing her marry someone else. Jerry couldn't bear to think about that.

# CHAPTER 9

The weeks flew by, and the homeless shelter was on track to open Christmas Eve. They'd completed the outdoor space first, and people flocked to sleep in the warm sheltered courtyard. Miriam couldn't believe how fast Mrs. Vandenberg's crews renovated the building inside and out.

All their newly hired helpers had been given the first available rooms, while those who remained at Miriam's house waited for the final spots. When they weren't working at the shelter, Grayson and Inez helped Miriam cook meals, and they all dined at the large oak table, filling Miriam's heart with gladness. She'd miss them when they moved out.

Although her family never decorated for Christmas, Mrs. Vandenberg put Miriam in charge of decorating the shelter and planning holiday gatherings. Boxes of lights and ornaments arrived along with a huge evergreen. While Miriam organized groups of people to decorate the lobby and hallways, Grayson and Jenece set up the tree and wrapped lights around it. The rest of the week, they all took turns baking their favorite Christmas cookies in the communal kitchen.

As planned, the shelter officially opened on Christmas Eve. All the new residents gathered around the lighted Christmas tree in the lobby to hang ornaments and sing while Jerry played Christmas carols. Her heart overflowing with joy, Miriam and her new friends passed around cocoa and cookies. It was amazing how much they'd accomplished in a few short weeks.

While she circled the room, Miriam couldn't keep her eyes off Jerry. Her heart ached that he'd strayed so far from the faith. If only. . .

Mrs. Vandenberg touched Miriam's arm. "Would you like to read the Christmas story to everyone?" She held out a Bible with an embroidered marker.

*Daed* always read the passages on Christmas morning after breakfast. A twinge of sadness shot through Miriam. He wouldn't be there tomorrow to do this. They wouldn't have their usual Christmas family celebration with all the relatives.

"You're missing your family, aren't you?" Mrs. Vandenberg's eyes shone with sympathy.

Miriam pressed her lips together and blinked her stinging eyes. "*Jah.*"

The elderly woman gave Miriam a side hug. "They'll be back soon."

Only a few more days. Miriam had been so busy the past few weeks, she hadn't had much time to think about her family. Every night, she fell into bed exhausted and drifted off into dreams of Jerry. Each morning, she captured her memories of Jerry in a sketch or two. Sometimes she also jotted down a poem.

She kept all the previous drawings lined up on the desk, because she loved how they revealed the changes in him. Over time, the haunted look disappeared from his eyes to be replaced by kindness and caring. He carried himself with more confidence. Now he radiated compassion and wisdom.

"Miriam?" Mrs. Vandenberg's gentle voice startled Miriam back to the room. "Let's start now."

Mrs. Vandenberg handed over the Bible, led Miriam to the front of the room, and stepped over to speak to Jerry. From here,

Miriam could look directly at him while Mrs. Vandenberg conversed with him and then called for everyone's attention.

"Because Christmas is to celebrate the birth of Baby Jesus," she announced, "I've asked Jerry to play 'Silent Night,' then Miriam will read the nativity story."

After the final strains of "Sleep in heavenly peace" faded, Miriam opened the Bible and read from Luke. A hush fell over the crowd, and they all listened intently.

After she finished, Mrs. Vandenberg stood beside Miriam and recited John 3: 16. Then she added, "At Christmastime, we celebrate this gift of God's Son." She bowed her head and prayed that each person in the room would experience this gift for themselves. Quietly and reverently, people slipped away to their rooms, and Miriam asked God to make His presence known in each one of their lives.

When she lifted her head, moisture glimmered in Jerry's eyes. Had the Christmas story touched him?

She whispered another prayer from the depths of her soul. *Lord, please touch his heart.*

THROUGHOUT THE EVENING, Jerry had tried not to look in Miriam's direction, but his gaze snapped to her like a magnet. Whenever she smiled at him, his pulse bounced along with the music. How different life might have been if he'd stayed true to the Lord. He and Miriam might be married by now and be starting a family.

He shook away that daydream. After all he'd been through, he'd never make a proper husband for anyone, let alone Miriam. He could never ask her to join him in the homeless shelter or, worse yet, on the streets. And he'd walked away from his faith, so she'd never consider him.

Over the years, he'd hardened his heart, but as Miriam read the familiar words of the Christmas story, it brought back

146

good memories, loving memories. And some of his resistance melted.

The holy silence that fell over the crowd after Mrs. Vandenberg's prayer stayed with the group as they traveled back to Miriam's house. Jerry was relieved, because chatter would have disturbed the reckoning in his soul. For the first time since he'd made the decision to reject the church's teachings and turn away from God, he faced some hard truths.

Jerry had struggled with being a mentor to Abraham the past few weeks. The teen seemed to be looking up to Jerry as an example. Yet, while he encouraged Abraham to stay on the straight and narrow, Jerry couldn't point to his own life as an example. *Do what I say, not what I do* wasn't an authentic way to live. And the more time he spent around Miriam, with her genuine trust in God, the more he felt like a fraud.

When he'd walked under the fallen tree in the barn, not knowing if it would crash down and crush him, he'd prayed for protection. He'd had no right to ask God for answers to prayer after he'd strayed so far from his faith. Yet, the Lord had answered his request.

The van pulled into Miriam's driveway, and Jerry lingered outside until everyone else had entered the houses. Logan had opted to stay at the shelter tonight, so Jerry was alone. An icy wind whipped through his coat, but he'd weathered much lower temperatures, and this cold didn't compare to the deep freeze in his heart.

Stars twinkled overhead in the darkness, tiny points of light in the blackness. Like the small pinpricks of God's light in his life. The Lord kept trying to show him the way back, but Jerry had ignored all the signals. Because if he'd acknowledged them, he'd have to confront the ugliness he'd buried deep inside. And he'd have to do something he'd vowed never to do: Forgive his father.

But right now, his heart compelled him to pray:

*Lord, please forgive me for my rebellion against You. And—*

Jerry drew in a shuddering breath. He'd recited the Lord's

Prayer every day of his childhood, and he'd heard countless sermons about forgiving others. How could he ask God for forgiveness unless he confessed all the bitterness he'd stored up against his father? But how could he let go of all that pain and anger?

A frigid gust sliced through Jerry's coat. He huddled deeper into the puffy parka, but he couldn't stay out here long. Dealing with his past might take days. Or even years. He slipped into the *dawdi haus*.

As always, walking into the warmth brought a rush of gratitude. Jerry had no idea where he'd sleep after Christmas. Perhaps in the courtyard behind the shelter. He didn't want to take up much-needed rooms for other desperate people. Tonight, though, his thankfulness spilled over at being inside this safe, heated space.

Jerry slipped out of his coat and sank onto the couch, tempted to forget about the roadblocks to returning to the Lord. He'd lived for years without facing them. In two more days, he'd no longer be here. He wouldn't be a mentor to Abraham anymore. Nor would Miriam's living example of God's love constantly jab at Jerry's conscience.

He tried to forget it all as he prepared for bed, but the minute he lay down, his prayer flooded back. He'd started to ask for God's forgiveness. But he also had to surrender his own will and do whatever the Lord required. For hours, he wrestled with his past, his stubbornness, his pride, his unwillingness to forgive, and the many, many sins that stood in the way of full surrender.

*Lord, I can't let go of this hatred and anger without Your help. Show me how to release it all. I'm turning it over to You. Please cleanse me of all my sins. Not my will, but Yours be done.*

And then a miracle occurred. The huge ball of resentment and rage strangling his heart unraveled, one tendril at a time. His lungs expanded in his chest. For the first time in ages, he could breathe deeply and freely. His soul expanded, leaving him uplifted and peaceful.

He drifted off into the most serene sleep of his life and woke at dawn, filled with radiant energy, excited to start the day. He began the day with prayer.

*Lord, lead my steps today. I long to live for You.*

Now that he'd gotten right with God inwardly, Jerry wanted an outer sign to reveal his changed heart.

Miriam had said to use anything in the house, so he opened the bathroom cupboard. The supplies he needed were arranged neatly on a shelf, but did he have the courage to use them?

He picked up the scissors. With shaking hands, he chopped at his shoulder-length locks and managed a passable, but ragged, Amish cut. Then, nervousness pooling in his stomach, he lathered his beard and mustache, and picked up the razor. Taking a deep breath, he removed the facial hair that had disguised him for the past few years. After he finished, he faced his reflection and cringed at how his bare face made him feel exposed. He squared his shoulders. Time to come out of hiding and present his real self to the world.

When he showed up for Christmas dinner, everyone did a double-take. Abraham's eyebrows shot up, but he shrugged. When Mrs. Vandenberg arrived with Logan, she gave him a thumbs up. Logan shot him an amused, but rueful, smile.

Miriam, though, seemed to be probing the change as if she sensed it held a deeper meaning. Jerry longed to share last night's experience with her. Of all the people here, she'd be the most likely to understand.

# CHAPTER 10

*A*fter they finished the delicious Christmas dinner, the women cleared the table. Jerry rose to help, but Inez insisted he sit.

She gave him a motherly smile. "You worked harder than anyone at the shelter. It's your turn to rest and be waited on."

Jerry settled back in his chair, uncomfortable about letting others do things for him, but he used the time to count his blessings. He had so many things to be grateful for in addition to getting right with the Lord. Jerry hadn't been this full in years. Or this toasty warm. Or this comfortable. Or surrounded by friends. Or this happy.

He'd spent the meal staring across the table at Miriam. She grew more beautiful each time he looked. Often, she'd be glancing at him, but before their eyes met, her gaze skittered away. She seemed to be fascinated by the change in his appearance.

If he'd known it would attract so much of her attention, he might have shaved and trimmed his hair weeks ago. That change made him less bogged down by the past. Of course, most of his lightness of spirit stemmed from his decision early this morning. His lips curled into a smile.

Miriam's eyes sparkled. He hadn't realized he'd beamed all his joy in her direction, but she responded with a heart-stopping smile. He couldn't look away, and neither did she. The stack of dirty plates in her hands trembled.

Jenece steadied the chattering china. "Thought you were gonna drop 'em."

"*D-danke.*" Miriam focused on her task, turned, and scurried from the room.

Jerry's spirits had been soaring. Now they crash-landed. Her smile had only been meant as an encouragement for his new look. Anything more was an impossibility. He had no future to offer her.

After Miriam and Jenece whisked the last dishes to the kitchen, Mrs. Vandenberg held up a hand. "Before you serve dessert, could everyone sit down for a minute?"

Miriam and the others scuttled to their chairs and turned eager eyes to her. Jerry expected a speech about the shelter opening or perhaps a *thank you* for the work they'd done. Instead, she reached into her gigantic purse and passed out thick manila envelopes.

All the shelter residents opened them to find checks for triple what they'd been promised for the past week's work. In addition, Mrs. Vandenberg had tucked a contract into each envelope. Gasps exploded around the table.

"Yes!" Grayson exclaimed. He and Jenece exchanged contracts, which they read, then hugged each other.

Chatter burst out around the table as they each shared the details of their contracts. Grayson accepted the job as head chef, and Jenece agreed to manage the kitchen staff. Logan had been offered the job of intake coordinator for veteran's services, overseeing a staff of ten. His eyes glinted as they met Jerry's.

"You can do it, man," Jerry insisted. He rejoiced when Logan accepted the offer. His friend had been getting medication and counseling as part of the many services offered at the shelter, so he'd be especially helpful to other vets who were suffering from PTSD.

Jerry opened his own envelope and stared in shock. "This check isn't right. I'm only supposed to get—"

Mrs. Vandenberg waved away his protest. "You earned every penny."

He shook his head, but he suspected she'd win. Then he turned his attention to the contract. This couldn't be real. Executive director of the shelter. Room and board in a private apartment. A salary that took his breath away.

"No arguments over any of that, young man," Mrs. Vandenberg told him. "You're the only one I'd trust in that position."

Still in shock, Jerry listened as one by one, each person at the table shared their contracts and accepted them. Until they came to Miriam.

"This is such a generous offer. *Danke.*" She folded the contract and returned it to the envelope. "I'll talk it over with my parents when they return and let you know."

"I understand you'll need to discuss it with others. It's a big step." Mrs. Vandenberg smiled at everyone. "I'm ready for dessert."

"But we don't have a gift for you." Miriam appeared distressed.

Willow hopped up. "I know what we can give her." She dashed from the table and ran upstairs.

Jerry longed to comfort Miriam. "You gave us all this *wunderbar* meal. That's enough of a gift."

Her grateful look sent a jolt through him. And he dreamed of a future with her. Now that he had a job and a lovely place to live. Once he took baptismal classes and joined the church, nothing would stand in the way of a relationship between them.

Except his past. After all the things he'd done and the rough life he'd lived, he'd never be able to ask her, despite all his fantasies.

Reality smacked him hard. She'd never consider him. She deserved better. A man who'd stayed true to his faith, who'd never disobeyed the *Ordnung*, who'd never been kicked out by his family, who'd never ended up a drunk, who'd never lived on the streets, who'd never. . .

$\sim$

"MOMMY, LOOK." Willow bounded downstairs with a handful of paper scraps. "I bet Mrs. Vandenberg would like these."

She fanned them out on the table. "That's Jerry."

Miriam sucked in a breath. She was too far away to grab them and hide them from prying eyes. Her eyes blurred. She squeezed them shut, but the hearts on one drawing pulsed behind her eyelids. Her private longings lay spread out in front of the whole table. If only she could sink through the floor.

"Where did you get them?" Jenece demanded.

Willow lowered her eyes. "In Miriam's room. She has lots of pretty pictures."

Miriam groaned inwardly. If there'd been any doubt who these belonged to, Willow had just erased it. Miriam couldn't look at anyone, so she kept her head down.

Grayson frowned his disapproval. "You know better than to go into people's private things. Put them back and apologize to Miriam."

But it was too late. Much too late. She'd been humiliated in front of everyone. Even worse, Jerry was examining the sketches.

She stood up to gather all her drawings, but Mrs. Vandenberg leaned over to stop her.

"Don't be ashamed of your talent," Mrs. Vandenberg said.

Miriam blinked to hold back tears.

"You drew these?" Inez's face reflected her amazement.

Grayson's eyes widened. "Wow, you're really good."

"I agree," Logan added, "You're super talented."

"Can you teach me how to draw this good?" Willow asked.

But the praise didn't soothe Miriam. She only cared about one person's reaction.

≈

Jerry homed in on the first picture of him as a teen. It had a heart in each corner. His chest expanded until it ached. She'd loved him years ago. If only he'd turned his life over to God back then, he might be sitting at this table with her as his wife. Who knows how his life would have turned out. Now he had too many scars from his past.

But while everyone else exclaimed over Miriam's artistic skills, Jerry saw something else. Something nobody remarked on. The recent sketches might not have hearts in the corners, but each line had been drawn with love.

"You see it?" Mrs. Vandenberg asked him.

Too choked up to answer, Jerry only nodded. A happy song vibrated in his heart. Maybe, just maybe. . .

With a rosy blush on her cheeks, Miriam stood and hurriedly gathered all the drawings. Jerry had never seen her look more lovely.

"Time for dessert," she announced.

Willow jumped up. "Can I carry in the shoofly pie?" She threw back her shoulders. "I made it all by myself." After a glance at Miriam, she added, "Well, almost."

"You did a lot of it," Miriam assured her. "You should bring it in."

Willow started around the table. "Oops. I dropped this." She bent to pick up a scrap of paper and laid it on the table.

Everyone gasped.

≈

As the table erupted into exclamations and questions, Miriam wished she could disappear. She'd gone to bed last night, praying the Christmas story had touched Jerry. When she'd opened her eyes this morning after a dream of him being transformed by God's love, she'd stumbled from bed and reached for her drawing supplies. Only half-awake, she'd doodled him the way she'd imagined him—with short hair, minus his beard and mustache, and a heavenly glow on his face. She'd pressed the paper to her heart. A sense of peace flowed over her, an assurance God would answer her prayers.

She'd drifted downstairs wrapped in the fog of her dreams and faced her drawing come to life. Jerry walked through the door, looking exactly like her sketch. Chills ran through her. She still couldn't believe it.

Inez interrupted Miriam's musings. "You saw Jerry before we did this morning?"

Miriam shook her head. She'd drawn what God had laid on her heart.

Across from her, Jerry, his eyes wide, stared at the sketch. Then he lifted his head, and their eyes met.

*You knew?* he mouthed.

Her logical mind hadn't known, but her heart and soul had. A part of her had always connected with Jerry. A connection that had only grown stronger as they'd worked together these past few weeks.

Jerry's expression signaled he felt the same way about her as she felt about him. A secret message passed between them, confirming what their hearts read in each other's eyes. Their love and connection transcended time and space. They made a silent commitment to each other and God. A commitment that would last the rest of their lives.

# EPILOGUE

*Three years later. . .*
Life had flowed so fast and joyfully since the Christmas Miriam and Jerry had made their wordless agreement to each other. They'd had many ups and downs, as well as a long wait until Jerry finished his baptismal classes and joined the church. They'd married a few weeks after that on a crisp November day.

One of their greatest joys had been working together. Miriam not only checked with her parents about the contract, but she'd also asked Jerry.

His eyes lit with joy. "*Jah*, I'd love to have you as director of transitions. If it weren't for you and your generosity, I might never have made my own transition off the street. You'll help so many people start new lives the way you did for everyone who stayed at your house."

She'd lowered her head. "You're giving me too much credit. God would have worked a miracle in your lives without me."

"I'm so glad his plan included having you in my life."

"Me too."

Although they couldn't date until he'd been baptized, they'd made a promise to each other for life, and they'd kept it.

Even now, three years later, Miriam still couldn't believe her girlhood dreams about Jerry had come true, and he was now her husband. She cherished their precious moments alone together, and her heart still fluttered when their eyes met across a crowded room. They fell more deeply in love every day as they worked and lived together.

She thanked the Lord daily that they had an opportunity to partner in this work that meant so much to them both. Miriam enjoyed the team meetings, where she admired Jerry's servant leadership. All of his friends had become close friends of hers, and she and Jerry depended on their staff to make good recommendations for improvements. She especially appreciated the way they all prayed together before making changes or adding new services.

Now, Miriam headed for the kitchen to see if they needed help preparing for Christmas dinner. She paused in the dining room to run her finger over the oak table, where she and Jerry sat every evening. *Dawdi* had custom made six tables for the shelter with *Daed*'s and Abraham's assistance. Tables exactly like the ones in the dining room at her parents' house. With extra leaves inserted, they expanded even more to seat many additional guests at the holidays.

Images of that Christmas three years ago flitted through Miriam's mind. She'd been so lonely and downcast as she'd run her finger over their family table. Little did she know how God would fill that table as well as her life. If she'd gone to Pinecraft, she'd never have met Jerry, never have found such a fulfilling life's purpose, never had. . .

She set a gentle hand over her middle.

Today, they'd expand all these tables to their greatest length. Her whole family, including *Mammi* and *Dawdi*, who'd recovered and now spent several months in Lancaster every year, would sit at this table with Jerry's family. Watching Jerry reunite with his family three years ago had filled Miriam with joy. Jerry's *daed* had apologized, and he and Jerry had worked on their relationship.

Since then, his parents had become a *wunderbar* support for the ministry.

Footsteps sounded in the hallway. Jerry came up behind her and enfolded her in his arms. She leaned her head back against his shoulder with a contented sigh. They rarely had time like this during their busy days, and Miriam savored the chance to be alone with him. He turned her to face him, so they could gaze into each other's eyes. She beamed up at her husband with all the love in her heart.

~

JERRY GAZED down at his beautiful wife. He'd never dreamed his life could hold such joy. He held the woman he'd loved from the time he'd been young. They had a close, loving relationship with each other and with God, and they had jobs helping others. He thanked the Lord daily for all his blessings, including a mended relationship with his family, a roof over his head, running water, and delicious meals.

Jerry inhaled the delicious aroma of crisp, crackling turkey skin along with the tang of onion and celery in the filling, the yeastiness of rolls, and the sweetness of freshly baked apple pies. His stomach rumbled in anticipation.

Yet, a lingering sadness touched his soul. He'd wasted so many years in rebelliousness, running away from God.

He confessed to his wife, "When I think of how many days I went hungry—both physically and spiritually—I could have. . ."

She touched a finger to his lips to silence him. "It's over. You've moved on. Leave it in the past."

"But I regret—"

Miriam waved a hand to cut him off. "Everything happened in God's timing."

Her understanding touched his heart.

"If you hadn't been homeless," she said, "you'd never have known what all these people need or how to help them. You've

158

been out on the streets yourself, so you know what they're going through and can show them how to get back on their feet."

Jerry had never thought about it like that. Leave it to his wife to come up with a positive spin on his past. "Do you know I love you?"

She laughed. "You tell me many times every day, but don't ever stop. I love it. And you."

"I don't know how I got so lucky." Jerry swept her into his arms and kissed her thoroughly.

"I do," she said breathlessly. "You turned your life over to the Lord. He's blessed us both."

Jerry couldn't agree more.

She stared up at him with sparkling eyes. "Are you ready for another blessing?"

"You mean. . .?"

When she nodded, he drew her close. "I thought no Christmas could compare to this one, but you and the Lord keep making them better and better."

"By next Christmas, we'll need another seat at the table."

"Good thing your *Dawdi* made extra leaves. A few Christmases from now, we might even need another table."

Miriam melted against him, and Jerry thanked the Lord for the first Christmas he shared with her, all the ones since, and every one to come.

\*\*\*

If you enjoyed Miriam and Jerry's story, you might enjoy reading about Jerry's band, The Amish Rebels, in "Hitting All the Right Notes" in the anthology <u>The Christmas Gathering</u>. And stories about Mrs. Vandenberg and the other couples she's matched at the Green Valley Farmer's Market can be found in the <u>Surprised by Love</u> series.

## Miriam's Homemade Bread

> 1 c. warm water
> ¼ c. sugar
> 2 pkgs. dry yeast
> 1 c. warm milk
> 1½ tsp. salt
> ¼ c. vegetable oil
> 6 c. bread flour

In a large bowl, dissolve the sugar in warm water, then stir in yeast. When it's foamy, stir in milk, salt, and oil. Add flour one cup at a time, then knead until smooth. Place dough in well-oiled bowl, and turn to coat. Cover with a damp towel. Let rise 1 hour. Punch down the dough and divide into 2 loaves. Place in greased loaf pans, and let rise 30 minutes or until dough is about 1" above pans. Bake at 350° for 30 minutes.

## Amish Cinnamon Rolls

> Miriam's Homemade Bread dough
> (see previous recipe)
> room-temperature butter
> sugar
> cinnamon

Let the dough rest for 10 minutes, so it almost doubles. This will make it easier to roll out. On a lightly floured surface, roll dough into a rectangle. Spread butter evenly over the surface, leaving a ½-inch border around all 4 edges. Sprinkle sugar over the butter, then lightly sprinkle cinnamon across the surface. Roll the dough into a log, starting from the longest end. Slice into rolls. Place the rolls in a greased baking pan touching each other. Cover and let rise in a warm place for 1 hour. Bake at 350° for 25–30 minutes. Ice when partially cool.

## Icing

2 c. powdered sugar
2 tbsps. melted butter
1 tsp. vanilla
2–4 tbsps. milk

Mix the first three ingredients. Add milk slowly until icing is the desired consistency.

## Miriam's Potato Rolls

2 pkgs. active dry yeast dissolved in ⅔ c. warm water
1 c. warm mashed potatoes (no milk or butter added)
2½ tsps. salt
⅔ c. sugar
¼ c. honey
⅔ c. milk, scalded and cooled
⅔ c. vegetable shortening
2 eggs, beaten
6–7 c. flour

In a small bowl, dissolve yeast in warm water. In a large bowl, combine milk, mashed potatoes, shortening, honey, sugar, and salt. Add yeast mixture and eggs. Stir in two cups of flour, then add flour a few cups at a time to make a soft dough. Shape dough into a ball. Place dough in well-oiled bowl, and turn to coat.

Cover with a damp towel. Let it rise until doubled, about one hour in a warm place. Punch down the dough, divide it into thirds, shape each third into 15 balls. Place in a 9" pan. Cover and let it rise until doubled, about 25–35 minutes. Bake at 375° for 20–25 minutes, until golden.

Yield: 45 rolls

# ABOUT THE AUTHOR

*USA Today* bestselling author Rachel J. Good writes life-changing, heart-tugging novels of faith, hope, and forgiveness. She grew up near Lancaster County, Pennsylvania, the setting for her Amish novels. Striving to be as authentic as possible, she spends time with her Amish friends, doing chores on their farm and attending family events.

Rachel is the author of several Amish series in print or forthcoming – the bestselling *Love & Promises*, *Sisters & Friends*, *Unexpected Amish Blessings*, *Green Valley Farmer's Market and Auction* (2021), and two books in *Hearts of Amish Country* – as well as the *Amish Quilts Coloring Books*. In addition, she has stories in many anthologies.

Rachel hosts the Hitching Post, an online site where she shares Amish information and her book research. She also enjoys meeting readers in person and speaks regularly at book events, schools, libraries, churches, book clubs, and conferences across the country. Find out more about her at: www.racheljgood.com

# TROUBLE AT THE CHRISTMAS TABLE

JENNIFER BECKSTRAND

# CHAPTER 1

*B*est day ever!

Alfie Petersheim merrily shoveled snow off the porch steps, whistling "Joy to the World" as loudly as he could, while Benji shoveled the sidewalk, singing along to Alfie's whistling.

Alfie thought he might burst with happiness. Christmas was coming, there were only three more weeks of school, and a new layer of snow had fallen over Bienenstock, Wisconsin, just last night. The sledding would be epic. "Epic" was a word his *Englisch* friend Max had taught him, and it meant the best thing ever in the whole world.

All of these were reasons to be happy, but the best reason of all was that after four long years of sleeping in the cellar, Alfie and his twin *bruder*, Benji, were finally getting their old room back. Joy to the world!

Campbell Smith had finally moved out of Alfie and Benji's room upstairs, and Alfie and Benji were moving back in today. There was ice on the sidewalk, it was thirty degrees outside, and Alfie's nose had started to drip. But he was just grateful to still have a nose after sleeping in the cold, damp cellar for four years. He could very well have lost his nose, his feet, and at least a few fingers to frostbite in that cellar in the dead of winter. *Four* deads of winter, to be exact.

Alfie had doubted that *Mamm* even cared about her two youngest sons.

But now, he knew. *Mamm* cared. *Dat* cared. Abraham and Andrew cared. Austin didn't care, but nobody but Austin's *fraa* liked him, so Alfie didn't care if Austin cared.

Four years ago, *Dawdi* David had a stroke, and *Mammi* and *Dawdi* had to move in with Alfie and Benji's family. *Mammi* and *Dawdi* slept in *Mamm* and *Dat*'s old bedroom because *Dawdi* couldn't climb stairs, and *Mamm* and *Dat* had moved upstairs to Alfie and Benji's room. Their older *bruderen*, Andrew, Abraham, and Austin, thought they were too good for the cellar, so *Mamm* had made Alfie and Benji move down there because they were just little kids and nobody cared about their feelings.

Alfie and Benji had worked very hard to find their *bruderen* girlfriends, so they would get married and move out of the house. After a lot of sneaking and scheming on Alfie's part, all three *bruderen* had gotten married. After that, Jerry Zimmerman, then Campbell Smith—they called him Soup—had needed a place to stay. Alfie and Benji had been stuck in the basement for another year because *Mamm* wouldn't think of making perfect strangers sleep in the cellar with the spiders, the smelly canned beans, and poisonous mold.

But all was forgiven now that Campbell had moved out. Alfie and Benji would be able to go to the bathroom without having to trek up the creaky stairs, which was very important if you had a sensitive bladder or you drank too much soda pop. He and Benji wouldn't have to streak through the house naked when they forget their towels after a shower.

*Mammi* Martha had caught Alfie more than once and had scolded him for dripping on the floor and giving her an eyeful. *Mammi* had no sympathy for Alfie's situation.

*Mamm* came outside to shake out a rug and examine Benji

and Alfie's work. "*Gute* job, boys. Be sure to sprinkle some ice melt so no one slips."

"I know, *Mamm*," Alfie said.

*Mamm* peered at Alfie over her glasses. "Do you? Because three days ago the ice was two inches thick on the steps, and your *dat* nearly broke his arm."

Alfie had accidentally run off to play with Tintin and forgotten about the ice melt. And Benji hadn't reminded him. Really, it was Benji's fault. But Alfie was in too good of a mood to care.

Alfie's *bruder* Andrew and Andrew's apprentice, Zeke Hostetler, drove up to the house in Andrew's wagon. Something very big sat in the back of the wagon, covered with a sturdy black tarp. Andrew waved to Alfie and pulled the wagon to a stop.

*Mamm* tiptoed to the wagon, making sure not to slip on the sidewalk Benji was still shoveling. "Did you come to move Zeke's things in? Alfie and Benji's room is almost ready."

Alfie's heart jumped like a skater bug on the water. "What do you mean, *Mamm*? The room is almost ready for *us*."

*Mamm*, Andrew, and Zeke acted as if Alfie hadn't made a peep. Benji was the only one who looked even mildly alarmed.

Alfie didn't want to overreact, but they were completely ignoring him, as if they knew they were doing something wrong and didn't want to face up to it. He yanked on *Mamm*'s apron. "Why are Zeke's things coming over here?"

It was like *Mamm* had suddenly gone deaf.

Andrew set the brake and jumped down from the wagon. "I've brought you an early Christmas present. We'll haul Zeke's things over on Tuesday."

*Mamm* drew her brows together the way she always did when she thought one of her boys might be playing a trick on her. "An early Christmas present? I don't need any presents."

Andrew grinned and glanced at Alfie. "After Mother's Day, we could all see that the old kitchen table wasn't going to last much longer."

Alfie nibbled on his bottom lip. Mother's Day had not been his fault, no matter what everybody else thought. Two big, squishy spiders had been hanging out on the ceiling, and Alfie and Benji had to climb on the table to kill them. They'd learned from sad experience that if spiders weren't killed immediately, they ended up in the cellar hunting for blood. One of the table legs collapsed, and Alfie and Benji had been tossed onto the floor like two sacks of flour. Benji had bruised his shin, and Alfie had gotten a goose egg on his forehead. But everybody had been more concerned about the table than Alfie's goose egg. Andrew had fixed the leg with duct tape and a couple of screws, and it seemed perfectly fine to Benji.

Zeke Hostetler laughed. It seemed like he was always laughing or looking for the next thing to make him laugh. "Andrew says the table won't hold a good-sized turkey."

*Mamm* blew air from between her lips. "That's why we had Thanksgiving at Andrew's house this year."

Andrew and Zeke untied the knots that secured the tarp. "Close your eyes, *Mamm*. I don't want you to see it until it's set up."

*Mamm* looked even more excited than she had when Alfie and Benji got their medals from the mayor. Come to think of it, the medals hadn't excited her at all. "I'll turn my back."

"*Gute*," Andrew said. "Alfie and Benji, you too."

Alfie scowled. "Why do I have to turn my back?"

"Just do it, Alfie, or you'll ruin the fun."

Alfie didn't see any fun in it, but he and Benji stood next to *Mamm*, staring at the wood fence, while Andrew and Zeke made a lot of noise behind them. The only *gute* thing was that now it would be impossible for *Mamm* to ignore him. "*Mamm*, what did you mean when you said not to move our things up to our room yet?"

*Mamm* acted as if she'd never done anything wrong in her whole life. "I've invited Zeke to stay with us."

"What?" Alfie shouted. Zeke lived with Andrew and Mary.

He was helping Andrew with his furniture-making business. "Zeke already has a place to stay."

*Mamm* folded her arms. "You don't have to throw a fit, young man. Mary and Andrew need to make room for the new *buplie*."

Benji didn't seem to realize that his whole world was about to come crashing down. "I like Zeke. He's funny and loud, and he can sing the ABCs with his mouth closed."

That was a cool trick, but Alfie would not be talked into thinking anything good about Zeke Hostetler. "But we need to get out of that cellar before we freeze to death, and *Mammi* Martha doesn't want to see any more naked boys."

"I should hope not."

"We need extra towels, *Mamm*," Benji said.

*Mamm* glanced at Benji. "I suppose I can spare a few towels."

Benji was a *gute bruder*, but he was too nice, and he was going to ruin everything. "We don't need more towels," Alfie hissed. "We need our own room."

"You have your own room. It's in the cellar, and your bed is not fifteen feet from the pellet stove. It's the warmest place in the house."

"*Nae*, it's not," Alfie snapped. "And our air mattress leaks. Why can't Zeke sleep in the cellar?"

*Mamm* shook her head. "I wouldn't make a guest sleep in the cellar."

Alfie's eyes widened in indignation. "But it's okay to make your sons sleep there?"

*Mamm* would not be moved. "You have a very comfortable arrangement in the cellar."

Alfie huffed so hard, his breath made a little cloud in front of his face. "*Mamm*, I've been a *gute* son. I do my chores, most of the time. Me and Benji saved two people from carbon monoxide poisoning. The mayor called us Bienenstock's finest citizens. We got medals, and you won't even let us wear them to school."

"Rebecca," *Dat* called from the porch. "Come see this."

*Mamm* had the nerve to smile as if nobody was mad about

171

anything. Without another word, she raced up the porch steps. Alfie and Benji didn't have any choice but to follow.

Andrew, Zeke, *Dat*, and *Mamm* stood around a sturdy, dark-stained wooden table. The top was made of eight long pieces of wood, shiny and smooth, fixed together with four solid pillars for legs underneath.

"We moved the old table out to the barn until you decide what to do with it."

It looked like a nice table, even though Alfie didn't particularly care about tables. He reached out to feel how smooth it really was.

*Mamm* shot out her hand. "Don't touch it!"

Alfie made a face. "Ever?"

*Mamm* went to the sink and washed her hands, then spent a very long time drying them on a clean kitchen towel. She ran her hand along the tabletop and traced her finger in one of the grooves between the boards. "Andrew, it's the most beautiful thing I've ever seen."

*Dat* clapped his hands. "Let's try it out. It's almost lunchtime."

*Mamm* positioned herself between Dat and the table. "*Nae*, Benaiah. We can't eat on this table. It will get scratched."

*Dat* opened and closed his mouth, like a fish out of water. "But Rebecca…"

*Mamm* motioned to Andrew. "Help me." She pointed to the cupboard above the LP gas fridge. "Can you reach the cookie sheets?"

Andrew was tall enough to reach anything in the kitchen. They probably should have asked him to kill those Mother's Day spiders on the ceiling. Andrew pulled a stack of metal cookie sheets from the cupboard and handed them to *Mamm*.

*Mamm* handed out the cookie sheets. "From now until Christmas, we eat on these cookie sheets."

Benji's eyes nearly popped out of his head. "Like you mean, on the floor?"

*Mamm* hesitated, then nodded. "*Jah*, like a picnic for breakfast, lunch, and dinner."

"What about *Mammi* and *Dawdi*?" Alfie said.

"They can sit on the sofa with their trays on their laps."

Well, that settled it. *Mamm* had gone completely crazy. She made her sons sleep in the cellar, and she didn't want to use the table for the only thing a table was for.

Zeke's gaze flicked between Andrew and *Mamm*. "You're not going to use it?"

*Mamm* sank into one of the new chairs that matched the table. Would she give Alfie the spatula if he tried to sit too? "I just…it's just until Christmas. Wouldn't it be *wunderbarr* to eat our first meal at this beautiful, flawless table on Christmas Day? There would be no spills, no Alfie and Benji handprints…"

"Hey!"

"…no dog scratches, nothing to ruin the finish. I can decorate the table with pine boughs and candles and festive placemats, and it will be the start of a wonderful *gute* Christmas tradition."

"I suppose it will," Dat murmured.

*Mamm* pointed at Alfie and Benji, as if they were the cause of all her problems. "I've lived through twenty-five years of rowdy boys, frayed furniture, bathrooms that smell like urine, and dented walls. I've put up with dog hair, police officers, and four near-death experiences. I want this one nice thing. Just this one nice thing."

Alfie didn't know what urine had to do with the kitchen table because there was no way *Mamm* knew about that accident five years ago.

Was there?

*Dat* didn't disagree with *Mamm*. Ever. He sighed softly. "Okay, Rebecca. It wonders me if it won't make for a very funny story in a few years."

*Mamm*'s brows crashed together. "What's so funny about it?"

"*Ach, vell*, I meant the urine and the dents and the dog hair." *Dat* cleared his throat. "Nothing at all, *heartzley*. What I meant to say is that it wonders me if it won't be a heartwarming story our children tell our grandchildren one day."

"*Denki*," *Mamm* said, clutching a cookie sheet to her chest. "This is just the prettiest table I've ever seen."

It seemed like *Mamm* loved that table more than she loved her whole family. For sure and certain, she would never make that table sleep in the cellar.

"I'm *froh* you like it," Andrew said. "Zeke helped me with the finishing work. He's just as *gute* as I am now."

Zeke laughed, loudly like he always did, and held his cookie sheet out in front of him as if he didn't know what he should do with it. "Not quite that *gute*, but your instruction has made me so much better."

Andrew placed a hand on Zeke's shoulder. "You're ready to go out on your own, if you want, but I wouldn't mind if you stayed on with me for the next fifty years."

Alfie folded his arms and gave Zeke the stink eye. "You're not planning on staying in our bedroom for the next fifty years, are you?"

"Oh, hush, Alfie," *Mamm* said, not taking her eyes from her precious table.

Zeke laughed even louder. "Don't look so concerned, Alfie. I'm planning to go back to Ohio as soon as I marry Sarah Zimmerman."

Andrew tapped his cookie sheet against his thigh. "Jerry's sister? Are you engaged?"

Grinning like a cat with a baby bird in his mouth, Zeke shook his head. "I haven't even asked to drive her home yet, but she's the one I want to marry, and I'm pretty irresistible when I want to be."

Alfie's heart did four somersaults. He glanced at Benji, who looked like he'd just swallowed a raw egg. Zeke wanted to marry Teacher Sarah?

Benji eyed Zeke with a look of horror on his face. He was obviously thinking the same thing Alfie was.

Sarah Zimmerman was Alfie and Benji's school teacher. She taught grades five, six, seven, and eight, and she was the best teacher ever. On Fridays she let the scholars have an extra ten minutes of recess. She played softball with them and sometimes let them do their lessons outside on the grass when the weather was warm. She never scolded Alfie when he missed a spelling word or fell asleep in class, and she sometimes brought sugar cookies as a treat. She was the nicest person Alfie had ever met, except for Hannah Yutzy, who had married Austin. Nobody liked Austin, and Hannah was an angel for marrying his annoying *bruder*.

If Zeke married Sarah, Sarah would have to quit teaching. It didn't seem fair, but those were the rules, and Alfie didn't know how to change them. He hadn't even been able to talk his *mamm* into giving him a real bedroom. Once Teacher Sarah left, the school board would probably hire someone with crooked teeth and bushy eyebrows who would cancel recess and make them recite their times tables three hours a day. For sure and certain, she'd never make sugar cookies.

*Mamm* eyed Zeke as if she didn't believe him. "You're wonderful confident for a boy who hasn't even asked to drive Sarah home. How do you know you'd suit? Sarah is quiet and serious. You seem to like being the center of attention."

"I can't help the way I am. I like to laugh. I get excited about things. I usually say the first thing that pops into my head."

"Zeke always gives you the truth, plain and straightforward, no matter what," Andrew said. "Sometimes that offends people."

Zeke laughed as if what Andrew said hurt his feelings. "My *Mamm* says I'm not everybody's cup of tea."

"I understand that," *Mamm* said. "I'm not everybody's cup of tea either."

Zeke shrugged. "I'm a handsome boy, and I have a *gute* skill and the potential for a steady income. I can build my *fraa* a fine house and make her very comfortable. I'm just being honest when I say I'm sure Sarah will say yes."

*Mamm* reached out and patted Zeke's arm. "Maybe don't tell Sarah that right off. Tread carefully. You can't be sure you're Sarah's cup of tea."

Zeke didn't seem concerned. "I am. We're perfect for each other. I've loved her since the first time I saw her."

"That's very sweet, but you might want to wait to hear what Sarah says about it." *Mamm* opened a drawer and pulled out a long cream-colored tablecloth. She spread it carefully over the table and pinned Alfie and Benji with the look she used for special life-and-death situations. "There will be no touching any part of this table until Christmas Day, do you understand?"

"We understand," Benji said.

*Mamm* must not have believed him. "There will be no sitting on this table, standing on this table, or brushing against this table any time, day or night. No letting the dog lick, chew, or scratch this table."

"*Mamm*, you won't even let Tintin in the house."

*Mamm*'s eyes flashed with indignation. "I believe you mean LaWayne."

Alfie pressed his lips together until they went numb. One of the rules *Mamm* had made when she let them have the dog was that they had to call him LaWayne. Alfie and Benji liked "Tintin" better, so they called him Tintin when *Mamm* wasn't around. Sometimes they forgot and messed up. "*Jah, Mamm.* I meant LaWayne."

"LaWayne is not to touch this table, and neither are you. Is that clear?"

Alfie nodded, feeling sullen and irritated. "You don't even want us to breathe on your table."

"That's right."

"Can we look at it?" Benji asked.

*Mamm* folded her arms. "Only when you're passing through. But don't linger."

Andrew swiped his hand across his mouth and erased what looked like a smile from his face.

Alfie didn't like to be laughed at, and he didn't like being the least-loved person in the family—tied with Benji. "We'll just head down to the dungeon where you put sons who aren't allowed to sleep in a decent room or breathe on your precious table."

"Don't get your germs on the table when you pass," *Mamm* said, proving what a cold heart she really had.

"Come on, Benji." Alfie stuffed his hands in his pockets so *Mamm* couldn't accuse him of trying to secretly touch the table, then clomped down the cellar stairs.

One nice thing about the cellar was that no one liked to go down there, so Alfie and Benji had a lot of privacy. They sat on the air mattress, facing each other. Alfie got right to the point. "We can't let Zeke marry Sarah Zimmerman."

Benji leaned closer. "I know. We still have three and a half years of school left."

"Maybe she doesn't know who he is. He's only been in Bienenstock since July."

Benji shook his head. "Zeke is tall and loud and can turn his eyelids inside out. For sure and certain, Teacher Sarah has noticed him."

They deflated like leaky balloons.

Benji suddenly re-flated. "If Zeke and Sarah get married, Zeke would move out, and we'd get our room back."

Alfie frowned. Would he rather lose his room or his favorite teacher? It felt like an impossible choice, until he remembered that they had been in the cellar for four long years. "It doesn't matter."

"It doesn't?"

"It doesn't matter if Zeke moves out. We're never getting our room back. *Mamm* thinks we make dents in the walls, stink up the bathroom, and breathe on her nice things. There will always be some excuse to keep us in the cellar."

Benji's bottom lip quivered. "Does she hate us?"

"I don't know. Maybe we're like gum on her shoe."

"Bubble gum or Fruit Stripe?"

"Teacher Sarah loves us just the way we are," Alfie said. "I've never heard her say the word *urine* in my entire life."

Benji nodded. "Remember when she gave us a box of dog treats for Tintin?"

Alfie squared his shoulders. "We have to save Teacher Sarah from Zeke. There's nothing else to do."

Alfie and Benji did their secret handshake and a double pinky swear. The double pinky swear was a binding agreement to never tell anybody.

"What do we do now?" Benji said.

Alfie rubbed his jaw where he hoped whiskers would grow someday. "We've got to think."

Alfie and Benji had a lot of experience helping people find spouses, but they'd only ever broken one couple apart: Austin and Scilla. But they had to set a lot of things on fire to do it. *Mamm* wouldn't like it if they set something on fire. She didn't even like it when they breathed.

Benji rested his head on his pillow. "Can't we help Zeke fall in love with someone else? Scilla Lambright still works at the library."

Alfie shook his head. "He says he's already in love with Sarah. Our best chance is to make sure Sarah doesn't fall in love with him."

"That's gonna be hard. Zeke has double-jointed elbows, and he can curl his tongue both ways. *And* he has an extra toe on his left foot. Sarah might think he's exciting."

"Then we'll just have to change her mind."

How hard could it be?

# CHAPTER 2

*Z*eke Hostetler strolled into the schoolhouse carrying a sturdy black toolbox, and Sarah Zimmerman crinkled her nose as if a bad smell had wafted in with him. It was a very uncharitable thing to do, but Sarah couldn't help her instinctive reaction. Zeke was handsome enough, with his chocolate brown eyes and dark, wavy hair, but she didn't especially like him, and she hadn't been looking forward to his arrival.

She had just excused the children for the day, and her classroom was empty except for Alfie and Benji Petersheim, who had volunteered to stay behind and clean the chalkboard and wash the desks. It wasn't typical of any child to want to stay after school to *redd* up, but Alfie had told her that they were trying to spread Christmas cheer by helping others, and Sarah definitely needed help. Today the scholars had made stars and sparkly paper chains for the school Christmas program, and there was glitter everywhere. She made a note to herself to never, *never* use glitter again at school. She'd be sweeping it up for months. Probably years.

"*Hallo*, Sarah," Zeke said in that booming voice that shook the windows and surely scared songbirds from their nests. He grinned as if he couldn't contain his excitement. "Did you know I was coming?"

Sarah wasn't excessively short, but she felt small and insignificant just being in Zeke's presence. He was so tall and boisterous that he seemed to fill whatever space he was in, as if he wanted to hog all the attention and leave none for anyone else. Not that Sarah craved attention. She'd gladly let Zeke take all of it. But she could never shake the feeling that every time he talked to her, he was secretly poking fun at her for being timid or laughing at her for not being as enamored with him as he was with himself. She'd rather he leave her alone and let her blend into the scenery.

Sarah laced her fingers together and drew even further into herself. "Rebecca Petersheim told me you were coming. *Denki* for your trouble."

Zeke seemed more than eager. "It's no trouble at all. I've been waiting for my chance to talk to you. I never seem to be able to get you alone."

Oh, dear. Zeke wanted to talk? How silly that she had thought he'd fix the desk without saying a word. She gave him what she hoped passed for a smile. "I'll show you the desk that needs repair."

"You sure look pretty today," he said, his eyes dancing.

Sarah's face caught fire. There was no call to make fun of her. "The desk is over here."

"You look as fresh as a daisy, even after a long day of teaching."

Thank *Derr Herr*, Alfie and Benji appeared at the back door, each carrying an eraser and sporting smudges of chalk on their cheeks. "Oh," Alfie said, as if he'd found something green and gooey on the sidewalk. "You're here."

Zeke's countenance fell. "*Ach*, you're here too."

Benji peered at Zeke with one eye closed. "*Jah*. We're helping our favorite teacher."

"We've still got three years coming to us," Alfie said. "Besides, we're boycotting our house."

Zeke set his toolbox on one of the desks. "Boycotting? That's a wonderful big word for such a little boy."

Alfie scowled. "I'm not little. I'm a preteen. And we're boycotting because every time we breathe, *Mamm* tells us to go outside and quit bothering her table. She loves that table more than she loves peanut butter."

Benji nodded. "More than she loves her children." He grabbed Sarah's hand and tugged her toward the front of the room. "Teacher, we'll help you clean the glitter now. I'm a *gute* sweeper."

Alfie brushed chalk dust off his hands. "I'll hold the dustpan."

Sarah gave both boys a smile. "I don't know what I'd do without the Petersheim brothers. Start over there, and I will join you after I show Zeke the desk that needs to be fixed. I'm afraid we might have to get down on our hands and knees and wipe up all the glitter with a wet rag."

"*Jah*," Benji said. "Teacher Salome called glitter 'devil's sawdust.'"

Sarah grinned. "*Jah*. I don't wonder but she did." She lost her smile when she looked at Zeke. Lord willing, he wouldn't be there very long. She much preferred Alfie and Benji's easy company to Zeke's teasing eyes upon her. "The broken desk is over here."

Zeke flashed his white teeth and motioned for her to lead the way. "How did the desk come to be broken?"

From across the room, Alfie snapped his head up to look at Zeke. "That's not important."

Sarah pursed her lips to keep from smiling. She adored Alfie and Benji and their impish grins and bountiful freckles, but they were too mischievous by half. The desks in Sarah's classroom were ancient, eighty years or older, probably brought in by the first Amish settlers to Bienenstock. They'd been through a lot of school children and had no doubt been repaired dozens of times. Each desk was made of wood with wrought iron legs and a chair attached to the front of it. The chair seat folded up when someone wasn't sitting in it, and the school board had all the hinges oiled thoroughly each year.

Three days ago, Alfie had been trying to stand on his chair too close to the back of the seat, and his foot had slipped down the crack, and the chair had folded on his ankle. The hinge had seized up, and Alfie had gotten his foot stuck in the crack. Sarah hadn't had the heart to scold him, even though Alfie knew the rule about standing on any part of his desk. He'd gotten a very nasty gash on his ankle, and Sarah had been forced to take a hammer to the hinges to get the chair to release him.

Sarah cleared her throat. "There was an accident, and I had to pound on the hinges to get a scholar's foot unstuck. Can it be fixed?"

Zeke smirked at Alfie, knelt down, and worked his long fingers around the damage. "You're pretty *gute* with a hammer," he said, chuckling and giving her a wink.

Sarah winced. She'd splintered some of the wood trying to loosen the hinge, but there was nothing else she could have done. Alfie had been caught like a fox in a steel trap. The seat was splintered beyond recognition.

"I might have to take it back to Andrew's shop and construct a whole new seat. Let me look at it and see if I can figure it out."

"Okay," Sarah mumbled. No use hovering over Zeke while he was trying to do his job. She'd much rather not be so close. She marched to the other side of the room, where Alfie and Benji had their heads together. Alfie had an impressive pile of glitter and dust in his dustpan. "*Gute* work. That's a lot of glitter."

Alfie's gaze flicked in Zeke's direction. "I'll throw this away and come back for another pile."

Carefully balancing the dustpan, Alfie walked down to the end of one row of desks and turned up the row where Zeke was working. Sarah gasped as Alfie tripped over his own feet and catapulted the dustpan and its contents into the air. A cascade of dust and glitter rained down on Zeke and Alfie, and the dustpan clattered to the ground even as Alfie tried to catch it.

"*Ach!*" With surprise exploding like popcorn on his face, Zeke jumped to his feet and hastily swiped his hands back and forth through his hair, sending glitter and dust in every direction. "Alfie, be more care…achoo!" Zeke's first sneeze was followed by another, which was followed by a violent sneezing fit. Five sneezes in a row, each one louder than the other. His eyes watered, and his nose turned red.

"Oh, *sis yuscht!*" Sarah said. "Are you okay?"

Sarah had never heard so many sneezes in succession. Zeke sneezed again and again before pulling a tissue from his pocket and pressing it to his nose. "I work…with…," more sneezing, "…sawdust all the time…and I've never…it's the glitter. I think it went into my sinuses."

Alfie spit dirt from his mouth and shook his head to clear the glitter from his hair. "Well, that was *dumm,*" he said, picking up his dustpan and looking very irritated with himself.

Zeke pressed the tissue to his nose and pointed toward the door. "The trash can is over there, Alfie. What were you doing in *my* row?"

Alfie drew a line in the dust on the floor with his foot and put the dustpan behind his back. "Taking a shortcut."

Zeke blinked and blinked, and his eyes watered and watered. "That's no shortcut."

Sarah stared at Zeke in concern. His face was covered in a light layer of dust and glitter, and water dripped from his right eye and made a trail down his cheek. "Did you get something in your eye?"

He blinked and then shut his eye. "It feels like it got poked with a stick."

Sarah frowned. "Let me look."

Alfie was rooted to the floor, his hair disheveled and dusty, looking at her as if very interested in what Sarah would do next.

"*Cum,*" she said. "Sit there so I can see better."

Zeke sat on the edge of her desk so she could look him in the eye. Drawing a deep breath, she gently pinched the top eyelashes of his right eye between her thumb and index finger. Zeke smelled of citrus and cedar, and it was the most pleasant scent she'd ever smelled on a man. The sensation threw her slightly off kilter, but she recovered quickly enough that he couldn't have noticed.

His lips twitched upward. "This is nice." *Ach, du lieva.* Maybe he had noticed.

She pulled on his eyelashes and looked under his upper eyelid. "*Ach*, I think there are two pieces of glitter stuck up there." She peered at him doubtfully. "I could try rinsing them out."

He didn't even hesitate. "Please."

"Is he going to be okay?" Benji asked.

Alfie poked Benji in the ribs with his elbow. "Don't you even care about me, Benji? I got glitter on my face too."

Benji scowled and poked Alfie back. "It's your own fault."

Sarah didn't want any distractions while she worked on Zeke's eye. "Alfie and Benji, why don't you go outside and see if Zeke's horse would like some water? Take the bucket."

"That's not Zeke's horse," Alfie said. "It's Andrew's horse pulling Andrew's wagon. Zeke takes everybody's stuff and doesn't even care that he's bothering people."

Zeke huffed out a breath. "I'm sorry if I'm bothering you, Alfie, when I'm trying to do you a favor. I just came to fix the desk you broke."

Alfie's eyes flashed with surprise. "You don't know anything."

Zeke made a face at Alfie. "I'm smarter than you think."

Benji picked up the bucket, grabbed Alfie's sleeve, and yanked him out the front door.

Sarah didn't know who'd gotten the better of whom in that conversation, but it made her smile just a little. Alfie had a way of getting under people's skin. She went to the closet and pulled out a fluffy towel, some wet wipes, and the first-aid kit. She was *froh* she'd talked the school board into buying the extra-large, well-stocked version of the first-aid kit. It was more like a first-aid suitcase. This year alone, she'd already used three instant ice packs, a whole tube of antibiotic ointment, the needle and tweezers, and five different sizes of bandages.

Zeke was suddenly right behind her, and she let out a little gasp. He was boisterous *and* sneaky. No wonder she didn't like him. He chuckled. "Sorry. I didn't mean to startle you."

"You're injured. You should probably sit down."

"Not too injured to help my angel of mercy."

Sarah's embarrassment went straight to her toes. "Don't... don't tease me," she mumbled, in hopes he wouldn't hear her. She rarely stood up for herself and always felt immediately sorry when she did.

He peered at her with his good eye. "I'd never tease about something like that." He took the clumsy first-aid suitcase from her hand. "Here, let me."

"*Ach...denki.* It is a little heavy." She motioned him back to her desk where he laid it open. She rummaged around in the compartments until she found the saline rinse solution. Lord willing it would clean the glitter out of Zeke's eye. It looked very painful, and she truly wanted to be rid of him.

She closed the first-aid kit and set it on the floor then lay the folded-up towel on one end of the desk. "Lie face up with your head on this towel. Let your legs dangle over the edge, and open your eye while I rinse it with this saline solution. It's the best way."

He ran his hand along his jawline. "I'd hate for your desk to get water damage. It's really pretty wood. I should lie on the floor."

That was unexpectedly nice of him to be concerned about her desk, but it made sense since he was a carpenter. "That's why I've got the towel. It will catch the water, and washing out your eye will be easier up here, like an operating table."

"I really appreciate it."

She handed him a wet wipe. "Clean your hands, then hold

your eye open with your fingers. Your reflex will be to close it as soon as I start rinsing."

"*Gute* thinking." He cleaned his hands with one wet wipe, and when that one turned gray, she handed him another. "I don't wonder but Alfie spilled that dustpan on purpose."

Sarah cleaned her hands too. "Oh really, Zeke, no need to accuse an innocent child."

Zeke scrunched his lips together. "You know Alfie and Benji. Can you really believe they're that innocent? Andrew says they like to set off smoke bombs. They once kidnapped a chicken and faked her death. They set fire to a Christmas tree and burned down Emmon Giles's shed."

Sarah found Alfie and Benji's hijinks adorable, though she was sure their *mater* didn't. "One time Alfie got stuck in Bitsy Kiem's tree, and my *bruder* Jerry helped pull him out." She frowned. Jerry had been a volunteer firefighter before he jumped the fence. He hadn't meant to hurt her, but his leaving had resulted in unhappy consequences for Sarah. "They also saved a homeless man from freezing and two *Englisch*ers from carbon monoxide poisoning."

Zeke shook his head. "With all the mischief they get into, they're bound to accidentally do a good deed occasionally. That doesn't mean they aren't a barrel full of trouble. Alfie especially doesn't like me. He's mad at me for stealing his bedroom."

Sarah laughed. "*Ach*, I've heard all about the bedroom. They thought they were going to get it back, and you dashed all their hopes."

Zeke flashed his straight, pearly-white teeth. "I really like it when you laugh."

Sarah ignored the heat that traveled up her neck. "No matter the trouble Alfie and Benji get into, I'll love them forever. They persuaded my *bruder* Jerry to come back to Bienenstock, and they somehow convinced him to stay. They gave me my *bruder* back, and I can never repay them for that."

Zeke studied Sarah's face as if trying to read her mind. "I'm *froh* Jerry came home, but I don't think you can give Alfie and Benji credit for that."

Sarah didn't care what Zeke thought. She knew the truth. "I've learned to never underestimate Alfie and Benji Petersheim."

He chuckled. "You're absolutely right. I'll never let my guard down again." He brushed his fingers through his hair, dislodging a few pieces of glitter in the process. "Especially since I think Alfie has it in for me." He grinned, as if Alfie's scheming to dump glitter on his head was a very funny joke.

Sarah's eyebrows traveled up her forehead. Zeke was more good-natured than she had thought. "Alfie tends to be quite stubborn when he thinks he's right."

"I can respect that. I'm the same way."

Sarah smiled to herself. "Lie back now so I can wash out your eye."

Zeke climbed on the desk and lowered himself until his head was resting on the towel. In this position, he seemed all arms and legs, but he still smelled *wunderbarr*, and Sarah had to concentrate very hard on his face to keep from staring at those muscles that rippled under his glitter-covered cream shirt.

"I hate for you to see me like this, with my nose running and my eyes swollen and puffy."

"I'm a teacher, Zeke. I've seen worse. Bloody noses, dislocated fingers, bee stings."

He cleared his throat. "I'm sure that's true, but a boy wants to look his best when he's trying to work up the courage to ask a certain girl if he can drive her home from the next gathering. What would you say if you were that girl?"

Sarah froze. How was she supposed to respond? Certainly not truthfully. But not with a lie either. "Pull your lids open, and I'll rinse your eye out. I've never done this before, so I can't promise to do it right."

"But did you hear me…?"

"I really need to concentrate on your eye, Zeke."

He hesitated. "Okay."

187

There was plenty of uncertainty in that word, but Sarah had spoken the truth. She couldn't come up with a way to refuse Zeke until she'd dealt with his eye problem. Maybe by the time she was done, he'd forget about it.

After opening the saline solution, she screwed the nozzle into place. She squeezed a bit of the water onto her wrist to test it, not exactly sure what she was testing for, but she'd seen it done with baby bottles, and it seemed like an important thing to do. She rested her arms on Zeke's chest and immediately stiffened. She hadn't realized what an intimate and awkward position this would put her in.

Zeke sucked in a breath and stared straight up at the ceiling. "I...uh...I...this is very kind of you. *Denki*."

The room suddenly got very stuffy. Sarah pressed the back of her hand to her forehead. She should definitely invite Alfie and Benji back into the classroom to witness that nothing inappropriate was taking place.

Those dear little boys appeared at the door as if she'd called them. "What's going on here?" Alfie said.

Sarah drew back momentarily. "Zeke has some glitter caught in his eye, and I'm washing it out." She leaned closer and gently squeezed the solution into the corner of Zeke's eye. He flinched but managed to keep his eyelid spread open as she worked. She ignored her irregular heartbeat and his warm brown eyes as she carefully attempted to rinse out the glitter. Water dribbled into his hair and onto the towel. "There's one piece of glitter!" Sarah said. "It's actually working."

Zeke's lip twitched upward. "I felt that."

Alfie and Benji drew closer.

"Is he going to die? It looks like maybe he's going to die." Alfie said, as if he were very hopeful of that outcome.

Sarah pressed her lips together to keep from smiling. Maybe Alfie really did want to get rid of Zeke. "He's not going to die."

"What will you do if his eye pops out?"

"That's not really possible," Sarah said, trying to keep her arm steady while shaking with silent laughter. "Oh, look. The other piece of glitter came out."

Zeke sat up, rubbed his eye, blinked, and bloomed into a very handsome smile. "I think you're right." He picked up the towel and pressed it to his eye. "You're a genius."

Sarah lowered her eyes. "Not really." She *was* patient, and most problems that seemed impossible only needed a little persistence applied to them. Of course, she would never tell Zeke that. She didn't want to sound like she was boasting, and her patience wasn't boundless.

Zeke scrubbed the towel through his hair and wiped the excess water off his cheek, his eyes never straying from Sarah's face. "Alfie and Benji, would you go outside and get my toolbox from Andrew's wagon?"

Sarah felt the sudden onset of a massive headache. Zeke didn't need his toolbox. He wanted to get the boys out of the room so he could have a private talk with Sarah. *Ach*! How would she dodge his question this time?

Benji pointed in the direction of the damaged desk. "Your toolbox is over there on the floor."

Zeke forced a smile that didn't fool anybody. "In that case, will you fetch my lunch? It's in a brown bag on the wagon seat."

Alfie folded his arms and spread his legs as if he were an immovable post. "It's not lunchtime."

Bless Alfie and Benji Petersheim for being diligent little imps.

Irritation traveled across Zeke's face. "Okay then, will you just step outside for a few minutes. I need to talk to Sarah alone."

Benji looked as if he were ready to defend Sarah to the death. "Anything you say to Teacher Sarah, you can say to us."

Sarah wanted to give that presumptuous little troublemaker a kiss on the cheek.

Zeke growled and glanced at Sarah as if expecting her to help him out. But he didn't realize she was on the boys' side. A trickle of water made its way down his neck. He pressed the towel to the side of his head, huffed out a breath, and regained his smile. "I guess it doesn't matter who knows, especially since I've already told Alfie and Benji."

It was Sarah's turn to be irritated. "You've been talking about me behind my back?"

"Sarah," Zeke said, ignoring her question, "will you let me drive you home from the next gathering?"

Sarah drew a long breath. She was acutely aware that she wasn't anything special, with mousy brown hair and a perky, turned-up nose. Why would Zeke want to drive her home, especially since she was sure they would never suit?

Aside from his obvious annoyance that Alfie and Benji were listening in on his private conversation, Zeke seemed very confident that she'd say yes. Could this conversation be any more unsettling? His self-assurance made everything worse. "Why do you want to drive me home from a gathering?"

His eyes twinkled. "Isn't it obvious?"

Oh, *sis yuscht*! He was mocking her. She could see the amusement in his eyes. "This isn't funny, Zeke."

That mischievous glint in his eye disappeared, and he acted as if she'd thrown a rock at his head. "What do you mean?"

"I may not be pretty or interesting or outgoing, but I'm smart enough to know when someone's making fun of me. I refuse to become fodder for a joke between you and your friends."

Alfie was quite offended. "*Jah*, don't make fun of her."

Zeke's eyes grew rounder and rounder. "What do you mean? You're the prettiest, most interesting, most delightful girl I know. I like you. A lot."

She got so worked up, she snorted. "That's a gross exaggeration, Zeke Hostetler. I'm not prettier than anyone, and it wonders me why the handsomest, most popular boy in the *gmayna* is asking such a thing. Is it so you and your friends can laugh at poor Sarah Zimmerman?"

"I…I don't understand. You must think very poorly of me if you believe I would ever do something so cruel." He seemed sincerely upset.

Had she misinterpreted his intentions? "You're not making fun of me?"

"As I've already said, I would never make fun of you. To be honest, I've had my eye on you for a long time." He grinned sheepishly. "It was overconfident of me, but I thought you were expecting me to ask."

She pressed her lips together, unable to wrap her brain around the thought that Zeke had ever had his eye on her. "Why would I expect that?"

A smile slowly grew on his lips. "You think I'm handsome?"

"Don't pretend to be surprised. You know how handsome you are."

He hesitated. "I could just as easily accuse you. Surely you know how pretty you are."

"Don't make fun of me."

Zeke fell silent, and his eyes bored two holes into her skull. "I had no idea." He sat on the edge of Sarah's desk and folded his arms across his chest. "You truly don't believe me."

*Ach, vell,* she hadn't intended to, but she'd knocked his confidence down a peg or two.

His lips curled upward. "I guess the only way to prove my sincerity is to drive you home and let you decide for yourself."

Sarah still doubted his sincerity, but it didn't really matter if he was being completely honest or not. She was very sure she didn't want to ride home with him. Zeke Hostetler was bold, boisterous, and arrogant. She did not want any sort of a relationship with him. Besides that, *Dat* would never allow it, and *Dat* had the final word on every choice Sarah made.

She wasn't very *gute* at being plainspoken and even worse at saying no, but she got the feeling he would tap dance his way around any excuse she gave him. Could she put him off without stuttering her way through a rejection? "Zeke, it's not…that I don't appreciate the invitation, but…I'm sorry. I'm not interested."

His forehead bunched in puzzlement, and his gaze flicked in Benji's direction. "Why not?"

"I'm just not. Interested."

Alfie and Benji looked at each other and smiled conspiratorially. Sarah was starting to believe Zeke was right. They were out to get him.

Zeke peered at her as if she'd lost her mind. A small muscle twitched at the corner of his mouth as he stared at her for what seemed like an hour. Was he angry? Arrogant *buwe* always got angry when they didn't get their way. "You don't like me," he said.

He wasn't angry.

He was shocked.

Sarah didn't want to be rude, but he'd already swallowed the hardest pill. "I...just want to be friends." She cringed at her attempt to soften the blow. They weren't friends to begin with, and she had no desire to start a friendship.

He surprised her again when his shoulders drooped and the light went out of his eyes. "Why don't you like me?"

Alfie smirked. "Because you steal people's bedrooms. And you don't care that me and Benji have to sleep in the cellar."

Zeke pinned Alfie with an exasperated look. "That's why *you* don't like me, Alfie."

Should she try to make Zeke feel better about himself? Or let him marinate in his disappointment? *Ach,* she couldn't let him marinate. Even though she didn't like him, she hated to see anyone so downhearted, shocking as it was that Zeke could be downhearted about her. "It's okay, Zeke. Who cares what I think anyway? Lily Ann Miller and Treva Nelson and all the other girls like you."

"I don't care about those other girls. I want to drive *you* home."

"But why? I'm nothing like you. I'm quiet and boring, and I don't like attention. You seem to crave it."

The intensity in his eyes made her uncomfortable. "Is that why you don't like me, because I attract attention?"

"I'd much rather that you attract the attention. I don't want to be noticed at all."

"That's an impossible request," Zeke said. "You're the only one I ever notice."

"Do you think it's funny to embarrass me?"

"Of course not. I think you're *wunderbarr*. There's no one as *wunderbarr* as you."

He was talking nonsense, and she didn't believe it, but Sarah was sure her face was bright red. "You try to embarrass me every time we're in the same room. You like to call everyone's attention to me, and then you and your friends laugh, like I'm the target of a private joke."

Benji frowned. "That's mean."

Zeke looked like he'd just been zapped by lightning. "Oh, *sis yuscht*! I've made a mess of things." He stretched out his hand to…Sarah didn't know what. Pat her on the head? But he pulled back before he embarrassed both of them. His voice took on a sense of urgency. "Sarah, Sarah, you've got it all wrong."

"I'm not going to apologize for my feelings."

He dabbed the towel at his drippy eye. "*Nae*, of course not. The fault is mine. I simply can't comprehend how I got it so wrong."

"You're as thick as a slab of pie," Alfie offered.

Zeke ignored the comments from the far side of the room. "I thought you enjoyed my teasing. Most girls like it when I pay attention to them."

Sarah had never spoken her mind so forcefully before. Maybe Zeke's arrogance made her just irritated enough to put him in his place. "You're stuck-up and overconfident, but I can't see as that's entirely your fault. The girls hang on your every word as if you were one of the blessed apostles. Of course you're going to get a big head."

He winced as if she'd pinched him. "I'm not trying to defend myself…well, I suppose I am trying to defend myself, but your cheeks turn a lovely shade of pink when I tease you. You're shy and quiet and very cute. You don't care about flirting or impressing anyone."

Sarah brushed an imaginary strand of hair from her cheek. There was such a pleasing timbre to Zeke's voice.

Alfie called from across the room. "Don't try to butter her up. She's not interested."

Zeke glanced at Alfie and then back at Sarah. They shared a smile at Alfie's expense. Alfie was lovable and persistent and a little bit of a menace. "Alfie, are you sure you don't want to go fetch my lunch? You and Benji can share it. I brought two Twinkies."

Benji's face lit up. "He's got Twinkies, Alfie."

Alfie shoved Benji away from him. "You'd betray Teacher Sarah for a Twinkie?"

Benji deflated slightly. "I guess not."

Zeke's eyes sparkled with amusement and sincerity as he turned to look at Sarah. "I apologize for being insensitive. I truly have been wrapped up in myself."

Sarah had said quite enough. She didn't need to grind Zeke's face into the dirt. Not even *Dat* would approve of that. "I forgive you. *Denki* for understanding."

He seemed relieved and very pleased. "Now that we understand each other, will you let me drive you home from the next gathering?"

# CHAPTER 3

*A*lfie rolled over in his sleeping bag and stared up at the ceiling. The house was completely quiet, except for the occasional creak and bump and the sound of *Mammi* Martha snoring in the bedroom. But Alfie wasn't scared of strange noises anymore. He'd been sleeping in the cellar for years. Nothing had more strange noises and poisonous spiders than the cellar.

He fluffed his pillow and propped his hands under his head. This was his best, most genius plan yet, and not even Benji knew about it. Benji was a *gute* spy partner, but he would have tried to talk Alfie out of his plan, and Alfie didn't want to be talked out of it.

He nestled deeper into his sleeping bag and smiled to himself. Wouldn't *Mamm* be furious if she found out that Alfie had been sleeping on her precious table for the last three nights? She'd be even madder if she found out he was planning on sleeping there until Christmas Day.

Of course, *Mamm* wasn't going to find out until Alfie wanted her to find out, probably on his wedding day when she wouldn't be able to punish him and she would have a day of reckoning for all the years she'd made her two baby boys live in the cellar. "Hey, *Mamm*, do you remember that one Christmas when you wouldn't

195

even let us breathe on your new Christmas table? Well, I fooled you! I sneaked up to the kitchen every night, spread out my sleeping bag, and slept on your table. I got my dirty hands all over it and breathed on it and slobbered and one time I even spit on it. And you didn't even know. Now you know how it feels to be disregarded and cast off like an old pair of underwear."

Alfie got a warm feeling just thinking about it. All the people who came to the wedding would gasp and say, "Rebecca, how could you love a table more than you love Alfie? How could you have made your own sons sleep in the cellar and let Zeke Hostetler have a real bed? Zeke Hostetler tried to steal Alfie and Benji's teacher. He didn't deserve a real bed."

His plan was working perfectly, even with the close call he'd had last night. *Mammi* Martha had shuffled into the kitchen in the middle of the night, pulled something out of the refrigerator, and gone back to her room without a sound. She hadn't even noticed Alfie perched on the table. She didn't see that well, and he'd held very still. If she'd seen him, she probably thought she was dreaming.

Every morning, Alfie got up and tiptoed back downstairs before sunrise and fell back asleep on the air mattress. Benji never even noticed he was gone. Alfie hadn't slept well on the table because it wasn't very comfortable, but it was the principle of the thing. He would suffer for his principles.

His heart lurched when the cellar door squeaked open and Benji emerged into the kitchen holding their emergency flashlight. "Alfie!" Benji hissed. "What are you doing?"

Alfie sat up, irritated that he'd been discovered. "What does it look like I'm doing? I'm camping out on *Mamm's* table."

"But why?"

"Why do you think? For revenge."

Benji moaned. "Oh, *sis yuscht*, Alfie. If *Mamm* finds you here, you'll get the spatula, and she'll probably put you up for adoption."

"*Gute*. If I'm adopted, at least I'll get a bed to sleep in."

"What if a robber adopts you and makes you steal things?"

Alfie folded his arms. "I don't care. *Mamm* needs to learn a lesson."

Benji screwed up his face as if he were going to cry. "I don't want you to get adopted. You're my favorite *bruder*. I'll have to sleep in the cellar alone."

"Go back to bed, Benji. This is none of your business."

Benji was a *gute bruder*, but he seldom followed orders. He set the flashlight on the counter, marched to the end of the table nearest Alfie's feet, and pulled on the sleeping bag. "Get off, Alfie. *Mamm* will catch you."

Alfie lay on his stomach and braced his palms on the table. "Stop it, Benji. I'm sleeping here until Christmas."

Benji tugged at the sleeping bag until Alfie's feet were within reach, then he wrapped his arms around Alfie's feet, still in the sleeping bag, and pulled even harder. Alfie did his best to stay on the table, but he didn't have anything but his pillow to hold onto, and Benji's feet were braced on the ground.

Alfie struggled and squirmed, and the sleeping bag zipper got caught between his hip and the table. He could feel the pull tab poking into his side and hear the hard metal scraping against the table. His weak hold slipped, and Alfie and his sleeping bag tumbled to the floor with a thud.

Alfie wrestled with the sleeping bag for a few seconds, then yanked out his feet and turned on Benji. "How *dumm* can you get?" he yell-whispered. "For sure and certain *Mamm* heard that."

Benji picked up his flashlight, grabbed the sleeve of Alfie's pajamas, and pulled him toward the cellar door. "Come on. She'll never know we were up here. She'll think it was *Mammi* or *Dawdi*."

Alfie snatched the flashlight from Benji's hand and picked up his pillow, which was balanced half on and half off the table. And then he saw it. His stomach did a somersault, and he thought he might lose his dinner and Zeke's Twinkie he'd eaten for dessert. "Benji, look what you did," he whispered, shining the flashlight on the surface of the table.

Benji's eyes almost popped out of his head. There in the middle of the table where Alfie's sleeping bag had been was a crooked, deep, three-foot-long scratch. It was the most horrible sight Alfie had ever seen, and that included the time when Tintin had thrown up all over *Mamm*'s new birthday quilt. It was the reason Tintin wasn't allowed in the house anymore. "I didn't do that!" Benji protested. "I never even touched the table."

Alfie thought he might choke on his own tongue. Strangling the flashlight in his hand, he lifted the sleeping bag from the floor and showed Benji the zipper. "Look. This got caught underneath me when you pulled too hard, and you made a scratch all the way down the table."

"It isn't my fault. *Mamm* told us not to touch that table, and you were sleeping on it!"

Alfie clapped his hand over Benji's mouth. "Quiet. You're going to wake the whole house."

"What are we going to do? If *Mamm* sees that scratch, she'll never forgive us. She'll probably sell us to the zoo."

"Benji, they don't take kids in the zoo."

"Maybe she'll call the police and ask them to put us in jail."

Alfie frowned. Calling the police was a lot more likely than the zoo. "Help me put the tablecloth back on. When *Mamm* takes it off on Christmas Day, maybe she'll be so full of Christmas cheer she won't be mad."

Benji sniffed. "She'll be mad, alright. But maybe she doesn't have to know it was us."

Alfie couldn't hope for any such luck. "She'll know." Alfie gave Benji the stink eye. "You wouldn't tell on me, would you?"

Benji burst into tears. "*Nae*. I love you, Alfie. I'll never tell, even if *Mamm* puts me up for adoption."

Alfie put his arm around Benji. He was the best *bruder* anyone could ask for, even if he didn't follow orders very well. "Maybe we can fix it. Andrew might let us borrow some sandpaper."

"How can we fix it? We don't know anything."

"We know a lot of things," Alfie protested, but Benji was right. They would never be able fix a scratch that deep and long. *Mamm* would notice.

Benji pressed his lips together and looked at the ceiling. "We could say a prayer. *Mamm* says *Gotte* is always listening."

"He might be listening, but He won't fix the table for us." Alfie's eyes stung just a little bit. "He's punishing us because we had a fight over the sleeping bag."

Benji shook his head. "*Gotte*'s really nice. I don't think He gets mad at anybody. Just disappointed."

"I still don't think He'll fix the table."

Benji picked up the tablecloth and spread it over the table. "Kneel down, Alfie. We need to pray."

It wasn't going to work, but Alfie didn't want to discourage Benji's faith, even if it was a little childish. Besides, he couldn't come up with a better solution. Alfie knelt next to Benji on the floor and silently asked Heavenly Father to fix the table. He and Benji finished at the same time. They both stood, and with hope shining in his eyes, Benji pulled the tablecloth off the table. Surprise, surprise, the scratch was still there.

Alfie placed a hand on Benji's shoulder. "I guess *Gotte*'s too mad at us to help."

"He's not mad. He's disappointed," Benji insisted.

"I heard a bump. Is everything okay?"

Alfie jumped out of his skin. Zeke Hostetler stood in the archway between the kitchen and the living room wearing an undershirt and long johns, his hair mussed and his right eye puffy and swollen.

Alfie yanked the tablecloth from Benji's hand and threw it on top of the table, but Zeke had already seen. His eyes widened like two open barn doors. "*Ach, du lieva.* What happened to your *Mamm*'s table?"

"You don't need to talk so loud," Alfie said. "We hear you."

Zeke came into the kitchen, pulled the tablecloth from the

table, and ran his fingers over the scratched top. "*Ach, du lieva. Ach, du lieva.*"

Benji's bottom lip quivered. "We accidentally scratched it."

Zeke nodded slowly, thoughtfully. He seemed almost as upset as Alfie was. "I can see that."

Benji caught his breath as if a spider had just crawled up his nose. "You helped Andrew build this table."

"I did. Andrew picked a beautiful piece of wood."

"Could you fix it? Without our *Mamm* finding out?"

Alfie's heart skipped three beats. Since *Gotte* wouldn't help them, Zeke was the next best thing. Benji was a genius.

Zeke scrubbed his hand down the side of his face. "*Ach, du lieva.* You think I can fix this without Rebecca noticing?"

Benji got more and more excited. "I bet you're a better carpenter than Andrew."

That was going a little too far, especially since Zeke was trying to steal their favorite teacher and sleeping in the room that rightfully belonged to them, but he was also the only thing standing between Alfie and the zoo.

Zeke was quiet for a long time. He took the flashlight from Alfie and shined it on the table, running his hand along the scratch and looking at it from about seven different angles. "You'd need to get your *Mamm* out of the house for seven or eight hours." He squinted in the direction of the clock. "I have to sand, then apply stain. The stain and varnish need time to dry."

"We can do it," Benji said, not even thinking to consult Alfie. "And we've got walkie-talkies like real spies."

One corner of Zeke's mouth twitched upward. "For sure and certain, the walkie-talkies will be helpful."

Benji pulled Alfie in for a bracing hug. "*Mamm* never has to find out. We're saved." He looked up at the ceiling and closed his eyes. "Never mind, *Gotte*. We found someone else to fix the table."

Zeke handed Alfie the flashlight, folded his arms, and leaned against the counter, as if he had nowhere else to go at two in the morning. "If I do this for you, I want you to do something for me."

"Anything you need," Benji said.

Benji was a *gute bruder*, but sometimes he spoke without thinking. Alfie wasn't so trusting. "It depends on what you want us to do. *Gotte* said not to steal or lie or kill. We won't do any of those."

Zeke chuckled quietly. "Okay. I'll agree to those terms." He tilted his head to the side and cleared his throat. "I hear you boys are wonderful-*gute* matchmakers. I want you to get Sarah Zimmerman to fall in love with me."

Alfie's heart sank to his toes. He was a very good spy, but even he couldn't do the impossible. And even if he could, their teacher would be lost.

They were doomed.

# CHAPTER 4

*S*arah was one of the *newehockers* at her *bruder* Jerry's wedding, which meant she got a tattcd handkerchief as a gift and sat at the front with the other attendants during the wedding ceremony. It also meant she had plenty of time to watch Zeke Hostetler out of the corner of her eye. It wasn't a bad view. Zeke might have been arrogant and loud, but he had dancing eyes and a lively smile. He really was very good-looking, even if Sarah didn't want anything to do with him.

Why was she letting him occupy space in her head? She was completely disinterested in Zeke.

The ceremony took place in the Yutzys' large barn, with four tall propane heaters spaced around the benches. Mary looked beautiful in an orchid-colored dress, white organdy apron, and black prayer *kapp*. The *newehockers*, or attendants, wore dresses or shirts the same color as the bride's dress. Mary had chosen a beautiful color of purple, and Sarah looked forward to wearing her attendant's dress for many years to come. Her *bruder* Jerry had always been of a serious and solemn disposition, but today he had a permanent smile on his face, and he looked like a young teenager again, full of love and hope for the future.

A few years ago, Jerry had jumped the fence and moved to

New York City to volunteer at a homeless shelter. He had returned a broken and disillusioned shell of himself. It was thanks to Alfie and Benji that he'd returned at all and thanks to Mary Yutzy that he'd decided to stay. Sarah could never begin to express her gratitude to the three of them for bringing her *bruder* home.

After the ceremony, some of the benches were reconfigured into tables, and the wedding dinner took place in the same space. Mary had rented bright white tablecloths and white stoneware for all the tables, with purple napkins and glasses with purple stems. Mary's family had done all the food preparation, and since the Yutzys owned a bakery, the pastries and rolls and desserts had been *appeditlich*. Mary's *schwester* Hannah had made twenty cakes, one for each table, decorated with purple frosting pansies and white roses. It was an absolutely beautiful wedding.

After the first meal, Sarah helped clear the tables so they could set up for the evening meal. Amish weddings were like family reunions, and most of the guests stayed all day and into the evening. Sarah carried the last of the plates into the kitchen where Hannah Yutzy and her *mamm* and several other relatives buzzed around like bees, washing dishes and preparing food for the next meal.

Hannah squealed when she saw Sarah, even though they'd talked only this morning. "*Ach*, Sarah, wasn't it the most beautiful wedding? I don't think I've ever seen Jerry so happy, and he never took his eyes from Mary for one second."

Sarah nodded. "So beautiful." Would Mary care if Sarah borrowed the exact color scheme for her wedding? She didn't have a groom picked out yet, but she had been planning her wedding day since she was six years old. She caught her breath as Zeke Hostetler's face intruded into her daydreams. Zeke was *not* groom material. He was loud and energetic and cheerful. *Ach, vell*, Sarah didn't mind cheerful. She liked *buwe* who were cheerful. She didn't mind energetic either, but Zeke's enthusiasm got a little out of control sometimes. Zeke as a husband? Heat traveled up her neck. What a strange and unwelcome thought.

*Dat* would never approve of someone who wanted to take Sarah to Ohio. She was safe in her daydreams, and Zeke never had to know that she'd thought of him thirty-seven times already today.

Saloma, Mary's *mater*, took the dirty dishes from Sarah and gave her a quick hug. "Oh, *heartzley*, you are such a dear to help, but you should be in the barn with *die youngie* playing games and singing." She nudged Sarah away from her. "Go, go now, and let the old ladies do the dishes."

Hannah's eyes twinkled, and she squeezed Sarah's hand. "Who are you coupled up with for the singing?"

"My cousin Norman."

Hannah's expression drooped. "Your sixteen-year-old cousin? That doesn't sound very fun."

Sarah wasn't offended at Hannah's reaction. "It's much more fun than trying to keep a conversation going with a boy I barely know. I always feel so awkward at weddings. I usually dread being coupled up, but Mary took pity on me and let me pick my partner. Norman is nice, and he can talk for hours about horses. I won't have to say a word."

Hannah scrunched her lips together. "But what if you're missing out on finding a new boyfriend? Wouldn't that be exciting?"

Sarah laughed. "I don't want exciting. I want easy and comfortable." And boring. She frowned to herself. Sometimes she wished she was more like Zeke, who could talk to anybody and never seemed to feel awkward about anything. His life was much more exciting than hers.

Hannah bloomed into a smile. "I just love you, Sarah. You're so honest, and you don't pretend to be anything you're not. I hope you have a wonderful-*gute* time with your cousin."

"I will."

"And it's not like you can't talk to other boys. Who knows who might be hoping they get to sit by you tonight?"

Sarah didn't reply. Hannah had come a little too close to the truth. Zeke Hostetler was interested, even though she'd told him in no uncertain terms she didn't like him. Thank *Derr Herr* she wouldn't even have to look at Zeke if she didn't want to. Her attention would be riveted to her cousin Norman.

Riveted.

As long as he didn't tell the story about how he'd gotten the scar on his armpit. She'd heard that one four times.

Sarah clutched the collar of her coat around her chin as she left the house and headed back to the barn. Alfie and Benji stood near the barn door like they'd been waiting for her. "Are you boys having a *gute* time?" she asked, because they were whispering to each other and casting sidelong glances in every direction.

Benji snapped to attention, as if Sarah had caught him smoking behind the barn. "*Hallo*, Sarah. *Vie gehts*?"

They were definitely up to no good.

Benji reached into his pocket and pulled out a pen, which he promptly handed to Sarah. "Jerry and Mary were giving these away after the ceremony."

"Very nice," Sarah said, a smile tugging at her mouth. The wedding favors were ballpoint pens, green ones for the groom and purple ones for the bride. "But I already have one of each."

"Are you going to play games with *die youngie* now?" Alfie asked, his eyes practically glowing with mischief.

Sarah nodded. "I've got to hurry in there. My partner is waiting."

Benji scratched the side of his head and squinted in Sarah's direction. "You should give him a chance. He's really nice."

How did Benji know Norman? *Ach vell*, Alfie and Benji seemed to know a lot of things no one would ever guess they knew. "I will."

Alfie stepped forward and blocked Sarah's way into the barn.

"We're doing a secret fireworks show after dinner. Will you come?"

A secret fireworks show put on by eleven-year-olds? That sounded dangerous and irresponsible and very cold. "Um, does your *Mamm* know?"

Benji looked positively panic-stricken. "Know what?"

"That you're doing fireworks?"

Alfie blew a puff of air from between his lips. "She doesn't care."

"How are you going to keep it a secret? There's nothing but pastureland for a mile."

Benji traced a circle in the dirt with his toe. "We're going behind the barn. *Mamm* will be in the house."

"I thought you said your *Mamm* doesn't care."

Alfie grimaced. "She won't care if she doesn't know. Besides, Zeke will be there. He says he has to supervise."

Nope. If Zeke was going, Sarah would pass. "*Ach, vell,* it sounds like you'll have enough watchers without me."

Benji looked offended. "Of course we won't have enough people. You have to come."

She hated to disappoint them. They were so cute and so persistent. "We'll see how the rest of the evening goes. I might have to help clean up. I'm one of the attendants, you know."

Alfie spread his legs and folded his arms. "It won't take very long, and me and Benji can help do dishes after fireworks."

Sarah was smart enough to be wary. No little boy in his right mind would volunteer to wash dishes. Alfie and Benji were scheming, and it seemed that Sarah was at the center of their scheme. She might have suspected they wanted to get her alone with Zeke Hostetler, but both twins seemed to dislike Zeke even more than she did. Surely that wasn't their plan. Sarah eyed the two adorable troublemakers. She loved them to the moon and back, and if they wanted her to see their secret fireworks show, she would show up. If they truly had fireworks, the show wouldn't be secret for long, and if she brought Norman with her, she wouldn't have to talk to Zeke at all.

"Okay. I'll come to your secret fireworks show if my *dat* says it's okay."

Benji clapped his hands and did a jig around Alfie. His glee seemed a little overdone. "Come out to the pasture behind the house after the evening meal. We brought our camp chairs."

Camp chairs. They'd put some thought into this scheme, whatever it was. But she was one step ahead of them. She would invite Norman and all the other attendants to come with her. There was safety in numbers. No matter what Alfie and Benji had planned, she could blend into the crowd like she always did.

She strolled into the barn where *die youngie* were coupling up and getting ready for the singing. After the singing would be games, then dinner, then a secret fireworks show. Were Alfie and Benji allowed to stay out that late?

Hay bales had been pulled down to form a semi-circle where couples could sit to sing. Norman sat next to Pauline Schmutz at the far end of the barn. They seemed to be engaged in a very lively discussion. Norman raised his arm and pointed to his armpit. Oh, no. Not the scar story. Sarah didn't really want to hear it again. Maybe she should just make herself comfortable until Norman remembered that he was her partner. She didn't mind.

Sarah sat down on the nearest hay bale, clasped her hands in her lap, and quietly watched *die youngie* gather. Sarah's *dat* stood in the center of the barn holding a clipboard, making sure all *die youngie* knew who they were coupled with.

Jerry and Mary sat on a hay bale off to the side, quietly whispering to each other. They looked so happy, it was a wonder they weren't both floating a few inches off the ground. Matt Gingerich and Sadie King were making eyes at each other, and Sarah wouldn't be surprised if there was another wedding come next year.

She flinched when Zeke Hostetler slid next to her on the hay bale, crowding her on the small space. "*Hallo*, Sarah. You look very pretty today." He grinned like a puppy with a new toy but said it softly, which Sarah appreciated because Zeke tended to draw attention with his booming voice.

Hay bales were just the right size for two people, *if* the two people liked each other and didn't mind that their sleeves brushed during the singing. Sarah's face warmed to a temperature between melted chocolate and hot *kaffee*. What did Zeke think he was doing? He knew she didn't like him. He knew that she would never, ever think of him as a groom. Then again, his closeness wasn't completely his fault. He was tall and broad, and all those muscles took up a lot of space.

Would it be rude if she stood up and walked away?

He must have seen something concerning in her expression. "Sorry," he whispered. "I know you don't like to draw attention. Am I crowding you?"

She cleared her throat. His eyes held real apprehension, as if he were only thrilled about sitting there if she was. "*Ach, vell,* you're kind of squishing me, but…"

"I'm sorry. That was inconsiderate of me to just plop myself down next to you like a fat tabby cat." His grin returned, and he slid off the hay bale and onto the ground, stretching his legs out in front of him and folding his arms across his chest. "This works. No one will notice me down here."

"*Ach, nae,* Zeke. That doesn't look comfortable. Norman and I can find another place to sit." She didn't mention that Zeke was the one who should find another place to sit. She'd been there first.

"Norman?"

"*Jah.* Mary and Jerry coupled me with my cousin." She lowered her gaze, suddenly embarrassed that she was too timid to be matched with somebody else, somebody exciting and daring like Zeke. She was a chicken, plain and simple, and everybody knew it. "It's just easier."

His expression softened like a mushy banana. "No need to be embarrassed. I think you're fascinating."

She couldn't tell if he was teasing her. "What is that supposed to mean?"

He paused, contemplating his answer, and his gaze was like warm butter dripping off a stack of whole wheat pancakes. "Well, you have this little dimple just to the right side of your mouth that only appears when you smile really wide. Your eyes are the color of a clear blue sky in January, and your hair shines like amber honey in the sunlight. That mole just below the corner of your eye is intriguing in a way I can't explain."

Sarah was struck completely mute. It was clear Zeke had spent way too much time thinking about her. She pressed her cold fingers to her warm cheeks. Way too much time.

"I've always liked the way you twirl the hair at the nape of your neck when you're thinking deep thoughts, or the way you nibble on your bottom lip when you disagree with someone."

"Do I do that? I don't think I do that."

He chuckled. "You're doing it now."

A reluctant smile tugged at Sarah's mouth. "That's because I always disagree with you."

"*Jah.* You've made that very clear." He didn't seem annoyed about it, so Sarah didn't feel bad she'd said it. "Your students love you, and I admire that you can control a whole classroom of children without raising your voice. You're thoughtful and cautious and always concerned that no one feels left out or overlooked. Like I said, I find you fascinating. Did I explain myself well enough?"

Sarah avoided Zeke's gaze and willed her heart to slow down. "I...I suppose you did." She smoothed her hand down her purple dress. "I don't mean to be rude, but I have to go now. The singing is about to start, and I should sit with Norman." She choked out his name. *Jah*, she was a lily-livered coward.

Zeke half grimaced, half smiled sheepishly. "Actually, I think you're coupled up with me."

209

Sarah shook her head. "*Nae*. I saw the list on Sunday."

His face turned one shade darker. "I, uh, they changed the list." He spread his hands as if presenting himself for inspection. "They coupled you with me."

It took all of Sarah's self-control not to jump to her feet and demand that Zeke take back such a horrible lie. She was coupled up with Norman, and she was looking forward to a very boring, very safe afternoon. Resisting the urge to shove Zeke aside to make room for Norman and his armpit scar, she pasted a smile on her face, rose calmly from her hay bale, and strolled nonchalantly to her *fater*.

"*Dat*, will you check the list for me and tell me who Zeke Hostetler is coupled with tonight?"

She could always tell when *Dat*'s hackles went up. "Why do you want to know?"

Sarah sighed inwardly. "Zeke thinks he's coupled up with me, and I just want to help him find his real partner."

"Aren't you coupled up with Norman?" Dat studied the list, written in Mary's chunky handwriting. "*Vell*, this will never do. It says you're with Zeke."

Sarah's heart skipped a beat. She grabbed the clipboard from Dat's hand. "That can't be right." But there it was, plain as day, Zeke's name next to hers where Norman's used to be. She could even see the faint letters of Norman's name erased from the page. Mary had replaced Norman with Zeke!

*Dat* shook his head. "I'm sure he's a nice *bu*, but he is not for you. He's too tall and lives in Ohio. I won't have my *dochter* paired with an out-of-stater. Where is Mary? I'll fix this right now."

"*Nae, Dat*. I'll talk to Mary. For sure and certain, it's a mistake."

Dat's frown took over his face, traveling clear to his hairline. "It doesn't look like a mistake. It looks intentional on Mary's part, or maybe Jerry's. He knows better than to pair you with someone I don't approve of."

Sarah didn't know why a heavy weight pressed into her chest, as if she suddenly felt very bad for herself and sorry for Zeke. She didn't approve of Zeke. Why did it matter what *Dat* thought?

Maybe because the situation felt so harsh and final when *Dat* said it like that. Would she forever be doing only what her *fater* wanted her to do? Was he going to insist on being in charge of her life until he died?

Sarah faked a smile and, trying not to attract attention, ambled toward Mary and Jerry, who were still sitting in the corner pretending they were the only two people in the world. "Mary," Sarah hissed. "What have you done?"

Mary was always so cheerful, and today, nothing could bridle her joy. She stood up, wrapped her arms around Sarah, and pulled her close. "*Ach*, Sarah, isn't it a *wunderbarr* day? Now we're officially *schwesteren*."

Sarah refused to be derailed, not even by a hug from her new *schwester*. "*Jah, jah*, a truly *wunderbarr* day, but Mary, I'm supposed to be coupled with Norman, not Zeke Hostetler."

Mary's smile twitched in confusion. "Alfie Petersheim told me you wanted to change to Zeke. Did I make a mistake?"

"What does Alfie Petersheim have to do with this?"

"He said you wanted to be coupled up with Zeke because the two of you are helping him with fireworks."

"What do fireworks have to do with this?"

"It didn't make sense to me either, but I wasn't all that curious. I had a few other things on my mind." She smiled at Jerry, who couldn't seem to take his eyes off her. "I never question Alfie and Benji's judgment. You know I'd do anything for them."

Sarah was beyond perplexed. "But what about Norman?"

"Oh, I asked Norman if he'd be willing to change partners. He was fine. He thinks Pauline Schmutz is cute, and he wanted to talk to her about horses."

Oh, bother. Pauline's *dat* bred horses. Sarah's hopes for Norman were thrown on the ground and trampled by a stampede of mustangs.

Sarah huffed out a puff of air that made her lips vibrate.

The lines around Mary's eyes deepened. "Oh dear. I guess I shouldn't be so trusting of Alfie Petersheim. But he's so cute. I can't resist his freckles."

Sarah didn't know whom to be angry with first. Had Zeke put Alfie up to this? Or had Alfie thought he was doing a *gute* deed? Did Alfie have a plan? Or was he just making mischief? Didn't he dislike Zeke as much as Sarah did? And how much did Sarah dislike Zeke? She liked him a lot better than she did half an hour ago, but that didn't mean she wanted to spend the next three hours with him.

Sarah couldn't begin to sort out the motives, and her options were dwindling. She could make a fuss and insist on a new partner. She could storm out of the barn and wash dishes to her heart's content. Or she could hold her nose and spend the afternoon with Zeke.

What she *would not* do was ruin Mary's perfect happiness with her selfish concerns. "Nothing to worry about, Mary. I was confused, that's all. I don't mind being coupled up with Zeke." When she said it out loud, it felt almost true. Only moments ago, Zeke had knocked her completely off-kilter with his genuine smile and staggeringly sincere compliments. Her stomach did a little flip.

Then again, what if he embarrassed her? He'd always been completely insensitive to her feelings. Her stomach did three more flips when she thought of Zeke and his loud friends making her look foolish in front of everyone. She squared her shoulders. For Mary and Jerry's sake, she'd quit being a baby and put up with Zeke's teasing. She refused to spoil her *bruder*'s big day, even if Zeke spoiled hers.

Sarah took the clipboard to her *dat*. "I guess I'm coupled with Zeke," she said.

She couldn't have hoped that was the end of it. Dat narrowed his eyes. "I will talk to Jerry myself."

"*Nae, Dat.* It's all been settled. Please don't make a fuss."

*Dat* grunted. "I'll always make a fuss where my *dochter* is concerned."

"It's only for the afternoon. I don't even like Zeke Hostetler."

He must have recognized her sincerity. Either that or he truly didn't want to make a fuss. He'd made enough of a fuss about Jerry to last all of them three lifetimes. "Don't disappoint me."

Everything was so dire with her *dat*. Why couldn't he stop worrying and trust her? No amount of worry on Dat's part had kept Jerry from leaving home in the first place. Worry was like praying for something you didn't want to happen. You only made yourself miserable for no reason at all.

Sarah marched back to her hay bale, agitation warring with anticipation in her chest. It was a strange combination of emotions, but Sarah could do nothing to sort them out right now.

Zeke's grin took her breath away. "You came back."

She wasn't sure what to do with his unbounded joy. "Uh, *jah*. There was a misunderstanding." She plopped herself down. "You…you really should sit next to me. I don't want to be accused of hogging the hay bale."

His smile grew wider, if that was possible. "*Denki*. I'd like that. But only if you're comfortable."

She nodded slightly. She was the furthest thing from comfortable, but it wasn't necessarily a horrible feeling.

He rose from the ground and slid beside her, being careful not to take up more than his fair share of space. "I'll do my best not to embarrass you, aside from the embarrassment of having me as your partner."

"Don't be silly," she said. "Every other girl in the barn is jealous."

His eyes glowed with warmth. "I don't care about any other girl in the barn."

She wasn't about to let him know that he had completely disarmed her. She nudged his arm with her elbow. It was one of the boldest things she'd ever done. "No teasing."

He held up his hands as if stopping traffic, his expression

open and honest. "I admit I like to tease you, but I wouldn't tease about something like this. The only feelings I care about right now are yours. I know I've been insensitive, but I really do want to do better. Will you give me a chance?"

She'd never seen a more eager look, not even on Benji Petersheim's face, and she surprised herself at how badly she wanted to give in. "I suppose so, but only because there are dirty dishes waiting for me if this doesn't work out."

"You have my permission to poke or kick me if I do anything to embarrass you."

Sarah stared at him in mock horror. "I've never kicked anyone in my life. Except, I guess I've kicked the rooster, but that was only because he attacked me."

*Dat* left the barn with the clipboard, and Sarah breathed a sigh of relief. What *Dat* didn't see wouldn't hurt him, and if she gave Zeke a little encouragement, *Dat* wouldn't be there to scrutinize her motives. Mary's *bruder* James came to the front. He was the *Vorsinger*, or the one who got them going on each line of the song. James started in on the first song, and no one needed to be told what to do. The voices floated to the rafters and back again, and Sarah found herself relaxing slightly. Zeke could be overbearing when he wanted to, but he behaved himself—not singing too loudly or in a way that drew attention to either of them.

Of course, he had *Sarah's* full attention. She'd always thought he was handsome, but she hadn't noticed how sincere and eager to please he was. Or how solicitous he was, as if everything depended on her good opinion. Oy, anyhow! A few days ago, she didn't much care what Zeke thought of her. Now she feared she'd break under the pressure of trying to make a *gute* impression.

She growled under her breath. Why was she getting so worked up? They had been coupled up for the singing and a few games. After today, they could go their separate ways, and she'd never have to speak to him again. But that thought only made her more discontented.

After the singing, they played a new game called *Chicken Taco*. They sat in a circle, clapping their hands, then slapping their thighs in unison. Going clockwise, the first person clapped and said, "Chicken!" The next person slapped his thighs and said, "Taco!" Down the line, they repeated "Chicken Taco" twice and then the next person said, "Boom." Around the circle they went, adding one more "Boom" between each two "Chicken Tacos."

The first person to break the rhythm was out of the circle, the circle would get smaller, and they'd start again.

Sarah was very *gute* at games because she played so many with the scholars at school, but Zeke, it turned out, was even better. He was the last person in the circle after the first round and one of three left at the end of the second round. His grin was so wide, Sarah could have counted all his teeth. In the third round, Zeke got out right after Sarah did. With exhilaration written all over his face, he jumped up and moved out of the circle. He seemed to smile with his whole body when he sat next to Sarah.

"I thought you were unbeatable," Sarah teased as they watched the rest of *die youngie* play.

He laughed. "*Ach, vell*, to be honest, I wanted to sit by you more than I wanted to win, so I messed up on purpose."

She didn't know what to say to that, so she checked that her hair was in place and wrapped her hand around the nearest pillar to keep from floating away. "How is your eye?" she said, because if he kept looking at her like that, she would hyperventilate.

"It's better. I still think Alfie dumped that glitter on me purposefully, but he's not so bad. I'm liking him better and better all the time."

After two more rounds of *Chicken Taco*, where Zeke purposefully messed up as soon as Sarah did, one of *die youngie* suggested they play *Charades*. They split up into teams and passed around pieces of paper to write clues on. *Charades* clues were things, people, or phrases they thought the other team would have a hard time guessing.

Sarah had never been *gute* at coming up with clues. She turned to Zeke, pencil at the ready. "What should I write?"

He showed her his piece of paper. It said *schoolteacher*. "I seriously can't think of anything else," he said, his eyes alight with mischief and tenderness.

Sarah held her breath. Zeke Hostetler was not talking about *Charades*.

"Oh, I see." She'd get no help from Zeke. He was too preoccupied with…her.

She pressed her hand to her cheek. Surely her face must have been glowing. Recovering some of her composure, she jotted down *milking the cow*. That was *gute* enough for a girl who, at this moment, could barely remember her own name.

Their team gave the first clue. James Yutzy pulled a piece of paper from the hat, looked at it, and grimaced. He thought about it for a few seconds and wiped any emotion from his expression. Then he pointed to his face.

"James Yutzy," someone yelled.

James frowned fiercely and waved his hand back and forth. He pointed to his face then took one step to his right and pointed to his face again.

"Standing in line?" was Matt Gingerich's guess.

"Getting your picture taken!"

"Two-faced?"

James shook his head but seemed encouraged by that last guess. He put two fingers in the air and pointed to his face again. Then he shaped his fingers to frame his face and smiled. He took another step to the right and repeated his action.

"Looking in the mirror!"

"Eating a sandwich!"

Both Zeke and Sarah turned to peer at Norman. How in the world had he come up with *eating a sandwich*?

Sarah caught her breath. She tugged on Zeke's sleeve and whispered, "Twins. It's identical twins."

Zeke's eyebrows shot up his forehead. "Say it, Sarah."

She pressed her lips together and jerked her head back and forth. "You say it."

Zeke threw his hand into the air. "Identical twins," he shouted.

"Yes," James yelled, clapping and jumping up and down. "Good job, Zeke!"

The whole team cheered.

Zeke turned to Sarah, seemed to think better of what he was going to do, and looked behind him. "It wasn't me. I heard someone else say it."

Sarah clasped her hands together and sat demurely on the hay bale like an innocent bystander. How kind of Zeke to divert everyone's attention without taking the credit for himself. She was really starting to like him. Not only had he not stolen the credit for her idea, but he'd taken her seriously when she'd told him she didn't like attention.

When the other team's clue giver stood up and pulled a paper out of the hat, Zeke leaned close to Sarah. "You should have told everyone it was your answer."

She grinned. "I'm just *froh* our team got a point."

He laughed. "I've never met anyone like you."

"Don't exaggerate." Her scold was accompanied by a warm and cozy feeling in her chest. "We'd just been talking about Alfie and Benji. The answer seemed obvious."

"Only obvious to someone as smart as you." He leaned back on his hands. "Speaking of Alfie and Benji, did they invite you to the fireworks show later?"

"*Jah.*"

He eyed her curiously. "The real question is, are you going to go?"

"Alfie says you'll be there."

"I'm only going if you're going."

What a lovely thought. "You really should go. Alfie said you agreed to help, and they definitely need adult supervision. It seems rather irresponsible to abandon them just because I'm not going."

His expression fell. "You're not going?"

Sarah's heart did a little flip-flop. "*Ach, vell,* since you're the only person standing between the twins and a forest fire, I guess I should be there."

Zeke laughed, and there was so much joy in the sound it took Sarah's breath away. "*Jah,* you should. You can hold the fire extinguisher."

Sarah's eyes went wide. "They brought a fire extinguisher?"

"Just in case. Years of hard experience."

She rolled her eyes. "For sure and certain. There's a rumor they set off a smoke bomb outside the library, though no one ever caught them. But Austin Petersheim's ex-girlfriend worked there, and Alfie and Benji didn't like her one little bit."

"I'll remember to stay on their good side."

The expression on his face made her laugh. "That's wise."

"We should invite Jerry to the fireworks. I hear he used to be a firefighter."

Sarah's chest tightened as if someone had snapped a rubber band around it. "*Jah.* That's what started all the trouble."

"Zeke, Sarah, pay attention," Matt Gingerich barked. "We need your help."

Sarah hadn't even noticed that Norman was up in front getting ready to act out a word. She had stopped paying attention altogether. Zeke crowded out every other thought.

Pretending to be engrossed in Norman's clue, Zeke folded his arms and leaned closer to Sarah. "All the trouble?" he whispered.

"Jerry met someone at the fire station who liked to talk about religion. They had some deep discussions that led Jerry to question his faith. He went to New York without telling anyone he was leaving, and *Mamm* and Dat were devastated."

"You and Jerry seem close. I bet you were devastated too."

She nodded slowly. "I was. It hurt that he didn't trust me enough to tell me how he was feeling, and it hurt that he didn't say goodbye. But he didn't even tell Mary his plans, so I tried not to take it personally."

"He must have been in a lot of pain."

Sarah heaved a sigh. "I suppose he was, but it wonders me if he realizes how much pain he caused the rest of us."

"Do you think he was being selfish?"

Sarah eyed Zeke's expression. He wasn't accusing her or Jerry. Simply making a statement that held no judgment. "I don't know," she whispered. Her voice cracked into a hundred pieces. Something in Zeke's eyes made her want to open her heart. "It felt selfish. Did he even care how his leaving hurt me? Before he left, I worked out for an *Englisher* at a grocery store. My *dat* made me quit my job, and I wasn't allowed to go anywhere but church for months. I got lecture after lecture about hell and choices and jumping the fence."

Zeke reached out and softly placed his hand over the top of hers. It was such a tender, kind gesture, she didn't pull away. They were sitting in the back, and no one could see their hands touching. "Your *mamm* and *dat* took out their frustration and heartache on you. That must have felt so unfair."

"*Dat* still monitors everything I do as if I were a six-year-old who doesn't know how to tie her own shoes. The families in the community trust me to teach their children, but my own *fater* doesn't trust me to go to a gathering by myself. I think he's afraid of being hurt again."

He squeezed her hand lightly. "Fear guides so many of our bad decisions. He's afraid of losing you, so he's smothering you."

"Sometimes I can't breathe." She'd said too much. What must Zeke think of her? "I sound like a bitter young woman who can't get over her own selfishness. I'm sorry."

Zeke puckered his lips as if he'd just eaten a lemon. "Why do you think you need to apologize? You haven't done anything wrong. Feelings are neither *gute* or bad. They just are, and it's okay to feel them." He smoothed his thumb over the back of her hand. "Though I wish you felt differently about me. I mean, what's not to like?"

Sarah giggled. Zeke, bless him, had brought the conversation back to something safer and less fraught with painful emotions. "There are many things not to like about you."

He cocked an eyebrow, and his lips twitched upward. "Really?"

"You're wonderful loud."

He grinned. "Can I help it that *Gotte* gave me this deep, booming voice?"

"Besides that, you don't have an ounce of fat on you. How do you stay warm in the winter?"

"I wear a coat."

She bit her bottom lip. "The nail on your right index finger is purple. You know fingernail polish is not allowed."

He laughed softly and examined his nail. "It's a very nice shade, isn't it? I clocked myself with a hammer."

"That doesn't seem very wise. Just another thing to add to my list."

"Ring around the Rosies," Mandi Glick called from the front, momentarily bringing their attention back to *Charades*. Norman was having a difficult time getting the team to guess the right word.

"Square dancing!" James said.

"Rounding up cattle."

Sarah startled herself when she threw up her hand and yelled, "Red Rover!"

Norman pointed to Sarah. "*Jah!*"

Sarah's team cheered, and Sarah found that she was more pleased than embarrassed. It wasn't that horrible to get a little attention, especially among friends, and being timid could be very inconvenient when you knew the answer to the *Charades* clue.

Zeke's smile was a country mile wide. "It's no wonder you're the schoolteacher. You're so smart."

She rolled her eyes. "No need to gush. A little notice goes a long way with me."

Zeke chuckled. "You don't know that I secretly shower you with attention all the time."

Sarah couldn't help but laugh. "No more teasing, or I'll have to put 'shameless flatterer' on my list."

He propped his chin in his hand. "I like that you're keeping a list. It means you think about me sometimes."

"I think about you approximately zero percent of the time, Zeke Hostetler."

His smile made her heart race. "See what I mean? You can do complicated percentages in your head. You're smart as a whip."

Sarah did her best to concentrate on the rest of the games instead of the interesting, aggravating, handsome boy beside her. She guessed two more *Charades* clues, and their team won. *Dat* came into the barn just as they were finishing up *Do You Like Your Neighbor?* and announced it was time to set up the tables for the evening meal.

He caught sight of Sarah and Zeke sitting together and frowned. They sat close, but it couldn't be helped. The hay bale wasn't that big, and Zeke had broad shoulders.

"Sarah," *Dat* said, motioning for her to come.

Sarah reluctantly rose to her feet. She couldn't remember when she'd enjoyed herself half as much at a wedding and was certain she'd never enjoy herself so much again. Unless…could she sneak away and go to the fireworks show without *Dat* knowing?

*Dat* must have seen something he didn't like on Sarah's face. "Go in the house and help with the food preparations. And Zeke?"

Zeke jumped to his feet as if he were eager to do whatever *Dat* asked. Sarah had lost that eagerness a long time ago. "*Jah?*"

*Dat* put a hand on Sarah's shoulder. "You seem like a nice boy, but we have better things in mind for Sarah. We don't want her seeing an Ohio boy. He'll take her away and settle her too far from her home. We won't allow it. I'll thank you to keep your distance."

Never pulling her gaze from Zeke's face, Sarah listened to her *dat*'s little speech in complete mortification. She wasn't interested in Zeke Hostetler, and even if she were, *Dat* had certainly just driven him away. What kind of man wanted a hostile *fater*-in-law?

Not that Sarah in a million years was thinking of Zeke as a husband.

But if she was, *Dat* had just dashed all her hopes.

Not that she had any hopes. Or dreams. Or wedding plans.

Not in a million years.

Zeke's shoulders drooped while *Dat* talked, then in an instant, he squared his shoulders and shook *Dat*'s hand as if they were the best of friends. "*Denki* for your concern, Wallace. Sarah most certainly attracts attention. I know you want to be vigilant."

Off he strolled, without another word. He didn't seem deterred or discouraged. In fact, Sarah could have sworn he had a spring in his step and a twinkle in his eye when he walked away. He hadn't agreed to anything, and Sarah wanted to jump for joy.

But why was she so happy?

She certainly didn't have any hopes for Zeke. Or dreams. Or wedding plans.

Not in a million years.

# CHAPTER 5

S arah's hopes fell off a cliff and were dashed on the rocks below as *Dat* pulled their buggy up to the barn door and waved Sarah over. "Sarah, go find your *mater*. It's time to go home."

But…

She didn't really want to argue with her *dat*, but it seemed rude for the groom's family to leave before the cleanup was done and especially rude to leave before the bride and groom did. The bride and groom were staying the night at the Yutzys' house, but they were still visiting and laughing and showed no signs of retiring for the night. *Dat* probably would have been persuaded to stay, except he'd caught Zeke and Sarah with their heads together after dinner, and making sure Sarah obeyed his wishes was his first priority.

He thought he was being protective, but he was trying to dictate her behavior, for sure and certain.

It was her own fault. She should have steered clear of Zeke after dinner, but he'd searched her out to reassure her that he'd brought plenty of blankets for the fireworks show, and then he'd made her laugh with a story about his stepping on a skunk on his front porch five years ago. "I can still smell the faintest hint of skunk when I blow my nose," he had said.

They definitely should have parted after that, but then he wanted to tell her about carpentry and ask her about teaching school. That boy was persistent and delightful and altogether too sure of himself. But he'd probably ruined everything by talking to her right out in the open where *Dat* could see and have a chance to get suspicious.

Now Sarah had a dilemma. She should honor her *fater*, but she also wanted to see that secret fireworks show more than ever. Maybe she'd get to sit by Zeke and watch the light from the fireworks reflected in his eyes. But really, Zeke was only ten percent of why she wanted to see the fireworks. Alfie and Benji had been so eager for her to come, and she needed to go if only to make sure they weren't killed or maimed for life.

Ten percent seemed low.

Maybe Zeke was more like forty percent.

Seventy percent at most.

But percentages didn't matter because *Dat* was sitting in the buggy ready to whisk Sarah away from Zeke Hostetler and the secret fireworks show, and it was definitely on purpose.

Sarah trudged into the house. *Mamm* was standing at the sink with a dishtowel in her hand drying plates that Rebecca Petersheim washed. "*Mamm*, Dat is ready to leave," Sarah said, feeling herself blush. The groom's family shouldn't have been leaving so early. And she really wanted to see those fireworks.

*Mamm*'s countenance fell. "*Ach*, we were having such a lovely visit."

Rebecca pressed her lips into a hard line and dried her hands on a towel. "I'll take care of it. Wait here."

Sarah and *Mamm* exchanged a look as Alfie and Benji's *mamm* marched out the door. "What do you think she's going to take care of?" *Mamm* asked.

"I have no idea." Sarah took off her coat and plunged her hands into the dishwater. Might as well make herself useful while she waited. Sarah could never be as brave as Rebecca Petersheim. She was a strict but loving parent who kept her boys in line with discipline and hard work. Alfie and Benji were mischievous, but they were also truthful, kind, and loyal. And Rebecca never took nonsense from anyone, even Sarah's *dat*. Over *Dat*'s objections, she had invited Jerry to sleep at her house when Sarah's *mamm* and *dat* had turned their backs on him. Rebecca had a *gute* heart and a brave soul.

Sarah's stomach clenched. Forgiving Jerry had taken *Mamm* and *Dat* a very long time. What would happen if Sarah went against their wishes? Would they kick her out? Maybe Rebecca would take her in. That thought almost made Sarah smile. Alfie and Benji would be very mad if yet another intruder took over their bedroom.

Rebecca was back not five minutes later. "You're staying. Benaiah is taking care of it."

*Mamm*'s eyebrows inched together in concern. "He is?"

"They're looking at Benaiah's new seed catalog. He takes it with him everywhere. You can never get too early a jump on seed selection." Rebecca gave Sarah her no-nonsense smile and nudged her aside. "Go have some fun before it's time to leave." She smirked. "I expect you've got about half an hour."

Sarah's heart leaped in her chest. Did Rebecca know about the fireworks? Did she know about Zeke?

Alfie and Benji had tried to hide it, but it was plain they hadn't told their *mamm* about the fireworks or the camp chairs or the fire extinguisher. But that didn't mean Rebecca hadn't suspected something.

Sarah didn't need to be told twice. She dried her hands and ran out the door as if a dog were snapping at her heels. She slowed down as she approached the barn. She didn't want to appear too eager. Zeke would think she liked him or something. Sarah glanced around her for any sign of *Dat*. He and Benaiah were nowhere to be seen, but the buggy sat right where *Dat* had left it between the barn and the house. In the gathering darkness,

Sarah slipped cautiously behind the barn where she saw three shadowy figures about fifty yards away in the snow-covered pasture. It looked like the fire danger would be minimal. The tallest figure waved a flashlight back and forth in her direction and made her pulse race double time. He'd been watching for her. It was just going to be her and Zeke, Alfie and Benji, and she had no desire to invite Norman or the other attendants or anyone else.

What had gotten into her?

She jogged toward Zeke, her shoes crunching in the thin layer of snow. "I've only got thirty minutes."

By the light of the flashlight, she could see disappointment travel across Zeke's face, but it was quickly replaced with a blinding smile. "It's not enough time, but it's better than no time. I'm just *froh* your *dat* let you come."

"What if I forgot to ask permission?"

He threw back his head and laughed. "I swear I just saw lightning shoot out of your eyes. I've never seen your headstrong side before. It's very attractive."

She shook her head. "It's all pretend. I'm terrified of getting caught."

"We know how that feels," Benji said.

The look Zeke gave her was pure melted Swiss chocolate. "But you came anyway."

"I wanted to see the fireworks show. I mean, there's camp chairs, blankets, little boys, and matches. It doesn't get more exciting than that."

"And sparklers," Benji added.

"And sparklers." Zeke's eyes flashed with amusement. "Who thought it was a *gute* idea to put fire on sticks and let small children wave them around? What could possibly go wrong?"

"They're safe," Alfie said, as if any child should know something so obvious. "And we borrowed four oven mitts from the kitchen so no one's hands will catch fire."

"I must admit, I didn't think you were smart enough to do

something so sensible, Alfie." Zeke winked at Sarah, picked up the thick quilt draped over the back of the camp chair, and wrapped it around Sarah's shoulders. She shivered just a little and sat down. "Your *dat* doesn't know you're here, and he never would have given his permission. If he did know you were here, he would probably get very mad and demand that I leave the state."

"That's about right."

His eyes danced. "It sounds dangerous and very exciting."

"Or foolhardy. I've got twenty-six minutes left." She wrung her hands. The only things keeping her from turning around and walking back into the house were Zeke's smile and his palpable confidence. He made her feel like there was nothing to worry about ever. If he wasn't worried about *Dat* or fire or getting in trouble, she would try not to worry either.

Zeke sat next to her and spread one quilt over his shoulders and another over their legs. "Nice and cozy," he said. "Are you warm enough?"

"Warm enough for twenty-five minutes' worth."

Benji stood in front of Zeke and Sarah and spread his arms in welcome while Zeke shined the flashlight on Benji's face. "*Denki* for coming to our fireworks show. We're *froh* you could make it."

Alfie handed Benji a pair of oven mitts, which Benji slid onto his hands. One was bright red, the other bright purple. Did Rebecca know her sons had stolen her oven mitts? Hopefully, she'd get them back, and they wouldn't be lost in the pasture in the dark. Alfie pulled two sparklers from a box and carefully tucked them between the thumb and pad of each of Benji's mitts. Benji held both arms wide, like a scarecrow, as if expecting they'd burst into flames at any minute.

Alfie pulled a click lighter from his pocket. Where had he gotten that? Did his *mater* know?

Sarah stifled a smile. There was no need to ask herself if Rebecca knew anything about the fireworks show. The answer was quite obviously no. Of the fifty things Alfie and Benji had to do to put on a fireworks show, Rebecca would probably say no to all of them.

It took five clicks, but finally the flame flickered from the lighter. Alfie held the flame to the first sparkler, and it hissed to life. He jumped back as if the ignition had startled him. Then he lit the other sparkler and stepped back. Benji proceeded to wave both sparklers in a circular motion and dance around like a bumblebee. In the meantime, Alfie put a bright yellow oven mitt on his left hand, put two sparklers into the mitt, and lit both of them with his other hand. This created a bigger hiss as both sparklers lighted at once. Alfie tossed the lighter on the ground, slid another oven mitt onto his right hand, and transferred one of the sparklers to his right oven mitt. He joined Benji in their strange dance. It was cute and weird, but also very pretty how the sparklers hissed and popped and gave off brilliant white light and dazzling sparks.

Sarah and Zeke oohed and aahed, and when Alfie threw his sparkler into the air, they didn't panic or scream. It landed mere inches from Zeke's foot, but the snow immediately snuffed it out, and Zeke pretended it was the most normal thing in the world to almost accidentally get his foot set on fire. The remaining sparklers burned out, and Alfie and Benji bowed as Sarah and Zeke clapped and cheered. Mostly they were clapping and cheering that no one had been injured, but the twins didn't need to know that.

Benji peeled off his oven mitts and once again spread his arms wide. "And now for our last firework."

Zeke grinned at Sarah. "Short and sweet."

"Lots fewer chances to set something on fire," she said.

Benji rolled his eyes. "We had a small budget."

Sarah reached out and squeezed Benji's hand. "The sparklers were lovely."

Benji turned to Alfie, who was fiddling with a stick with what looked like a red piece of chalk on the end. Alfie tinkered with the stick for a minute then motioned for Benji to come closer and help. They put their heads together and whispered.

Sarah clenched her teeth. "Nineteen minutes."

Zeke chuckled quietly. "What is waiting for you at the end of your thirty minutes?"

"Benaiah and my *dat* are looking at the seed catalog. Rebecca put Benaiah up to it, and she says I only have thirty minutes before *Dat* will be ready to go."

Zeke turned to look behind him. "I can take you home if your *dat* wants to leave."

Sarah scrunched her lips together. "I'd like that, but *Dat* would never agree. He told you to keep your distance, remember?"

He bloomed into a smile. "You'd *like* it if I drove you home? This is progress."

Sarah cuffed him on the shoulder. "It doesn't matter, because *Dat* won't allow it."

"It matters a great deal. Last week you told me you didn't like me. Now you'd like it if I drove you home. Huge progress."

Sarah rolled her eyes. "I'm *froh* you can see the positive side of it."

"You say your *mamm* and *dat* have been directing your every move since Jerry jumped the fence. I don't wonder but that's been hard."

"Very hard, but it's my own fault. I've held onto this resentment when I should have let it go. I'm not a *gute* person, Zeke. I hold too many bad feelings in my heart. I'm an ungrateful *dochter* and a terrible *schwester*. I'm *froh* Jerry is home, but there's still part of me that can't forgive him. My parents were devastated when he left, and they took out their anger on me. I suffered for Jerry's actions."

He turned so he could look her in the eye. "I don't know Jerry well, but I can't imagine he would do anything to intentionally hurt anyone. I'm sure leaving was a heart-wrenching decision."

"I don't wonder but he was trying to figure things out in the best way he knew how. But he still hurt me."

Zeke nodded adamantly. "Of course he did. I don't blame you for that. You're living with the consequences of Jerry's choices. And it doesn't make you a bad person if you're still carrying the hurt."

He said it so decidedly, Sarah believed him. At least she believed that he believed it. A ribbon of warmth trickled down her spine.

Alfie and Benji were still fiddling with the long stick, which was presumably a mini firework. Alfie set the stick on the ground and frowned at Zeke. "We have to go find a bottle. Wait here. We'll be back." Without another word, the boys took off across the pasture toward the house.

Zeke grimaced. "It looks like the fireworks show isn't going so well. Do you think they'll be back or leave us here in the pasture to fend for ourselves?"

"Whatever they do, it needs to happen in the next fifteen minutes."

"The fireworks show ruined due to the lack of a bottle." Zeke leaned back in his chair and looked into the sky. "Do you think Jerry would have left had he known how it would hurt you?"

"*Jah*. It truly was a heart-wrenching decision. He just couldn't take it anymore. It's exhausting trying to earn *Dat*'s love. Jerry grew tired of trying. When he left, I worked harder to win *Dat*'s approval. Jerry hurt me, but I'm also envious he had the courage to go. I just can't be that brave. I'm afraid of what *Dat* will do if I go against his wishes."

Zeke's eyebrows traveled up his forehead. "You think he'll throw you out?"

"I don't know, but I'm too afraid to find out."

"But don't your parents care what you want?" Zeke asked.

"They think they know what's best for me, and maybe they're right. When Jerry finally came home, he was a miserable shell of what he once was."

Zeke pulled the quilt closer around him. "But if he hadn't made his own choices, he would have wondered forever about what he should have done. Everyone should choose their own path. How can they truly be free if they don't?"

A smile tugged at Sarah's lips. "You're much wiser than I give you credit for."

He acted as if she wasn't saying anything he didn't already know. "*Denki*. You should put that on your list."

"*Nae*. It's a list of your bad qualities."

"You really need to start another list of my *gute* qualities."

Sarah laughed. "It would be very short."

Zeke's jaw fell open in mock indignation. "I don't think so. I have nice thick hair, all my teeth, and an extra toe."

"You have eleven toes?"

"I'm also really fun to be with and very even-tempered."

Sarah tilted her head to the side and studied his face. "You *are* very even-tempered. In the barn, when my *dat* told you to keep your distance, you didn't seem upset at all. Why? He was very rude."

Zeke shrugged, that irrepressible grin stretching across his face. "Because I haven't done anything wrong, and you haven't done anything wrong either. Not in sitting by me in the barn, not in coming outside to see a fantastic fireworks show, not in wanting your own dreams. Your *dat* has his opinion, I have mine, and you have yours. What you want is just as important as what your *dat* wants. Actually, it's more important because it's your life, not his."

She felt the conviction in his thoughts clear to her toes.

He wiped his hand across his mouth and frowned. "I'm sorry. I'm sharing an opinion that you didn't ask for and probably don't want."

What she really wanted was for him to keep looking at her like that. "I wish I were as unconcerned about everything as you are."

"I'm not unconcerned about *everything*. I'm very concerned

that you're having a *gute* time at the secret fireworks show and that you might grow to like me just a little."

"I'm having a *wunderbarr* time at the fireworks show, and I suppose I like you well enough."

He whooped so loudly, his voice echoed off the barn behind them.

She showed him a tiny space between her thumb and index finger. "Maybe this much."

He grabbed her hand and laid a quick kiss on her knuckles. She felt so light, she could have flown into the sky like a firework.

Alfie and Benji came running back to the pasture. "We had to get a bottle to set the rockets in," Benji said. He held up a glass milk bottle, and Sarah didn't want to know where he'd gotten it or if Rebecca knew about it.

"I've only got about five minutes," Sarah said.

Zeke stuffed his hands in his coat pocket. "It might take your *dat* some time to find you out here. I'd bet you've got at least ten."

And what would she do when he did find her? She certainly wasn't ready to be brave. "I think I'd rather not take any chances."

Alfie set the tiny rocket in the bottle and put the bottle on the ground. "Get ready." He pulled a pair of lab glasses from his coat pocket. "Benji, put on your goggles."

Zeke raised his hand. "Can we have goggles?"

Alfie groaned as if Zeke had asked him to donate a kidney. "You don't need goggles. You're the watchers."

Zeke eyed Alfie suspiciously, stood up, and scooted his camp chair back about five feet. Then he grabbed the back of Sarah's chair and pulled her back to be even with his chair as she held on tight. It was an amazing show of strength. He sat down and smiled at her. "I don't trust Alfie as far as I can throw him."

She giggled, then swallowed past the lump in her throat. "Um, are you sure this is safe?"

"Nope."

The look on his face made her laugh harder.

Alfie clicked the lighter and lit the tiny fuse at the bottom of the tiny cylinder. It was so small, how dangerous could it really be? Surely it wasn't big enough to kill anybody, but it could possibly take out someone's eye. Thus, the goggles. Sarah was impressed with how sensible and cautious Alfie and Benji were being. It was very uncharacteristic of them.

The tail flared to life like an oversized sparkler, then erupted, catapulting the rocket straight into the sky. She followed the faintest speck of light as it went up and up. Then it burst into a blaze of fire with a little *plip-plop*. Considering its size, the rocket was quite impressive.

Sarah and Zeke clapped in appreciation, and Alfie and Benji jumped up and down as if they were just as surprised as anybody. Alfie placed another rocket in the milk bottle and lit the fuse. This one went even higher, exploding with a *plip-plop-plip*. Alfie and Benji cheered and patted each other on the back.

Zeke glanced at Sarah. "I underestimated Alfie and Benji. Fireworks were a pretty *gute* idea."

The only lights they had were Zeke's flashlight and an ample sliver of moon. Sarah gazed up at the sky, then at Alfie and Benji getting another rocket ready to launch, then back at Zeke, his handsome face illuminated in the glow cast by his flashlight. A slight breeze chilled her cheeks, and she snuggled deeper into the warm, soft quilt Zeke had draped over her shoulders. "It's perfect," she said.

Zeke had never looked so happy. "*Jah*, it is."

Alfie cupped his hands around his mouth and shouted, "I'm going to do two at the same time."

Zeke stiffened. "That doesn't seem like a…"

Before Zeke could finish his sentence, Alfie lit the two rockets in the bottle and quickly jumped back. The first rocket shot into the air, causing the bottle to tip over just as the second rocket ignited and launched straight at Sarah and Zeke.

Zeke threw himself in front of Sarah, his back to the rocket, his hands clutching the poles on either side of her backrest. He smelled of pine and citrus, though why Sarah noticed at a moment like that was anybody's guess.

The rocket hit Zeke's back with an underwhelming plink, followed by a swooshing sound that could only mean the blanket had caught fire. Zeke jumped to his feet and threw his burning blanket to the ground. Sarah popped up and jerked away from the flames. Alfie and Benji came running, Benji screaming at the top of his lungs, Alfie lugging a substantial fire extinguisher.

Alfie pulled the fire extinguisher's pin, pointed the nozzle at the blanket, and squeezed the lever. A loud hiss was accompanied by a burst of foam that Alfie deftly pointed at the fire. Hmm. Apparently, he'd done that before. Did Rebecca know?

The fire was out in a matter of seconds.

Zeke growled in exasperation. "Alfie, you got my feet."

Benji examined Zeke's shoes and made a face. "For sure and certain, you'll have to get new ones. Fire extinguisher foam doesn't come out easy."

Zeke growled louder. "That was the quilt from my bed. Your *mamm*'s quilt."

Did Rebecca know?

Sarah should really stop asking that.

Alfie's eyes got wide. "You brought *Mamm*'s quilt to a fireworks show? *Ach*, she's gonna be mad at you." Alfie sounded almost relieved that Rebecca was going to be mad at someone besides him for a change.

Sarah caught her breath. There was a singed circle of fabric on the left shoulder of Zeke's coat, obviously right where the rocket had hit him. That rocket could have taken out Zeke's eye. "Are you hurt?" she gasped. "Take off your coat."

Zeke reached his hand over his shoulder and felt around for the hole. "That's gonna leave a bruise." He slipped his coat off his shoulders, and Sarah examined the spot where the rocket had hit. There wasn't a mark on the shirt underneath. Thank *Derr Herr*.

Of course, all that noise was bound to attract attention, and they soon had a kerfuffle on their hands. Even in the darkness, Sarah could see half a dozen people running out to the pasture, and she heard her *dat*'s voice among the murmuring questions. She stiffened and grabbed Zeke's arm as she saw them approach.

Zeke put his coat back on and smiled playfully, as if he hadn't a care in the world. As if Rebecca's quilt wasn't a pile of ashes and fire extinguisher foam. As if he hadn't nearly been maimed by a firework. "You should go while you have the chance. Your *dat* doesn't need to know you were here."

Sarah nearly swooned with gratitude. "*Denki*. That's a very *gute* idea." She shoved her blanket into Zeke's hands and took five steps away before stopping in her tracks. The anxiety in her chest nearly suffocated her, but she turned around and snatched the blanket from Zeke. His eyes flashed with surprise. "I'm not leaving," she said. "I haven't done anything wrong."

"Of course you haven't," Zeke said, blooming into an attractive grin. "But are you sure? Your *dat* isn't going to like it."

"It's time he learned to manage his disappointment instead of counting on me not to disappoint him."

His expression made her heart do a tap dance on her ribcage. "Good for you." He pointed to the smoking pile of fabric. "I'm the one who should worry. Rebecca is not going to be happy about her quilt."

"Rebecca might huff and puff, but I think she'll just be grateful her boys still have all their fingers."

Rebecca came marching across the snow, ten yards ahead of everyone else. It was too dark to make out her features, but Sarah would recognize that angry, purposeful stride anywhere. "Alfie and Benji Petersheim, what have you done?"

Alfie slid the remaining rockets behind his back. "We were doing a fireworks show, but there was an accident, and Zeke ruined your quilt."

"Fireworks! Who said you could do fireworks?"

"*Mamm*, we were doing it so Sarah and Zeke could fall in love."

Sarah's heart did a flip-flop. Was Alfie just blowing smoke, or was he telling the truth? Earlier she'd had a suspicion that the twins were scheming. Was matching Zeke and Sarah what they'd been scheming about? And did that make her happy or uncomfortable? She looked at Zeke's face.

Happy. It definitely made her happy.

Rebecca drew in a deep breath, obviously getting ready for a long tirade, then glanced at Zeke and Sarah and let all the air out again. "Sarah and Zeke, how sweet. You two make a very cute couple." Then, as if Sarah and Zeke had completely disappeared, she started in on Alfie and Benji again. "I've told you not to play with matches a hundred times."

Benji showed Rebecca the lighter. "It's not matches. It's a lighter. *Dawdi* David gave us permission to use it."

"*Dawdi* David can't even talk!" Rebecca yelled.

"He blinks once for yes and twice for no."

Rebecca launched into a very impressive lecture about fire and lighters and the grievous sin of manipulating *Dawdi* to get what you wanted. But Sarah didn't hear much of it because *Dat* found her, yanked the blanket from her hands, and tossed it on the ground. *Ach*, Rebecca's quilts were not faring well tonight.

"Sarah, tell Zeke goodbye. We're leaving."

Thankfully, Zeke kept his mouth shut. She was glad he didn't try to convince *Dat* of their innocence.

The surge of courage she'd felt just moments ago abandoned her, and she didn't know how to stand up to her *fater*. She didn't want to stand up to her *fater*. Not tonight. She was proud of herself that she hadn't run away, but it was late, and there really was nothing left to say. She'd taxed his patience, and he wasn't ever interested in listening to reason. Her resentments and his disappointments would have to wait for another day when they weren't worn out and two dozen curious eyes weren't trained on them.

*Dat* jabbed a finger in Zeke's direction. "I told you to keep your distance, but it seems you are determined to go against me. Another reason I don't want you seeing my *dochter*."

Irritation swelled in Sarah's chest like fast-rising yeast. It was one thing to boss Sarah around. It was quite another thing to pick on an innocent bystander. "*Dat*," she snapped, surprising herself with her boldness. "There is no need to talk to Zeke that way. I'm old enough to make my own choices. I wanted to see Alfie and Benji's fireworks."

Zeke held out his hand in a gesture of peace. "*Nae*, Sarah. It's okay. Tempers are hot, and I don't want any of us to say something we'll regret later."

"I regret nothing," *Dat* said.

"Of course you don't," Zeke countered, in that cheerful, nonthreatening way that Sarah was coming to appreciate more and more. He smiled at Sarah, which considering the tension among them was a huge feat. "I had a wonderful *gute* time tonight. I will see you at the school Christmas program."

Sarah's tongue tied itself into a very complicated knot. *That would be glorious*, she wanted to say. *It would be the best Christmas gift ever. I think I love you.*

*Ach, vell*, she wouldn't say *that*. But she was thinking it.

She frowned. Her heart was running away with her common sense. How could she love Zeke Hostetler? She didn't even like him.

"There…will be a lot of glitter," she stuttered.

*Dat*'s eyes nearly popped out of his head. "You will not be attending the school Christmas program. I've made it very clear. Stay away."

Zeke's eyes flashed with amusement, and he acted as if *Dat* hadn't just bitten his head off. "I'd better go sort things out with Alfie and Benji before Rebecca cancels Christmas altogether." He winked at Sarah and turned away. "*Guti Nacht*. Drive home safely," he said over his shoulder.

"That boy is not coming to the school Christmas program. He doesn't have any *kinner*."

It would be silly to argue with *Dat* about that. He had no say in whether Zeke came or not. And despite his wishes, there was no doubt Zeke would show up. Sarah had seen the determination in his eyes.

*Dat* curled his fingers around Sarah's elbow and pulled her toward the house. "Your *mater* is waiting. Your disobedience has broken her heart and ruined Jerry's wedding day."

Until today, Sarah would have burst into tears and melted into a puddle of shame, but although Dat seemed very angry, she didn't believe him. She believed Zeke. She hadn't done anything wrong. It had been a *wunderbarr* day for Jerry and Mary. They had barely noticed Sarah at all. She certainly hadn't ruined their wedding. And if her spending a few hours with Zeke Hostetler was all it took to break *Mamm*'s heart, then Sarah would be better off not even trying to make *Mamm* happy.

She hadn't done anything wrong.

Sarah couldn't be responsible for her parents' happiness anymore. *Dat* meant for her to feel guilty so she would behave the way he wanted her to, but his expectations were very unfair, as if Sarah's happiness didn't matter at all.

Still, she kept quiet. Let *Dat* accuse her all he wanted. She wasn't going to let it upset her. Not tonight. Not after Zeke Hostetler had smiled at her and saved her from a renegade firework and made her feel like a bowl of quivering gelatin. Not after he'd looked at her like she was the only girl in the world and made her feel as giddy as a lightning bug.

Not after the fireworks going off inside her head.

# CHAPTER 6

*S*arah's heart tried to claw its way out of her throat as she waded through the snowy pasture. She wasn't exactly sneaking away, but *Mamm* and Dat hadn't exactly approved of her escape either. *Dat* was milking the cow, and *Mamm* was still in bed, enjoying her annual Christmas morning sleep-in. Sarah wasn't needed in the kitchen until noon when preparations for family dinner would begin in earnest. Maybe *Mamm* and *Dat* wouldn't even notice she was gone.

She pulled the collar of her coat around her neck. She'd left *Mamm* and *Dat* a note so they wouldn't worry, though they'd be more angry than worried when they found out where she was headed.

Zeke had invited Sarah to Christmas breakfast at the Petersheim house, and Sarah had bravely agreed to go. Rebecca wanted Sarah to see the new table, and Zeke wanted Sarah to sit next to him and let him hold her hand under the table. She knew that because he'd told her so last week. That boy didn't have a hesitant bone in his entire body. He just sort of plowed ahead with his plans and assumed everything would work out. He was too confident by half.

He had more confidence in his little finger than Sarah had in her whole body. She liked him so much. She had always envied her *bruder* Jerry for his courage to defy their *dat*, and she was tired of the oppressive resentment. Did she have the courage to be with Zeke or not?

Despite *Dat*'s stern warning, Zeke had come to the school Christmas program. He sat next to Rebecca and Benaiah Petersheim and beamed at Sarah until the program started. It was a *gute* thing the scholars knew their parts so well because it was almost impossible to concentrate on anything with Zeke that close.

*Mamm* and *Dat* hadn't attended the program, probably because they'd seen some version of it for the last twenty years. Sarah had been a little surprised that *Dat* hadn't come to make sure Zeke stayed away, but *Dat* wasn't used to being overruled, and he probably had no idea how determined Zeke could be.

After the program, Zeke had stayed late and helped Sarah and some of the parents clean the classroom. Then he'd offered to drive Sarah home, so the Millers didn't have to. Surely *Dat* would have come if he'd known how Zeke had plotted against him. Zeke had walked her right up to the front porch, given her a peck on the cheek, and sprinted down the steps as if expecting *Dat* to burst open the door and chase him with a shotgun.

Sarah's feet had not touched the ground for over a week.

And now she was doing something so daring and foolhardy, she feared she was going to get anxiety hives or a heat rash or some other unpleasant skin disease.

Zeke pulled up in his buggy and waved enthusiastically at Sarah. Thank *Derr Herr*, he was prompt. It was cold out there, and the sooner she got in his buggy, the less likely *Dat* would be to catch her. He gave her a playful grin. "*Frehlicher Grischtdaag.* I'm so happy to see you. I feared you wouldn't come."

"So did I. I almost turned back halfway across the yard. It's easy to think about being brave. It's harder to actually do it."

He gazed at her as if she had the answers to all the questions in the world. "Much harder. I'm proud of you."

Sarah lowered her eyes. "You shouldn't be. I didn't even tell my parents I was coming. I left a note. It was cowardly."

He laughed. "I'm *froh* you came, even if you had to write a note."

They pulled up to the Petersheims' house, and both of them slid out on Zeke's side. He held her hand to help her out, and she'd never been so glad she hadn't worn gloves. She loved the feel of his callouses against her skin.

Alfie and Benji were halfheartedly playing in the snow with their dog Tintin. Tintin had a bright red bow tied around his collar, and Benji had a sprig of something green tucked in the top buttonhole of his coat. The boys immediately rushed at Zeke when he got out of the buggy. "Zeke," Alfie moaned. "*Mamm* is in there right now setting the table, and for sure and certain she's going to send us to the zoo right after breakfast."

Benji sniffled into his sleeve. "Or put Alfie up for adoption. You said you'd help us. Why didn't you help us?"

"We helped you," Alfie said, and it sounded like an accusation.

Benji nudged Alfie with his elbow. "We should have prayed harder. You didn't even try."

Sarah glanced at Zeke. "What's wrong?"

Zeke patted Tintin on the head then tapped Alfie's hat down over his eyes. Alfie growled and nudged his hat upward.

"I'm sorry I haven't been here," Zeke said, a smile tugging at his lips. "I helped Andrew make a rocking chair and a cradle this week. I was busy."

Alfie glared at Zeke. "Not too busy to make eyes at Sarah during our Christmas program."

Zeke glanced sheepishly at Sarah. "I guess I was."

A single tear trickled down Benji's face. "And now *Mamm* is going to give Alfie away."

Alfie turned on Benji. "It's not my fault. You're the one who pulled me off the table. Maybe *Mamm* will give you away and keep me to scrub the toilets."

241

Zeke knelt down in the snow next to Benji and put his arm around his shoulders. "I'm sorry I've been busy, but you boys have helped me more than I can ever repay. I told you I'd fix the table, and I'm as good as my word. I fixed the scratch last week."

It was as if somebody flipped a switch. Alfie and Benji squealed and catapulted themselves into Zeke's arms, laughing and showering Zeke with all sorts of affection.

"I told you, Alfie. He kept his promise."

"Zeke, you are the best friend in the whole world. I don't even care if you steal our favorite teacher."

Sarah looked away and tried to pretend she didn't know who their favorite teacher was. The boys' unbridled joy made her smile. She must hear this story.

Did Rebecca know?

Zeke seemed as happy as Alfie and Benji were. His laughter came from deep in his throat. "I would feel terrible if your *mamm* gave you to the zoo, though I bet it would be fun to ride the giraffes."

Benji took Sarah's hand. "Come and see what *Mamm*'s cooking. We're having two kinds of pancakes, bacon, and eggnog. I hate eggnog, but I love bacon."

"I hate eggnog too," Alfie said, "but *Mammi* Martha says it's a Christmas tradition. She's got some crazy ideas."

The boys led the way into the warm house where the heavenly smell of apples and cinnamon, hearty wheat and maple syrup greeted them. Alfie and Benji's *Mammi* and *Dawdi* were already sitting at the table. *Dawdi* David couldn't talk, but his eyes twinkled merrily as if he had many pleasant secrets to keep. He probably did, especially because he and Alfie and Benji seemed to be partners in crime. He sat next to *Mammi* Martha, who was as different from David as she could be. Her gaunt face was dripping with wrinkles, and she had a severe brow and thin, judgmental lips.

Rebecca stood at the stove tending to some pancakes. When Sarah walked into the kitchen, Rebecca turned and pointed to her new dark cherrywood table. "What do you think? Isn't it beautiful?"

"Gorgeous," Sarah said. Fragrant pine boughs ran the length of the table atop a burlap runner trimmed with cream-colored lace. Pinecones and fat, unshelled walnuts were artfully placed amongst the pine boughs, and five candles in brass candlesticks glowed and danced with bright yellow light. The plates were cream-colored stoneware with green napkins and stemmed glasses. "The decorations are stunning."

Rebecca was pleased. "I got the idea from a magazine at the library. But really, the table is so nice, it doesn't need decorations."

Alfie nodded so hard he fanned up a breeze. "It's the prettiest table we've ever seen."

"And not a scratch on it," Benji said.

Alfie nudged Benji so hard, he nearly fell over.

Rebecca ran her hand along the smooth wood. "I should hope not."

*Mammi* Martha laced her fingers together. "You got a bit carried away with the pinecones."

Rebecca picked up her spatula. "I suppose I did, but you can never have too many pinecones. I'm *froh* you could come, Sarah. I hope your *Mamm* can spare you this morning."

Sarah's heart skipped a beat. "I hope so too."

Rebecca's lips twitched as if she was stifling a smile. "She doesn't know you're here?"

"*Nae.*"

Rebecca scrunched her lips together. "*Ach, vell,* I suppose those chickens will come home to roost soon enough. *Cum* and sit." Rebecca pulled out a chair for Sarah at the table. "The German apple pancakes are just about done, and I have a stack of peanut butter pancakes warming in the oven."

"With cream syrup," Benaiah said.

*Mammi* Martha sighed. "Maple was always *gute* enough when I raised my children."

Benji sat next to *Dawdi* David. "We have maple too, *Mammi*." He seemed very happy, apparently because Alfie wasn't going to get sent to the zoo. Or maybe simply because they had two kinds of syrup.

Benaiah sat next to *Mammi* Martha. "You should feel honored, Sarah. This is our first time eating at this table, and you're here to witness it."

"I do feel honored. *Denki* for the invitation."

Rebecca pulled a light-yellow German apple pancake from the oven and set it on a trivet on the table. It smelled heavenly and looked even prettier. A stack of pancakes came next, followed by bacon and a steaming plate of hash browns. "Sit, Zeke, Alfie. Let's pray, Benaiah, before the food gets cold."

Everyone took their places at the table, and Benaiah said, "*Handt nunna*." Sarah bowed her head and prayed that she'd get through breakfast and make it home before *Dat* discovered her absence. It was too late to reconsider her decision now. Her throat constricted. What had she been thinking?

They finished the prayer and passed around the food.

Sarah drizzled a small amount of cream syrup on her pancakes. It looked *appeditlich*, but she didn't want to be greedy. Zeke smiled at her. "I think you're going to want more of that," he whispered. Sarah obliged him by pouring a more generous amount on her plate. She did love cream syrup, and there was a whole pitcher of it. How did Zeke know so much about her without even asking? "These taste so *gute*, Rebecca."

"*Denki*. The pancakes are made from Petersheim Brothers peanut butter."

"My fay-vite," Alfie said, shoveling food into his mouth.

*Mammi* Martha patiently fed David a pancake, while Benji periodically wiped David's mouth and gave him lots of encouragement. "You're doing *gute*, *Dawdi*. Do you want some orange juice?"

Martha glanced at Benji. "Did you wash your hands?"

"Where is the rest of your family today?" Sarah asked.

"They're spending most of the day with their in-laws' families. I suppose it's only fair to share, but I do miss seeing the grandbabies. Lord willing, we'll see them tomorrow for Second Christmas. I'm *froh* you're here, though. I wanted to celebrate Christmas Day with the new table, and it's nice to have a guest. I suppose I was too cautious, but I haven't let anyone touch my new table for almost four weeks."

"Except for Alfie," Martha said. "He's been sleeping on it."

Benji gasped and clapped his hands over his mouth as if he was the one who'd just revealed the horrible secret. Alfie froze like an icicle, and Zeke grinned like he hadn't a care in the world. Everyone fell quiet, and all eyes turned to Rebecca, who was staring at Alfie so hard, she could have seared a hole through his skull.

Sarah flinched when a sharp knock on the door broke the silence. Her heart sank to her toes. She knew exactly who was on the other side of that door. Zeke grabbed her hand under the table. That small gesture gave Sarah a measure of courage, but hardly enough to stand up to her *fater*.

Rebecca pried her gaze from Alfie and looked at Sarah, pasting a painful smile on her face. "The chickens are here to roost."

"Chickens can't knock on doors," Benji said, trying to be helpful.

Benaiah jumped from his seat and raced to the other room, as if he wanted to be anywhere but the kitchen. Sarah heard the front door open. "*Hallo*, Wallace. *Hallo*, Erla. *Frehlicher Grischtdaag.*"

Sarah's chest tightened at the sound of *Dat*'s unyielding tone. "We've come to fetch Sarah. Will you send her out, please?"

Benaiah was a quiet, passive man, who didn't seem to have one assertive bone in his whole body. Was he even aware of the situation between Sarah and her parents? "She's in here just finishing her breakfast."

Sarah thought she might be sick. What had she been

thinking? She shouldn't have come. It would be better if she left so the Petersheims could finish breakfast in peace. *Dat* wouldn't hesitate to make a fuss to get his way. She turned to Zeke. "I...I should go."

"Don't you dare," Rebecca murmured under her breath.

"I don't want to ruin your Christmas," she said weakly.

Rebecca smirked. "Oh, *heartzley*, you can't ruin Christmas. Not even King Herod could ruin Christmas. It's time your *dat* learned to bend." Her expression softened. "Of course, it's your choice, not mine. I should keep my nose out of your business. Heaven knows, I have plenty of my own problems." She gave Alfie and Benji the stink eye.

Sarah looked at Zeke. His gaze was sweet and gooey like creamy pancake syrup. "It's up to you," he said. His calm assurance was one of the things she loved most about him. No matter what, he wouldn't be mad at her or try to get her to change her mind. He wouldn't get his feelings hurt or pout about not getting his way. "Do you want me to talk to your *dat* so your pancakes don't get cold?"

One more thing to love about him. He'd stand up for her if she asked him to.

But she didn't want that. It was time she stood up for herself. She hated being a chicken, and she hated always giving in to her *fater*'s wishes. If she truly wanted to change, if she truly wanted to be brave, what better time than now? And what better reason than Zeke?

She squared her shoulders. "He needs to know how I feel, and he needs to hear it from my own mouth."

Zeke smiled. She could swim in those eyes for a week.

"*Cum reu* and see Rebecca's new table," she heard Benaiah say.

"No need to bother your family. We want to get going."

"It's no bother at all. *Cum reu.*"

Benaiah was like a brick wall, though he surely wasn't trying to be one. If *Dat* wanted to talk to Sarah, he'd have to come in and face everybody. It gave her a measure of comfort. Zeke was a steadying presence, and Rebecca was a fighter. They were on her side.

*Dat* and *Mamm* marched into the kitchen with Benaiah close behind.

Rebecca didn't seem intimidated in the least. "*Frehlicher Grischtdaag*, Wallace, Erla. Don't you love my new table? Andrew and Zeke made it for me."

"It's...very pretty," *Mamm* said, her eyes darting back and forth between *Dat* and Sarah.

*Dat* wasn't about to be distracted. "Sarah, it's Christmas Day. Everyone knows you should be with your family on Christmas Day. Come home now." He put some concern in his voice, probably because there were so many people watching and he wasn't in his own home. Sarah pressed her lips together. Dat loved her, and he was doing his best.

But she refused to live for her *fater* anymore.

Sarah held tightly to Zeke's hand and mustered every ounce of courage she had. It wasn't more than a penny's worth. "Don't worry, *Dat*. I'll be home in plenty of time to help *Mamm* with Christmas dinner." She coughed into her napkin to hide her trembling. "I want to have breakfast with Zeke. Then I'll come home."

*Dat*'s eyes flashed with annoyance, and he lost any pretense of trying to get along. "Sarah Jane Zimmerman, I made myself very clear about that boy."

"He can turn his eyelids inside out," Benji said. "And he likes broccoli."

Zeke's mouth curled upward. "I have very talented eyelids."

Dat pointed at Zeke. "That boy is not for you, Sarah. He's not one of us. You're coming home with us right now."

"He's sitting right here, *Dat*, and his name is Zeke."

"I know what his name is. You will come home now, and you will not see him again."

Zeke's steady, kind gaze never left Sarah's face, but his grip was like a vice around her fingers, and his lips pressed together so tightly, they turned white. He was probably dying to say something, only remaining silent because Sarah had asked him to. The thought warmed her heart. "I already said I'd be home in time to help with Christmas dinner. And I will see Zeke as often as I want. He's a bit too loud at times, but he's *gute* man with a *gute* heart."

Zeke chuckled under his breath. "Is that on the list of things you like about me or don't like about me?"

Sarah nudged his arm. "Both."

*Dat's* face turned bright red. "How dare you contradict me? I am the *fater*, and what the *fater* says is the law of the home. Honor thy *fater* and thy *mater* that thy days may be long upon the land."

Rebecca's lips turned white too. She and Zeke were showing amazing restraint.

"I will always honor you, *Dat*, because it is my duty as your *dochter*, but nowhere in the commandments does it say I must always do what you say."

Dat sputtered on his reply. She had surprised him. She was usually so compliant. "But...but your *mamm* is devastated. She's been crying all morning. Isn't that right, Erla?"

*Mamm* always took Dat's side, but often only half-heartedly. "Won't you please come home? I need help with the pies."

Sarah picked up her fork. "I'll be home at noon, *Mamm*. That will give us plenty of time."

*Dat* narrowed his eyes. Sarah could feel his frustration building like a teapot about to whistle. "Sarah, I didn't want to have to do this, but you come home with us right now, or don't bother coming home at all."

Sarah's heart disintegrated like a smashed bug on the sidewalk, even though she'd been expecting such a threat. She looked at Zeke, who had lost his smile quite some time ago. He smoothed his thumb over the back of her hand.

*Mamm* eyed *Dat* in shock and distress. "But, Wallace, it's Christmas."

"I don't care. She must learn to obey her parents or suffer the consequences."

Sarah took a deep breath and made her choice, suddenly feeling as light as a helium balloon. "Then I won't be coming home. It doesn't matter what you say. I love Zeke, and I'm going to marry him."

*Dat* protested loudly. *Mamm* looked as if she'd just been struck with a dread disease.

Zeke caught his breath and burst into the most beautiful smile Sarah had ever seen. "Really? Are you sure?"

"This is unacceptable," *Dat* interjected.

Sarah ignored her *dat*. "Of course I'm sure. Will you have me, even though I'm mousy and timid and don't have a place to live?"

Zeke laughed. "Will you have me, even though I'm loud and boisterous and you think about me zero percent of the time?"

Sarah had never felt so much happiness. "I have to confess it's more like a hundred percent of the time."

Zeke raised his fist in the air and whooped, then grabbed both of Sarah's hands and kissed them. "I am the most blessed man alive. I'll never need to ask *Gotte* or Alfie and Benji for another thing the rest of my life."

Sarah laughed just for the pure joy of it. "Alfie and Benji?"

"It's a long story," Zeke said, "and you were right. I underestimated them."

Alfie folded his arms. "But you're not grateful enough to get out of our bedroom."

Benji scrunched his face in confusion. "But aren't you glad they love each other?"

Rebecca eyed her boys, a mix of irritation and affection on her face. "You boys did a *gute* thing, but that doesn't excuse your sins." She gave them one last menacing look and turned to Sarah. "You can stay with us, Sarah. We have plenty of room."

*Dat* protested more loudly.

*Mamm* squeaked out her opposition. "It's Christmas. She needs to come home."

Alfie's ears perked up. "Plenty of room? Where will Zeke sleep if Sarah stays here?"

Rebecca cocked an eyebrow. "In the cellar with you."

"What! *Nae, Mamm.* He's too tall, and he stinks."

"Oh, *sis yuscht*, Alfie, have a little compassion. Sarah and Zeke are both welcome here. Sarah shouldn't be thrown out in the cold because her *dat* is too stubborn to let her make her own choices."

*Dat* harrumphed in indignation. "You find it impossible to keep your nose out of our business, don't you, Rebecca? You let Jerry stay here when you knew he wasn't welcome in our home. You went against our wishes and undermined our authority. You should be ashamed of yourself."

*Dat*'s scolding didn't seem to hurt Rebecca's feelings. She heaved a sigh. "For goodness' sake, Wallace, sit down, take a deep breath, and have a pancake before you dig yourself any deeper."

Unsurprisingly, *Dat* did not budge. *Mamm* was also unmoved, but she eyed the peanut butter pancakes as if she thought she might enjoy eating one.

"I will not hear you, Rebecca Petersheim," *Dat* said, trying to look and sound as immovable as a post cemented into the ground. "Unlike your husband, I am the law in my own home."

Benaiah calmly studied his glass of orange juice, as unconcerned as an old work horse after a long day. "If you feel the need to lay down the law, Wallace, then you have lost your authority already. Everything a *fater* does should be done in meekness, persuasion, and sincere love. If you can't bring up your children that way, then you have no authority to begin with."

Rebecca smiled for the first time since *Dat* and *Mamm* had come in the kitchen. "Benaiah is very wise, Wallace. Being Sarah's *fater* does not give you leave to bully her."

*Dat* wilted like a daisy in the heat. "I would never bully my *dochter*. I love her."

Zeke wrapped his arm protectively around Sarah.

Sarah settled into his embrace. "I love you, *Dat*. Everything I've done has been to try to earn your love. But I will never be *gute* enough for you. Jerry found that out when he came home. He had to rely on the kindness of others because his own parents wouldn't forgive him."

*Dat*'s hands trembled. "Jerry hurt us very deeply."

"He hurt me too, but the hurt was doubled because you heaped all your disappointments and fears and expectations on me." Sarah looked at her *dat* and felt nothing but compassion. "I won't give up the man I love to earn your approval. I'm going to live my own dreams and give up trying to live yours."

*Dat*'s eyes were dull, as if he were too tired to fight anymore. "He'll take you to Ohio, and we'll never see you again."

"You've kicked me out of the house. What does it matter how far away I live?"

*Dat* and *Mamm* met eyes. "You know I didn't mean that. We want you to come home. We made so many mistakes with Jerry that after a while, it felt impossible to make up for them."

"It's never too late to make up for a mistake," Rebecca said.

*Mamm* blinked back tears. "We just...we just didn't know how to bear the pain."

Sarah stood and threw herself into her mother's arms. "I know, *Mamm*."

They held each other for a good long time, *Mamm* crying, Sarah basking in the warmth of her *mater*'s touch.

*Mamm* kissed Sarah on the cheek and pulled away. "Can we maybe start over?"

Sarah glanced doubtfully at *Dat*. "What do you think?"

Sarah recognized the moment *Dat* swallowed his pride. "I would like that," he said.

Everyone at the table let out a collective sigh.

"*Vell*, then," Rebecca said. "Do you want to go outside and knock on the door again?"

Dat huffed out a breath. "Can we just eat? I'm starving, and those peanut butter pancakes smell *appeditlich*."

251

Rebecca nodded. "Made from Petersheim Brothers peanut butter."

"Nothing better," *Dat* said, and with that, all was forgiven. Praise Rebecca's peanut butter, and she was your friend for life.

*Mamm* and *Dat* sat down, and *Dat* forked four pancakes onto his plate along with two pieces of bacon and a healthy serving of hash browns. *Mamm* took two pancakes and drowned them in cream syrup.

"The table is beautiful, Rebecca," *Mamm* said. "I love the natural decorations and the chunky candles. So pretty."

Rebecca's lips twitched upward. "*Denki*. It is just how I imagined it." She glanced at Alfie and Benji. "But I must apologize to my family. I should have let you all eat at the table from the very beginning. I've been overly concerned with earthly possessions, when my real blessings are *Gotte*, my family, and my friends. I'm sorry I forgot that."

"We forgive you, *Mamm*," Alfie said.

Rebecca jerked around to look at Alfie. "No need to be so smug, young man."

Benji burst into a grin. "Alfie! Just a minute, Alfie. When Zeke and Sarah get married, we'll get our room back." The twins stood up, wrapped their arms around each other, and jumped up and down.

Zeke's smile was blindingly brilliant. "It's nice to be the reason for so much glee."

Rebecca folded her arms across her chest. "Alfie, Benji, sit down and mind your manners. You will not behave like a pair of wild animals in my house."

"Can we behave like a pair of wild animals outside the house?"

Rebecca leaned forward. "Before you get carried away, I'm warning you that tomorrow you will be cleaning toilets every week for a year."

Alfie's face contorted in surprised indignation. "But *Mamm*, it was just a little jumping around."

Rebecca laced her fingers together and leaned forward, pinning the twins with her sternest expression. "I don't care about the jumping around. What I do care about is someone sleeping on my table and leaving a three-foot long scratch down the center. Three. Feet. Long. Did you think I wouldn't notice the feathers from your pillow on my floor?"

Alfie stretched a horrified smile across his face. "Maybe those feathers were from the chickens who have come home to roost."

"They certainly have," Rebecca said.

Sarah smiled. Did Rebecca know?

Yes.

\*\*\*

Want more of the Peanut Butter Brothers?

Check out more hijinks and mischief from Alfie and Benji Petersheim in The Petersheim Brothers series: <u>Andrew</u>, <u>Abraham</u>, and <u>His Amish Sweetheart</u>.


Yes, she did

# CHRISTMAS PEANUT BUTTER PANCAKES

## Ingredients

- 1 cup flour
- 2 tsps. baking powder
- ½ tsp. salt
- ½ cup Petersheim Brothers creamy peanut butter
- 2 ½ Tbsps. sugar
- 2 Tbsps. avocado oil (or vegetable oil)
- 1 egg
- 1 cup milk

## Instructions

- In a large bowl combine the flour, baking powder, and salt. Set aside.
- In another bowl mix the peanut butter, sugar, and oil until smooth. Add in the egg and milk and mix until well blended.
- Add peanut butter mixture to the dry ingredients and stir until blended, but don't overmix.
- Grease a pancake griddle and heat to medium-medium high heat. Pour batter onto griddle. Flip pancakes when bubbles appear on the surface and the edges look slightly dry. Cook on the other side until golden brown.
- Serve with your favorite syrup, butter, bananas, or berries, or anything else you want.

# ABOUT THE AUTHOR

Jennifer Beckstrand is the *USA Today* Bestselling author of clean romantic comedies, sweet historical Westerns, and Amish romances. Her popular books include *Dandelion Meadows*, *The Matchmakers of Huckleberry Hill* series, *The Honeybee Sisters* series, *The Amish Quiltmaker* series, and *Cowboys of the Butterfly Ranch* series. Jennifer is a two-time RWA RITA® Award finalist, a Carol Award® finalist, and a #1 Amazon bestselling Amish author.

# LOVE BENEATH THE PINE

## TRACY FREDRYCHOWSKI

# CHAPTER 1

$\mathcal{H}$annah Schrock maneuvered her buggy on the slippery blacktop road as the early morning light filtered through the bare maple trees that lined Mystic Mill Road. The snow had fallen gently overnight, adding a fresh layer of white to the Pennsylvania landscape as Hannah rode along the familiar road to the Amish Market and Dry Goods Store, where she worked as a clerk.

Even as dawn started to paint an array of colors above the horizon, Hannah's mind was elsewhere, clouded with worry, prohibiting her from enjoying the start of a new day. Lost in her own thoughts, the rhythmic clip-clop of her horse's hooves failed to calm her anxiety as she tried to concentrate on the puffs of vapor her buggy horse exhaled as he made his way up the slow hill to the market.

Her *grossmommi's* health had been declining steadily, and with it, the medical expenses had grown, threatening to overwhelm their modest means. The thought of her dear *grossmommi* Ellie suffering, both in health and financially, was more than her twenty-year-old body could bear.

Hannah pulled the buggy off to the side of the road to let a few cars pass before turning onto Main Street. The downtown area of Willow Springs would soon be a bustle of activity, with many residents preparing for the upcoming holiday season. The light poles were beautifully decorated with pine boughs, and each store's windows were highlighted with a colorful Christmas display. She would have loved to linger long enough to take in the beautiful displays any other time, but today was different. This year, the worry about their finances troubled her even more fiercely.

The decision to move from her parents' home in Sugarcreek, Ohio, to northwestern Pennsylvania to care for her aging grandmother was easy, but finding the means to do so proved daunting. Although she had always been resourceful, the pressure of the situation weighed heavily on her shoulders, making finding a solution prevalent in her mind.

As the market came into view, Hannah's heart was heavy with the knowledge that her job, though fulfilling, wasn't enough to cover Ellie's growing doctor and medicine expenses.

After securing her horse in one of the stalls behind the market, Hannah pulled her scarf tight and took a determined breath, forcing herself to put her troubles aside to tackle the tasks awaiting her inside.

Stepping into the market, she was immediately immersed in its comforting familiarity—the sights and sounds of the bustling store, enhanced by the cozy warmth from the woodstove situated at the heart of the store. The old-fashioned setup, surrounded by a collection of mismatched rocking chairs, offered her a brief refuge from her whirlwind of worries.

In a matter of minutes, the chairs would be occupied by the local Main Street merchants, a daily ritual as they gathered there before opening their businesses. The constant hum of their friendly chatter would add a sense of community to her day.

Just thinking about how much she loved Willow Springs shifted something within her. The pressure of her responsibilities didn't disappear. Still, they faded momentarily with the realization that she wouldn't need to face the challenges alone, reinforcing the knowledge that her neighbors would rally around her if the need arose. Praying she wouldn't need to go to her *bruder* Henry, the local bishop, for help impelled her to press forward for a solution.

Hannah carefully arranged the rows of neatly stacked preserves and packaged dry goods on the shelves while conjuring every possible resolution. *There must be something more I can do,* she thought, pondering her skills and what she could offer beyond her duties at the market.

Susan Slabaugh, the store's owner, approached Hannah, her steps firm and purposeful. Susan was known in the community for her no-nonsense attitude and keen business sense. Her presence was commanding, yet she had a soft spot for Hannah and her grandmother.

"Hannah, you've been stacking and restacking that shelf longer than the preserves have been in the jars," Susan observed, her voice trickling with an edge of sarcasm.

Hannah finished placing a jar, a faint smile gracing her lips as she turned to face her. "Oh, Susan, it's just… I'm worried about Ellie's medical bills."

Susan looped her arm in Hannah's and guided her to the row of rockers. "Why are you fussing about such things? You know the community will help; all you need to do is go to your *bruder*."

"I know the *g'may* will help, but I want that to be my last resort. I want to find a way to take care of things myself first."

Susan's expression relaxed. "You have a kind and responsible heart, but worry alone won't fill your purse. Let's think practically. There must be a way to generate some additional money quickly."

Hannah nodded, eager for any help Susan could suggest.

"You're good at so many things. What do you enjoy? They say if you do what you love, it won't be like a job."

Hannah rested her chin in her hand. "I don't know. I love gardening, but that won't help, considering it's months before we see the likes of spring."

"*Jah*, not much opportunity there," Susan replied. "Have you considered using your baking skills?" She crossed her legs and propped her elbow on her knee as she thought briefly. "Your frosted cookies are always the talk of the town when you leave a plate on the counter. Why not bake extra and sell them? I bet the *Englisch* would go crazy for them, especially during the holidays."

Hannah's eyes lit up at the suggestion. "Do you think people would really buy them?" she asked, hope seeping through her words.

"For sure and certain," Susan affirmed. "Why don't you make a couple of batches people can sample? We could make a sign and take orders."

The idea sparked a glimmer of hope in Hannah's mind. The thought of using something she loved doing to help support her grandmother filled her with determination, but suddenly, a sinking worry made her frown. "Thank you, Susan. I hadn't considered baking, but…"

Susan held up her hand. "Before you say another word, I know exactly where that worrisome look is coming from. You take whatever you need for supplies from the store."

"Susan, I couldn't!"

"You can and you will. Consider it my investment in keeping my favorite employee rooted in Willow Springs."

Hannah smiled and followed Susan to the counter to wait on a customer. Stepping in closer, Hannah whispered, "I won't take away your blessing, but I'm not sure how I'll ever repay you."

"That's good, because I'm not asking you to," Susan replied joyfully.


IN THE QUIET moments between customers, Hannah's mind raced with the possibilities that lay before her. The idea of baking cookies, not just to ease the financial burden but as a creative endeavor, gave her a sense of purpose she hadn't felt in a long time. She imagined each cookie beautifully decorated like a canvas waiting to be painted.

As she mulled over the flavors and designs, a secret whispered through her mind—a splash of almond flavoring in both the cookies and frosting. It was her secret ingredient, one that made her cookies stand out. She knew that to achieve cookie perfection, she would need to experiment with a few different recipes.

Her mind swirled with possibilities: snowflake shapes dusted with sparkling sugar, delicate angels with wings of white icing, and vibrant Christmas trees adorned in green and red for her *Englisch* customers. Hannah couldn't wait to get home and share the idea with her grandmother, Ellie. She imagined their kitchen transformed into a bustling workshop of confectionary delights, the air teeming with the sweet scent of sugar and spice.

The prospect of turning Susan's suggestion into a tangible reality filled Hannah with hope and determination. As she made her way home, even the brisk evening air couldn't dampen her thoughts of those first cookies emerging from the oven, ready to be shared and savored throughout the community.

Isaac Kauffman stood near the frost-covered window of his mother's kitchen with a mug of steaming coffee, watching Hannah across the street prepare to leave in the early morning light. The snow blanketed outside in a silent beauty, but his heart was anything but quiet. As Hannah guided her horse out of the driveway, Isaac's mind was consumed with an unwavering desire to see that she was taken care of. With each passing day, his love for her grew deeper and deeper. The problem was—she didn't know he existed.

"Whatcha studying so hard?" Isaac's mother followed his stare out the window.

Isaac tipped his chin in Hannah's direction. "I was just

making sure the neighbor didn't need any help getting out this morning."

His mother gave him a sly smile. "I'm certain she won't have a bit of trouble since you keep her driveway cleaner than ours."

Isaac vaguely heard the rest of his mother's comments as he watched Hannah pull out onto the road. To him, she was the essence of perfection. From her bluebird eyes and wheat-colored hair to her infectious smile, her face stayed embedded in his mind from sunrise to sunset. Every part of her radiated a sureness and dedication to her grandmother like nothing he had ever witnessed. That alone left him feeling intimidated, unsure how he could ever measure up to her strength of character.

As her buggy disappeared over the ridge, he wished for the courage to express his true feelings, to step boldly into the role of someone she could spend time with—someone other than just the milk delivery man. Doubt clouded his thoughts, questioning his confidence and making him wonder what someone as special as Hannah Schrock could possibly find in him.

Despite these insecurities, Isaac's deliveries had become the highlight of his week. He cherished the brief interactions with her, holding onto them long after they were over, hoping for a sign that she might one day see him as more than just the boy across the street.

Today, however, Isaac quietly promised to start looking for ways to show Hannah how much he cared, to convey his interest in her somehow. The task almost felt unreachable, but the thought of continuing to watch her from afar, never taking the chance to share his heart's desire, was even more so.

As he put on his barn boots to head outside, he vowed to spend extra time with her this afternoon during his delivery. Then, he could look for any small opportunity to help her and her grandmother. He hoped that small acts of service would show the kindness and nature of his character, laying the foundation for something more to grow between them.

With a new sense of persistence, he stepped outside, letting the crisp morning air fill his lungs. His heart lifted with a twinge of hope. Today might not be the day he confessed his feelings, but it would be a step toward showing her the extent of his affection, one delivery at a time.

~

Isaac walked across the road to Hannah's, carrying his delivery just as the sun set behind the storm cloud brewing in the west. The evening air was biting, making his breath visible as he approached the door. Hannah greeted him with a warmth that seemed to scatter the chill, her smile melting any hint of winter's cold.

"Isaac, come in, come in! You must be freezing," Hannah said, stepping aside to let him enter the cozy kitchen. "I was just about to make us some hot chocolate. Would you like a cup?"

Like a blessing from the Lord, her invitation came unexpectedly, and his heart skipped a beat with the thought of extending his visit. "*Ach... jah*, thank you. That would be wonderful," he managed to say, his voice steadier than he felt inside.

Stepping out of his snow-covered boots, Isaac tipped his head toward Hannah's grandmother, noticing her eyes full of joy, untouched by her illness. "Good evening, Ellie. It's good to see you up and about with a smile on your face."

Ellie's laughter was infectious, much like Hannah's. "Oh, Isaac, my boy, when you walk in faith as I do, there's no room for anything but cheer. The Lord has his plans, and I trust in them."

Isaac couldn't help but marvel at Ellie's strength and faith. Her sincere acceptance of her cancer diagnosis was a testament to her deep spiritual strength. It was a moment of revelation for him, a glimpse into the unwavering faith he saw in Hannah. Undoubtedly, she had a wonderful influence on Hannah, and he found himself more drawn to both women.

"It smells wonderful in here!" Isaac exclaimed.

"*Jah*, my girl's been busy perfecting her recipes all day," Ellie noted.

"All I know is I can't taste another bite of batter, or I'll burst," Hannah added. "My sweet tooth has been pushed to the limit, and I need some fresh tastebuds." Hannah busied herself with preparing the hot chocolate and gracefully placed two trays of cookies in the center of the table. "Susan suggested I make frosted Christmas cookies to sell for the holidays," Hannah explained, her voice bubbling with excitement. "I've tried a couple of different recipes. Would you like to help us taste-test them to see which is best?"

The request, simple as it was, felt like a precious gift to Isaac. It was the opportunity he'd prayed about all day—a chance to be a part of Hannah's world, to share his opinion on something that mattered to her. He eagerly accepted the suggestion, his heart grateful for the unexpected moment.

Isaac sensed Ellie watching them with a knowing smile as they sat around the small table. Isaac tasted each cookie, savoring its flavors and the companionship. He genuinely and enthusiastically offered his thoughts, praising Hannah's knack for making the lightest sugar cookie that melted in his mouth that he had ever tasted.

Without warning, Ellie patted Hannah's hand. "I think the two of you can handle this decision. I'm retiring for the evening." As Ellie stood up slowly, the air in the kitchen shifted to a quieter, more intimate setting. With a gentle smile and a word of thanks for the company, Ellie excused herself, leaving Hannah and Isaac alone in the friendliness of the kitchen, surrounded by the soft glow of the overhead oil lamp.

Hannah filled their cups with fresh hot chocolate, adding a heaping spoon of whipped cream to each mug. It wasn't long before she told him about the reason behind her newfound baking venture. "I thought maybe if I could take orders for cookies, it could ease some of the financial burden."

Isaac listened intently as Hannah revealed her plans. He

fought to remain silent, reminding himself that she didn't need a problem solver, but a supportive friend. Yet, as he listened, he began to see the value of simply being there for her.

He continued to let her pour her heart out to him, his admiration for her growing with each word. The determination to support her grandmother's needs and her willingness to share her concerns with him touched a deep chord within him. He wanted to help and be part of her solution.

"The only issue," Hannah continued, gesturing toward the cramped space of the small kitchen, "is the size of this table and the lack of storage space." She pointed to the boxes of baking supplies littering the floor. "I wish I could figure out how to organize my baking supplies and have more room to roll out cookies. I also need a place to let them cool before frosting them."

Ever the problem-solver, Isaac finally spoke up after seeing the opportunity to propose his assistance. "I'm sure we have extra shelving in the storage barn that would work perfectly for storing your supplies and leaving some shelves in the middle to cool cookies." He stood up and walked off the measurement of the empty wall. "And maybe, if we can find another table, you could move this small table to the end of the counter to extend your workspace to the corner."

The idea seemed to light a spark in Hannah's eyes. "That's a wonderful idea," she said, her spirits visibly lifted until she considered the cost of such changes. "But… I wouldn't have any extra money to buy a bigger table."

Seeing the distress suddenly etched on her forehead, Isaac quickly added, "Now, let's not get ahead of ourselves. Let me look around the farm first. I'm certain my *datt* would be happy to donate anything we're not currently using for a good cause like this. I'm almost certain I saw an old table in the back of the barn at one point."

Hannah's smile at his response was all the confirmation he needed. The thought of working together on this project gave him a sense of purpose and joy he hadn't expected when he'd delivered her order earlier.

As his visit ended, Isaac wished he didn't have to leave. He wanted to explore his new connection with Hannah and their plans to improve her baking setup. He offered a heartfelt "good night" as he prepared to leave, his mind racing with ideas for the kitchen project.

~

HANNAH CLOSED the door behind him, and an awareness of wonder engulfed her. His bid to help lingered in the air like a promise of spring in the depths of winter. She leaned on the door for a moment, allowing herself to process the evening's events, the heat of his presence still heavy in the room.

His kindness surprised her, adding a light she hadn't noticed before. It was as if she had seen him for the first time in the two years she had lived in Willow Springs. Suddenly, he was not just the young man who delivered eggs and milk, but someone with a heart of kindness. Something stirred and shifted inside her, leaving her unsettled. How had she overlooked his gentle demeanor and his thoughtful nature when he'd been right there, across the road all along?

It was more than his willingness to help that touched her so deeply; it was his uncanny way of not rushing in to voice his own opinions. It was a rare quality in a young man she hadn't experienced before.

She replayed their conversation, each word, each gesture. His hazel eyes seemed to dance before her in the quiet of the night; his hair, the color of autumn leaves, curled just slightly at the edges of his hat, a detail she hadn't noticed before. The image of him, so vivid and so real, accompanied her into her dreams, clouding her sleep with curiosity at his sudden interest in her.

As the first light of dawn crept through the window of Hannah's room, she awoke with a start, the lingering dream mixing with the reality of life. The thoughts of Isaac, which lured her to sleep, now felt like a luxury she couldn't afford. She lay there staring at the ceiling, trying to recreate the affection she felt toward him last night with the cold, hard duties that awaited her that morning.

Her mind raced as she considered her grandmother's frail health, the endless list of chores, and the financial strain they were under. The idea of allowing Isaac into her life seemed almost selfish, given her commitment to Ellie. The very thought made her feel guilty about thinking of her own happiness.

With a heavy heart, she pushed Isaac from her mind, tucking him away until another time. She reminded herself that she'd promised to care for her grandmother, which took precedence over fleeting schoolgirl emotions. The vow hardened something within her, creating a barrier against the longing in her heart.

Preparing for the day, she consciously decided to distance herself from him. She would be polite, of course, but she promised herself that she would keep their interactions friendly at most. She couldn't afford to let his kind and gentle demeanor sway her from her current path. Though the thought ignited a silent passion within her, they were distractions she couldn't afford.

# CHAPTER 2

$\mathcal{H}$enry Schrock, Hannah's oldest *bruder* and the local bishop, made his presence known with a deliberate stomp of his boots on the porch to shake off the snow before knocking on the door. Upon Hannah's invitation inside, he stepped into the kitchen's warmth, hoping his visit would be well received. The familiar scents of baking cookies and brewing coffee surrounded him, a comforting reminder of the many visits to their grandmother's home.

After exchanging morning pleasantries, he removed his black wool hat and pulled out a chair, accepting Hannah's cup of coffee. "Hannah, we need to talk," he began. "It's come to my attention that you're struggling to care for Ellie and her unexpected expenses." He paused to take a sip of the steaming liquid. "I wish you would have come to me..."

Hannah interrupted, "It's not your responsibility. I took on the job as her caregiver, knowing that came with supporting her financially."

Henry quickly added, "That's not how this family works, and you know it. Let alone the *g'may* not stepping up to help cover medical costs."

"But I didn't want to burden the community unless necessary."

"Hannah... now come. You know, asking for help is not a burden to anyone in our church district. It's the heart of our existence."

"That's beside the point," Hannah mumbled. "I'm plenty capable of taking on some extra work to make sure things are taken care of."

Henry picked up a warm cookie off the center of the table and nibbled on it before replying, "I'm sure you are, but Maggie and I have been discussing it, and we think we have a solution. Our home is big enough for all of us, and if you move in with us, Maggie can help you care for Ellie."

"Oh, Henry. We couldn't. Maggie has enough to do with your *kinner*; she doesn't need two more mouths to feed."

Henry nodded. "Then perhaps it might be time for you both to consider moving back to Sugarcreek, where *Mamm* and *Datt* can help more."

Hannah paused, her hands still dusted with flour, as she processed his words. "I appreciate your offer, I really do," Hannah answered, her voice unsteady. "But I can't take Ellie away from her home, not at this time in her life. I promised to take care of her, and I intend to do just that, even if it means I do without a few things and do it alone."

Henry felt a familiar heaviness in his chest at his youngest *schwester's* stubbornness. "Hannah, we're family. You shouldn't have to face these challenges by yourself. Why won't you let me help the best I can? Or at least let me go to the deacons and ministers to seek support."

The conversation between them grew tense, a clash of wills surrounded by love and concern for their grandmother's well-being. After a moment of silence, complete with the soft ticking of the kitchen clock, Hannah relented, but only partially. "I'll accept some financial help, but only with her medical costs. The care of the house, the groceries, that's on me. I'll find a way to manage, support Ellie, and honor the responsibility I've taken on."

Henry sighed, respecting Hannah's decision. "I admire your stewardship, but please remember you're not in this alone. Our community is here to help and share in each other's trials and difficulties. You and Ellie are no different."

"Thank you, Henry. I know you're right. It's hard to admit when we need help, but I promise to remember our values and traditions are there for a reason—to lift one another up when needed."

As Henry prepared to leave, he placed a reassuring hand on Hannah's shoulder. "Ellie is blessed to have you."

"*Jah*, and I'm honored to be her caregiver." Hannah smiled up at him. "Thank you for checking on us, but really, Henry, I'm capable of caring for her needs, even if it means I must work a little harder."

"You'll make someone a fine *fraa* someday, little *schwester*," Henry replied.

Hannah giggled. "Being someone's wife is the furthest thing from my mind right now." Hannah held out her flour-dusted hands. "I can't see past cookie orders at the moment."

Henry pulled his wool jacket on and snagged another cookie off the table before leaving.

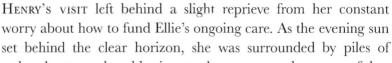

HENRY'S VISIT left behind a slight reprieve from her constant worry about how to fund Ellie's ongoing care. As the evening sun set behind the clear horizon, she was surrounded by piles of order sheets, each a blessing to the unexpected success of her Christmas cookie venture.

The overwhelming response had caught her completely off guard. What had started as a small addition to her clerk's job at the market had ballooned into a daunting challenge. With each new order, her doubt grew. The fear of being unable to fulfill all the orders started to weigh heavily on her.

The sound of Isaac's delivery wagon pulling next to the kitchen door tore her away from the stack of orders scattered across the table. Silently remembering the vow she had taken just that morning, she greeted him with a smile that didn't quite reach her eyes, a clear signal of her intention to maintain a pleasant but firm distance as she opened the door.

Three wire storage racks were strapped down in the back, which he quickly undid and carried to the small porch outside the kitchen door.

"What's all this?" she asked curiously.

"The shelves I mentioned. *Datt* was happy to lend them to you for as long as needed."

Hannah stepped back and held the door open as he carried the first one in. He placed it against the far wall and added, "I'm pretty sure all three will fit perfectly in this space."

Hannah waited until he placed the other two before shutting the door. She mopped up remnants of snow that he had carried in on his boots and stood back to admire the new addition to the small kitchen. "*Ach*, Isaac, I can't thank you enough. This will be such a big help in organizing supplies and orders."

Isaac removed his hat and coat and hung them on the peg by the door. "Are those orders?" he asked, his tone hopeful.

Hannah let out a small sigh, gesturing toward the sea of paper. "All these orders came in just this week—I didn't expect so many. I'm worried I won't fill them all in time."

Before Hannah could continue, Ellie chimed in from her chair in the living room. "Hannah, my dear, we're a team here, and I'll help."

Hannah looked at Isaac, her eyes conveying doubt about how much help her grandmother could offer. Ellie's simple words, lined with love, brought a flicker of hope to Hannah's heart. Despite her grandmother's limitations, it reminded her how much Ellie lived for the moment.

"I'm not sure how she does it," Hannah whispered. "Her mind says she wants to help, but her body isn't cooperating much these days. I let her do what she can, but she tires quickly."

"Maybe that's all she needs," Isaac murmured quietly, "reassurance that she's still useful."

Hannah sucked in a silent breath. "You're so right."

Isaac wasted no time securing the shelves together to prevent tipping and leveling them to perfection before allowing Hannah to add her supplies. Before long, they had organized all the baking supplies and left a few shelves open to be used for cooling racks.

Hannah turned up the oil lamp above the table as the sun finally set over the snowy landscape between her home and the Kauffman farm across the street. She looked in on Ellie, who was napping, and then offered Isaac a glass of milk to wash down the cookies he was snacking on. A sense of accomplishment and order warmed her heart as she sat at the table across from Isaac.

"How will I ever thank you for helping me get organized?" she asked as she sipped her tea.

ISAAC TOOK a moment to savor the milk, a perfect complement to the warm cookies he had happily sampled. The warmth of Hannah's kitchen, the company, and the sense of purpose he felt by helping her created an atmosphere that was hard to leave.

"Well, you could start by not allowing me to eat any more of these cookies," Isaac joked, gesturing to the plate between them. "I'll be rolling out of here if I keep this up."

Hannah giggled, her voice sweet to his ears. "And here I thought I was doing you a favor, letting you taste-test. I'll have to find someone with more self-control next time."

The easy banter between them added a new layer to their relationship, which he found surprisingly comfortable. "Seriously, though," Isaac continued, leaning back in his chair, "how can I help you with these orders?"

Hannah raised her eyebrow. "You want to help me bake?"

"If that's what you need me to do. I'm a quick learner."

"I can see it now—frosting on the floor, flour in the rafters, and sugar coating every surface."

"Now come, Hannah, you're not giving me much credit. I can be a lot of help in the kitchen. Just ask my *mamm.*"

HANNAH LET OUT a nervous sigh and reminded herself of the importance of her responsibilities. She felt a twinge of sadness before refusing his help. "Sounds wonderful, but there's hardly enough room in this kitchen for me, let alone stumbling over you." Hannah waved a hand toward the shelving units. "Just being able to see what I have has helped immensely."

Isaac's shoulders sank slightly before he replied, "I almost forgot. I've stumbled onto something in the storage barn that might work perfectly for you. It's an old table, but it needs some work. It's much larger than what you have now, and I reckon it could fit right in here with a bit of cleaning and fixing up."

Hannah looked at him, surprised at his find. "You'd do that for me? I surely don't want to add more to your workload than I already have."

"It's no imposition at all," Isaac assured her. "Consider it my part in helping you make your cookie business a success."

"Your *datt* won't mind me using it indefinitely?"

"I already asked him, and he told me that the old table has already passed through most of his family, and it's only right that it should find a new purpose."

"I must admit I love restoring old things and breathing new life into pieces that hold a history. How big is it?" she asked.

"I didn't measure it, but if you have time, we can look at it before you go to work in the morning. Then I can work on getting it out of the back room after my morning chores."

Hannah sighed with relief but knew she shouldn't encourage spending more time with him than necessary. "I'm not sure I'll have time."

Isaac stood and took a few seconds before he responded, "I promise it will only take a few minutes."

"Okay, then," she answered, unsure of her decision. "I won't have but a few minutes before I need to head into the market."

As Isaac left for the evening, Hannah felt a surge of sadness and gratitude. She marveled at his willingness to give more of himself than was expected but was ashamed that she had disappointed him.

A WINTER HUSH covered the air as Hannah crossed the road to meet Isaac at the storage barn early the next morning. The beam of her flashlight cut through the predawn darkness. The world was waking up around her as a distant rooster welcomed in the day.

As they entered the barn, a sense of anticipation hung in the air, mixed with the musty smell of hay and old wood. The barn, a treasure of memories and forgotten items, held a special silence that spoke of the Kauffman family's history.

Isaac led the way, his memory guiding them to the corner where the antique pine table was stored. "It should be right over here," he said. He moved aside a few boxes, revealing the table under a dusty canvas.

With eagerness, they pulled off the covering, exposing the table to the dim light of their flashlights. "It's larger than I expected. Are you sure it will fit?"

"I'm almost certain of it," Isaac pointed out.

"It's beautiful," Hannah whispered, running her hand over the well-worn pine planks.

Isaac smiled at her reaction. "I thought so, too. With some work, I think it can be the perfect worktable." He brushed a few cobwebs from the legs and looked at her tenderly. "I thought… maybe we could work on it together."

His simple yet profound proposal sent her heart fluttering, but she had to stop any inclination he had about the two of them quickly. "I really don't think I have the time for such a project," she ran her hand over the aged wood again. "I suppose I will have to make do with what I have. But I certainly appreciate you going to all this trouble of showing it to me."

Rays of sunlight danced in the gaps of the barn, highlighting the dust particles floating like little stars in the air as Isaac disclosed his vision for the old table. He tried to convince her that the table could be just like new with a little sanding and a new coat of varnish. His excitement was contagious, and he turned to her with hopeful eyes, asking again if they might tackle the project together. Hannah felt a tug in her heart.

"It's not much now, but it could be beautiful and wouldn't take long if we tackled it together," he said.

Hannah stepped over a couple of boxes and moved away from the clutter. "I think it's a fine table." Yet, as they stepped out of the barn, her responsibilities pressed down on her shoulders with a harsh dose of reality. The notion of spending time together, working side by side with him, was tempting, offering a glimpse of what could blossom into something deeper if she would allow such things.

Gathering her nerve, her voice cracked with regret as she responded, "I appreciate your offer more than you know, but… I… I can't. My responsibilities to my grandmother, my job, and caring for the house are too great, and I must focus all my energy there. I can't allow myself to be distracted, not even by something as generous as your proposition."

With disappointment in his eyes, Isaac replied, "I understand. I just thought it might be nice to work on something together."

Hannah felt a pang of guilt, knowing his intentions were pure but also knowing the stakes were too high for this time in her life. "Your kindness means the world to me, but the less I divert my attention, the better I'll be able to concentrate on my grandmother's needs." She waited and looked to the ground, refusing to meet his eyes before adding, "It's just not the right time for me to consider such notions." As she walked away, she prayed her words expressed her appreciation, and explained her refusal.

∼

AFTER WATCHING Hannah's buggy disappear into the landscape, Isaac returned to the day's chores, a familiar routine that kept him grounded yet allowed his mind to wander. The few minutes he spent with Hannah had left a mark on him; a sense of disappointment pumped through his veins, chilling him deeper than the coldest morning of December thus far.

As he settled onto his stool beside his favorite dairy cow, his thoughts drifted back to Hannah. He imagined them working together, sanding and repairing the old pine table, sharing stories and laughter. The image was so vivid in his mind that a hopeful glimpse of his longed-for future faded in a sea of sadness.

The rhythmic motion of streams of milk hitting the aluminum bucket provided a backdrop to his daydreams. Each squirt of milk reminded him of the life he hoped to share with a *fraa* someday—one deeply rooted in the traditions of Amish life. His only desire was it would include Hannah.

Guiding his delivery wagon through the back roads later that morning, Isaac couldn't help but daydream about Hannah. But after her refusal and determination to shoulder life's burdens alone, he struggled with feelings of rejection and disappointment. *Is it really so impossible for her to see a future for us?* he wondered with a heavy heart. *Or is it that she won't even consider the possibility?*

Maneuvering his delivery cart to his next stop, his mind kept

278

returning to the same thought. *I must be patient. I need to show her that I'm here, not just for the moment, but for all the moments to come.*

He stopped at the home of one of his elderly neighbors to deliver a small order—just a quart of fresh milk. Despite the cold, the man was sitting on the porch wrapped in a heavy quilt, smoking a pipe. His eyes twinkled when Isaac walked up the stairs.

"Isaac, come sit a moment. You're always in a rush," he said.

Respecting the man's request, Isaac joined him on the porch, settling the milk near the door. "Good morning. How are you today?" Isaac inquired.

The man waved the question off with a chuckle. "Oh, the same as yesterday and the day before that. But tell me, boy, when are you planning to settle down?" Without letting Isaac answer, he blew out a puff of smoke and continued, "By the time I was your age, I had two little farmers to trip over. The Lord tells us to be fruitful and multiply, *jah* know?"

Isaac felt a sudden rush of warmth land on his cheeks at the unexpected direction of the man's question. It wasn't common for men to talk about such things, and he was caught off guard by the man's forthrightness.

Isaac stuttered an answer, "That's… well, that's a matter for the Lord to decide, I'd say." He paused and took a silent breath before continuing. "Right now, I'm focused on helping my family build our delivery business and helping in the community where I can."

"Hogwash!" the old man declared. "I was young once. I know there's more on your mind than milk and eggs." The old man snickered and rolled his eyes in a manner that left little to Isaac's imagination… to a point he felt his face flush yet again.

The elderly neighbor leaned forward and whispered, "You know the Lord helps those who help themselves, and you're not going to find a *fraa* by sitting back and letting life pass you by."

Isaac shifted uncomfortably, aware that further discussion

might stray too close to his private thoughts concerning Hannah. "I appreciate your concern. But these things are in *Gott's* hands."

The man nodded, his expression softening. "Of course they are. Just don't forget to listen when He speaks. Sometimes, the heart hears before the head understands."

Isaac waved to the old man as he climbed back into his cart, hoping the true condition of his heart wasn't evident on his face at the man's questions.

~

HANNAH STOOD BEHIND THE COUNTER, her hands busy filling containers with bulk foods, trying not to stare at the young couple in the corner. As they spoke in hushed tones, their eyes locked on each other, and smiles played on their lips, the space around them seemed to fill with tenderness.

As she watched them, an unfamiliar longing tugged at her heart. She couldn't help but notice the couple lean towards each other; the tender way they communicated without words left her yearning for something she did not know. Suddenly, the market around her came alive with expressions of love and connection. Customers warmly chatted privately with an unspoken admiration for each other. Unexpectedly, she ached for companionship and love.

*Why now, Lord?* she wondered silently. *Why show me these things when my life is full of responsibilities?* The questions lingered in her mind, unanswered as she returned to her duties.

Susan moved to her side with a knowing look.

"Did you need something?" Hannah asked a little too quickly, trying to mask her brooding.

Susan tipped her chin toward the young couple in the corner and asked, "I was just wondering when you'll settle down and start your own family."

The question invaded Hannah's thoughts. "Susan! You know we aren't to talk of such things... those things are private," she replied, her cheeks coloring slightly. "And besides, with everything going on with Ellie, I hardly think now is the time for me to consider… such things."

Susan chuckled, not unkindly, and placed a hand on Hannah's arm. "Love, family… it's all part of *Gott's* plan, even when we're busy with other responsibilities. That's usually when the good Lord tries to get your attention the most."

Hannah was silent for a moment, contemplating Susan's words. The truth was undeniable, yet the timing felt all wrong. How could she think of herself when her grandmother needed her more than ever? "I appreciate your concern, but my focus is on Ellie and filling these cookie orders and nothing else."

Susan nodded and gave her a slight elbowing. "Of course. But remember, the heart has a way of making its own plans, even when we think we're too busy for them."

Trying not to let her irritation show, Hannah replied, "I know, but now's not a good time to consider such things. Besides, it's all I can do to get through each day. Anything more seems… impossible."

The conversation ended when a customer called Susan away, but Hannah continued to ponder Susan's words. They only magnified what had been stewing in her mind all morning. Despite her resistance to his attentions, Isaac's presence in her life was becoming more meaningful. The mere thought was both daunting and wistfully appealing.

# CHAPTER 3

resh snow covered the ground, and the final remnants of light tucked themselves behind the horizon as Isaac made his way to the storage barn. His earlier visit with Hannah had left him more determined than ever to prove he was worthy of her attention. He navigated to the back of the barn, where the table lay hidden under years of accumulated dust and forgotten memories.

The workshop, usually used for farm equipment repair, was quickly converted into an area that allowed plenty of room to restore the antique table, regardless of Hannah's lack of interest in helping. He could almost hear the sandpaper against the wood and the smell of pine filling the air as he stripped years of wear from the forgotten piece of furniture.

Isaac and his *bruder* maneuvered the table into the newly cleared workshop, and Isaac concentrated on positioning it at the perfect angle to utilize the shop for his restoration project. He was putting a lot of hope onto the table; however, his *bruder* had other ideas.

"You're putting a lot of effort into this old piece of wood. All for Hannah, huh?" His *bruder's* tone was skeptical, questions hanging between them.

Isaac wiped his brow on the back of his hand and took a shop rag to wipe the dust off the tabletop. "*Jah*, for Hannah. She needs more workspace, and this will work perfectly for her needs."

His *bruder* crossed his arms, leaning back against the workbench. "I saw a notice at the market. She's opening a cookie business, isn't she? Seems like she's got ambitions beyond what you're offering. If you ask me, she's too wrapped up in her job, caring for her grandmother, and now this new business venture to consider anything else. Maybe you're wasting your time."

Isaac's jaw tightened slightly, but he kept his composure. "Her dedication to Ellie and her passion for baking… that's part of why I… admire her," he chose his words carefully, not wanting to reveal the true condition of his heart. "She's got a good heart and a strong spirit, and that's just as important. *Jah?*"

"But don't you want someone who'll focus on home and family?" his *bruder* pressed. "Someone without all these crazy notions about running a business?" His *bruder* propped himself up on the workbench. "If I were you, I'd be looking for someone with a little less responsibility and someone who took more interest in supporting my work than starting her own."

"I'd say that might be why you still aren't married either, ain't so?" Isaac snapped back.

Without adding more fuel to his *bruder's* obvious warnings, Isaac didn't want to get into a heated conversation about the real reasons why Hannah was starting a cookie business. "It's not a silly notion. It's something meaningful to her, and I want to help however I can."

His *bruder* sighed, shaking his head. "Well, it's your life… I hate to see you put so much time into something that may not go anywhere besides this old table."

After his *bruder* left the workshop, Isaac returned to the table, running his hands along the worn wood. Regardless of the outcome, he was determined to put forth the effort. He knew it was right no matter how much time he invested into the project.

After turning off the kerosene oil lamp, he returned to the

house, his mind churning with thoughts of the table and its potential. The evening's work had left him feeling connected to the old table, but he realized he knew little of its history. Seeking answers, he found his parents in the living room, the glow of the woodstove heating the large room.

"*Datt*, I moved that old table we're giving to Hannah from the back of the barn to the workshop." Isaac sat on the edge of the coffee table and asked, "I'm curious about how it ended up there. I don't remember it ever being in the house. Where did it come from?"

His father looked over his wire-rimmed glasses perched on the tip of his nose and replied, "It belonged to my grandparents some seventy years ago."

A hint of nostalgia tickled his mother's voice as she inserted, "We started our marriage around that table."

His father nodded, a gentle smile on his lips. "*Jah*, then we had too many kinner to fit around it, and I had to buy a bigger one."

"After his grandparents, the table went to his parents. It served them well during those hard times," Isaac's mother said.

"Exactly," his father affirmed. "But once my father built a new table, it went to your Uncle Jacob and ended up here some thirty years ago." He winked at his mother and stated, "It was where your mother served me our first meal together. Chicken and dumplings if I remember correctly. The best meal I ever had!" he exclaimed as he patted his expanding waistline. "And one too many after that."

Isaac smiled and nodded, absorbing the table's history. *Hannah would love to hear this*, he thought.

As their conversation wound down, a flick of intrigue sealed the air as Isaac's father leaned in slightly, gave his wife a knowing smile, and declared, "You know, that table holds more than memories and meals. There's a reason it's been passed down through our family and found a spot in the storage barn until the right time came along."

"What do you mean? Is there something I should know about the table?"

A smile played on the corner of his mother's mouth. "The table… it's been said to carry secrets of its own. Secrets that are only revealed to the keepers of the table in due time."

Isaac's curiosity was piqued. "Secrets? What kind of secrets could a table possibly hold?"

"*Ach*, Isaac, some things are meant to be discovered, not told," his mother whispered. "When the time is right, you will uncover what's meant to be revealed." A glow Isaac couldn't explain spread across his mother's face as she explained the importance of the table's history. "Just remember, the table has been a silent witness to the lives gathered around it. It's more than wood and nails; it's the keeper of stories preserved in time."

Isaac's mind raced with the possibilities. What could these secrets be? And how would they be revealed? The idea that the table he was about to restore might hold a mystery added a new, exciting layer to the project.

"Thank you," Isaac replied.

His father nodded, satisfied. "Good. Remember, every piece of our past has something to teach us. And if you let it, honor it and be open to the lessons it has to share."

As he made his way to his upstairs bedroom, Isaac was more eager than ever to begin the restoration, not just for Hannah, but for the secrets it might reveal.

A FEW DAYS LATER, Isaac stepped into Hannah's kitchen with an order of eggs and butter. Once inside, a comforting blend of sugar and spice lined the air. The kitchen was a flurry of activity, with Hannah amid her baking, her focus unwavering on the orders demanding her attention.

Sitting at the table, filling small white boxes with cookies, Ellie offered Isaac a weak but sincere smile, a gentle reminder of her current condition. "Isaac, dear, it's good to see you," she greeted him softly.

"Good to see you too, Ellie. How are you feeling today?"

"Ready for a nap," she replied, using her cane to direct herself back into her chair near the stove in the front room. The kitchen suddenly felt smaller; the space between him and Hannah charged with an unspoken connection.

"I moved the table to the workshop at the front of the barn," Isaac said, hoping she would be interested in its progress.

Hannah, apron-clad and dusted with flour, barely paused stamping cookie designs into the rolled-out dough. Without looking up from her task, she said, "Isaac, I already said I don't have time to devote to the table right now." Her voice edged with frustration. "I can't think about anything but what's in front of me."

Taken back by her brisk attitude, Isaac tried to ease her irritation. "Then let me help you with these orders. It'll be quicker with two pairs of hands," he suggested, eager to find a way to ease her burden.

But Hannah was unwavering, her walls firmly built. "Thank you, but no. I've got this under control," she insisted.

"Hannah, I'm just trying to find a way to be helpful. I don't understand why you have to be so hardheaded." The refusal stung more than Isaac wanted to admit. He had come with hopes she would have changed her mind, only to find the wall she had erected around herself was sturdier than before.

With her hands still on the dough, her irritation at his persistence was evident. "Because this is my responsibility, my burden to bear," she spat. "I don't need your help, and I don't have the time or energy to explain why," she said sharply.

Isaac tried hard not to let his disappointment show, but he added, "Have you ever heard the term *gracious receiver*?" When she didn't respond, he turned toward the door and accepted her decision, though his disappointment was evident. "Alright, but if you change your mind about the table... or need my help with anything, you know where to find me."

THE STORM DOOR banged so violently that Hannah crumpled in a chair, burying her face in her hands. She couldn't help but think she'd just pushed him away for the last time. Her heart ached with the realization that she had isolated herself from the possibility of love and companionship in her attempt to prove to herself that she could do it all without anyone's help. She cared more than she dared to admit, but the fear of relying on someone else and being vulnerable held her back.

"Why bring Isaac into my life now?" she whispered in the kitchen's quiet. The question hung in the air as she wrestled with her doubts and fears. When the buzzer rang to signal another batch of cookies was ready to be removed from the oven, she began to ponder whether perhaps the greater risk lay not in opening her heart but in keeping it closed.

AFTER FINISHING HIS AFTERNOON CHORES, Isaac worked alone in the workshop; the quiet of the winter afternoon surrounded him with the fading sun. The silence was only broken by the soft scraping of sandpaper against the aged wood. The forgotten table succumbed to his gentle touch to bring it back to life. His father, a sturdy pillar in the Amish community, entered the barn, his broad form filling the doorway.

"How's it coming along?" he asked, scanning the progress Isaac had made on the table.

"Good. I think it will be beautiful when I'm finished."

His father nodded, appreciating all the hard work his son had put into it thus far. After a moment, he ventured further, stopping at Isaac's side. "I've noticed you've taken a special interest in our neighbor that may go beyond repairing this old table. Ain't so?"

Isaac stopped his work, the question catching him off guard. He looked up, meeting his father's eyes with a question of his own. "Isn't that what the Lord calls us to do... to help our neighbors?"

The old man's long-grayed eyebrows danced as a smile spread across his face. "I feel your plans go further than neighborly kindness, son."

"If you're asking me if my intentions are honorable, I can promise you I want to respect our ways and take things slowly... one step at a time."

His father studied him briefly before asking, "And Hannah, how does she feel about all this?"

Isaac felt uneasy as he admitted her reaction to his latest offer to help ease some of her burdens. "I doubt she has the same thoughts in mind."

His father listened intently, the lines on his face etched with wisdom, before responding, "Son, attracting the attention of a good woman, someone like Hannah, isn't just about grand gestures. It's about showing her your steadfastness and reliability."

Isaac brushed sawdust off his pants and leaned against the workbench, trying to absorb his father's sound advice.

"Be a constant presence in her life, offering support and kindness, even when she's not asked for it."

Isaac sighed and wiped his brow. "You're saying I should continue to be there for her even when she pushes me away?"

"*Jah*," his father nodded. "True affection and friendship are built over time. Daily acts of kindness and the willingness to be there for her will show her your sincerity. And remember, whatever the outcome, it's in *Gott's* hands. Trust in his plan for you, Hannah, and your future together ...if that's what He has in store."

"Is that what you had to do with *Mamm*?" Isaac asked.

His father gave a jolly giggle. "She was a tough bird, your *mamm*. Set in her way long before I came along."

Isaac smiled and asked. "How so?"

"Let's just say, being the oldest of ten, she had a way of needing things in order, including me." He snickered and continued, "I won her over with kindness, and eventually, she lightened up some."

Encouraged by his father's advice, Isaac turned his attention back to the table. Flipping the table over to secure the wobbly legs, his fingers brushed against a seam he hadn't noticed before —a hidden compartment. Curiosity piqued, he carefully opened the hidden spot to discover a stack of letters, their edges worn, the handwriting faded by time. He gently pulled them out in anticipation of uncovering the table's secrets.

"*Datt?* Is this what you and *Mamm* were referring to?"

His father placed a hand on his shoulder, offering a nod of encouragement and a soft smile on his lips. "Sharing our family history and stories is a way to keep our heritage and all we've been through alive. They remind us of where we come from and the bonds that tie us to our past and each other."

Overwhelmed by the history in the letters, Isaac said, "I'd love to read them with Hannah if she'll let me."

"I think that sounds like a fine idea," his father declared as he stepped out of the workshop.

With the letters still folded in his hands, Isaac devised an even better idea. But that would first require some planning.

WARMED BY THE CRACKLING WOODSTOVE, Hannah stood by the window, her eyes fixed outside where Isaac was busy plowing snow from their driveway. He maneuvered the plow horses so easily that she could not take her eyes off him. Wrapped in a warm shawl, Ellie sat in her favorite chair nearby, knitting needles in hand, watching Hannah more than the scene outside.

"He's a good man," Ellie commented, breaking the silence, her eyes not leaving her granddaughter. "Look at him out there, taking care of us without being asked. It speaks volumes about his character, *jah*?"

Hannah watched, her heart taking on a new beat as she watched him. "*Jah*, it does," she admitted, her voice cracking with the turmoil inside. "He seems to keep showing up and doing things for us when I least expect it."

Ellie set her knitting needles aside and patted the seat next to hers, inviting Hannah to sit. "Come here, child. Let's talk." Hannah reluctantly moved away from the window to sit beside her grandmother, the warmth of the woodstove taking the chill off her heart.

"Hannah, my dear, why do you push him away? He continues to make his interest obvious, and yet you hold back. What are you afraid of?"

Hannah sighed. "It's complicated. With your health, my work at the market, and the cookie orders, there's so much I need to handle that I don't have time for what he might be expecting from me."

Ellie reached for her hand, her soft fingers cool against Hannah's skin. "Nothing in life is sure, but one filled with love and joy is what makes our time here incomparable to anything else we know in this world. I've lived a long life, my dear. I loved your grandfather deeply, and he was a lot like Isaac—persistent, kind, and tenderhearted."

Watching Isaac outside, Hannah longed for the kind of love Ellie described. "He has been so kind to me, even when I've been snappy and ungrateful."

Ellie snickered. "I can guarantee it will take more than a few snippy remarks to chase Isaac Kauffman away. He has an internal strength and determination that goes far beyond his gentle manner."

"I don't know, *grossmommi*, I've been short with him. I haven't shown him my good side for sure and certain."

Ellie smiled, picked back up her knitting, and laid it across her lap. "You're too hard on yourself. I see how that boy looks at you, and a few harsh words won't chase him away quickly."

As Hannah thought over her grandmother's words, the room grew silent for a few minutes, except for the crackling woodstove. Ellie smiled, squeezing Hannah's hand. "Love is a journey, my dear. And every journey begins with a single step. He's been out there in the cold working for some time now. I bet he would enjoy some of your famously good hot chocolate."

Motivated by Ellie's gentle encouragement and the warmth spreading through her chest, Hannah rose from her seat, her breath catching in her throat with each step toward the door. She opened it, the cold air brushing against her face, a harsh adjustment to the warm room behind her. Isaac was focused on his task and didn't notice her at first, the steady sound of the horse and scraper filling the air.

"Isaac!" she called out, her voice fighting the wind.

He stopped, looking up in surprise, a slight flush on his cheeks from the cold.

"Would you like to come in for hot chocolate when you finish?"

His face lit up with a grateful smile. "I'd like that," he responded. "Let me put this away, and I'll be in shortly."

As she closed the door and headed to the kitchen, she found herself praying, a silent plea whispered in the solitude of her heart. She prayed that her offer of hot chocolate would clear the air after her recent unfriendly response to his offer of help.

She busied herself making hot chocolate, a familiar and comforting routine that allowed her mind to wander. She thought of his smile, the way it reached his eyes and seemed to light up when he spoke to her. The thought warmed her from the inside, much like the milk she heated on the stove, and she found herself smiling.

She chose two mugs from the cupboard, each simple yet sturdy—much like his ever-present presence in her life. As she stirred in cocoa, her mind turned to Ellie's words about love being a journey… one she never allowed herself to consider much before now.

When Isaac stepped into the kitchen, shedding the cold and snow at the door, Hannah greeted him with a hot mug, her hands slightly trembling as she offered it. She pointed to a chair, and they sat silently as the sudden awkwardness wrapped them in a thick blanket. It was Isaac who finally broke the stillness.

"I found something in the table," he said, taking a second to wipe chocolate from his upper lip before continuing. "It was a hidden compartment filled with old letters from the previous keepers of the table."

Hannah felt a twinge of regret and asked, "You decided to work on the table anyways."

Isaac offered a reassuring smile, brushing off her concern with a wave of his hand. "It's all right. I know you're busy. I just thought I'd work on it when I can. It's really a pretty piece, and I want to see it restored. Besides, it's winter, and I don't have much else to do on these long nights."

Hannah balanced her chin in the palm of her hand and leaned in to ask. "So, what do the letters say, and who are they from?"

He shrugged his shoulders. "Don't know. Haven't read them yet."

Confused, Hannah giggled. "If it were me, I would've dropped everything to read them right then."

Isaac smiled and waited for her to finish before he replied quietly. "I thought it might be nice to read them together. I figured you'd want to know about the people who owned the table before you."

Hannah could hardly believe her ears. There he was again, putting her needs above his own and considering what she might like. "I would," she said softly, a smile breaking through her initial hesitation. "So, you know who had the table in the past?"

"I do," he answered. "It's been in my family for three generations. And some of the table keepers are still alive."

As Isaac started to explain everything his parents had revealed to him, he couldn't help but notice Hannah's sudden change in demeanor. Her initial resistance to helping with the table suddenly melted away, and he couldn't help but ask, "Hannah, if you don't mind me asking, what's changed? You seemed so adamant that you didn't have time to think about the table. Why the sudden interest?"

Hannah paused and looked down at her hands wrapped around the now-empty mug. "I guess… it was seeing you out there in the cold, taking care of things without even being asked. And the thought of you working on the table, even when I said I couldn't… made me realize how much I was holding back. Not just from the table, but from… us?"

She lifted her eyes to meet his and continued, her voice soft and thoughtful. "And then seeing how excited you are about the letters and the history surrounding the table… it's not just a piece of furniture. It's part of your family's story. And maybe, in a small way, I wanted to be a part of that too." Hannah waited for him to respond, and she could tell he was trying to absorb all she had explained.

~

Isaac's heart swelled at her admission. "Hearing you say that… it's more than I could have hoped for. The table is an important part of my family's history. Being able to share it with you, to have you be a part of it, makes everything more meaningful. And the table is just the beginning." He smiled, a wave of contentment settling over him before he replied. "It means a lot to me that you want to be a part of it. It's only fitting since you will be the next keeper of the secrets."

Hannah nodded, returning his smile with a comforting

agreement. As they stood to clear away the mugs, the air between them felt lighter, filled with hope of new discoveries.

# CHAPTER 4

*I*saac quickly shut the workshop door as the winter wind seeped under his wool coat. Stoking the small woodstove to warm the space, he wiped a fresh cloth over the newly stained and polished table. He'd labored over restoring the old table for the past week until it looked new. He sat at the workbench and carefully penned a short note to Hannah before placing the stack of letters in his jacket pocket.

*Hannah,*

*Please don't open these letters until we can read them together tomorrow. I've added a few new orders for your wonderful cookies. If you're willing, I've made plans to deliver the cookie orders tomorrow on our off-Sunday visiting day. Please meet me outside at nine tomorrow morning. I pray you'll agree to spend the day with me.*

*Isaac*

He peered out the window when he heard the clip-clop of her buggy horse making his way out of her driveway and past his house on her way to work. He had already planned with Ellie to deliver the new table after Hannah had left for work. With his *bruder's* help, he loaded the table in his open cart to make the short trip across the road.

The morning was quiet except for the crunch of snow under

the cart's metal wheels as he made his way to Hannah's. This was more than just a delivery to him; it was the start of, hopefully, something wonderful between them. Excitement was bubbling inside him as he thought about the plans he'd laid out for the following day.

Once he situated the shining new table in the center of the tiny kitchen and moved the old table to the end of the counter, he stood back and admired how at home it looked. He placed the stack of letters at the center and positioned his note to Hannah so it could be easily read.

Stepping back, he imagined her surprise when she returned from work later that afternoon. Before he could slip away unnoticed, Ellie emerged from her bedroom.

"Isaac, it's beautiful!" Ellie exclaimed joyfully.

He smiled, wiping a spot of snow off the corner with the back of his coat sleeve. "It turned out wonderful and fits the space perfectly."

Ellie winked and tipped her chin toward him. "You care for her deeply, don't you?"

Isaac nodded, hoping his eyes didn't tell too much of his heart. "I do. But she's a little hesitant, and I understand she has responsibilities to you and this house."

Ellie used her cane to move toward the table and sat before adding, "My health is in the Lord's hands. Don't you let her use my illness as an excuse not to explore all life has to offer the both of you."

He dared not assume anything about Hannah's feelings and changed the subject. "I admire your faith, Ellie. Despite everything, you walk with the Lord with such devotion. It's inspiring."

Ellie's face took on a serious edge. "Faith carries us through, no matter what circumstance we face. And faith will guide Hannah too; although she may need a little nudge along the way."

Isaac still felt uncomfortable speaking to Ellie about Hannah's feelings. He took a long breath and headed to the door, but as he passed Ellie, she reached out and placed a frail hand on his arm. "Be patient and pray. The Lord has a plan for you, and He'll reveal it in His own time. Hannah's heart will open in due course. Just wait and see."

HANNAH RETURNED HOME JUST as the afternoon sun started to warm the icicles hanging from the corner of the house. Preoccupied with the list of tasks awaiting her, she didn't notice her surprise at first. Nothing could have prepared her for the sight, and she stood in awe of the polished pine staring back at her. The last rays of sunshine streamed in the window, highlighting its beauty. On top of the table lay the stack of letters, Isaac's note, and three cookie orders.

She was momentarily speechless, amazed by Isaac's hard work, which spoke volumes about his character. She approached the table slowly, her fingers tracing the smooth surface before picking up the letters. Holding them close, she read Isaac's note, and her heart fluttered to a new beat. She read his instructions closely, excited that she would get to spend the whole day with him.

Setting the letters aside, she got busy filling the orders. The anticipation of the following day gave her a surge of energy, and she found herself smiling and humming one of her favorite hymns. As she worked, her mind wandered to the surprises the letters might hold. She imagined the stories of love, hardship, and joy they contained. Stories that had been part of Isaac's family for generations. The history they represented drew her in, making her all the more anxious to uncover the secrets within.

Snowflakes gently danced as Isaac helped Hannah into his enclosed, brown-capped buggy the next morning. Inside, bricks warmed in the fireplace were wrapped and carefully placed at their feet to ward off the winter chill. Hannah, in turn, brought a thermos filled with hot chocolate, a small gesture that spoke of her growing fondness for him.

Once settled, Isaac turned to Hannah, a gleam in his eye as he outlined his plans. "I thought it'd be special to visit some of my relatives who have owned the table. To hear their stories and maybe understand more about the letters we found."

Hannah's heart skipped a beat at Isaac's plans. "That sounds wonderful. I brought the letters. Are we going to read them before we get there?" she asked.

Isaac took a few seconds to guide his horse safely across a patch of icy blacktop before he responded. "I thought it might be nice if we let them read their letter to us."

Hannah clapped her gloved hands. "I'm so looking forward to hearing the stories in the letters... and I'm so happy you invited me to do this with you."

The journey to Isaac's grandparents' house was anything but quiet as the two exchanged sweet memories of their childhood.

"Did I ever tell you about the time I tried to milk a goat and ended up being headbutted into the barn wall?" Isaac began, a mischievous glint in his eye.

Hannah chuckled, shaking her head. "*Nee*, but please, do tell."

He recounted the tale with animated gestures, describing how his youthful confidence soon turned into a valuable life lesson. "Let's just say the goat and I reached a mutual understanding that day. And to this day, I prefer cows to goats."

Hannah laughed, her tone turning severe but playful. "I have one better for you. Did I ever tell you about the time when I fought with a rooster, and the rooster won... or so he thought?"

Isaac leaned in closer, intrigued by her story. "Oh? What did he do?"

Hannah sighed dramatically, the memory still haunting her like it was yesterday. "One morning, I was minding my own business, just happily skipping through my mother's flower garden, when out of nowhere, our king rooster decided to claim his territory. He chased me from the garden all over the yard, squawking and flapping like I had insulted him somehow."

Isaac couldn't help but chuckle. "What happened?"

"Well, in my desperate bid to escape his spurs, I ran up on the porch, and he continued to chase me. I tripped and fell through my mother's front window. Glass was everywhere, and I was in the middle of it all! Surprisingly, I didn't get hurt."

Isaac laughed. "I can only imagine it was quite a sight."

"My *datt* didn't think so. I refused to go back outside until he dealt with that rooster."

"What happened?"

"Let's just say I never looked at chicken stew the same for a long time."

Isaac raised his eyebrows in surprise. "That's one way to solve a problem."

Isaac pulled up to his grandparents' tiny *doddi haus* just as Hannah pulled the stack of letters from her bag. "Do you know which one belongs to them?" Hannah asked.

He reached over, sifted through the letters, and pulled one from the stack. "I'm pretty sure this is my *grossmommi's* handwriting," he said.

Hannah handed him a neatly packed box of iced cookies before stepping down from the carriage. "You never told me how you got your relatives to order cookies?"

Isaac smiled. "They didn't, I did. I figured it would be a sweet thank you to them for sharing their stories with us."

"Great idea!"

As they made their way to the small front porch, Isaac kept a hand on Hannah's elbow, guiding her along the slippery walk. "Thank you again for spending the day with me," he whispered as they walked up the stairs.

Hannah smiled and gave him a knowing nod as she knocked on the front door.

The elderly couple met them at the door, and their faces lit up with joy for the unexpected visitors. "Isaac, what a wonderful surprise. Come in, sit. We were heading to the kitchen for tea and a piece of apple pie."

After Isaac introduced Hannah, he explained that she made the best cookies in Willow Spring, and they'd brought a box for them to have for the holidays. After his grandmother served them pie and tea, they settled around the table for a friendly chat.

Isaac cleared his throat and pulled the letter from his jacket pocket. "We've come today because we found something very special in an old table I've been restoring, and we thought it would be nice if we shared it with you."

His grandmother's smile widened, and she asked, "Would it be an old pine table with one mismatched leg?"

"*Jah*," Hannah nodded.

"Well, I'll be," his *doddi* exclaimed. "I'd almost given up hope we'd hear who the next table keepers might be."

Isaac's grandparents exchanged a look of fond remembrance before his grandfather leaned forward with a twinkle in his eye. "Ah, that table has been a silent witness to many a tale in the Kauffman family."

Hannah spoke up. "We thought it might be nice if you read us your letter."

"Oh, child. These old eyes aren't good for reading anymore. How about you read it instead?"

Isaac handed the letter to Hannah, and she slowly unfolded it and turned so the light coming from the window landed on the page.

*Dear Keeper of the Table,*

*As you unfold this letter, we pray you'll discover a piece of history you'll cling to as you find comfort around this treasured pine table.*

*This is our story...*

*Our marriage was one of tradition, a path chosen not by us but by our* families, which was not uncommon in our community at the time. In the early days, this table stood as a meeting place, a spot where we learned to love one another. The careful exchange of words and uncertainties about our life together filled the space between us when we barely knew one another. It was in this kitchen that the foundation of our life together was built.

We fell in love here amidst the clatter of dishes and the glow of the oil lamp. Night after night, we sat across from each other, not in the fiery passion of our youth but in a slow-burning flame nurtured by shared experiences and mutual respect.

This table has seen many family meals, moments of happiness, and tears of sorrow. It has felt the warmth of hands clasped together in prayer and the cold touch of absence when we were apart.

One memorable evening, with a house full of guests, one wayward child let loose a tiny field mouse, sending a fury of chaos into our orderly home. The laughter that followed, even as we discovered the leg of our cherished table had been broken, reminded us of the bliss that can be found in life's unpredictable moments.

As you become one of the keepers of this table, please remember it's more than just wood and nails; it's a vessel for our family history, a keeper of our love passed on to the next rightful owner.

We leave this letter to you, praying that the table will continue to be a place of love and laughter. A place where your family is woven together... forever in time.

With all of our love and affection to the next table keepers,
Melvin and Martha Kauffman

Hannah, touched by the sincerity of the letter, asked, "How did you manage to find love in such a situation like yours? It must have been challenging."

Isaac's grandmother chuckled softly. "Love can find you when you least expect it."

Hannah and Isaac listened to more stories about how the table came to be in their possession and what a hard decision it was when it was time to pass it to their son Jacob and his young family.

"Thank you for sharing your stories with us," Hannah said. "I'll treasure them and the table always."

~

With great anticipation, Hannah and Isaac approached Uncle Jacob's cozy home beneath whispering pines laden with snow. His uncle, a man who had outlived two wives, welcomed them with open arms. The warmth of his woodstove invited them in from the cold.

Jacob greeted them, his voice tinged with gladness. "I hear you've been working on restoring the family table," he said.

Isaac nodded, taking a seat next to Hannah on the sofa. "*Jah*, we found a collection of letters hidden inside the table, and there was one from you and Aunt Maggie."

Hannah gently unfolded the old letter as Isaac continued. "We thought it would be nice if you read the letter to us."

Jacob sat back in his rocking chair and moved it with the ball of his foot. "I don't need to read it. I can tell you everything in it."

Hannah crossed her legs and laid her coat on the back of the well-worn couch as Isaac got comfortable.

Jacob tapped his thumbs on the chair arms and said, "After all those years of being a widower, I didn't think love would happen to me again. But then Maggie walked into my life... like the first spring flower," his voice cracked slightly, "she brought color into my life and expressed love when I didn't expect it." He paused and wiped the moisture from his weathered eyes. "It was the only piece I could save when our house caught fire. Maggie didn't care about anything else but saving the table. It took the both of us to drag it out into the snow on that cold January night. We all sat on top of it and watched our home burn to the ground. We held our babies on our lap and soothed their cries while waiting for the fire department to come."

A small smile appeared on his lips as his memory changed to

something lighter. "One November, on the first day of deer season right after Thanksgiving, I nicked the table while butchering a deer. Your Aunt Maggie was none too pleased at first, but that cut became a cherished mark over time. A reminder that life, with all its imperfections, was still beautiful."

Hannah smiled, touched by the memories their visit evoked. "I love hearing how much the table meant to you and Maggie," she said.

Jacob nodded and settled his eyes on them both. "I'm glad it's finding a new home after all these years."

Hannah sighed slightly. "I surely hope I can live up to the responsibility of being the table's new owner, even for a short time."

As Isaac gathered their coats, a small part of him agonized over Hannah's statement that the table was only hers for a short time. Passing on the table to her was more than a temporary assignment... in his heart, it was a lifelong commitment, and he was determined to prove that to her.

WRAPPED IN BLANKETS, with the thermos of hot chocolate between them, Hannah felt a warmness that wasn't just from the bricks or the drink. A budding affection seemed to grow stronger with each moment.

When they finally opened the thermos, the hot chocolate took the chill off amidst the snowy landscape. Hannah poured the steaming liquid into two cups, the chocolate's rich aroma mingling with the air, and offered one to Isaac.

"*Denki*," Isaac said, accepting the cup with a smile that reached his eyes.

Hannah nodded, her heart full. "Where next?" she asked.

Isaac smiled as he pulled into his parents' driveway. "My folks are the last on our list of table keepers." He pulled the buggy into the barn and disclosed, "*Mamm* is expecting us for supper."

Hannah couldn't contain her sudden rush of unease. The thought of spending the evening with his parents was an important step for Isaac, and she prayed she wouldn't disappoint him.

Sensing her abrupt change, Isaac reached over and squeezed her gloved hand. "There is nothing to be nervous about. You've spoken to my mother a hundred times."

"*Jah*, I know it's just that…"

Isaac interrupted her thoughts. "They're looking forward to seeing you, and you have nothing to be anxious about."

With the day fading beyond the horizon, they entered Isaac's parents' home. Warmth greeted them as they stepped inside. The aroma of tomato soup and freshly made sandwiches covered with a towel in the center of the table filled Hannah with a sense of belonging, which left her speechless for a few minutes. After removing her coat and stepping from her boots, she handed Isaac's mother the last box of cookies, which was tied with a pretty Christmas ribbon. "I brought you a little something to enjoy."

Isaac's parents, Alvin and Mariam, were already sitting at the table enjoying a cup of coffee, and they welcomed them in with big smiles. Set for a simple, yet heartfelt, meal, stories about the table led the conversation easily as they talked about their visits with Isaac's grandparents and Uncle Jacob.

Mariam took the box and peered inside, oohing at the wonderful smell emulating from the opened lid. "Is that almond I note?"

"*Jah*, I add just a touch to enhance the flavor."

"*Ach*… Hannah, Alvin will gobble these up in no time at all. Thank you so much for sharing some with us. I've heard nothing but praise about them for weeks."

After the meal, Hannah carefully pulled the last letter from her bag as they settled into a comfortable silence. The anticipation in the room was evident as Hannah handed the letter to Mariam.

"This letter," she added, trembling, "we wrote it together at the table before moving it to the barn." She tenderly unfolded the crisp paper, took a deep breath, and giggled slightly with recalled memory. "I asked your *datt* to paint the legs of the table black. I'd seen a shiny new table in the window of a fancy *Englisch* furniture shop in town and thought it was the most beautiful thing. We couldn't afford a new table, so he spray-painted the legs black for me."

Alvin chimed in with a joyful groan. "I got spray paint everywhere that day. I was smart enough to pull it outside but failed to put anything behind it and got more paint on the house than the table."

The room erupted in laughter before Mariam cleared her throat and began reading the letter.

*Dear Table Keeper,*

*As we sit and add our own letter to this family heirloom, our hearts are filled with years of emotions. This table has seen its share of laughter and tears. It has sat in this spot for twenty years, and it's like we're letting go of a trusted confidant. How can we measure a lifetime of memories in one letter?*

*Happy times have grown around this table. Hundreds of pies and cookies, weddings and babies, hands busy but hearts full. It's hosted many work frolics, sisters' days, birthday and funeral dinners, each adding another memory to its trusted pine.*

*With gladness comes pain. We grieved our youngest son, Abel, around this table as his little life was cut way too short. His absence has left a void in our hearts, reminding us of the fragility of life, and our only daughter, Sarah, chose a path away from our community in search of herself. Her seat at the table was forever empty as she ventured to live among the English. Her departure was a sorrow that we carry with us forever, a silent prayer for her return always on our lips.*

*Despite its scratches and stains, this table has been an anchor for our family. Now it's time we gladly send it on its way to stand as a silent witness for the next generation.*

*As you take possession of its importance to the Kauffman family, we pray you'll never forget the stories it holds, the laughter shared, the tears shed, and the celebrations lived. Cherish it as we have, and let it be a place where prayers are prayed, new memories are made, love grows, and family is everything.*

*Forever an honored keeper of the table.*

*Alvin and Mariam Kauffman*

With the visit to Isaac's parents still lingering in the air, Hannah pulled her heavy brown bonnet close to ward off the wind. "Your parents are lovely, and I enjoyed listening to them talk about the table."

Isaac moved closer to shield the swirling snow from her and answered, "*Jah, Mamm* can get a little sentimental sometimes, but it was nice listening to them reminisce."

As they walked across the road to Hannah's house, Isaac used his flashlight to light the way to the porch. Hannah stopped for a second and said, "Ellie must have gone to bed early. There isn't a light on in the entire house."

Isaac looked up toward the chimney. "I don't smell smoke. She must have let the fire go out too."

With concern etched on her face, Hannah ran up the stairs, threw open the door, and cried out, "*Grossmommi?*"

# CHAPTER 5

*T*he return home was supposed to be the end of a wonderful day exploring the history of the table. However, the moment Hannah and Isaac stepped through the door their reminiscing was replaced with instant dread. Ellie lay, still and quiet, on the living room floor.

Hannah's heart tumbled into her stomach as she raced to Ellie's side, gently cradling her grandmother's head in her lap. "*Ach, Grossmommi*, I'm so sorry," she cried, her voice filled with guilt.

"I'll run to the phone shanty. We need to get help," Isaac said as he rushed out into the cold night.

Left alone, Hannah tried to assess Ellie's condition, her hands trembling as she ran them along her grandmother's legs and hips. "Is anything broken?" The house was usually warm but felt unbearably cold, a true reflection of the fear gripping Hannah's heart.

Ellie, her eyes fluttering open, managed a weak smile. "Hannah, my dear, don't fuss. It's just a little fall. I couldn't get up, is all."

"But I shouldn't have left you alone. It was selfish of me to leave you all day like this—"

307

Ellie cut her off, her voice gentle but firm. "Now stop. Today was important for you. I'm fine. It's just a little mishap, is all. Now help me up."

"No, not yet. I'd feel better if we wait for help to ensure nothing is broken." Hannah scooted across the floor and grabbed a quilt to warm her grandmother. All the while, Hannah whispered apologies and promised never to leave Ellie's side again.

When Isaac returned, breathless from sprinting to the phone, he knelt beside them and offered support. "Help is on the way, Ellie. You'll be all right."

Hannah motioned her head toward the cold woodstove, and Isaac went right to work, filling the house with heat.

Within minutes, an ambulance arrived, and Hannah and Isaac moved off to the side as the emergency team worked efficiently around Ellie. The fear and tension of the moment left Hannah's mind spinning aimlessly into a sea of shame.

"I should have been here," she murmured, barely audible over the sound of the medical team's movements. "I shouldn't have left her alone. This is all my fault."

Isaac felt the distance growing between them as he tried to ease Hannah's worry. "This isn't your fault. We couldn't have known this would happen."

"But I chose to leave her, to spend the day away... for what?" her voice cracked under the pressure. "So, I could be selfish and think of my own needs before hers."

A pang of fear entered Isaac's heart at Hannah's comment. "You're not being selfish by wanting to experience life—that's not selfish. It's human. Ellie wouldn't want you to blame yourself like this."

Hannah shook her head, tears brimming in her eyes. "But she's, my responsibility. And when she needed me the most, I wasn't here."

As the paramedic assessed Ellie's condition, checking for breaks and ensuring she didn't have a concussion, it became clear that, despite the fall, Ellie was adamant about not going to the hospital.

"I'm fine, really—just a little tumble. I don't need to go to the hospital," Ellie insisted, her voice firm, despite so many people hovering over her.

Hannah, torn between relief that Ellie wasn't seriously injured and concern over her refusal to go to the hospital, approached one of the EMTs. "Are you sure she's, okay?"

The EMT, a young man with a calming presence, offered Hannah a reassuring smile. "There are no breaks and no signs of a concussion. But we need to get her to sign a release to refuse the trip to the hospital. It's protocol."

Hannah turned to her grandmother, who was already reaching for the pen, her independence as strong as her spirit despite her weakened state. With the release signed, the EMT helped Ellie to her bedroom, making sure she was comfortable and settled before preparing to leave.

As the emergency team left, closing the door slowly behind them, Hannah and Isaac were alone in the quiet house. The fear and uncertainty of the past hour gave way to a heavy silence. They both walked solemnly into Ellie's room. Hannah moved to sit on the edge of her grandmother's bed and took her hand.

Ellie, now comfortable, looked up at them both. "Now stop that worrying. I'm tougher than I look," she said, a faint smile gracing her lips.

"We know, but we're going to take extra good care of you, just to be sure."

Ellie's eyes softened a bit before closing them gently. "I'm blessed to have you both," she whispered before drifting off.

They waited a few minutes to be sure she was asleep before slipping out of her room and closing the door behind them. Moving to the kitchen, Hannah began to tidy it, moving the chairs back to their original place around the table and wiping down surfaces. The simple chore contrasted sharply with the turmoil of her emotions.

Breaking the silence, Hannah's voice was firm as she directed her words to Isaac. "I've realized something today. I can't... I can't let myself be distracted again. My place is here, taking care of Ellie. I can't afford to entertain any schoolgirl notions of... whatever this is between us."

Isaac hovered nervously near the door, twirling his hat in his fingers. Hannah refused to look at him, refused to acknowledge the sharpness of her words, and continued cleaning up the counter.

"You don't have to choose between caring for Ellie and exploring us," he replied, his voice tinged with desperation. "We can find a way to do both, and I want to be here to help you."

Hannah paused while cleaning, with her back still toward Isaac. "It's not that simple. Today showed me just how fragile Ellie is. I can't... I won't risk being distracted, not when Ellie needs me. My focus must be on her, completely." She turned to face him to be sure he understood, fighting the pool of tears threatening to spill over her cheeks. "It's not the right time for me... for us."

With apparent distress etched on his face, Isaac nodded and said, "I'll respect your wishes. Just know that I'm here whenever you need help. With Ellie, with anything."

The silence that followed was deafening, and Isaac lingered for a moment before he glanced at her one last time with a profound sense of loss and left, letting the storm door slam with his departure.

Suddenly, the welcoming kitchen felt cold in his absence. Alone with her thoughts and the sleeping house, she couldn't shake the gnawing feeling that in her determination to protect her grandmother, she might have sacrificed something precious, something that might never be recovered.

≈

THE SUN barely made its way up over the shadows of the barn when Isaac found himself at odds with his routine. His harsh movements and clumsy hands left the cows sensing his foul mood. It wasn't long before his *bruder*, attempting to lighten his mood with some harmless bantering, received Isaac's sharp tongue.

The argument was petty but loud enough to draw their father's attention. With a stern look and a gesture for Isaac to follow, his father led him away from the cows and the brewing tension.

Once out of earshot, his father's voice cut through the morning chill. "What's gotten into you today? This isn't like you at all."

Isaac propped his foot up on a bale of hay and sighed. "It's Ellie. She had a fall yesterday, and Hannah is taking it hard and blaming herself. She's pushing me away again, claiming she only has enough time to care for Ellie and nothing else."

His father listened intently. After a moment, he asked, "Do you remember our conversation about you being a steady, reliable force in her life? This is part of that. She's facing a tough time coming to terms with Ellie's failing health. Give her the space she needs."

Isaac nodded, though the disappointment in her pushing him away was hard to swallow. "But what if she decides she's better off without me? What if the space she needs pushes us further apart?"

"Isaac," his father began, "you can't control how Hannah feels or what she decides, but you can control how you respond. Continue to show up and stay involved in her life, even when she doesn't want you to. Be that person she can count on without her realizing she needs you."

His father paused, letting his words of wisdom sink in. "And you can start by delivering that box of eggs and milk. It won't make its way to her kitchen on its own."

With the box on his hip, he set off across the road to Hannah's, the early morning light guiding his way. The journey was short and unsure, but he held tight to his father's advice and was determined to be a steady force in her life whether she wanted it or not.

~

HANNAH ARRIVED AT THE MARKET; her mind clouded with worry. After the scare with Ellie, Hannah couldn't bear the thought of leaving her alone again. Despite the financial strain, she employed a caregiver to stay with Ellie while she was at work. The cost of hiring someone weighed heavily on her, but the peace of mind it brought her was worth every penny. She couldn't risk another fall, couldn't risk the guilt that came along with it.

The market bustled with last-minute shoppers and was filled with the scent of cinnamon and fresh pine boughs. But Hannah hardly noticed the festive atmosphere. Her attention was immediately drawn to the stack of new cookie orders waiting for her. Seeing them, each order a promise she had made, left her anxious and overwhelmed. How would she fill all these orders, especially now, with her mind preoccupied with Ellie's care?

As she unpacked a new order of local honey and arranged it on the aisle's end cap, lost in thoughts and the daunting task ahead, Susan stepped up beside her and whispered as she handed her jars of honey.

"I saw you out with Isaac Kauffman yesterday." Susan beamed, her tone lighthearted. "Did you have a nice time?"

Hannah felt tense, as she wasn't ready to relive the flood of memories that suddenly invaded her mind. "It was nothing," she muttered quickly. "Besides, I don't have time for such things." Hannah sighed and continued, "There's too much to do here, the cookies, and with Ellie... I just can't."

Susan furrowed her brow and laid a hand on Hannah's arm, stopping her from picking up another jar. "Life is so short. Why would you want to push matters of the heart aside?" Without letting Hannah reply, Susan added, "Love is a gift, not a burden, and besides, what would your grandmother say if she knew you were giving up a chance for happiness because of her?"

Hannah knew Susan was right. Her grandmother had always encouraged her to embrace happiness where she found it and not let fear dictate her choices. "I know you're right, Susan. It's just hard to let go and trust everything will be okay."

Hannah paused as Susan's words stirred a fresh wave of guilt. She settled her eyes on Susan and let the older woman continue to give her unsolicited advice. "Nobody ever feels truly ready for love. It's a leap of faith. As for making mistakes, they're part of life. And remember, if the Lord ordains a relationship, He'll guide and protect it through all circumstances, not only when everything goes smoothly."

Susan walked away, leaving Hannah to her ponderings. The idea that love was a journey, not a destination, and that it required faith, not just in the other person but in herself and *Gott's* plan, was a comforting thought.

However, the cost of the caregiver, the orders, and Ellie's health seemed to fall on her all at once. Suddenly, her mind wandered back to the stories around the table, giving her a glimmer of hope. Maybe, just maybe, there was a way to navigate her responsibilities without completely closing the door to her own happiness. Was it too late to consider the possibility of love? To trust that whatever the future held, she could face it with someone just like Isaac.

About ready to call it a night, Isaac glanced out his bedroom window and noticed the light still burning in Hannah's kitchen. A twinge of concern entered his mind and nudged him to check on her, especially given the late hour. Bundling up against the cold, he crossed the road to her home.

He lightly knocked and pushed the door open, without

allowing her time to answer. The scene before him made him stop in his tracks. Hannah, dusted in flour and green frosting, a bin of flour overturned on the floor by her side, was focused on decorating a row of Christmas trees, each one a small masterpiece.

Isaac couldn't help but chuckle at the sight. "Looks like a flour snowstorm has hit!" he joked as he stepped out of his boots.

Hannah looked up, her expression shifting from surprise to mild irritation. Then, seeing his broadening smile, she snapped, "Isaac! What are you doing here? I'm a bit, as you can see, busy."

"I can see that," he muttered. "It looks like you could use an extra pair of hands."

Hannah hesitated and gave him a wary glare. "I don't know. I have a method to my madness, and I don't have time to explain."

"*Jah*, the famous flour-on-the-floor system. Very innovative, if I say so myself," he teased, already taking off his coat and hat. "Come on, let me help. I promise to follow your lead."

He noticed her reserve soften, and soon, she gave him instructions on how to package orders properly. Isaac tried to keep the banter light as they worked, determined to show her how well they could work together.

After placing a batch of cutouts in the oven, he reached over and wiped a dollop of frosting off her cheek, licking it off his finger. "I should have left it there," he teased. "It made quite a colorful statement."

Hannah grinned, wiping her cheek only to realize she was using a frosting-stained finger and adding another streak. They both laughed and went back to work.

As they worked to navigate the chaos, the antique pine table stood at the center of their efforts. Its surface now became an expansive workspace that Hannah appreciated.

"You know," Hannah began, pausing to glance over at him as he sat at the end of the table packing boxes, "this table... it's changed everything. I can't believe how much more I can get done with all this space."

Isaac carefully stacked the completed orders on the corner of the table, looked up, and smiled, his affection for the table evident. "I'm happy it found a new home, and I think it's happy to be useful again."

Hannah rolled out another batch of dough and asked, "I wonder how many loaves of bread have been kneaded here and how many meals it served over the years. I understand now why your family keeps saying it's the keeper of stories. Just think of how many memories have been made around it."

The conversation shifted as they worked, and Isaac exclaimed, "And to think it could have stayed hidden in the barn for years without anyone knowing its secrets." He paused momentarily, and Hannah heard him take a quick breath and hold it before continuing, "Bringing it here... to you, it feels right. Like it was meant to be a part of your journey."

He didn't hide his words, which seemed to affect her in ways that filled him with a sense of wonder, especially when she added, "I'm glad your family trusted me with it."

Trying to lighten the moment, Hannah admitted, "You know... you might have a future in the cookie business."

"Only if you're by my side," Isaac joked, his words carrying a hint of his deeper feelings.

Hannah busied herself, wiping the table and filling the sink with dirty dishes before approaching him. "I can't thank you enough for tonight. I couldn't have finished all this without your help."

Isaac tied a ribbon around the last box of cookies and stretched just as the first hint of dawn began to paint the sky. The night had been long, soaked with hard work and laughter as they stood back to survey the fruits of their labor.

Hannah moved to the stove to brew a pot of coffee. The aroma saturated the kitchen within a few minutes, a welcome scent after hours of sugary sweetness. "Coffee's ready. How about breakfast before you go?" she offered, turning to him with a tired but genuine smile.

"Sounds good, but I need to do chores. But I'll take you up on the coffee," he conceded, accepting the warm mug from her hands. Their fingers brushed briefly, a spark of connection in the quiet of the morning.

Sitting together for a few minutes at the now-cleared table, they discussed how she would deliver all the orders before Christmas. Isaac, the ever-thoughtful friend, offered his assistance. Hannah didn't answer right away and contemplated a response. A streak of independence flittered across her mind, making her wary of relying on him too much. After a moment of pause, she accepted. "Thank you. I could use the help," she admitted, a small smile breaking through her fatigue.

Isaac finished his coffee and stood to leave. The promise of the next day lingered between them as he stepped back into his boots and slipped away.

After he left, Hannah remained seated, the quiet kitchen surrounding her with a sense of peace and accomplishment. Her body ached from the night's work, but there was satisfaction in her heart that hadn't been there before Isaac showed up. With the task behind her, she took a few minutes to clear away their early coffee break and ran a loving hand over the polished pine table, feeling the smooth wood and the occasional indent of scratches beneath her fingers.

She allowed herself a moment to reflect on the significance of the table in her life. It was more than a workspace; it was becoming a connection to Isaac and his family, one she couldn't deny much longer.

# CHAPTER 6

The sweet rolls and milk tea aroma warmed the air as Hannah and Ellie enjoyed an early breakfast in the kitchen. Hannah couldn't help but notice her grandmother's reflective mood as she stirred honey into her tea. It was Ellie who finally broke the silence.

"Hannah, my dear, you know I won't be around forever," she started, her hands shaky as she took a long sip from her cup. "And I can't bear the thought of you putting your life on hold because of me."

Hannah opened her mouth to protest, but her grandmother raised a hand, signaling her to listen. "Let me tell you about a young man I knew when I was about your age. We were close, very close, and I thought the world of him. But I pushed him away, thinking I needed more and that there were things I had to do before I let myself love someone."

Ellie wrapped both hands around the warm mug, and Hannah leaned in as she absorbed her grandmother's tale.

"By the time I realized my mistake, it was too late. He moved away and found a *fraa* in a neighboring community, and I was left with nothing but a broken heart and questions about what might have been," Ellie continued with a distant look in her eyes.

317

Hannah reached across the table, covering Ellie's hand with her own. "But you met *Doddi*," she said softly.

Ellie smiled. "*Jah*, I did, and he blessed me with a wonderful life and ten *kinner*. But the what-ifs… they lingered." Ellie took her other hand and covered Hannah's, lightly squeezing her fingers. "I don't want that for you. Isaac is a good man, and I see how he looks at you. Don't make my mistake. Don't let fear or duty keep you from following your heart."

With her grandmother's words still fresh in her mind, a distant jingle called her to the door, and she swung it open, letting the crisp air welcome in a hint of evergreen. She stepped out onto the porch, and her breath formed small clouds in the air. There before her was Isaac in a horse-drawn sleigh. The sight of it, adorned with festive ribbons and a fresh layer of snow on the ground, felt like she had stepped into a Christmas card.

"Isaac! A sleigh?" The festive red scarf he wore fluttered in the gentle morning breeze, adding a sense of wonder to her surprise.

"Thought we'd make our deliveries in true holiday style. I even picked up some candy canes to hand out." Isaac's grin matched her excitement as he hopped down from the leather seat and followed her inside. Staying put on the rug by the door, he nodded to Ellie and warmly greeted her.

WITH THE SLEIGH packed and ready, they set off, the gentle jingle of sleigh bells accompanying their journey. The world around them was a blanket of white, the trees frosted with snow and bearing the weight of winter. As they made their way from house to house, reactions to the sleigh were priceless—surprise, delight, and the sincerity of community spirit with each delivery.

Making their way back to the sleigh from one of their stops, Isaac turned to Hannah with a mischievous glint in his eye. Without warning, he dug deep past the fluffy snow to the heavy snow below to scoop up a handful, shaping it quickly before lobbing it in Hannah's direction. The snowball hit its mark, and her surprised yelp was quickly followed by laughter.

The day passed in a blur of laughter, looks, and the pleasure of giving. As the afternoon began to fade, they found themselves on the last delivery, reluctant for the day to end. Sitting side by side in the sleigh, Hannah shivered when the sun disappeared behind a cloud.

"I have one more surprise for you. I hope you're up to it."

Hannah turned to him with a mix of concern and wonder. "It's been a wonderful day, but I should really get back to Ellie."

"You don't need to worry about Ellie. I asked my mother to check in with her throughout the day."

Before she could thank him, he slowed the sleigh and headed down a hidden alley that emerged into a small opening where a bonfire cracked invitingly, melting the snow surrounding the clearing.

Hannah pressed her gloved hands to her lips and whispered, "It's beautiful."

After pulling up next to a nearby tree and securing the sleigh to a hanging branch, Isaac helped Hannah down, his eyes shining with anticipation. "I wanted our day to end with something special, just for us—a moment to enjoy the season in a way you'd never forget."

Hannah gasped in delight as she noticed a cozy picnic had been laid out. A thick layer of blankets was spread out on the snow, and a thermos of hot cider peeked out of the top of a picnic basket lined with treats.

"Who did all this?"

"I had a little help from my *bruder* and his *fraa*."

Isaac's smile widened as he led Hannah to the blankets, the warmth of the fire inviting them to sit close. He poured them each a cup of cider, the steam mingling with the crisp winter air. "I just wanted to create a moment that was as special as you are to me," he confessed.

Hannah was at a loss for words. The beautiful picture he

painted by going out of his way to create a memory for them overwhelmed her. "Isaac, this is… it's wonderful," she managed to say, her heart swelling with emotion.

As they sat beside one another, Isaac gathered his courage, set his cup aside, and picked up her hand, turning to face her. Taking a deep breath, he brought her hands to his lips, allowing them to land lightly on her knuckles. "Hannah, I need you to know how much you've come to mean to me over the last few weeks. It's changed me, and I can't imagine my life without you."

Hannah lifted her face to his, the flickering flame reflected in his eyes. The feeling she'd been fighting for weeks spilled out into an apology. "Isaac, I… I feel the same way. I was so caught up in my responsibilities that I almost missed the delight of being with you. I can't imagine my life without you either. I hope you can forgive me."

Their joint confessions hung between them, allowing them to pause. The bonfire crackling was the only sound in the quiet of the winter afternoon. "Then let's not imagine it," Isaac exclaimed. "Let's make it our reality. We'll have challenges, but let's face them together."

Hannah nodded, a smile breaking through the crisp air. "*Jah.* Together sounds perfect."

# EPILOGUE

*Christmas, one year later…*

Hannah and Isaac busily supplied their home with the kindness and cheer of the holiday season as they prepared to host their first Christmas game night as a married couple. The antique pine table, now a cherished part of their family, stood ready in the center of the room, with an array of board games and snacks filling every inch of the polished wood.

As their friends and family began to arrive, the room buzzed with excitement, and laughter moved through the small home with joy. Amidst the activities, Isaac pulled Hannah aside, his eyes gentle and serious. "Ellie would have loved to see all these people in her home enjoying each other's company."

Hannah nodded, her own heart heavy with the memory of her grandmother. "She would have. I miss her and her wisdom, but most of all, her strength and faith." Hannah let Isaac pull her close, and she rested her hand on her protruding tummy. "She certainly taught us a lot through her last few months, and I pray I can pass on some of that wisdom to our *kinner* someday."

Isaac took her hand, squeezing it reassuringly, leading her into the front room. "She left us something. I wanted to give it to you later, but I can't wait."

Hannah looked up at him with curious eyes. "She did? What was it?"

"While she was so sick, I completely forgot to put the letters back in the hidden compartment. After she passed, I turned the table over to secure the letters in their hiding spot before they got lost. When I did, I found that she had added one herself."

"How on earth did she do that?" Hannah asked.

"I'm not sure, but she did." Isaac retrieved the letter from the table near his chair and handed it to Hannah. "I didn't read it. I thought we could do it together."

The envelope bore their names in Ellie's familiar handwriting. As she unfolded the paper, Hannah's eyes pooled with tears.

*My dearest Hannah and Isaac,*

*If you're reading this, it means I've embarked on my final journey. Know that I leave this world with no regrets and filled with love for both of you.*

*Thank you for taking such good care of me during this season. It brought me much joy to watch your love blossom.*

*My final advice is to cherish each moment, to support one another through life's trials, and to always keep laughter in your home.*

The letter continued, offering blessings for their future and reminding them of the strength they found in each other. Ellie's words were a bittersweet delight for their first Christmas together without her.

*Your journey together will not always be easy. There will be times of hardship and moments where your path seems uncertain. Lean on that love, and let it be the one thing that holds you together to weather life's storms.*

*I've witnessed how you look at each other, how your hands find each other at the end of a long day, and how your laughter fills a room. You both remind me so much of your grandfather and me and the love we shared.*

*Never forget the importance of forgiveness. There will be times when you need to offer it and others when you need to receive it. Let your hearts be generous with one another.*

*My final advice to you, my dear grandchildren, is to cherish each moment. Lean on each other, draw strength from your love, and never forget the power of a smile.*

*And when the time comes, as it surely will, to add your own letter to the table, write it with hearts full of love and hands aged by a lifetime of holding each other.*

*With all my love and blessings,*

Grossmommi *Ellie*

Hannah nestled closer to Isaac and whispered, "I can't wait to write our own letter someday. And when we do, we'll mention all the lessons Ellie shared with us, how her belief in love's power saw us through times when I doubted our path."

Isaac smiled, his heart full. "We will, and we'll mention our first Christmas together and how the table was the beginning of us." The room filled with the quiet elation of understanding between them. They basked in the happiness of their first Christmas together, surrounded by friends.

As the hours passed, the table came alive with new memories, echoing laughter and future dreams. With glances across the table, Isaac and Hannah silently knew that the time would come for them to pass the table onto new keepers, but until that moment arrived, they would fill its surface with love, faith, and the laughter that now defined their home.

DID you enjoy your visit to Willow Springs?

Discover more stories from this quaint Amish community nestled in Northwestern Pennsylvania by diving into the first book of the Willow Springs Amish Mystery Romance Series, *The Amish Book Cellar*.

# HANNAH'S FROSTED SUGAR COOKIES

## Cookies
$\frac{1}{2}$ cup butter-flavored shortening
$\frac{1}{2}$ cup softened unsalted butter
1 cup sugar
2 eggs
1 teaspoon almond extract
3 $\frac{1}{4}$ cups all-purpose flour
$\frac{1}{2}$ teaspoon baking soda
$\frac{1}{2}$ teaspoon baking powder
$\frac{1}{2}$ teaspoon salt

## Frosting
2 cups sifted confectioners' sugar
1 tablespoon milk (more as needed for consistency)
1 tablespoon light corn syrup
$\frac{1}{4}$ teaspoon almond extract

## Directions
For the cookies, combine sugar, shortening, eggs, vanilla, and almond extract and beat using an electric mixer on high speed until light and fluffy.

In a separate bowl, combine the flour, baking powder, baking soda, and salt. Gradually stir into the butter mixture until well blended.

Cover bowl and chill for two hours.

Set oven to 400°.

Line cookie sheet with parchment paper.

Roll out dough into 1/4-inch thickness and cut into desired shapes.

Bake 4–6 minutes until lightly browned around the edges.

For the frosting, in a small bowl mix confectionery sugar with milk, (start with 1 tablespoon and add more as needed) until spreading consistency.

Beat corn syrup and almond extract in icing until smooth and glossy.

Add in food coloring until the desired color is achieved.

Frost and let cool on wax paper.

# ABOUT THE AUTHOR

Tracy is an award-winning and *USA Today* bestselling author, homesteader, and lover of all things simple living. As a country girl at heart, her passion lies in capturing the essence of a simpler way of life, much like the one she enjoyed growing up in rural Pennsylvania.

Her life has always been intricately linked with Amish culture, fostering a deep love for their simplicity, sense of community, and God-centered living. Growing up in Northwest Pennsylvania, the rhythmic clip-clop of horse and buggies was a familiar sound throughout her childhood.

Now residing in South Carolina, Tracy frequently travels through Amish regions in Pennsylvania, Ohio, Indiana, and Wisconsin. These journeys are not just visits but also opportunities for research, allowing her to write Amish fiction that authentically represents their culture, thanks to invaluable insights from friends within these communities.

Made in the USA
Middletown, DE
07 December 2024

66350803R00196